Fourth Strike

Book Four in The Family or Foe Saga
J. T. Bishop

Eudoran Press LLC

Eudoran Press LLC

6009 W. Parker Rd. Su. 149, #205

Dallas, TX 75093

www.jtbishopauthor.com

Publisher's Note: This is a work of fiction. Names, characters, places, and incidents are a product of the author's imagination. Locales and public names are sometimes used for atmospheric purposes. Any resemblance to actual people, living or dead, or to businesses, companies, events, institutions, or locales is completely coincidental.

Author Photos by Nick Bishop and Mayza Clark Photography

Book Editing by P. Creeden and G. Enstam

Cover Design by ebookorprint

Updated Cover by J.T. Bishop

Cover photo credit merrydolla, aetb, Aivolie

Fourth Strike/ J.T. Bishop -- 1st ed.

ISBNs 978-1-7325531-5-6, 978-1-955370-06-6

To Christine.

A dear friend.

Whether it's Gandhi, explosive feet, or back boobs,

you always keep it fun.

Love you.

Other Books by J. T. Bishop

Chapter One

RETIRED JUDGE MARTIN HENDRIX adjusted his tie in the mirror. He'd chosen the red one with the gold golf tees because his wife of forty-eight years had given it to him on his previous birthday. Smoothing his hair in the mirror, he observed the gray sprinkled within it and the minimal, but deep wrinkles on his dark skin. "You still got it, Martin," he said to himself in the mirror. His friends had told him he didn't look a day over sixty. He chuckled.

"Are you talking to yourself again?" Martha entered the bathroom.

"Just telling myself how handsome I am." He took a last look and faced her.

She gave him a quick kiss. "You are pretty handsome."

"Not as good-looking as my wife though. She's something else."

Martha grinned. "Still a charmer after all these years." She eyed his outfit. "Where are you going with a tie and all? I haven't seen you wear a tie since you left the bench."

He adjusted a sleeve. "It's been six months, and I have a closet full of them. I figure I should wear at least one a year. I'm having lunch with Frank Lozano. Thought I should look respectable."

"Frank? We haven't seen him in a while. Tell him we need to have him and his wife over for dinner sometime soon. I'll make some pot roast."

"He'd love that. I'll mention it. You headed out?"

She checked her makeup in the mirror and added some lipstick. "Yes. I have my ladies' group lunch today." She checked her watch. "I better get going or I'll be late."

"You tell those ladies to have a drink on me."

"Oh, Martin. It's lunchtime."

"We're not getting any younger, Martha. Time to live it up a little." He reached low and squeezed her butt.

Martha jumped and swiveled. "What are you doing?"

"Just admiring my wife's fine traits."

Her eyes widened. "You are a mess today. You better behave yourself at lunch."

"I'll behave myself until you and I come home, then..." he moved closer, "...who knows what might happen."

She smiled, reached around, and pinched his rear end. "We'll see if you have the strength."

"Oh, I'll have the strength. In fact, if you have the time now—" He pulled her closer.

She giggled and swatted him. "Would you stop? I have to go, and so do you." She gave him a quick kiss. "You be safe out there, my dear."

He held her hand. "You sure? Those ladies will live if you're a little late."

She giggled again. "You can still make me feel like a schoolgirl." She gave him another kiss. "I love you, man of my dreams."

"I love you, too, light of my life."

She stepped away. "I'll see you later."

He winked. "See you."

He watched her leave and after taking a last look at himself, left the bathroom, hearing her go out the back door. Having a few minutes before he had to depart, he went into the kitchen and poured himself some milk. The paper sat on the counter from when he'd brought it in earlier and he opened it, scanning the headlines.

The door opened from the back and he heard it close. "You forget something, Martha?" he asked, reading an article.

There was no response and hearing footsteps encroach, he looked up. A man walked into the kitchen.

"Hello, Judge."

Hendrix lowered the paper. "Who the hell are—"

The man pulled out a weapon and fired.

· · · ● · ● · · · ·

Detective Aaron Remalla stared into the closet. The first thing he saw was the sweater. Taking it down from the shelf, he held it, inhaling its scent. It was musty, just like any sweater would be after sitting in a closet for two years, but beneath the mustiness, he detected just a trace of what he'd been hoping for—a whiff of her perfume. Maybe he was just making it up in his mind, but it didn't matter. That one whiff brought Jennie back, and he closed his eyes, thinking of her.

He'd been putting off this task for some time, but with the two-year anniversary of her death approaching next month, he decided he had to face it. Having the day off, he'd taken the morning to relax and sleep in. He and his partner, Gordon Daniels, didn't get many of those days. Daniels was taking his fiancé and son to the park, and Remalla figured this would be as good a time as any to face the closet.

Not long after Jennie had died, he'd taken everything he could find of hers that was in his apartment and stored it. It had been too painful to see every day, and back then, any reminder would spiral him into depression, so he'd hid her things away, out of sight and out of mind. After moving into his Aunt Audrey's home once she'd gone into assisted living, he'd taken Jennie's things out of storage and put it all in this upstairs bedroom closet. He wanted it near, but not too near that he had to think of her every day.

But now, after two years, he needed to deal with it.

He'd taken a stiff drink at lunch and then, after eating, had come upstairs. He'd brought the bottle of vodka with him, fully expecting to drink a lot while he finished the task.

He folded the sweater and put it to the side, not knowing yet if he would donate it or keep it. He wondered if her family would want it. Going back to the closet, he scanned it, unsure what to pull out next. There were plenty of clothes, some scarves and a couple of jackets, plus her shoes. The memories swirled, and he forced himself to not think, but just do. Sometimes, that was all he could trust.

Seeing a box on the floor, he squatted down and picked it up. He brought it out and set it on the bed in the room. Having some idea what was inside, he poured himself a shot of vodka, but didn't drink it. It would be there when he needed it.

He stared at the box and slid his hand over the top. Memories of the night she'd died reared up. The phone call. Hearing about the accident and the drunk driver who'd hit her. Going to the hospital. Identifying her body.

Clenching his jaw, he closed his eyes and fought to stay calm. After several seconds, he took a deep breath and opened the box. The first thing he saw was her makeup. He remembered swiping it in here not long after the funeral. There was her perfume, bottles of shampoo and conditioner, and her soap. The box smelled of lavender. He swallowed. He'd have to toss most of it.

He reached in and dug around, and seeing something small and delicate, he picked it up. Holding his breath, he pulled it out, knowing what it was.

The silver bracelet had darkened with exposure, but the inscription remained. He read it. *To my angel. From your devil. I love you.*

The memory of him giving it to her on the anniversary of their first date reared up and hit him in the gut like a gunshot, and he dropped it on the bed, grabbed the vodka, and downed it in one gulp.

The liquid burned his throat, and he poured another when his cell rang. Unsure he could answer, he let it go to voicemail. Taking a few shaky breaths, he eyed the liquor, debating whether to drink it, when his cell rang again.

Cursing, he pulled it out of his pocket, and saw it was his partner, Daniels.

He inhaled and exhaled several deep breaths, trying to pull it together, and answered. "Yeah."

There was a brief pause. "Rem?"

He cleared his throat and forced some levity into his voice. "What's up?"

"You okay?"

He shut his eyes. Sometimes their friendship could be a pain in the ass. "Yeah. I'm fine. How's the park?"

"It was nice, but I'm on my way home. Lozano called. Judge Hendrix is dead. Gunned down in his home. He wants us there."

Rem opened his eyes. "What? Judge Hendrix?"

"I know. Hard to believe. So much for the day off. I'll text you the address. I'm dropping Marjorie at home and heading over."

Rem rubbed his face, glad he hadn't taken the third shot of alcohol. He'd have to get some coffee on his way. "I'll meet you there."

"Okay."

Rem hung up and turned back toward the box, seeing the bracelet on the bed. He sighed again. "You'll have to wait, Jennie. Sorry."

He left the room, closing the door behind him.

Chapter Two

CAPTAIN FRANK LOZANO STOOD outside Judge Hendrix's home, holding his phone and pacing. The forensic team and coroner had arrived and were inside. His detective, Gordon Daniels, pulled up. Daniels stopped at the curb and got out, wearing his customary ironed slacks, collared shirt and leather jacket. His normally gelled blonde hair was windblown, and he brushed it back with his hand. He jogged over.

"Captain."

"Daniels. Where's your partner?"

"On his way. What happened?"

The captain huffed, feeling the weight of what he'd seen on his shoulders. "The judge and I were due to have lunch. He never showed and wouldn't answer his phone. He's more punctual than a clock, so I headed over and found him in the kitchen. Looks like he took a round to the chest." He rubbed his temples.

"I'm sorry, Cap. I know you two were friends." Daniels gestured to a porch chair. "Why don't you sit?"

Lozano nodded, wanting to tell his detective he was fine, but conceding his fatigue. "Yeah." He walked over and sat.

Daniels sat beside him. "Where's his wife?"

Lozano sighed. "On her way. I didn't have her number, but I called in at the station. Had someone find it for me. She's on her way."

"Does she know he's dead?"

Lozano grunted. "I didn't want to tell her over the phone, but she kept asking if he was okay." He paused. "I didn't want her driving, but a friend is bringing her back."

A car pulled up and stopped and Lozano saw Martha get out of the passenger side, her face stricken.

Lozano stood. "Give me a second."

"Yeah," said Daniels.

Remalla's car pulled up and parked behind Daniels. He got out, holding his customary cup of coffee, wearing ripped jeans, sneakers and an old Metallica t-shirt with a navy hoodie. His long dark hair blew in the wind, and he wore a Mariners baseball cap over it.

Lozano approached Martha, who ran up to him and burst into tears. She wanted to run past him, but he stopped her and took her in his arms.

Remalla hesitated when he walked by, but Lozano shook his head, and Remalla walked past, heading up toward the porch.

· · • • • • • • · ·

Daniels watched his partner approach the house, remembering his tone on the phone. "Hey," he said.

"Hey." Remalla came up the porch steps. "Is that the wife?"

"Yes. Her name's Martha."

"Hell."

"I know. Lozano was supposed to have lunch with the judge. Ended up finding him instead."

"Lozano found the body?"

"Yeah."

Rem eyed the house. "Forensics inside?"

"Yeah. So's the coroner. Lozano said it looked like he took a shot to the chest."

"Who the hell would want to kill a retired judge?"

"Good question. Maybe a robbery, or somebody who didn't like what happened in his courtroom."

Rem rubbed his neck. "Guy sat on the bench for over thirty years. That could be a lot of people."

Daniels sighed. "It sure could. Maybe they'll find something inside that might give us some help."

On cue, the door opened and a thin, bald-headed man with spectacles stepped out. "You guys here for the case?"

"Yes," said Daniels. He introduced himself and Rem. "You filling in for Ibrahim today?"

"I'm Villanueva. Ibrahim's on vacation. Took his wife for their anniversary to Hawaii. You two want to check out the scene?" He held out shoe covers and gloves.

"Thanks," said Remalla, taking the items.

A few minutes later, they stepped into the house.

"Looks okay in here," said Rem, entering the living area.

Villanueva followed them in. "Everything is undisturbed from what we have seen so far, but we'll dust for prints. It's the kitchen where it happened."

Daniels followed Rem into the kitchen area, seeing a covered figure on the floor. Blood spattered the refrigerator door and a pool of it lay beneath the body on the linoleum. A shattered glass lay beside the covering, and white liquid dotted the floor and cabinets.

"The white stuff is milk," said Villanueva. "Looks like he was drinking it when he was hit." He pointed. "The door leading into the garage was open. We're assuming that's how the perp got in," said Villanueva.

Daniels squatted and lifted the cover, seeing the remains of the judge. Rem squatted next to him. "Yeah. Looks like a round to the chest," said Rem. "Any casings?"

"One," said Villanueva. "Over by the dining table."

"Any forced entry?" asked Daniels.

"Not that it looks like. Door may have been unlocked though."

"Nothing stolen?" asked Rem.

"His wallet's in his pocket. Bedroom looks undisturbed. We did find something of interest though."

Daniels dropped the cover back over the judge and stood along with Rem. "What's that?"

Villanueva nodded over to a Ziploc bag on the counter. "A piece of paper with a number on it. We bagged it, but have no idea what it means."

Rem walked over and picked up the bag. "0212," he read. He looked at Daniels. "Any idea?"

Daniels shook his head. "No clue. A date? A case number?"

"Maybe Lozano knows," said Rem. He put the bag down. "Anything else?"

"Nope." Villanueva sighed. "Damn shame to see this, though. Judge Hendrix was a legend in the legal world. He once gave my nephew probation when he could have given him three to five, with the stipulation that he go work for the people he stole from. Changed my nephew's life."

Daniels eyed Rem. "Yeah. We worked with him a few times, too. Testified in his courtroom more than once over the years."

"Lozano, too," said Rem. "I hear that's how they became friends."

"You seen enough?" asked Daniels.

"More than I wanted to," said Rem. "Let's go check on the widow."

"We'll get you our report as soon as we have it," said Villanueva.

"Thanks," said Daniels. They turned and left the house.

Chapter Three

REMALLA SAT ACROSS FROM Lozano's desk, his partner sitting beside him. Lozano looked tired, his eyes worn and red.

"Why don't you head home, Cap? You've had a hard day. Go be with your wife," said Rem.

"I'll go home when I feel like it, Remalla," said Lozano. He clenched his hands together and rested them on his desk. "I want to be sure we're covering our bases on this one. No one saw anything?"

"No, Cap," said Daniels. "Not from what we can tell. Nobody we talked to even heard anything."

Lozano groaned.

"What about that number left at the scene? It mean anything to you?" asked Remalla. He sipped from a cup of coffee.

"Not a thing." Lozano sat back in his seat and swiveled, looking out the window behind his desk. "Who the hell would want to kill the judge? That man was well-respected and beloved in his community. He sat on that bench for thirty-two years." He hung his head. "And he was a good friend." He paused. "Poor Martha. They'd been married almost fifty years."

Remalla glanced at Daniels. "Sorry for your loss, Cap. We promise we'll find this guy, though. If somebody targeted him for some purpose, we'll figure it out."

"That number means something," said Daniels. "The killer left it for a reason."

Lozano turned back, his eyes glittering. "I need you two laser-sharp on this one. Everything by the book. I don't want any kind of reason for a defense attorney to claim we cut corners. Once we find this guy, he's going to prison. You got it?"

"We got it," said Daniels.

"Hendrix deserves our full commitment on this. If some perp who held a grudge came back to seek revenge, then we need to find him."

"We haven't ruled out a random robbery gone bad, Cap. Or maybe an angry family member," said Remalla.

Lozano glared. "That man's family worshiped him, and this is *not* a robbery gone bad. I don't want guesses, Remalla. I want answers."

Rem sat up. "I'm not guessing, Cap, I just think—"

Lozano pointed. "Stop thinking and do your job. I don't need you wasting you and your partner's time going off on some half-assed theories. This ass-hole is out there, and he doesn't deserve to be."

Daniels straightened. "That's not fair, Cap. Rem is right..."

Lozano aimed a sharp stare at Daniels. "Don't tell me what's right or wrong, Daniels. I'll decide that. Just get your butts out there and do what you have to do."

The room went quiet, and Lozano breathed heavily.

"Cap...," said Rem. "You going to be okay? Maybe you shouldn't be—"

"When I want your opinion, I'll ask for it." Lozano stood. "Now get your asses out there and get to work. And be ready to work weekends, cause until this is solved, there are no weekends."

Rem nodded, and Daniels pushed himself out of his seat. "Okay," said Daniels.

Rem stood too. "Okay," he repeated.

Lozano sat again, swiveled in his chair and resumed his stare out the window. Rem followed Daniels out of the office and shut the door behind him. "He's upset."

"Sure is," said Daniels.

"You think he should be leading this, considering his connection to the judge?"

"You want to tell him that?"

"I tried," said Rem.

"Didn't go over too well."

"Obviously."

Daniels sat at his desk. "So much for our day off."

"Or any future ones." Rem sat, too.

Daniels opened up his laptop and looked around the edge of it, his eyes curious. "Did I interrupt anything when I called earlier?"

Rem sipped his coffee, remembering the bracelet. "Nothing important. How was the park?"

Daniels narrowed his eyes at him, and Rem flipped through a file on his desk, not even sure what it was, but still feeling his partner's attention.

"Park was great. Beautiful day."

"Great. J.P. and Marjorie have fun?"

"Sure. J.P. played in the sandpit. Got sand in every crevice."

"Great." Rem opened a drawer and found a pencil. He tapped it on the desk. "So how do you want to start with this?"

Daniels paused, and Rem waited to see if his partner would answer, or if he'd pursue the subject Rem hoped to avoid.

Daniels gave him a look that told him the topic would be tabled for now, but not forever. "Well, the Captain doesn't want us to pursue the robbery or family theory. I guess that leaves us with someone who's pissed with the judge, maybe from one of his cases."

Rem twirled the pencil through his fingers. "That's a lot of cases."

Daniels rocked in his chair. "We'll have to start somewhere. We could go back and find the ones where he was threatened, or where the guilty defendants were violent offenders who may have been recently released. Omit anyone who's non-violent, or non-threatening, or maybe released more than a year ago."

"That's still a long list."

"We can send it to Research. I bet they can come up with something. Once we have that, maybe we can cross-reference that number from the scene. See if anything pops up."

Rem pursed his lips. "Well, like you said, we got to start somewhere." He glanced back toward Lozano's office. "In the meantime, we should still do some checking on the family. Just in case the judge has some pissed cousins we may not know about."

"Probably a good idea. Cap may not like it, but he also said not to cut corners."

"And we won't. I'll also check to see if there have been any robberies in that area. Maybe some nut job is running around breaking into houses, and the judge surprised him. My bet's on that."

Daniels nodded. "Yeah. Maybe." He tipped his head toward the coffeepot. "Better get that going, partner. We're going to need it."

"I'm on it," said Rem, standing.

Daniels jabbed a pen at him. "And don't think I don't know something's bugging you, but you're getting a reprieve for now."

Rem raised a brow. "I'm fine. No need to worry." He grabbed the grounds and opened them, still feeling Daniels' hard stare. "Really." He glanced back, making himself look relaxed. "You want one cup or two?"

"Two."

"Great. The rest of the pot is for me."

Chapter Four

ENTERING HIS HOUSE, REMALLA tossed his keys on the front table and closed the door. Exhausted, he went to sit on the couch. After kicking off his sneakers, he flipped on the TV. He and Daniels had spent the rest of the day checking for robberies in the area, and potentially murderous family members. They'd had no luck with either. Forensics had sent their initial report, which didn't tell them much more than they already knew. They'd sent the research request and hoped to have a report of potential suspects to work with the next morning.

Mentally and physically wiped, he watched an episode of *Seinfeld* flicker to life on the screen. Too tired to care, he lay back on the couch, knowing he should go to bed, but thinking of the bracelet.

Before he fell asleep on the couch, he made himself move. He stood and went up the stairs to the bedroom with Jennie's things. He opened the door and flicked on the light. The box still sat on the bed, and he saw the bracelet where he'd left it. The closet door stood open, and he went over and glanced inside. Cleaning out Jennie's things would have to wait. Glancing to his right, he saw the vodka bottle he'd opened that afternoon.

He flicked his eyes between the bottle and Jennie's jewelry, and walked over and picked up the bracelet, sliding his fingers over it. The memories surfaced again, and he wondered why he was doing this to himself. He realized the looming anniversary was to blame. The first anniversary had been plenty rocky. He'd gotten drunk and locked himself in his room. Daniels had to use his spare key to get into the house and then sat outside the door talking to him, gently trying to coax him out. After puking his guts out, Rem had taken a shower and reemerged from the bedroom, trying to act fine, but looking like hell. It had taken everything he had to keep it together so Daniels would leave and go home. His partner worried about him enough and he didn't want to make it worse. It took a few hours, but finally he'd left, and Rem had let himself lose it, and cried himself to sleep on the couch, watching some sappy rom-com. It had taken a full week to pull it together.

Holding the bracelet, he grabbed the vodka bottle, flipped the lights off and closed the door. He headed down the stairs, went into the kitchen, found another shot glass and was about to fill it when his doorbell rang.

Rem checked the clock. It was a little after nine o'clock. "What the hell?" he mumbled to himself. Wondering who would come knocking, he put the bottle and glass down and slid the bracelet into his jean pocket. He went to the door and opened it, half expecting to see Daniels. But it wasn't. "Jill?"

Jill Jacobs stood at his door. "Hey, Rem." She held a backpack and a small overnight bag.

"What are you...did I know...?" He rubbed his head. Was he that out of it that he'd forgotten his girlfriend was visiting?

"No. I'm sorry. It's an impulse visit."

He widened the door. "Come on in."

"Thanks." She entered and put her bags down. "It's good to see you." She looked him over. "You look tired. Long day?"

Her visit threw him. "Uh, yeah. You could say that. You okay? How's your dad?"

"Hanging in there. Still grumpy as hell. Hates his doctor visits."

"I bet. I haven't talked to you in a while. We keep playing phone tag."

"Yeah. I know."

He sensed an underlying hesitation in her he couldn't quite put his finger on. "Come here." He leaned in for a hug, and she returned it, but he felt her stiffen and he pulled back. "What is it? Something's wrong. Why'd you show up at my door without telling me you were coming?"

She sighed, and he noticed the strain in her face. "Can we talk?" she asked.

His heart fell and his chest tightened. *Great, she's breaking up with me,* he thought to himself. *Perfect timing.* "Sure. Have a seat." He mentally prepared himself.

They went into the living area, and Rem muted the tv. "What's up?"

She sat on the couch. "There's a reason I went quiet for a while."

"What's that?" He took a seat next to her and clenched his fingers together. Could this day get any worse? He considered retrieving the vodka.

She ran a hand through her long hair, and he remembered the last time she was here and he'd run his fingers through it while they were in bed.

"I, uh, had a visitor. A couple of weeks ago." She bounced her knee.

"A visitor? Who?"

She hesitated. "Sonia Vandermere."

His heart leaped up into his throat. "Are you serious?"

"I'm serious," she said. "You remember her?"

Rem stared. "Uh, yes. You could say that." *Shit*, he thought to himself.

"Have you seen her since the Makeup Artist? When she was a witness?"

He couldn't tell if she was testing him to see if he would tell the truth. He had no idea what Sonia may have told her, but he didn't see the point in hiding it. "Yes. I have."

"She told me quite a story."

"She did?" He held his breath. At least she wasn't breaking up with him.

Jill stood, her body tense. "Is it true that someone else may have killed Rick?"

He went still.

"Don't you dare lie to me, Aaron Remalla," she said. "If it's true, I need to know. I should know, and you should have told me."

He jumped up. "Jill, listen. It's a long story..."

"Don't tell me to listen. Is it true?"

He debated what to say, but she didn't leave him much choice. "Yes, it's true."

Her eyes narrowed. "How long have you known?"

He sighed. "We couldn't be sure..."

"Daniels too, huh?"

"Yes. But Jill, we don't have any evidence..."

"How long?" She spoke louder.

Frustrated, he thought back to Madison Vickers' case and mentally calculated. "Five months?"

She snickered. "All this time, and you couldn't even mention it to me?"

"It's not that easy—"

"Not that easy? We spent the holidays together. Did you think of mentioning it then? Or gee, I don't know, how about on one of our phone calls?"

"I didn't want to upset you."

"Upset me? What do you think I am now?"

"What did you expect me to say?" He threw out his hand. "Guess what? Your old boyfriend may have been murdered by someone other than some serial killer, but we can't be sure, because we don't have the evidence, and we can't catch him?"

"Yes," she said, her voice rising. "That would work. You know I would have been on the first flight out."

"And do what?" His own voice rose. "You think Daniels and I haven't tried to move heaven and earth to get this guy?" He paced beside the coffee table. "What exactly did sweet Sonia tell you, anyway?" He began to wonder if Sonia was more a devil in disguise than the sweet, angelic, grandmotherly type.

"She told me enough."

"Enough? What does that mean?"

"Are you saying there's more to tell?"

He stopped, telling himself to stay cool. "Be careful what you wish for. You want to jump down this rabbit hole, be prepared to fall for a while."

She set her jaw. "Don't act like I can't take it, Rem. You know what I've already been through. Anything else pales in comparison."

"You might be surprised."

She snorted. "Please don't tell me you believe the same crap that she does. That this mystery man's got some kind of superpowers? Come on. I think Sonia, as sweet as she is, has the early signs of dementia."

"Sonia's as smart as they come. She knows exactly what she's doing." He gripped his forehead. "Which I'm sure part of which is to drive me crazy."

"I'm so sorry you're having a difficult time with this, but you see why I just might be a little pissed. There's a man out there running around, free as a bird, who killed Rick, and you guys haven't said a word to me, nor have you caught him. Then some sweet little old lady, who I thought was just a witness in a case, shows up at my doorstep, telling me these crazy things. That I'm related to two strangers named Madison and Jace, and my parents and siblings aren't biological, and how Madison, Jace and I share these ridiculous abilities." Jill paused, breathing hard. "I think she's completely certifiable. But then she knows things about me too. Things that I can do, which I can't explain either, so she's not totally insane. Not yet, anyway." She pulled her hair back and wrapped it up into a messy bun with a band from her wrist. "Then she tells me about this psycho running around, and how he killed not just Rick, but others, too. Others related to these two people I'm supposedly related to. And I had to come here and ask you to confirm it. I was hoping this was some crazy story she'd made up in her head, but guess what? It apparently isn't. So now I have to figure out what to believe."

"Sonia knows more than you realize. More than we both realize."

"You don't believe what she says about this guy, do you?"

"What did she say?"

"That he's got some kind of crazy combination of telekinesis and psychic ability."

"You have psychic ability."

She paused. "It's a big leap from being a psychic, if I'm even comfortable with that term, to being able to bend a spoon with your mind."

Rem chuckled with annoyance. "It's a little more than that."

Her jaw fell. "You believe her?"

"It's hard not to believe what you've seen with your own eyes. Why do you think we haven't caught him?"

She stood for a moment, her eyes cautious. "Exactly how close did you and Daniels come to getting this guy?"

His memory flicked back to Madison Vickers and Secret Lake, and Jace Marlon and running after the perp through the construction site. He almost audibly moaned. "A few. Rutger made a point of talking to us a few times, but he always got away from us."

Her brow knitted. "You know his name?"

"No. We don't know his name. But he looks like a young Rutger Hauer. The name stuck."

"And you spoke to him a few times?" She glared. "Why the hell didn't you just ask for his address during your one of your visits?"

Rem set his jaw. "He didn't feel like sharing. I told you it's a long story."

She walked away from the couch, her head down.

"If you want to sit, I'll tell you the whole thing."

She turned abruptly. "I don't want to sit. This whole thing is ridiculous. Sonia shows up out of nowhere, telling me crazy things. You lie to me about Rick—"

"I didn't lie to you, Jill. When I went up for the holidays, you were happy. We were happy. You hadn't had that in a while, and I didn't want to ruin it."

She held up a hand. "There have been opportunities since then for you to tell me, but you didn't."

"Jill, there is nothing else we could have done. What would telling you have accomplished, other than this?" He gestured toward her. "If we could have arrested this guy and brought him in, of course I would have told you."

She yelled. "That is not the point. The minute you had an inkling that this might have been possible, you should have said something." She took a step forward. "You think if I had any sort of knowledge that something else had happened to Jennie, that I wouldn't have told you, and that you wouldn't have insisted on knowing?"

The mention of Jennie's name felt like another punch to the stomach, and he deflated. "I don't know what else you want me to say."

She stood unmoving, her face flat. "I wish you would have had the guts to tell me. And I wish you would at least say that you're sorry you didn't mention it sooner."

"I honestly thought I was doing the right thing, but I am sorry if I screwed up."

She nodded, her eyes shiny. "Me, too."

He closed his eyes and opened them. "What do you want to do now?"

She let go of a deep breath. "I'm going to go." She walked over to her things.

"You're leaving?" He followed her.

"I can't stay here."

"Why not? That's silly."

She grabbed her backpack and threw it over her shoulder. "No, it's not."

"Where are you going?"

"I'm going to do what I need to do to find this guy."

He frowned. "What? Are you serious?"

"I'm completely serious. You guys had your shot. Now it's my turn." She picked up her bag.

"Jill, listen. You have no idea what you're dealing with here. This guy...he's not..."

"He's a guy, Rem. Flesh and blood. And if he had a beef with me and took it out on Rick for some misplaced slight, I'm going to find out why." She adjusted her backpack and walked toward the door. "And I don't need your, or Daniels', approval."

"Jill, he's dangerous."

She swiveled. "So am I."

"Jill, please...just let me tell you..." He took her by the elbow, but she pulled away.

"No. You had your chance. You had five months, and you blew it."

His anger bubbled up. "I wanted to protect you."

She scowled. "How long would you have kept this a secret, huh? If you were to never catch him, would you have ever told me?"

He studied her angry face. "Hell, Jill. I don't know."

"I think I do." She opened the door and walked out.

"Where are you going?" he asked. "How do you plan on finding a ghost?"

She stopped. "Sonia gave me a few ideas. I'm starting with Madison Vickers. I'm going to Secret Lake."

He dropped his jaw. "Madison Vickers?"

"I'm going to get to the bottom of this, Rem." She stomped down the front stairs.

He moaned. "Jill, wait. You shouldn't be doing this alone."

She got to her car and opened the door. "I don't need, or want, your help." She threw her bags in. "Not anymore." She slid into the seat and closed the door.

Rem's heart sank as he watched her drive away.

Chapter Five

SITTING IN THE QUIET squad room early on Sunday morning, Daniels sat at his computer, reading the report. The printer whirred behind him, printing the potential list of suspects. It was long, and it would take time to check everyone on the list, but it was a start. The printer stopped, and he pushed back with his seat, pulling the report from the tray. He eyed the time, debating whether to call his partner. He was thirty minutes late. Thankfully, Lozano was spending the morning with Martha Hendrix and her family and wouldn't be in until after lunch.

Sliding back to his desk, he reached for his cell when he heard the squad door open. Rem entered, wearing dark sunglasses. His hair was unkempt, and Daniels was pretty sure he had on the same clothes as yesterday. He trudged to his desk, where he sat wearily. He kept the sunglasses on.

"Good morning," said Daniels.

"Mornin'," said Rem. He turned. "Any coffee?" Eyeing the half-filled pot, he pushed up with a groan and poured himself a cup, adding his customary healthy dollop of cream and sugar.

"You okay?" asked Daniels.

"Great. Just great," said Rem, sipping his coffee with a grimace.

"Headache?" He knew enough to know his partner was hungover.

"Just a touch."

"Hmm. Need some aspirin?"

Rem sat with his coffee. "Tried earlier. Couldn't keep it down."

Daniels leaned in, his elbows on his desk. "Are you sure you should be drinking coffee, then? Maybe water would be better?"

Rem held his head. "Don't start, okay?"

"Start what?"

He waved his fingers without looking up. "You know. The mother hen routine."

Daniels nodded. "Okay."

"I'm fine. I just need a minute." He sipped his coffee.

"Yeah. You look fine. If Lozano were here, he'd kick your ass to the curb."

Rem looked over. "God. Is he here?"

"No."

"Thank God for small favors." He took another sip.

Daniels studied his partner, wondering what was eating at him. When he'd called the previous day, he'd caught something in his partner's voice, but hoped it was temporary. Obviously, it wasn't. "We got the report back from Research. It's got thirty-two potential suspects' names on it."

Rem blanched, his face paler than when he'd entered, and he held his stomach. "Hold that thought." He jumped from his seat and ran out of the squad room.

"Told him he should have had water," said Daniels to himself. Tapping a pencil against the printed report, he wondered what to do. Rem was obviously in no shape to work. He wanted to be pissed because they had a lot to review, but he also knew this wasn't Rem's normal routine. Daniels tried to think about what could have triggered Rem's mood swing. Thinking of the date, his heart fell. Jennie. The anniversary of her death was coming up in a few weeks. Could that be it? But why this early? Recalling the previous year, Rem had fallen into a tailspin the week of the anniversary. Daniels knew, though, that grief could hit at any time. All it needed was the slightest trigger.

A few minutes passed, and Rem reemerged, looking worn and tired, his cheeks sunken. He sat at his desk and tossed out his coffee. He still wore the glasses. "Sorry about that."

"You going to keep wearing those?" He waved a finger towards the shades. "You look like you should either be singing karaoke to a Bob Dylan song or wearing a motorcycle jacket."

"If you saw me without them, I'd think you'd prefer the Dylan look." He rested his forehead on his desk.

"What's going on, Rem? It's not like you to get trashed on a work night."

"Yesterday was Saturday, so technically not a work night."

"You know what I mean."

Rem looked up and pulled his glasses down. Squinting, he looked around. "Is there any water around here?" His eyes were bloodshot and dark semi-circles creased his skin below his eyes.

Daniels stood. "You're right. I prefer the Dylan look." He walked over and grabbed a disposable cup from the counter and filled it with water from a large dispenser. He handed it to Rem. "Here. Water. From the big bottle that sits right behind you every day."

Rem took it. "Oh, yeah. Thanks." He sipped it slowly.

Daniels sat again, rubbing his jaw. "What's eatin' at you?"

Rem moaned and slid his glasses back up. "Do we have to talk about it?"

"Well, we could work on this case, but considering the state you're in, I don't see much of that happening."

Rem waved him off. "I'm good. I'm fine." He dug a thumb and index finger into his temples. "Except for this massive headache."

"Sip your water. You're likely dehydrated." He was afraid to ask when his partner had last drank a cup of regular, plain water.

Rem sipped some more, still holding his head.

"This have something to do with yesterday?"

"It's nothing."

"Come on, Rem. I've known you too long for you to pull that crap—"

Rem put the water down. "It's Jill, okay? She showed up last night. On my doorstep, after an already shitty day."

"Jill?" Daniels raised a brow. "Was she supposed to visit?"

"No, dammit, she wasn't." Rem pulled the glasses down again and rubbed his eyes. "She just dropped in without telling me."

"Why?"

Rem groaned. "Sonia. Sonia showed up and talked to her."

"Sonia was there?"

"No, bonehead. Sonia showed up at Jill's in Seattle a few weeks ago. Told her about Rutger and what he's done and what he can do. Told her about Rick, too. And mentioned Madison and Jace. The whole nine yards."

Daniels exhaled. "Everything?"

"Everything. Jill's furious with me that I never told her about Rick. And now she's gone off to look for Rutger. She doesn't really believe everything Sonia told her, so she wants to do her own digging. She's going to find Madison Vickers and basically told me...or us, to stay out of it."

"Wow. I don't believe it. Why would Sonia do that?"

Rem pushed his glasses up. "I don't know, but if I ever see that woman again, she's going to hear it from me. I could kill her right now."

Daniels paused. "You sure about that? Maybe you should thank her."

Rem's head shot up and Daniels saw his eyes crinkle with a wince. "What do you mean?"

"She told Jill what you couldn't. Now you don't have to."

Rem hesitated. "Are you saying I should have told Jill first? About Rutger and his antics?"

"Probably."

Rem sat up, his shoulders straighter. "Oh, come on. You know why I didn't want to tell her. We know nothing about this guy. We don't know who he is, where he comes from, his real name. Nothing. And he's making these crazy assertions about who his family might be, and let's not forget those weird abilities of his." He shoved his messy hair back away from his face. "Why would I tell her all that when she'd finally pulled her life back together after the Makeup Artist?"

"Would you have wanted to know if it were you?"

Rem stood but wobbled some and gripped the desk. "Not you, too. She threw the same thing in my face."

"Because you know it's true."

Rem's shoulders fell.

"Listen. She's pissed, but she'll get over it. Just give her some time. Deep down, she'll realize you were trying to protect her, but it's not going to help right now. Maybe it's a good thing she's going to see Madison. She might get the answers that we couldn't."

"And if she runs into Rutger?"

Daniels tapped on his desk with his fingers. "Let's hope she can handle him."

"That's your answer? Let's hope she can handle him? That's great. That's just great." He scowled and turned away. "Thanks for the help."

"What else do you want us to do, Rem? We can't go charging after her. We have a case to handle. Besides, if Rutger shows, he typically involves us..."

"So far, but that doesn't mean he will again."

"I know, but we have to assume it. There is only so much we can do. If he's disappeared and doesn't want to be found, I doubt Jill will find him, either."

Rem studied the ground. "But what if he wants to be found? What if Sonia did this knowing that Jill would go after him? What if she's using Jill to find him?"

Daniels sighed. "I don't know. It's a risk. All we can do is be there if she needs us. And if Rutger shows, we can try again to catch him. Maybe with Jill's help, we can have some success. Something tells me though, that Jill, Jace and Madison, if they really are related, are necessary to locate him. Assuming that's what he ultimately wants, which is to bring his 'family' together."

"Don't you want to catch him? This guy has put us through the wringer."

"Of course, I want to catch him. You know I do. But we can't keep running around in circles. Rutger has some plan, but what that is, we don't know. We could spend months or years waiting for him to show his face again. But we both have lives to live, you know?"

Rem stilled. "I know that. But my life...my life..." He paused and shook his head. "If Jill's a member of his so-called family, then it could cost her her own life. I know she's a former detective and I know she can handle herself, but I also know that's a false sense of security. She doesn't understand the stakes here." He faced Daniels, deflated. "We know what he's capable of... and if—" He stopped, his jaw clenched.

Daniels leaned in, finally understanding. "You're worried you might lose her, too?"

Rem straightened, taking a deep shuttered breath. "And it will be my..." He couldn't finish. Dropping his head, he went quiet for a moment before he cleared his throat. "You know what? It doesn't matter. You're right. There's not much I can do about it, is there? She's a big girl." He reached into a front pocket and dug around, pulling something out. "It's not my fau...problem...if she gets herself killed." He held the object in his hand, running his fingers over it.

"What's that?" asked Daniels.

"Nothing." He tossed it in the trash. "It doesn't matter anymore." His voice trembled, and he walked away.

Daniels stood and watched Rem head toward the doors. Looking over, he reached into the trash can and pulled out a silver tarnished bracelet. He turned it and read the inscription. His heart thumped. *Hell*, he thought. *No wonder he's drunk.* He jogged after his partner, putting the bracelet in his pocket.

Catching up to Rem before he could walk down the stairs, Daniels put a hand on his arm. "Hey, hold up," he said. Rem wobbled, but stopped. "There's that cot in the locker room. Why don't you go get some shuteye? Lozano won't be back till lunch." He checked his watch. "That'll give you a couple of hours to rest and sober up."

Rem eyed him through the glasses, and Daniels had no doubt that if he could see past them, he would know Rem was on the edge of losing it. "I should just go home," Rem whispered.

"You go home, and Lozano will kill you. Me, too." He guided Rem by the arm. "If you get a little sleep, you'll feel better, and I'll get you some lunch. And then we'll talk."

"Talk about what? There's nothing to talk about."

"Then we won't talk, but at least you'll be sober."

"I'm sober now."

"Of course you are."

Rem moaned and rubbed his neck. "You sure?"

"Yes. I'll wake you in two hours. I promise." Rem swayed on his feet, but Daniels held onto him. "Let's go."

Daniels led him down the hall to the locker room. A cot sat beside the wall and was typically used when someone pulled an all-nighter. "Here. Lie down. The room shouldn't be busy this time of day. I'll pull the shades. Just get some sleep."

Rem sat on the cot. "You'll wake me?"

"Sure will. Let me take those glasses for you."

Rem took off the shades and handed them to Daniels. He lay down on the cot, his head on the pillow. Daniels put the glasses on top of a locker and pulled a blanket from a shelf, and covered him. "Just rest, partner." He patted Rem's arm, and Rem closed his eyes, barely able to keep them open. "Just rest."

He stood for a minute, listening to Rem's breaths become deeper and finally, a soft snore. Pulling out the bracelet, he looked at it again, remembering when Rem had bought it for Jennie. Sighing, he took a last look at his slumbering partner and quietly left the room.

Chapter Six

Jill got out of her car, eyeing the town home. She'd spent the morning trying to track down Madison Vickers. She'd found the cabin where Madison supposedly lived, but after knocking on the door, a man had answered. He'd told Jill that Madison had sold the cabin recently and had moved, but he didn't have a forwarding address. Jill had spent the next two hours talking to neighbors until finally finding a friend who knew Madison's new address and was willing to give it to her.

It was only a fifteen-minute drive from the lake, so Madison hadn't gone far. The townhome was in a wooded area with a pretty park nearby. Jill verified the address, took a deep breath, walked up to the front door, and knocked. According to Sonia's wild story, the woman she was about to meet could be her sister.

She waited several seconds, and then knocked again, hoping Madison was home. After another several seconds went by, she almost knocked once more, when the door opened.

A pretty woman, shorter than Jill, with blonde hair and blue eyes, stood at the entry. *She certainly doesn't look like me*, thought Jill. Her hair was pulled back with a bandana, she was wiping her hands with a towel, and she had what looked like a speckle of paint on her chin.

"Hi," said Jill. "Madison Vickers?"

"Yes," said Madison. She flipped the towel over her shoulder.

Now that Jill had found Madison, she felt tongue-tied. What exactly should she say? "Uh, my name's Jill. I was hoping we could talk."

"Jill?" She frowned. "Do I know you?" She looked out toward the street, maybe to check to see if Jill was alone.

"It's just me, and no, we don't know each other, but we have a friend in common."

"We do? Who?"

"Sonia Vandermere."

Madison's eyes rounded. "Sonia? You know Sonia?"

"Yes, I do." She paused. "You mind if I come in?"

"Not at all." Madison held the door wide, and Jill entered.

"Thank you." Jill walked into a small living area adjacent to a dining table and open kitchen. It was furnished, but cardboard boxes took up some extra space. "This is nice."

Madison closed the door. "It will be nicer once I get everything unpacked. I just moved in a month ago." She tossed the towel on a dining chair. "Can I get you something to drink?"

"Water would be great. Thanks."

While Madison went into the kitchen, Jill scanned the room, seeing the artwork on the walls. "You got your paintings up. Those are usually the last thing on the list after a move." She eyed an abstract piece above the fireplace. "These are beautiful."

Madison returned with a glass of water. "Thank you. They are actually my work. I'm a painter."

Jill took the glass. "Really? Well, these are amazing. You're very talented."

"I was working on a piece when you knocked, and had the music on and headphones. I tend to zone out when I paint. I almost didn't hear the door."

"You have a studio here?" asked Jill.

"Well, it's really the second bedroom, but it works."

Jill nodded. "I went to your cabin on the lake first, but the man there told me you'd sold it. I have to say I am surprised. It was a beautiful piece of property."

Madison's face dropped. "Yes, well. Considering everything that happened there, I couldn't really stay."

Jill had familiarized herself with Madison's past, and knew about her husband's murder, Rem and Daniels's subsequent involvement, and what had culminated in the murderer's death at Madison's home on the lake. It was no surprise to Jill that Madison had moved. "I get it."

"You know what happened?"

"I do. I...uh...I'm a friend of Detective Remalla and Detective Daniels."

Madison dropped her jaw. "Remalla and Daniels? Those two saved my life."

Jill's chest constricted, thinking of Rem. "Yeah. They're good at that."

"Wait a minute..." Madison squinted, and she appeared to think back. Pointing, she asked. "Are you JJ?"

The name JJ startled Jill. Only the Artist had used that name, at least that she knew of. She tried not to react. "My name's Jill Jacobs, so yes, I guess one could call me JJ, although most just call me Jill."

Madison gestured toward the couch. "Why don't you have a seat?"

Feeling oddly anxious, Jill turned toward the couch. "I think I will."

Jill sat on the sofa, and Madison joined her. Jill sipped her water and put it down on the coffee table.

"So, how do you know Sonia?" asked Madison.

Jill chuckled. "It's a long story."

"She's an interesting lady."

"That she is," said Jill.

"She gave me this." Madison touched a purple-stoned bracelet on her arm.

Jill stared at the bracelet and pulled out her black-stoned necklace from beneath her shirt. "And she gave me this. It's tourmaline."

"Mines Fluorite."

Jill held her necklace, disbelieving that Sonia had given both of them jewelry. So far, Sonia's story was holding together. "When did you meet her?"

Madison smiled softly. "In jail."

"In jail?"

"Yes. I'd been arrested for my husband's murder." She shook her head. "God. That was a crazy time."

"She just came out of nowhere?"

"Yes. She visited me. Told me I was stronger than I thought, and more capable that I realized."

The chills grew stronger and ran down Jill's back. "She told me the same thing, basically."

Madison stopped fiddling with her bracelet. "When did you meet her?"

Jill recalled her introduction to Sonia during the Makeup Artist investigation. "She came forward as a witness when the Artist was killing women in San Diego. I'd come to help Rem...Remalla and Daniels. I'd been a detective in Seattle, and I'd had some past involvement with the killer. Sonia had seen him, and she helped provide a sketch."

"Lady gets around."

"That she does."

The two sat quietly while Jill sipped her water, and Madison scrubbed some paint off of her finger. The paint flaking off, Madison finally spoke. "Why are you here, Jill?"

Jill debated how to explain it. She didn't want to sound as kooky as Sonia, but she wasn't sure how to avoid it. "Um, well, that's a great question." She bounced her knee. "After the Artist was caught, I went home to Seattle. My family's there and I was a bit of a mess and I needed to get my head clear about a lot of things."

Madison made a soft chuckle.

"What?"

"You and I have a lot in common."

"We do?"

"It's why I sold the cabin. I had to create some space in my head and my heart. It used to be my dad's, but we never had a great relationship. Then me and my husband lived there and, well, that was a disaster. It just seemed that once I was cleared and had my life back, it was time to start over."

Jill smiled, appreciating Madison's honesty. "We do have a lot in common."

"What happened in Seattle? Did you find the peace you were looking for?"

Jill thought of her dad. "Things were better. I've been able to spend more time with my family, and just take some time for myself."

"That's exactly what I'm looking for. To take some time for myself. I've never been really good at being alone, so now's the time, I suppose." She sighed.

"I hear you." Jill shifted in her seat. "Anyway, a couple of weeks ago, Sonia showed up out of nowhere."

"She did? What for?"

Jill played with a hair tie around her wrist. "She wanted to tell me a few things."

Madison's forehead furrowed. "What did she tell you?"

Jill fought the urge to get up and leave. For a moment, an odd sense of dread came over her, and a sharp pain shot through her skull. She winced and rubbed her forehead, and the pain vanished. But she had an ominous sense that if she continued, Rem would be right. She'd be jumping into a hole that might be too deep to jump out of. But she'd never been one to shirk from fear. Not usually, at least.

She faced Madison. "During the Artist case, one of the victims was a man named Rick. He and I were close." She closed her eyes and paused, trying to just tell the tale without getting emotional. "I thought the Artist killed him, but it turns out he didn't." She opened her eyes. "Somebody else did."

Madison sat quietly, but her face paled. "Who?"

"I'm not sure exactly, but he wrote something in blood on the wall at the crime scene. He wrote 'I did this for you.'"

Madison's face went white and her hands clenched. "Oh, my God."

"Is that phrase familiar to you?"

Madison nodded, and the crease between her brows deepened. "There was a man after Donald was murdered. He followed me, I think, and I saw him watching me." She paused and nibbled her lip. "He said the same thing. 'I did it for you.' I think he killed Donald, although the police disagreed. I heard that same phrase in my head after I'd been arrested, but was out on bail. I told Remalla and Daniels. It was like this man was speaking directly into my brain. I can still hear that whisper like it was yesterday." She held the bridge of her nose. "Remalla got angry with me. He thought I was lying, but I wasn't."

Jill could imagine Rem's response. She put her hand on Madison's wrist. "I believe you."

"They chased him into the woods."

"Who did? Remalla and Daniels?"

"Yes. They were both injured by him and he...they called him Rutger...got away."

"He looked like Rutger Hauer?"

"That's what I told them. I guess the name stuck."

"They confronted him?"

Madison nodded. "Yes, but he somehow escaped."

Jill wondered how that could be possible. Rem and Daniels were relentless when it came to pursuit.

Madison's jaw fell. "Are you saying this is the same man that hurt Rick? He killed two people that we were close to?"

"I think so."

"But why?"

Jill took a deep breath. "According to Sonia, it's because you and I...we're somehow related. And so is this man you call Rutger."

"Related? How? I don't know you. And I certainly don't know him."

Jill eyed the artwork on the wall. "Well, he certainly believes he knows us."

"God. This is crazy. Are you saying he's still out there and he could be dangerous?"

Jill weighed her next words. "It's possible, yes. That's why I'm here. I wanted to tell you what Sonia had told me, and to ask you an important question. Actually, two."

Madison wrung her hands. "What are they?"

Jill hesitated, but pushed forward. "Apparently, this Rutger has some abilities, at least according to Sonia, and Remalla and Daniels."

Madison tensed and then stood, staring up at a painting. "Really?"

Jill detected the shift in Madison's demeanor. "You okay?"

Madison held her elbows. "They told you, didn't they?"

Jill felt that odd chill again. "Who told me what?"

"Remalla and Daniels. At my cabin. The night we caught..." She stopped and chewed her lip again. "... a vase moved on its own, and a picture frame. I'm not exactly sure how it happened, but it did. I think I had something to do with it, but my logical side tells me no. But weird things have happened around me my whole life. I can't explain it." She came back and sat on the couch. "Are you saying this Rutger can do the same thing?"

Jill stared, unsure of what to say. Madison obviously believed that she could somehow move objects without touching them. Maybe the stress of the situation had played tricks on her mind and what likely had an obvious explanation seemed implausible at the time. Had Rem and Daniels believed the same thing due to the same stress? "I don't know," she said.

"What about you? Are you saying you can do it too?"

Jill shook her head. "No, Madison. I can't. I'm more..." She thought about how to explain it. "...in my head. More so than I should be."

Madison studied her. "You can see things, can't you? In your mind?"

Chills ran up and down Jill's arms and she rubbed them. "You're pretty intuitive." Jill swallowed. "People call it a gift, but it's more of a curse."

"Can you see him? Rutger?"

Jill's stomach dropped. "I don't know. I haven't tried. I think I'm afraid to."

"Because once he's in there..."

Jill met her gaze. "I may not get him out." She recalled her visions of the Artist and couldn't avoid a shiver.

Madison massaged a shoulder, her face pinched. "We're a pair, aren't we? Maybe we are related, even though it's impossible."

Jill held her breath. "Is it?"

Madison stilled. "What do you mean? Of course, it is. I have a mom and dad, as I'm sure you do too. Sonia must just be confused, and so is this Rutger. He thinks we're someone else."

Jill took her wrist. "Madison, listen. I thought Sonia was crazy too, but after I heard her story, I sat with it for a while, and I did a little investigating. I mean, that's my background, right?" She bounced her knee faster.

Madison leaned in. "What are you saying?"

"I talked to my dad and asked about my birth. He went quiet on me, and basically told me I was nuts, but I thought he'd reacted strangely. Something didn't feel right. That sixth sense of mine kicked in. I researched my background. I have an older brother, Brian. At the time, my parents lived in Oklahoma and his birth certificate lists Tulsa as his place of birth. My mother had a heart condition and after she had Brian, her health deteriorated, but according to my dad, they decided to have me. But my birth certificate doesn't say Tulsa. It says a city in Connecticut. Dad says it's because they were traveling and I was delivered early. But now, I'm not so sure."

Madison frowned. "Why not?"

"Dad didn't like me asking these questions, and I wondered why. I started calling around to family. Aunts and uncles, talking to them and trying to figure out what was bugging me." Jill paused, remembering the phone call she'd had with her aunt a week ago. It was still jarring to her, and she still wasn't sure whether to believe the woman. "I found my Aunt Emily, who still lives in Tulsa. She and my dad are estranged and haven't talked in years. I asked her about my birth, and she told me how I was such a surprise. I asked her why, and she said because no one expected me. My mother had gone out of town for a while, presumably for medical care. The doctors had told her not to have any more children because it would be too stressful for her heart. She was gone for six months, then my dad went out of town to meet her, and they came back with me."

Madison's eyes shimmered. "Oh, hell."

Jill exhaled slowly, feeling the emotion swell almost as strongly as when she'd talked to Emily. The shock still swirled. "Right after that, they moved to Seattle. Emily and Dad rarely spoke afterwards, and he was always tight-lipped when it came to my birth. But Emily said she knew my mother had never had a baby, because she was beaming when she'd brought me home, when it had taken her weeks to recover after Brian."

Madison put her hand over Jill's. "You believe her story?"

Jill didn't want to, but she nodded. "I think I do. It felt true. And my gut is usually accurate."

"I'm so sorry."

Jill felt a tear escape and trickle down her cheek. She wiped it away. "I hate to admit this, but I'm pretty sure if I were to do a DNA test, I would not be my parents' child." She sniffed. "It stuns me and I'm still dealing with it, but now, I have to wonder..." She eyed Madison. "Where do I come from?"

Madison squeezed Jill's fingers. "I don't know what to say."

Jill shifted on the couch, blinking back her tears. "Madison, if this is true for me, then you have to consider the fact that it may be true for you."

Madison scoffed. "No. That's silly."

"Is it? What do you know about your birth? Is it at all possible that something just as strange could have happened to you? This Rutger. He targeted you for a reason. Think about it. Did your dad or mom ever say anything that seemed strange or out of place?"

"My father raised me, Jill. I was born in San Francisco and raised in that cabin outside San Diego. Dad never for one second said anything to me about being adopted. And I never knew my mother. She died in childbirth."

Jill raised a brow.

"That doesn't mean anything. That happens. In fact...." She stood. "I actually found my birth certificate while I was packing. Dad had kept the original in his safe. I threw it in one of these boxes...hold on." She went to a cardboard box and dug through it. She pulled out a file folder and opened it. "Here it is." She pulled out a worn piece of paper. "See. Look—" She read it and froze, the color draining from her face.

Jill stood, walking over. "What is it?"

Madison didn't answer.

"Madison..."

"How is that possible? I thought...." Madison mumbled, her face flustered. "Where did you say you were born?"

Jill came up next to her and studied the certificate, reading the place of birth. An ice-cold sliver of shock shot through her belly. The location was New Britain, Connecticut.

"Holy shit," said Madison, quietly. "We were born in the same city?"

Jill read the whole certificate. "It's not just that. Look." She pointed to the date of birth, her finger shaking. "I was born on the same day."

Chapter Seven

A LOUD HARP-LIKE SOUND reverberated in Rem's ears and played in a continuous loop, the noise aggravating his slumber and his aching head. He swatted out with his hand, trying to find whatever was making the noise and shut it off, but found nothing. The annoying sound wouldn't stop, and Rem reached out again, but couldn't find the source. Where the hell was it?

Reluctantly, and with great effort, he opened one eye. The surroundings were unfamiliar. After opening his other eye, he blinked, trying to focus. His eyes were crusty, his tongue felt like a dry sponge, and his temples throbbed. Raising his head, he looked around and remembered. He was in the locker room down the hall from the squad room. Murky light from the perimeter of the window shade illuminated enough of the room for him to see lockers and a couple of benches. He had a vague recollection of Daniels guiding him back here. Rem groaned into the pillow. He'd been emotionally and mentally exhausted, and still was, but he felt marginally better. At least he no longer felt the urge to throw up.

His muscles protesting, he sat up and pushed the blanket back. He swung his legs over and put his feet on the ground. Pushing his hair back with his hands, he saw his vibrating phone on the floor and a bag at the foot of the bed. He reached down, picked up his cell, and turned off the alarm. The room went quiet. The bag was the reusable kind you used for the grocery store, and he leaned down and pulled it over. Opening it, he saw some clothes, a lunch bag, and a note on top. He opened the note and read it.

I ran to your place and got you a change of clothes so you can take a quick shower. There's a ham and cheese sandwich and chips in the bag and a bottle of water on the locker beside the bed, along with two aspirin.

Rem looked up and spotted the bottle. He smirked.

Drink ALL of the water, and then come get some more. And take the aspirin. Lozano will be back at 1:00. I set your phone alarm for 12:30, so make it quick. D.

P.S. I put the bracelet in the bag. I figured you'd rather keep it.

Rem crumpled the note, the emotion returning. His partner took better care of him than he did, and the guilt washed over him. Daniels shouldn't have to be responsible for his reckless behavior. Yes. Rem had lost Jennie, but people died and left grieving loved ones behind every day. Daniels had lost people in his life too, and he didn't fall apart every time the breeze blew.

Moving slowly, Rem dug through the bag and pulled out the clothes. The locker area had a shower with shampoo, and he couldn't wait to get cleaned up. He felt like shit and probably looked it too. He thought of Jill and wondered where she was, hoping she was okay. He debated whether he should call her at some point and try again to talk to her, but his head hurt when he thought about it, so he stopped.

Pushing off the bed with a curse, he stood, swayed for a second, but found his balance. He grabbed his clothes and went into the bathroom.

Fifteen minutes later, he reemerged, feeling much better. His headache remained though, and he opened the water and downed the aspirin, then took several more gulps of the water. He knew he needed it. Seeing the sunglasses he'd worn earlier, he picked them up. His reflection in the mirror after his shower still revealed his red eyes, but the bags under them were less droopy, and he didn't look as haggard. He tied his wet hair back and figured it would have to do.

Holding the glasses, he grabbed the bag and was about to dump his dirty clothes and shades in it when he saw the bracelet at the bottom. Not wanting to fall back into his hole of grief, he hesitated, but after deciding he could certainly be strong enough to pick it up, he did. He took out his lunch and dropped the dirty clothes in the bag. Without looking at it, he put the bracelet in the pocket of his clean pair of jeans, picked up the bag, water and his lunch, and headed out. Checking the time, he saw he had eight minutes until Lozano's return. He could eat his lunch at his desk.

He returned to the squad room, feeling better physically, but remorseful. Daniels sat at his desk, a half-eaten apple beside him, and holding a pencil, with his head bent over a file. He looked up when Rem returned and put the pencil down. "My suspicions are confirmed. You are human."

Rem dropped the bag and shoved it under his desk. He put the lunch bag down and held the water. "I was a little dubious myself." He drained the rest of his water.

"Good boy. Now drink some more. And eat. It will help."

Rem nodded and refilled his water at the dispenser. He figured now was not the time to argue with his partner.

"Feel better?" asked Daniels.

"I couldn't feel much worse." He returned to his desk and sat. His head still throbbed, and he grimaced, but he opened the lunch bag and pulled out the sandwich and chips.

"You get the bracelet?"

Rem figured Daniels was probably waiting to see if he would melt down again. "I got it. Thanks for getting it out of the trash."

"You're welcome."

Rem's stomach rumbled, and he bit into his sandwich, taking a deep sigh of pleasure that he didn't feel like throwing up.

Daniels checked his watch. "Good timing. Lozano should be here at any..."

On cue, Lozano walked through the squad doors. He looked tired, but less worn than the previous day. "Remalla. Daniels."

"Hi, Captain," said Daniels.

"Cap," said Rem, taking another bite of his sandwich.

"How's Mrs. Hendrix?" asked Daniels.

He stopped by their desks. "She's doing her best, but it's hard."

"How are you?" asked Rem.

"I'm doing my best, too." He slid his jacket off. "Can I see you two in my office, please?"

He walked away and Daniels raised a brow at Rem. "We got a 'please.' I wonder what that means?" He stood.

Rem stood, too, holding his sandwich and grabbing his chips. "He's either got a full stomach, or we're about to be fired."

Daniels grabbed Rem's water. "Don't forget this."

Rem didn't object. "Thanks."

They walked into Lozano's office and took a seat. Rem chewed the remains of his food and drank his water. Lozano put his jacket on the back of his chair and sat.

"You get any lunch, Cap?" asked Rem.

"There was a ton of food where I was. The Hendrix family knows how to cook, especially when they're grieving." He sat back and held his stomach. "I'm stuffed."

Rem made eye contact with Daniels.

"Good to know," said Daniels.

"How are you two doing? You make any progress this morning?" He waved a finger at them.

Rem took another bite of his sandwich and tried not to sink in his chair. Daniels answered.

"No luck on robberies in the area, and we don't have any knowledge of any family members who might have a grievance."

"At least none that we've found," said Rem, adding what little he could.

Lozano grabbed a pen and scribbled something on a pad of paper. "I might have something for you on that. This morning, I learned about a grandson of the judge. Michael Jamison." He pulled the paper off and handed it to Daniels, who took it. "Apparently, he was in and out of juvie as a teenager, and he's recently been in trouble for domestic abuse and auto theft. He got into an argument with the judge a few months ago, after asking him to call in a few favors to help him out. Martin said no. Said it was time for Michael to start acting like a man. They argued and Michael left. He wasn't there today. I want you to check him out."

"Will do, Cap," said Daniels.

"What about the report from Research? Did you get it?" asked Lozano.

Rem bit into a chip and held his water. He remembered Daniels saying something about the report this morning, but couldn't recall what.

"We did," answered Daniels. "There're a lot of names on it, though. It's going to take time to go through it, and there's no guarantee our guy's even on it."

"That number pop up? Any connections?" He looked at Rem.

Rem glanced at Daniels and caught the movement of his finger, indicating no. "Nope, nothing so far," he said.

"Can we whittle it down more? What were the parameters?" asked Lozano.

Daniels leaned on his armrest. "Any violent offenders found guilty in the judge's courtroom, including anyone who threatened the judge, who were released in the last year."

"Hmm. I've been thinking," said Lozano. "Does that include anyone who died in jail before they were released?"

Rem tipped his head. "You think that's important?"

"It can't be many," said Daniels. "You think it should be in there?"

"Yes, I do." Lozano put his pen behind his ear. "That number. It could be a date. And if it is, that date was just last week. It could have been a trigger for the killer."

Daniels nodded. "That's a good catch, Cap. We'll check it."

"If someone died in prison that Hendrix put away, it could be a motive. Anger and grief can do funny things to a person," said Lozano.

Rem gripped his water, and his stomach curdled.

"That it can," said Daniels.

Lozano eyed Rem. "You okay, Remalla? You look a little pale this morning. And I haven't heard a single smart-ass comment." He squinted. "And why is your hair wet?"

Rem sat up straight. "I, uh, didn't sleep too well last night, Cap. Didn't feel too good this morning, either."

"I told him to take a quick shower," said Daniels. "Thought it might help him feel better."

Lozano nodded. "I'm sorry you two have to come in on a Sunday, but the sooner we can find this guy, the better. Especially for Martha and her family."

"We get it, Cap," said Daniels.

"Try narrowing your report to the last three months. Maybe that will help. If nothing turns up, we can extend the timeline." Lozano sat up. "Hope you feel better, Remalla. I'll let you guys out of here earlier today."

"Appreciate it, Cap, but I'm doing better," said Rem. He held up the last bite of his sandwich. "Daniels got me some food, and I'm keeping it down."

Lozano nodded at his bottle. "And you're drinking water. That's how I know you don't feel well."

"We'll check out Michael and rerun the report with the changes," said Daniels. "You need anything else?"

"No. You can go," said Lozano.

Rem and Daniels stood.

"Just one thing." Lozano took the pen from his ear. "I was short with you yesterday. I was a little harder on you than I should have been. I apologize."

Daniels and Rem regarded each other. "It's okay, Captain," said Daniels. "Yesterday was a hard day. No apology needed."

Rem tossed his empty chip bag in a trash can by the door, feeling that familiar constriction in his chest. "Like you said, Cap, grief can do strange things."

Lozano grunted and leaned back in his seat. "Get back to work and keep me posted."

"Thanks, Cap." They left and Daniels shut the door behind them.

Rem returned to his seat. Even though he'd slept a couple of hours, he still felt drained. He chewed the last bite of his sandwich and finished his water. He eyed the coffee machine.

"You should drink some more water," said Daniels. He sat at his desk.

Rem fiddled with the empty bottle. "Thanks for covering for me in there, and for this morning."

Daniels nodded. "You're welcome. Glad you're feeling better." He opened the file he'd been studying earlier. "I guess we can just mark out the cases that are over three months and come back to them later if we need to."

"Hey," said Rem.

Daniels looked up.

"I was an ass this morning. If Lozano had been here—"

"But he wasn't, so don't worry about it."

"I'm sorry I did that to you. I should have…" He scratched his head, which still throbbed. "I should have held it together."

Daniels put his forearms on the desk. "You don't need to apologize. Like Lozano said, grief can do crazy things. Combine that with Jacobs showing up on your doorstep throwing Rick in your face and going off to find Rutger, and you've got a royal shit storm waiting to blow."

"And I blew it all over you."

"Believe me, you smelled like it."

Rem rested his head in his palm.

"Hey," said Daniels. "You would have done the same for me. And have."

"Not at work, I haven't."

Daniels shrugged. "Not yet, anyway."

"I promise. I'm going to find a way through this. I just…I shouldn't have…"

"Gone through Jennie's things?" asked Daniels.

Rem raised a brow.

"I know where you put her stuff. I was there when you did it."

"I just thought, with the two-year anniversary and all, that maybe it was time."

Daniels studied him. "Maybe. Maybe not. Maybe you need to just take it in stages. Just one thing at a time." He closed the file. "But do me a favor."

Rem straightened.

"Don't do it alone. That's a recipe for disaster. Invite me over, I'll bring pizza and some beer. We'll share memories of Jennie and get drunk together."

Rem smiled. "What are friends for?"

"Exactly." Daniels relaxed back against the seat. "How's your stomach?"

"Better."

"Great." He pulled out the paper he'd been studying, creased it, laid it against the edge of his desk and split it in half. He handed one side to Rem, who took it. "Then let's get busy."

Chapter Eight

PETER TAPPED SOFTLY ON the bedroom door, holding a cup of tea. He heard a soft 'come in' and entered. Sonia sat at a desk with various papers and files in front of her. A laptop was open, and she closed it.

"Here you go. It's Earl Gray."

"Thank you, dear. I appreciate it."

He scanned her messy desk. "Are you making any progress?" She sipped her tea and he noted her fatigue.

She held the bridge of her nose. "Would you mind handing me my peppermint oil?"

"Not at all." He went to a side table, found the oil, and brought it to her. She opened it and dabbed some on her temples, third eye and back of her neck, then rubbed her hands together and smelled it, taking deep breaths. "Thank you, Peter."

He noted her tired features. Her usual cherub face was drawn, and her twinkling eyes drooped. A big chunky necklace of white stones encircled her neck, and she ran her fingers over a smooth one. "Are you all right?"

"I'm fine."

"Were you able to meditate today?"

She nodded. "Yes."

"You seem…" He searched for the word. "Unsettled."

She took another sip of her tea and set it down. "Are you worried about me?"

He decided to be honest. "I am."

"Why? I'm just sleepy."

He pulled the empty chair beside her up closer and sat. "Ever since your injury, you haven't been the same."

She nodded and patted him on the wrist. "Not to worry. Don't count me out yet."

"Have the meditations helped?"

Her face dropped. "On the contrary, they've been...as you say...unsettling."

"Have they revealed anything?"

"Nothing of value." She picked up her tea and took another sip.

He eyed her desk. "What are you working on?"

"Research."

He debated asking her what she was researching, but doubted she'd answer. "Sonia..."

"Yes?"

"You told me that the next time I had a concern or issue to bring it to your attention."

She put her cup down. "What is it?"

He took a deep breath, hoping he was doing the right thing. Sonia didn't like her actions questioned. "Do you think it was the right thing to tell Jill Jacobs everything? I'm worried she'll get hurt, or worse."

Sonia studied him and looked away. "I considered that many times before telling her, but intuitively, I knew I had to." She returned her attention to him. "And I always trust my gut."

"You want her to find Madison and Jace? You want her to tell them?"

"I fear it is the only way to end this."

"Won't it make it worse? He could retaliate."

"How much worse could it get?"

He considered his response. "Much worse. So far, he's only killed people close to those three. At least, as far as I know. What if he decides to hurt others?"

"That's exactly why the three of them need to come together. As a team, they are stronger. Individually, well, I don't think they could stop him."

"Then perhaps we should have told them sooner."

She offered him a soft smile. "It's hard to know what would have been best. Unfortunately, their shared pain is what gives them their strength."

He tensed. "Are you saying they benefited from his revenge?"

She shook her head. "In a strange way, yes. His rampage and anger could ultimately result in his own destruction." She gripped her necklace. "I'd hoped I could reach him another way, but I failed. Now we have to go with what we have."

"Sonia, I have to ask. Are you getting weaker because of your injury or because of something else?"

She waved a hand. "You worry too much, Peter. That's always been your weakness."

A wave of sadness washed over him. "You know why I worry. I've known my own pain. I don't want to lose anyone else."

She turned in her chair, her face sympathetic. "I know, dear. It's why I asked for your help specifically. I knew you would be an asset, despite your worries."

"I don't want to be your burden. I want to help."

She put a hand on his cheek. "You are a kind and gentle soul, Peter. I know that. You are far kinder and gentler than me. In many ways, your presence here reminds me of who I should be and what I should aspire to."

A swell of emotion made his heart swell. "I appreciate you saying that. I've wished I could be more like you."

"Be careful what you wish for, Peter." She dropped her hand and turned back to her desk.

"Is there anything I can do to help you? With your research?"

"No."

"Why not? Why can't I help you? Isn't that why I'm here?"

She started to speak, but then hesitated. "I'm uncertain."

"About what?"

"About how much to involve you." She touched her throat. "I am not the only one at risk. Those who are close to me could also be targeted."

He sat forward. "I didn't sign up for this just to bring you your tea. Tell me what I can do." She eyed him, and he could see her concern, but also her weariness. "You're obviously exhausted. Let me take some of the work. I might be able to see something you may not."

She waited, and he knew she was considering it. After a long pause, she huffed. "Very well." She dug through her papers, pulling out certain ones and gathering them together. She placed them in a file and handed them to him. "Here. Take this."

He took the file. "What is it?"

She rubbed her hands on her thighs. "I have decided that perhaps meditation is not enough. I do trust my instincts, but I also have to trust my intellect. The two should function together. I've written down everything I know about this man, from my earliest memories to the latest. His childhood and teenage years. His strengths and weaknesses. Who he knew and who he interacted with until the day he disappeared. And then I listed everything I knew about what he's done since. I'm trying to compile a profile of him. Something that might give us some insight into what he might do next, or what he might want from us. Anything that might help us find him or reveal some of his thinking."

"What do you want me to do with it?"

"Go through it. See if anything sparks something. If there's a name you know, then tell me how you know it. If there's a name you don't know, then research it. He's out there, so he's got to have money. He's got to have shelter and food. He's got to be using a name. If he's bouncing from place to place, I want to see if there's a pattern. Is he following someone? Is there another person on his list? The smallest detail is important."

He ran his hand over the file, feeling oddly proud. "I will. I'll check everything." He paused. "Thank you for your trust."

Her face fell. "Peter, listen. There are things you will read that you will find disturbing. You will learn things about me and others that will surprise you. If you take this on, you will be expected to keep anything you read confidential. It's between me and you only. If you can't honor that, then give me back the file. Not only that, but there are risks inherent with this research. The more you know, the more dangerous it becomes. Do you understand that?"

He took a steady breath. "I understand."

"Do as much as you can from home. It makes it harder for him to find you if you stay in."

A whisper of fear curled up his spine. Should he be doing this? Was it worth his life? "I can do that."

"Keep me apprised of everything. No delays. You know something, you say something."

"I will."

She nodded, her face drawn. "Please be careful."

"I'll do everything you ask. I promise." He touched her elbow. "Why don't you lie down for a bit? Let me review the files. When you wake, I'll order some dinner, and I can let you know if I have any questions."

She hesitated, looking at the file and then at him. "I think I will. I'm feeling a little tired." She picked up her tea. "You'll wake me if you need me?"

"Of course," he said, knowing he had every intention of letting her sleep. "Get some rest."

"Thank you, Peter." She stood. "Feel free to use the laptop." She walked to the door and looked back, her face clouded, and for a moment he wondered if she'd changed her mind.

"Everything will be fine," he said, trying to ease her fears. He realized he wasn't the only one who worried. "Go lie down."

She smiled sadly, holding her tea, and left the room.

Chapter Nine

JILL PULLED UP AND parked on the side of the street. She turned off the engine and undid her seatbelt. Madison did the same from the passenger side.

"This is it?" asked Madison.

Jill eyed the bar across the road. The sign *Brando's* in neon sat above the door but the lights were off. It was still early for the bar crowd. "This is it." Sonia had provided little information about Jace Marlon, but she knew he owned a bar named Brando's. Jill figured she'd find him here after she'd located Madison.

She regarded Madison. "You sure you want to go in? You can stay in the car if you want."

Madison bobbed her head. "Of course, I'm going in. If this guy is my brother, I want to meet him with you there. We should do it together."

Jill was glad Madison felt that way. It felt better to do this with someone else by her side. She thought of Rem and a heavy weight hit her heart. She missed talking to him. Now that her anger had cooled, she wondered if she'd been too hard on him.

"You ready?" asked Madison.

Jill came back to the present. "Yes. Let's go."

They opened their doors and got out, and jogged across the street. Approaching the front door, she saw the open sign was not on, but she pulled on the door and it was unlocked. Madison followed her in.

The bar was quiet and small. A few four-top tables and a few more two-tops to her right took up much of the space, and a long bar with barstools on her left took up the rest. There was a door to an office to the left of the entrance, but it was closed. "Hello?" she asked. "Anyone here?"

A man emerged from an area behind the bar. He was tall and thin with dark hair and probably in his thirties. He held a bar towel and threw it on the counter. "Sorry. We're closed. We'll open in an hour, though."

Jill wondered if this could be her brother. He favored her more than Madison did. She and Madison walked up, and her heart skipped with nervousness. "We're looking for Jace Marlon. You him?"

The man chuckled. "Hell, no. I wish. He's not here."

"You know when he'll be back?" asked Madison.

"No to that, too. He's out on a road trip. Probably be back this week, but who knows?" He picked up a glass from a drainer and the bar towel and dried it. "Who's asking?"

"Um, we're a couple of friends. Haven't seen him in a while. Thought we'd drop in and say hello," said Jill. She looked for a nametag but didn't see one. "You work here?"

"No, I just walked off the street, decided to do some cleaning." He paused and smiled when Jill and Madison didn't respond. "I'm just messing with you. Yeah. Jace just hired me. I run the bar when he's not here and bartend. It doesn't pay much, but I need the experience."

"What's your name?"

"Terrence. What's yours?"

Jill and Madison made eye contact. "I'm Jill. She's Madison."

He looked between the two of them. "Friends, huh?" He put the glass down. "You know he's got a girlfriend now, don't you?"

"Girlfriend?" asked Madison.

"Yeah. Danni. They've been spending a lot of time together, so if you're looking to hook up—"

"Hook up?" asked Madison with a grimace.

"No. That's not why we're here," said Jill. "Really."

Terrence shrugged. "Sorry. We get women in here who want to have his babies, so you know, I just figured..."

"Believe me, that's the last thing we want," said Jill. "You know how we can reach him?"

Terrence picked up another glass to dry. "Sure. Wait until he returns."

"We're sort of in a hurry, Terrence. We need to tell him something and it's not something that should wait," said Madison.

"It's urgent," said Jill. "You have a phone number for him?"

Terrence put the glass on the bar. "Sorry, I can't give out his personal information."

Jill sighed and pulled out her billfold. "Is it worth twenty bucks to you?"

Terrence grinned. "Have you seen how big that man is? I value my physical health more than twenty bucks."

"Make it forty," said Jill.

"I've got a twenty," said Madison, digging through her purse. "Make it sixty."

Terrence widened his eyes and whistled. "You ladies are desperate." He put down the glass and towel. "Listen. I'd love to help you, and I'd love to take your money, but I need this job. I can't afford to lose it over this. Money or no money. If you want to leave your contact info, I'd be happy to give it to him when he comes back." He adjusted a pile of napkins on the countertop. "That's the best I can do."

Jill debated her next step. She didn't want to wait a week or more for Jace to show. There had to be a way to find him. "Here." she grabbed one of the cocktail napkins Terrence had straightened and pulled a pen from her purse. "This is my name and number. Please tell him to call when he comes in. Or better yet, contact him and let him know we were here." She wrote down her name and number and slid it over to Terrence, who took it and dropped it into a top drawer under the bar, making Jill doubt Terrance would be getting in touch with Jace with the information any time soon.

"Will do. I'll make sure he gets it."

"Thanks," said Jill. "The sooner, the better."

"Thank you," said Madison.

Terrance picked up the towel and waved it. "You ladies have a nice day. You want to come in for a drink later, I'll give you the first one on the house."

Jill shook her head and exited the bar with Madison. They returned to the car and got in. Jill sat thinking and drummed her fingers on the steering wheel.

"What do you want to do now?" asked Madison.

"We need to figure out where he lives."

"You heard Terrance. He may not be back for a while."

Jill crossed her arms. "Or he could be at home, holed up, playing house with his girlfriend."

"Maybe we should have asked for his girlfriend's info?"

"I doubt Terrance would have been any more forthcoming with that information."

"Probably not."

Jill considered her options. She knew from Sonia that Jace had lost someone, too. His best friend. And it had been recent.

"You're a former cop. Don't you have connections?" asked Madison.

Jill shut her eyes and cursed just as Madison came to the same conclusion. "What about Daniels and Remalla? We could ask them."

Jill opened her eyes and gripped the wheel. She moaned out loud.

"What is it?" asked Madison. "It's a good idea."

Jill stared out the windshield, thinking of Rem and their argument. "No. You're right. It's a good idea."

"Then what's the problem?" Madison swiveled to face her. "Is something wrong? I thought you guys were close..." She paused and her eyes widened. "Wait...Are you dating one of them?"

Jill huffed loudly. "Kinda, sorta. Yes."

"It's Remalla, isn't it?" She clapped her hands together. "Oh, you lucky lady, you. I always thought he was good-looking. Daniels is more my type, but still."

Jill squinted. "Daniels is engaged."

"So? A lady can look and appreciate, can't she? Besides, I'm not interested in dating right now." She rested her elbow on the back of the seat. "Give me the scoop. What's the story between you two?"

Jill gawked at her. Having grown up with two brothers and being a tomboy, she'd never experienced a sisterly type of bond, but now Madison was giving her the full rundown.

"Seriously?" asked Jill.

"Seriously. Come on. What else do we have to do with our time?"

Jill grunted, but seeing Madison's eager look, realized she didn't have much choice. She gave Madison the background on her and Rem, and how they'd connected during the pursuit of the Artist and their shared bond of losing someone they'd loved. Just going through the story reminded her of how Rem had pulled her through some ugly times and how strong he'd been for her, and how he'd saved her life.

She finished the story with their argument, telling Madison how she'd left things with Rem and why she was reluctant to ask him for help.

Madison ran her hand over the armrest. "You were a little tough on him, don't you think?"

Jill dropped her jaw. "Excuse me? You're taking his side? He lied to me about Rick."

Madison scrunched her face. "He didn't exactly lie. He just didn't tell you."

"Isn't that a lie?"

Madison stared off, thinking. "I kind of have some experience with this myself. I guess it's how you look at it, isn't it?"

"Yes. I think so. He should have told me."

"I don't disagree. But I can also see his side. It's difficult telling someone something like that. He probably wanted to catch this Rutger guy first and then tell you. But it just took longer than he thought. And I don't think he was planning for this Rutger fellow to be a part of something as strange as all this." She raised a palm. "I mean it's a little crazy."

Jill smacked the steering wheel with her palm. "It just pisses me off."

"Consider this too. I've got some idea of how intense you can be, and I suspect I've just touched the surface. He knew if he told you that, you'd do exactly what you're doing now, which is going after Rutger."

"Of course, he knew that. So?"

Madison tilted her head. "You're zooming right past something important here, Jill. He's already lost one woman he loves. Don't you think he might not want that to happen again?"

Jill stilled, and her heart fell. "He worries too much. Nothing's going to happen to me."

"You sure about that?"

"If this Rutger was going to hurt us, he would have done it by now. I think he wants some sort of reunion."

Madison frowned. "If you're expecting us to be the Waltons, I think you're going to be disappointed. Don't forget. Remalla has seen what he can do. He's pursued him in three different cases. Yours, mine and Jace's. That's three dead people that we know of. You and I have no idea what Rutger wants or what he will do if we chase him down and confront him. Say what you want, but I think you know that you and I are risking more than a bad family reunion. We might not come back from this."

Jill stayed quiet and massaged her tense neck.

"He and Daniels are on the hot seat, too. How would you feel if something were to happen to Remalla?"

An angry heat pulsed through Jill, and she knew she'd fall apart, but not before taking the life of the perpetrator. She sunk into her seat, feeling miserable.

"That's just my two cents, though. I'll shut up now." Madison faced forward but checked her watch. "Just keep in mind. The clock is ticking. But I don't mind waiting for Jace to come back if you don't." She exhaled, her arms in her lap.

Jill studied her, exasperated. She knew when she'd been defeated. Considering the day and time, Jill decided to contact Rem and Daniels first thing in the morning. "You know, I always wondered what it would be like to have a sister." She started up the car.

"How is it?" asked Madison, offering a sideways glance.

"Just as irritating as I thought it would be." She put the car in drive.

Madison smiled. "I'm actually rather enjoying it."

Jill snorted, hit the accelerator and headed out into the traffic.

Chapter Ten

REM SIPPED FROM HIS coffee cup and relaxed against the sink. This morning was already a billion times better than the previous morning. He felt ill just thinking about yesterday. But after getting home at a decent hour, eating a solid meal, taking a nice hot shower, going to bed and sleeping for a solid twelve hours, he felt light years better. He could even think about the bracelet and Jennie without tearing up.

When he'd come home after a promise to Daniels not to go into the upstairs bedroom, he'd put the bracelet in the drawer by his bedside table and left it. He hadn't had the strength to do much else. He figured he'd deal with Jennie's stuff and the rest of the closet later. It might be a year later, but right now, it didn't matter. He was just glad his headache was gone, and he could drink his coffee again without it coming back up.

His cell rang, and he saw it was Daniels. He answered. "Good news. I'm up, I'm sober, and I'm about to head out. In fact, I might even be early."

"Glad to hear it," he responded. "Only don't go to the station."

"What do you mean?"

"We've got another body. Same M.O."

Rem put his coffee down. "You're kidding."

"No. And you're not going to believe who it is. Lyla Alba."

Rem dropped his jaw. "The D.A.?"

"One and the same."

"We just worked with her last month on that robbery arrest over on Fifth."

"I know. Looks like she was shot sometime last night. Her housekeeper found her this morning. The press is going to be all over this, especially with the judge's death, too. I'll send you the address. Meet you over there."

"Yeah. Ok. See ya."

He hung up, shocked. Lyla Alba had worked for the city for almost as long as the judge, or at least to Rem it seemed that way. Hardworking, tough as nails and relentless, she usually got her man. Rem and Daniels had worked with her as a prosecutor on several cases, and she'd just recently become the District Attorney. Gripping the counter, he couldn't believe she was dead. Obviously, somebody was pissed with the county's judicial branch. Shaking his head, he finished his coffee, grabbed his jacket, and headed out the door.

· · · • • · • • · · ·

Thirty minutes later, he pulled up to the house. Yellow tape surrounded the entrance and a coroner's wagon, police cars, a forensic unit and three press vans were on the scene. Reporters stood at the edge of the tape, likely broadcasting for the early morning news. Rem cursed and parked. Seeing Daniels' car, he got out.

Flashing his badge, he went under the tape and up to the entrance. Daniels met him at the door with gloves and shoe coverings.

"What have we got?" he asked, putting on the gloves.

"Just like the judge. One shot to the chest. Up close."

"Shit."

"Tell me about it."

His shoes covered, he followed Daniels inside. The house was elegant and refined, much like Lyla. Artwork covered the walls, and the furniture was plush and velvety, the kind of stuff where you could take a good nap or read a good book. He walked into the living room and saw a covered form lying on a cushy rug stained red with blood. His stomach clenched, and he put his hands on his hips. "Ah, hell."

Daniels stood beside him. "I know."

Rem squatted and lifted the cover. Lyla was in her robe, a gaping wound in her chest, her face a grimace. He dropped it back down and stood. He scanned the room and didn't see anything else out of place. Smelling coffee, though, he turned and saw the kitchen and coffee machine on the counter. A full pot had been brewed.

"Looks like she got up, put on her robe, went to get some coffee, and met her assailant, who shot her in the chest," said Daniels.

"Any forced entry?"

"No."

"Casing?"

"Found it on the carpet. Forensics has it. Oh, and there's something else."

"Of course, there is."

"Guy left a piece of paper with the same number on it."

"Of course he did."

"It's on the counter."

Rem walked over and saw a bag with a piece of loose-leaf paper. 0212 was written in a rough scrawl in pencil. Rem picked up the bag. "At least we know it's the same guy."

"And he's pissed at Alba and Hendrix, but for what?" asked Daniels.

Rem put the bag down. "Guess we're going to have to find out. If nothing else, I think that list we're working on is going to get a lot smaller."

"Let's hope." Daniels patted Rem's shoulder. "Let's get out of here."

· · · ● ● · ● ● ● · ·

After arriving back at the station, Rem parked and got out of his car. He met Daniels at the entrance, and they entered. A tall, slim policeman with a narrow mustache stood at the front desk. "Hey Shorty," said Rem.

"Shorty," Daniels said with a wave.

"Hey guys. I heard about Alba. Hard to believe," said Shorty.

"I know. Crazy world. Hopefully, we'll catch the guy quick before he hits again," said Daniels.

They headed toward the stairs.

"Hey, you two got visitors. I told them to wait upstairs for you."

Rem stopped on the first step. "Visitors?" He eyed Daniels, who shrugged. "Who?"

The phone rang, and Shorty answered. Rem looked up the stairs, but they hooked left, and he couldn't see.

"Guess we're about to find out," said Daniels.

"Guess so."

Rem headed to the second floor and Daniels followed. He saw no one, until he got to the top and stopped, seeing Jill sitting on a bench. She stood, her face unreadable. "Hey, Rem."

He went still. Some part of him wanted to take her in his arms, but he silenced it. He doubted she wanted the same. "Hey."

Daniels stopped suddenly beside him. "Hey, Jacobs."

"Hey, Daniels. How are you?" said Jill. "It's good to see you. How's J.P. and Marjorie?"

"They're great. How are you?"

She started to answer when another woman came around the corner. "Daniels? Remalla?" She came closer, and Rem recognized her.

"Madison?" he said, stepping toward her. He remembered the last time he'd seen her, cold, shivering and teary-eyed on her front lawn at Secret Lake. She looked much better now.

"Hi, Detectives. It's nice to see you." She came up and gave them both hugs.

"How's the art world?" asked Daniels.

Madison smiled. "It's going great. I'm selling some pieces, so I'm excited."

"Good for you," said Rem.

"Rem told me you're engaged. Congratulations," said Jill to Daniels.

"Thank you," said Daniels. "We're pretty excited, too."

Rem waited, wondering why they were here. The four of them sat in uncomfortable silence before Jill finally spoke. "Do you guys have a minute?"

"Uh, sure," said Daniels, eyeing Rem, probably wondering whether Rem was up for it.

"Why not?" said Rem. He gave Daniels a slight nod, assuring it was okay.

"Great," said Madison. "Thanks."

Daniels led them into a nearby interrogation room.

Jill walked in. "This brings back memories. This is where Sonia gave her description of the Artist."

"Yeah, it is," said Rem. "Have a seat."

Madison took a chair, but Jill stood. Feeling a little shaky, Rem took the other seat.

Daniels closed the door. "I'd ask what we can we do for you, but I think I'm afraid to."

Rem spoke to Jill. "It didn't take you long to find her, did it?"

Jill crossed her arms. "I knew where to start. I knew she lived at Secret Lake."

"She's tenacious," said Madison. "I'd actually sold the cabin and moved, but she found me."

"Tenacious is a good word," said Rem.

Jill frowned.

"You two helping each other out?" asked Daniels.

Jill and Madison held eye contact, and Madison hugged herself. "Yeah, well, when you find out you're sisters, you kind of want to get to know each other."

Rem sat forward. "Really? You're sure?"

"Pretty damn," said Jill.

"How do you know?" asked Daniels.

Jill sighed. "I talked to my dad and asked a lot of questions about my birth, most of which he did not want to answer. I got a hold of a relative who confirmed my birth story was suspicious. Long story short, Madison and I compared birth certificates. We share the same place of birth and same date of birth."

"What? Are you serious?" asked Rem.

"You're twins?" asked Daniels, his eyes wide.

"Obviously fraternal," said Madison.

"Obviously," said Jill.

Daniels' jaw fell open. "So Rutger is family?"

"We don't know who the hell he is, or what his connection is to us, but I plan to find out," said Jill.

Daniels straightened. "Jill, be careful. Rutger is not somebody to mess with."

"I've heard. He killed Rick, so yeah. I think I get the picture. Too bad it was later rather than sooner." She shot a look at Rem.

A sliver of anger bubbled up inside Rem, but he stayed quiet. Now was not the place for an argument.

"This man is not who you think he is. I doubt the timing would have mattered," said Daniels.

"We'll never know, will we?" Jill turned and ran a hand through her hair.

Daniels glanced at Rem, who shook his head. Daniels spoke to Madison. "What do you think about all of this?"

Madison sat up. "You guys know what this man can do better than any of us. You've seen things I know you're not comfortable talking about. You know Sonia and you know Jace. You probably have a better understanding of Rutger than anybody. What do you think we should do?"

Jill snorted. "Come on, Madison. He's just a guy with a penchant for murder. Why is everybody treating him like he's some sort of evil superhero?"

"Because he sort of is," said Rem. "He took me and Daniels out without touching either of us."

"Broke my ribs and gave him stitches in his head. Took our guns, too. Right out of our hands," said Daniels.

"Hell," said Madison, clenching her hands.

"How much had you two had to drink at the time?" asked Jill.

Daniels put a hand on the wall and kept a relaxed posture. "Believe us or don't, but I think Madison knows what we're talking about."

"Don't you, Madison?" asked Rem.

Madison dropped her head. "Yeah." She nodded. "Yeah, I do."

"Oh, come on. You guys are not really buying this, are you?" asked Jill. She looked at all three, but no one responded. "Fine. You believe whatever you want. That's your choice. But let me ask you something. Have you told Lozano any of this? Does he know why this guy 'supposedly' gets away all the time?"

"It's not exactly something that can go in a report," said Rem.

She smiled and her eyes glimmered. "I bet. And you know why? Because it's crazy."

"Jill—" started Madison.

"Madison," Jill interrupted. "Let's just ask about what we came here for. Then we will deal with finding this guy."

Daniels leaned against the wall. "What do you need?"

Jill adjusted a necklace around her neck. Rem recalled it was the one Sonia had given her. "Jace's contact info," she said. "We went to his bar. The guy there wouldn't give it to us, and he didn't know when Jace would be back."

"We want to talk to him," said Madison. "If he's our brother, we need to confirm it."

"And then what?" asked Rem.

"We'll gather around a campfire and roast marshmallows," said Jill. Rem caught Daniels' glare. Jill caught it too and huffed. "Fine. I don't know. We're just playing this by ear. But something tells me this Rutger guy might be a little curious if we suddenly become...become..." She shook her head.

"A family?" asked Daniels.

"Be careful what you wish for," said Rem.

Jill held his stare. "Can I get Jace's info? Or not?"

Rem debated what to do. If he gave it to her, he could be sending her on a collision course with Rutger, and that scared him, but if he didn't, then he'd be on the collision course. He couldn't be sure which was worse. Deciding, he pulled out his cell. Jill pulled out hers too, and he gave her Jace's cell number.

"You have his address?" she asked.

"Not in my phone," said Rem.

"It'll be in his file," said Daniels. Jill straightened and waited. Daniels eyed Rem. "I guess I'll get it."

"Thanks," said Madison.

Daniels stepped out of the room.

"If he, Rutger, shows up, what do we do?" asked Madison.

Rem considered that. "Keep him talking. He likes to talk. We still know nothing about his background or how you guys are connected to him, and something tells me he might want to share. Maybe if you can create a bond with him, he might keep you alive."

"Until we can bring him in," said Jill.

He held his breath. "Nobody's bringing this guy in unless you kill him first."

Jill scowled. "You're just trying to scare her."

"I'm trying to scare both of you. My hope is if you're family, he won't hurt you, but no one can guarantee anything at this point. Madison should know the risk."

"He killed Donald," said Madison. A strand of blonde hair fell in her face, and she tucked it back. "I know the risk."

The door opened and Daniels returned with a file. He put it on the desk. "Here it is."

Jill leaned over and read where Daniels pointed and typed it into her cell. After typing, she stopped. "Hell. Madison look." She pointed.

"What?" Madison stood and came over, checking the file.

Rem stood and did the same. "What is it?" He leaned in, reading where Jill pointed. It was Jace's date-of-birth.

Madison sucked in a breath. "Oh, my God. It's the same as ours."

Chapter Eleven

Jace put the plates in the sink and ran them under the faucet, then put them in the dishwasher. He thought of Danni as he worked, thinking about their past week. After he'd hired Terrance, he and Danni had gotten on the bike and disappeared. They'd spent some time at the beach and up in the hills, enjoying each other and their time together. After almost dying, Danni was slowly recovering, and so was Jace, but the mental injuries were taking a lot longer to recover from than the physical ones.

The bathroom door opened, and Danni emerged, wearing jeans and a t-shirt with a towel wrapped around her hair.

"Feel better?" he asked.

She came up behind him and put her hands around his mid-section. "Much. Thanks for breakfast. You make a mean pancake."

He shut off the water and swiveled in her arms. "You make a mean O.J."

She grinned and hugged him. "I bought it at the store."

"But you poured it with love."

Danni smiled up at him and pulled off the towel. Her hair fell in her face, and she brushed it back. "You going into work today?" She dropped the towel on the counter.

He pushed a lock of her hair back. "Nah. We just got back last night. Terrance can handle it."

Leaning against him, she put a hand on his chest. "You don't have to keep taking care of me. I'm okay."

A vision of her dangling from his grasp made him shiver. "You may be fine, but I still may need some time."

Sighing, she put her forehead on his chest. "It's hard, isn't it? The minute you think you feel better, the memories tell you otherwise."

"We'll get there." Jace stroked the back of her neck. "Baby steps."

They held each other for a moment before she pushed back. "Do you want to go back to work?"

"I do. I guess I hate the thought of leaving you alone. It still scares me."

"You can't stick to my side forever."

He leaned against the counter. "It's Rutger. He's still out there."

"You think he'll come back?"

"I know he will."

"What about Jill and Madison? Are you going to look for them?"

Jace ran a hand up her arm to her shoulder. "I thought maybe we could focus on you first before we deal with my family."

"Me?"

"How's your dad? Have you talked to him since we visited?"

She nodded. "He called me."

"And?"

"He invited me to Brad's ninth birthday party. It's next month."

"You want to go?"

She stared off. "I don't know. I just reconnected with my father after years of estrangement. I think going to his son's birthday may be asking a little too much right now."

"You got time. You can think about it. And I can go with you if you want."

She smiled. "Brad would love that. I think he's enamored with you."

Jace chuckled. "I think he likes the bike."

"And the fact you let him ride it. I think he would have come home with you if his parents would have let him."

Jace grabbed a kitchen towel from the counter and wiped up some spilled water. "I think you're right. He's a nice kid."

"Crazy what can happen when your parents are there for you." He looked back at her, and she shook her head. "Old grudges die hard." She walked out of the kitchen.

"Yeah. I know." He tossed the towel onto the counter and followed her into the living room. "You want to get out of here today? Go to a movie? Get some lunch?"

She went to the window and looked out. "You didn't really answer my question. Do you plan on looking for Jill and Madison? And don't divert the subject back to me. We've talked about me enough."

Jace picked up a pair of folded jeans from the floor that had fallen from the couch and tossed them back on the sofa. He didn't answer.

"What's holding you back?" she asked.

He raised his hands. "I don't know."

"Are you scared?"

He joined her at the window and stood in the sun, warming his face. "Were you scared when you met your dad?"

"Terrified."

Fiddling with a blind, he thought about it. "I don't want to meet them and find we hate each other, or that they're not really my siblings. Or worse, Rutger shows and..."

"Hurts them? Like your dreams? Did you have another one?"

He studied the parking lot outside, recalling his nightmare from last night. "Yeah."

"You should have woken me."

"And what? There's nothing you could have done."

She came up to him and slid her arms around him. "Oh, I can think of a few things."

His heart skipped, and he debated picking her up and taking her to the bedroom. He slid a finger down her cheek and kissed her gently. "Something tells me we're not going to make it to the movies."

She raised up on her toes and kissed him back, the heat quickly building. She spoke against his lips. "I need to go brush my hair."

Her breath mingled with his, and his hand traveled to the back of her neck. "Okay." He kept kissing her.

Danni raised her arms and encircled his neck. "It will tangle if I don't."

He trailed his lips down her cheek to her jaw. "Don't let me stop you."

She sighed, and her head fell back. "You're a bad man, Jace Marlon."

His tongue slid to her ear, and he nibbled her lobe. She shivered against him. "I know," he said. "We keep going and your lovely locks will be a complete mess."

"They will." She ran her fingers up into his hair as he lavished kisses on her neck and collarbone. "You won't be able to take me anywhere." She moaned.

"Guess we'll have to stay inside all day then." He slid his hands down her back and cupped her butt.

"Oh, God," she said. She moved against him and spoke into his ear. "You did it again. You keep changing the subject."

Jace nibbled her shoulder. "The force is strong in my family. You have no power against me."

She giggled, and his heart thumped. "You're crazy."

He trailed his mouth back to hers. "And you're beautiful. Tangled hair and all."

Her lips grazing his, she ran her hands down to his shoulders and caressed them. "How about I go find a comb, and I'll meet you in the bedroom?"

"How about I pick you up, carry you to bed, ravish you, and then you can find a comb?" He tickled her nose with his growing stubble.

The doorbell rang, and he groaned.

Her lip turned up. "Is that being saved by the bell?"

"More like tortured by it." He pulled her close. "Let's ignore it.'

"Maybe it's a delivery."

"They can leave it at the door."

The bell rang again, and she wriggled from his arms. "Answer it. I'll go deal with this." She pointed at her head. "And I'll meet you in bed, and if you're lucky, I'll be naked."

He took a ragged breath and let her go. "Oh, I better be lucky."

Grinning at him, she walked into the bathroom.

The doorbell rang again. "I'm coming," he said, imagining Danni waiting for him between his sheets. "Keep your shorts on." He opened the door and froze.

Rutger stood at his doorstep, his eyes glittering in the hazy light. "Hello, brother. Did I come at a bad time?"

· · • • • • • · · ·

Standing in the interrogation room, Daniels closed Jace's file and Rem frowned. "You guys are triplets?"

Madison sat again, her face pale. "Even better. If Rutger is related and shares the same birthdate, then that makes us quads."

"You think that's possible?" asked Jill. "I mean, all four of us?"

"Yeah, it's possible, but not common. It's rare for it to happen naturally." Madison rested her elbow on the table and held her head.

"You're thinking this wasn't natural?" asked Jill.

"It's more common with in vitro fertilization," said Daniels.

"Shit," said Jill. "What were we? Some sort of experiment?"

Rem tried to wrap his mind around it. "This keeps getting crazier."

"If it's true, then who? And why?" asked Daniels.

"I suspect Sonia knows. Did she enlighten you with anything other than all the stuff I didn't tell you?" Rem asked Jill.

Jill's face fell. "I didn't think to ask her about crazy in vitro science experiments."

Madison sat up. "You know, I've heard stories about the military trying to create some sort of superhuman fighter. You think it could be something like that?"

Daniels chuckled. "Sonia doesn't strike me as military."

"Me, neither," said Jill. She gripped her temples and grimaced.

"You okay?" asked Rem.

She dropped her hand. "Just a headache."

Rem knew there was more to it than that. He'd seen that expression before.

"I agree with Daniels," said Jill. "Sonia's not military. It doesn't feel right. This is..." Her face clouded. "It's something else."

"What are you picking up on?" asked Madison.

"I don't know." Jill squinted. "It feels smaller than some sort of military operation. This is personal. Intimate. Maybe a group of people."

"That's a hell of a group," said Daniels. "They've got to have a shit ton of cash and resources, and for what purpose?"

"Guess we're going to have to find out." Jill took a deep breath and eyed Madison. "Feel like finding Jace?"

Madison hesitated, and Rem wondered if she might back out—almost hoped she would. After a few moments, she stood. "What the hell. Let's go talk to him."

"You two sure about this?" asked Daniels. "You could be walking into a firestorm."

Jill put her phone in her pocket. "We've gotten this far. I'm not stopping now."

Rem blew out his cheeks. "Daniels and I want to help, but if we do, you'll have to wait. This case we're on just exploded."

Daniels nodded. "We've got a dead D.A. on our hands. Lozano's proba-bly waiting for us right now."

"No need. We're good," said Jill. "You ready?" she asked Madison.

Rem slumped, but his stomach tightened in worry. He wanted to pro-tect Jill, but knew he couldn't. And although he'd offered help, and she'd refused, he realized if something happened, he'd still blame himself. An image of Jennie flashed in his mind, and he almost audibly cursed.

Madison spoke. "Just about. Daniels, you have a second?"

Rem saw Daniels raise the side of his lip, and Rem understood Madison's intent. "Sure." Daniels lifted a hand. "Why don't you join me outside?"

Jill's shoulders sagged. "Madison—"

"I'll be just a minute. I want to ask Daniels about...I don't know...guns. I'm thinking of buying one. I live alone, you know." Madison walked to the door.

"Happy to help," said Daniels.

"You could ask me," said Jill.

"Not today, I can't." Madison flicked her eyes at Rem and if Rem had felt better, he would have smiled.

"We'll be right back," said Daniels. He followed Madison out of the room and shut the door behind them.

The room went quiet, and Rem returned to his seat, wondering what to say. Jill paced.

"I'm still pissed at you," she finally said.

"Believe me. I know."

"You should have told me."

"I wish I had."

She kept up her pacing.

"You sure about this?" asked Rem. "About tracking Jace down?"

"I've come this far. I don't plan to go home."

Rem nodded. "Will you promise me you'll be careful?"

She stopped and studied him. "Nothing is going to happen to me."

"You don't know that."

Something in her softened. "You don't need to worry. I can take care of myself."

Rem picked at a fleck of debris on his jeans. "Normally, that's true, but this is different. I know what you're dealing with here, and that's why I'm scared."

Jill made an exasperated sigh. "If this guy wanted me dead, he's had ample opportunity. He's come after each of us, exacting some sort of ill-directed revenge. He's pissed at something and supposedly, whatever happened to him was far worse. For some misplaced reason, he's directed his anger at me, Jace, and Madison. But he hasn't killed us. Why not?"

"I don't know. Nobody does. And if Sonia's not telling, it's probably because she doesn't know either. We can only hope he's done, but I think you and I both know that he isn't."

Jill squirmed and looked away.

"I saw that look on your face. Are you picking up on something? Are you connecting with him?"

She touched her forehead, and her brow furrowed. "No. Not yet at least, but I think he wants to."

"Why do you say that?"

"It's just a feeling, but I've learned how to close up, so I'm not making it easy for him."

"You worried about what will happen if you do?"

She made eye contact, looking weary. "Maybe a little. You know what happened with the Artist. Once he was in, I couldn't get him out. And this guy, he feels a lot stronger."

Rem traced a crack in the table with his nail. "You still having dreams?"

She tilted her head as if surprised he remembered. "Yes."

"Bad?"

"They're not fun."

He paused. "I wish I could help or knew what to do."

"I know."

Rem debated his next words. "I don't want you to walk out that door still pissed at me. If something happens, I'm going to feel bad enough."

"If something does happen, which it won't, it will not be your fault."

"That's easy for you to say. You'll be dead."

"Rem—"

"I know you still feel guilty about Rick, and you didn't kill him. That wasn't your fault, either."

She bit her lip and crossed her arms. "I have to do this."

"I know." He rubbed his jaw. "And in some crazy way, it's why I love you."

Her eyes widened. "You what?"

"You heard me. And you don't have to return it, but it makes me feel better to say it, because I'd regret it if I didn't."

She set her jaw. "God. Why do you have to choose the craziest time to drop this shit on me?"

"I think the timing is perfect."

Her eyes shimmered. "Damn it. I'm trying so hard to stay mad at you."

"I'm determined to wear you down."

She dabbed her eye with a shirt sleeve. "It's really irritating."

"I know. I have lots of practice with Daniels."

"You tell him you love him, too?"

"It takes him by surprise, which is why it's so effective."

"I bet."

He stood, wondering when he would see her again. "I suspect you want to get going."

A tear fell, and she wiped it away. "Oh, hell," she said, and walked into his arms.

He held her, and the smell of her shampoo reminded him of better days. "You promise me you'll be careful. Don't do anything stupid. And call me and keep me up to speed. You don't, and I'm going to call you and keep calling until you answer. Okay?"

She nodded into his neck. As much as she portrayed a tough woman with an even tougher exterior, he knew how fragile she could be, and he held her tighter.

A few seconds passed, and she wiped her face on his shirt. "Sorry," she said, pulling back. "I schmutzed on your sleeve."

"It's not the first time."

She smiled softly. "I know." She took his hand and held it. "I'm not mad anymore, even though I want to be, but I don't want you to worry."

"Thank you."

Her thumb traced the back of his hand. "You're a good man, and I know you're trying to watch out for me."

Rem let out a shaky breath. "And I know why you have to do this, and I know I can't stop you."

She paused. "You should know something else." Her fingers tightened over his hand, and she spoke, her voice cracking. "I love you, too."

His heart pounded, and he smiled. Before he could respond, she stepped close to him, her body against his, and ran her other hand behind his neck. She pulled him near and whispered into his ear. "Very much."

Her breath against his skin made his heart pound harder, and he wanted to hold her, but she gave him a quick kiss and stepped away. "And if I don't leave now, I never will." She wiped her eyes and composed herself.

"Jill—"

"Rem, I have to go or I'm going to lose it, and I don't need Madison harping all over me. She's bad enough as it is. I had no idea that's what sisters did." She walked to the door. "I promise I'll be careful. And I'll call you tonight." Turning, she offered him a quick glance before she opened the door and left.

Chapter Twelve

JACE THREW THE DOOR closed, but it hit an invisible barrier and bounced back, almost hitting him.

"You mind if I come in?" asked Rutger. He stood in his jeans and sweat-shirt, with no hoodie, and Jace saw his full head of hair for the first time. Blonde, long and wavy, it stood up in spikes as if he'd gelled it and went out in a windstorm. His blue eyes were piercing, and Jace wondered who he resembled, because it wasn't him.

"What the hell do you want?" He tried his best to keep his composure since Danni was in the bathroom, and he didn't want her to get hurt, but his heart raced and he fought the urge to reach out and strangle the man who'd killed his best friend, Justin.

Rutger's eyes narrowed. "Oh, you are mad, aren't you?" He offered a veiled smile. "That's good. It works in my favor. Makes you easy to manipulate."

Jace glared, drawing himself up to his full height, which intimidated most. "Get out of here."

"I want to talk."

"No."

"We can meet later, when you're more...available."

"No."

"I can tell you things you want to know."

"No. You're a liar."

His face twisted. "You and me. We have things to work out. Jill and Madison. They've met, and they're looking for you. Did you know that?"

Jace heard the hair dryer turn on in the bathroom.

Rutger heard it too. "Our time is short. I think you'll want to hear what I have to say. Come with me now. Leave Danni here. She'll be safe."

Jace's mind whirled. Something told him to get Rutger out of the building and away from Danni, but something even stronger told him Rutger could not be trusted. He'd already killed Justin. Did he want Jace to leave Danni alone as he'd done before?

"I'm not leaving here, and I'm not going with you."

Rutger studied him, his body rigid. "Oh, you'll be doing one, but preferably both."

"I don't think so. You're used to pushing people around, but I don't push easy, *brother*."

Rutger's eyes glittered like the shiny steel on Jace's motorcycle. "You really want to play this the hard way?"

Jace fought to buy time. How the hell was he going to protect Danni? "You mentioned Jill and Madison. They're looking for me. But you got here first. Why is that?"

Someone walked on the stairs below, and Rutger eyed the hallway. "I don't like standing out here. I'm not an errand boy. Perhaps you should invite me in?"

"If you don't like it, then leave."

"Not until we've talked."

"Unfortunately, we're talking right now."

They stood facing each other, and Jace could feel the energy heighten and swirl around them. He wondered if he was doing the right thing, but he had few options.

The dryer turned off, and before Jace could say anything, he heard Danni. "Who was at the door?"

"Fine with me," said Rutger. "The hard way, then."

From the corner of his eye, Jace saw Danni emerge from the bathroom, but then she was shoved back forcefully before the door slammed shut on her. He heard her scream. That was all it took for his composure to snap, and he reached out and grabbed Rutger by his sweatshirt, pulled him inside and slammed him against the wall.

Rutger gasped as the air left his lungs, but before Jace could slam him back again, Rutger pulled a fisted hand back and slugged Jace hard in his lower ribs. Jace heard and felt a rib give way. Rutger was stronger than he looked. The impact caused him to loosen his hold, and Rutger shoved him back and kicked out, hitting Jace in the stomach.

"I'm not as weak as you think," he said. "Just because you're big doesn't make you better."

Jace doubled over, and he heard Danni banging on the bathroom door. "Jace? What's going on? Jace?"

"You should have left with me," said Rutger. He glanced at the door. "Maybe I'll talk to her instead."

Jace launched himself at Rutger, hitting him in the midsection and slamming him back into the wall. A landscape picture popped off its perch and fell to the ground. He half-expected to be pulled back by some invisible force, but it never came. Rutger struggled against him, and Jace reared back and punched him in the face. Blood spurted from Rutger's nose, and Jace prepared to hit him again. Anticipating the blow, Rutger ducked low and wrapped himself around Jace's belly, hitting him again in the ribs. Jace cringed in pain and pulled Rutger to the floor, knocking over a lamp and toppling the coffee table.

Danni continued to scream from the bathroom, but he was glad she couldn't escape. Falling on top of Rutger, he punched again, contacting Rutger's jaw and cheek. Rutger bucked beneath him, but Jace stayed on. He hit Rutger again. The blood ran down Rutger's face and onto the carpet. Jace's side ached, but he ignored it, and prepared to hit Rutger once more when Rutger grabbed his wrist and delivered a vicious blow to Jace's damaged ribs. Jace cried out, and Rutger swiveled, getting a leg free and shifting his weight. Jace fell to his side and Rutger wiggled free, knocking over the dining table. A knife Jace had used earlier to open a box slid onto the floor.

Rutger grabbed the knife and stood. As Jace got to his knees, Rutger slashed with the knife, catching Jace on the side of his arm. His skin opened and blood spewed. Jace didn't hesitate, though, and as the momentum of the swing moved Rutger's arm away from him, he leaped up, grabbed for the knife and caught hold of Rutger's wrist.

Danni continued to scream and pound on the door, but Jace could not afford to lose his focus. He used his other hand to grab Rutger by the throat and shoved him against the wall, applying pressure.

Rutger cursed, his bloody face grimacing.

Jace, his ribs screaming in pain, held him and squeezed. "Why don't you want me to meet them?" Jace had some sense that's why Rutger had showed.

Rutger, despite his injuries, gasped and smiled, his teeth red from his bloody lips. "Sonia. She was smart to use Jill. But I'm smarter."

"Jace. Please. Let me out." The doorknob turned, and Danni banged desperately on the door. "What's happening?"

The distraction gave Rutger the slightest advantage, and he shifted his weight enough to relieve some of the pressure on his throat. He fought to escape from Jace's grip on his wrist, but Jace swiveled, turning his back to Rutger, and rammed an elbow into Rutger's gut. Rutger dropped the knife as he doubled over with a sharp groan. Jace picked up the knife and slashed at Rutger just as Rutger darted back, but Jace still caught him in the belly, carving a wicked slash into his abdomen. Rutger bellowed and gripped his stomach. His fingers turned red with blood.

Sweat dripped down Rutger's face and anticipating he was spent, Jace made one last lunge with the knife, intent on ending this, but Rutger turned at the last moment, and using Jace's momentum against him, brought his knee up and into Jace's midsection. Jace gasped as the air left his lungs. He buckled to his knees but kept his grip on the knife. A stab of pain shot through his side, and his ribs shifted in a way they weren't meant to. Holding his gut in agony, and forcing himself to breathe, he pushed himself up to face Rutger again.

Danni screamed from the bathroom, and sweaty and bleeding, Jace faced an empty room. The door stood open, and Rutger was gone.

Chapter Thirteen

Jill stopped at the light, double-checking the map on her phone for the next turn.

"Are you sure we shouldn't just call him?" asked Madison. "At least give him a heads up that we're about to turn up at his doorstep."

"I don't like phone calls. People can hang up. If you're standing at their door, it's hard for them to ignore you." The light turned green, and Jill drove on.

"You think he'd ignore us?"

"No. I don't. But it's still a shock. Besides, face to face is better. Let's just rip this bandage off."

"He may not even be there. You heard what Terrance said."

"If he's not, then we'll call." Jill flicked on her turn signal and turned right. Her cell phone rested in the center console and it buzzed and chirped, signaling a text. Taking the turn, she didn't look at it, but Madison did.

"Who is Neil?"

Jill glanced down. The notification was still up, and she read the message. *Share a glass of wine tonight? I have a great red.*

The sender was Neil Wilder. The man she'd met about a month ago at a bar. She swiped at the message, and it disappeared. "Why are you reading my text messages?"

Madison stared, her jaw hanging. "Are you cheating on Rem?"

Jill rolled her eyes. "No. I am not cheating on Rem. It's a text message, for God's sake. Let's not assume the worst."

"He's asking you to share a glass of wine with him. That sounds like a date."

"He's just a friend."

"Does *he* know that?"

Jill hesitated.

"Exactly what I thought."

"Madison, please. It's no big deal. He's just a nice guy I met in a bar. We had coffee and dinner. It's nothing."

From the corner of her eye, Jill could see Madison's eyes narrow and she almost moaned. Madison shifted toward her. "Let me ask you then. Have you told this good friend about Rem?"

Jill studied the road, thinking of Rem and him telling her he loved her, and guilt washed over her.

"You didn't, did you?"

Jill sighed. "Madison, it's just friendly."

"Have you kissed him?"

"What?"

"You heard me."

Jill glanced out the window, wishing she could divert the subject. "I didn't kiss him. He kissed me, but I deflected."

"You deflected?" Madison's voice raised. "What the hell does that mean?"

"It means what it means. I deflected. Pulled back. Moved away."

"But your lips touched his?"

Jill couldn't believe they were having this conversation. "Oh, dear God, Madison. It's not like I slept with him."

"Do you want to sleep with him?"

"No. Of course not."

"Then why haven't you told him about Rem?"

Jill turned onto Jace's street. Seeing the address and Jace's set of apartments, she pulled up and parked. She faced Madison, who did not look happy. Jill wondered how to answer. "I don't know. A month ago, when I met him, he was just a nice guy. Someone to talk to. I hadn't seen Rem in a while, and I guess..."

"What? You were lonely? So you decided to hook up?"

Jill held her head, exasperated. "I did not hook up. He was just nice, and I like him."

"Listen, Jill. I like Remalla, and if you're yanking him around by the chain, then I'm not okay with that."

"I'm not yanking him around by the chain, okay? I guess I just thought, back then, that maybe we weren't going to last."

"And you needed a back-up plan?"

Jill expelled a gust of air. "I don't know. Maybe I just liked the attention."

"That's not fair to Neil or Rem. You need to tell Neil, unless you plan to break it off with Rem, in which case you need to tell Rem."

"I'm not breaking it off with Rem. I'm in love with him."

Madison's face fell and then brightened. "You love him? Does he love you? Did he tell you?"

"Oh, dear God, help me. I'm sorry I said anything. Can we go in now? We have things to deal with other than my love life."

Madison grabbed Jill's cell from the console. "You're going to deal with this?"

Jill reached for her phone and took it back, thinking maybe she should have met Jace first instead of Madison. Brothers she could handle, but this sister thing was frustrating. "I'll deal with it."

"Good."

Shaking her head, Jill opened the door and got out. Madison did the same. Jill came around the car and stood beside Madison.

"Which apartment is it?" asked Madison.

"248," said Jill.

Madison pointed. "That's building two."

They walked over to the set of apartments in the two hundreds and faced the stairs. "You ready?" asked Jill.

"What are we going to say?"

"I figure I'll do what I did with you. Wing it. According to Rem and Daniels, he knows about us, but just isn't sure if he really believes it. It's why the pop-in works. It's hard to ignore two women standing at your door."

Madison nodded. "Then let's go see if our good brother is at home."

Jill took the stairs up to the second floor and found 248. It was a corner apartment with a view of the parking lot. Jill took a breath. "Here goes." She knocked.

They stood there for a moment but heard nothing. Jill knocked again.

"Shoot. He's not home," said Madison.

Jill waited again and knocked a third time. A neighbor opened the door next to Jace's and emerged holding a trash bag. He saw Jill and Madison and scowled. "You see Marlon, tell him to keep it down. I almost called the cops." He walked off without even a hello, looking irritated.

"Nice neighbor," said Madison.

No one answered, and Jill almost left, when the neighbor's comment stopped her. She reached for the doorknob.

"What are you doing?"

"It's just a hunch." She turned the knob, and it opened.

Madison looked around. "You can't just walk in."

The minute the door opened, a chill slid up Jill's back and her hair raised. "Stay here, Madison." She pushed the door, and it swung open.

"Jill, where are you going?"

Because she was a former cop, Jill's instincts were on high alert. Something didn't feel right. Another sharp pain in her head made her wince, but she stepped into the apartment, careful of her surroundings.

"Jill..." said Madison, following her in.

Jill motioned for her to stay back, but Madison followed anyway.

Jill saw the fallen picture of a landscape first. Sensing the emptiness, she scanned the room and checked behind the door. Seeing the mess, it was clear a scuffle had taken place.

"What the hell...?" asked Madison.

The coffee table was on its side, and a broken lamp lay on the floor. The dining table was upended, and there was a broken plate on the floor.

Jill moved farther in. The kitchen appeared undamaged, and she saw a bedroom and a bathroom. "Hello?" she asked. "Anybody here?" No one answered.

"Jill, look."

Jill stopped.

"I think that's blood," said Madison.

Jill moved closer. Red droplets dotted the carpet and there was a decent pool of it beside the dining table.

"What happened here?" asked Madison.

Jill squatted and gently touched the liquid. It was still wet. She rubbed it between her fingers and smelled it. "It's blood." She straightened, wiping her fingers on her jeans and went still, opening up her senses. She hadn't done much of that since the Artist case, but now was as good a time as any to start. Closing her eyes, she quieted her mind and took a deep breath. The chill up her back became a tidal wave, and she put her hand on a wall to steady herself. That pain in her head flared, her heart raced, and then a face appeared, and she could clearly see a man with blonde hair that bore a strong resemblance to Madison.

She opened her eyes, feeling disoriented, and Madison took her by the arm. "You okay? You're super pale."

Breathing deeply, Jill got her bearings and let go of the wall.

"What did you see?" asked Madison. "Do you know what happened?"

Jill nodded. "Rutger's what happened. He was here." She'd never seen him, but she knew it was him.

"Where's Jace? Is he okay?"

Jill squeezed her temples. "I don't know."

Madison pulled her cell out. "What's his number?"

Still feeling shaky, Jill retrieved her phone. She found Jace's number and told it to Madison, who dialed.

Madison held the phone to her ear. "C'mon. Answer," she whispered.

Jill waited, but Madison shook her head. "Nothing. Not even a voicemail option. It's just ringing."

"Keep trying." Jill shook out her hands, trying to rid herself of the negative vibes she'd felt from Rutger. She'd never sensed him that way before, but now that she had, he would be hard to ignore.

Madison kept the phone to her ear. "What do we do now?"

Jill studied the damaged apartment and the blood on the carpet and wondered the same thing.

Chapter Fourteen

DANIELS HUNG UP THE phone and studied the sheet in front of him. Tapping his pencil against the names, he glanced at Rem, who was still on a call. After Jill and Madison had left, they'd returned to the squad room to give Lozano a quick update of the latest crime scene, before Lozano had left to meet with the chief again about the D.A.'s death. The chief would be holding a press conference later in the day, and Lozano needed to give him the latest update.

Daniels had then contacted Manafor in Research to pull a new list of suspects, one that now only included names that both Hendrix and Alba had a connection to. They'd rushed it and it had taken about an hour, but Manafor had called back with the new list.

Daniels didn't have files for the names yet, but after talking with Manafor, he had enough initial information to get an idea of what they were dealing with, and it was interesting.

Rem hung up. "Well, the neighborhood canvas around Alba's didn't help. No one saw anything or anyone strange this morning. And the initial dusting of prints seems to be all Alba's, at least at the entry points, but they're still checking. Looks like the same gun was used for both Alba and Hendrix, too. There are no prints on the casing, though."

"Guy's careful," said Daniels. "But how did he get in? Alba had an alarm."

Rem shrugged. "Maybe Alba knew him and opened the door? Who knows?" He stretched his neck and reached for his coffee. "You get anything?"

"Yeah. A new list."

"I hope it's smaller than the last one."

"Considerably, and it's got some intriguing stuff on it."

"Really. Why?"

The squad door opened, and Lozano returned, looking tired.

"Captain, how'd it go with the chief?" asked Rem.

He stopped by their desks. "About as well as could be expected. The press is having a field day with this. I hope you two have some leads because we need to catch this guy fast, otherwise our judicial system is going to grind to a halt. I've already had four calls from attorneys asking if it's safe to go to court."

Daniels picked up the sheet of paper. "Well, we might have something. I asked Manafor to pull a new list of names with perps who had connections with both Hendrix and Alba over the past year."

Lozano raised a brow. "And?"

"Manafor just called back. He's going to email all of us with the basics, but I got a list of six names." He waved the paper.

Lozano waved a hand. "Bring it into my office."

Rem grabbed his coffee. "Six is a lot better than before. Maybe we'll get lucky and our guy will be on it."

They followed Lozano and sat in his office. Lozano slid off his jacket and loosened his tie. He pulled out his seat, threw his jacket on it, and sat at his desk. "What do we have?"

Daniels held the paper. "Okay. Based on what I requested, these people were in court with Judge Hendrix presiding and Alba as the prosecutor. They were either threatening or violent offenders or both and were recently released."

"We got that much," said Lozano. "Who's on it?"

Daniels read from the paper. "First guy is Foster Jackson. Convicted of breaking and entering and assault with a deadly weapon. Did three years. Threatened Alba when he was found guilty."

"Just three years?" asked Rem.

Daniels nodded. "Maybe he got out for good behavior. I don't have their files yet. This is just Manafor's preliminary report."

"Got it," said Lozano, finding a pencil and writing on a piece of paper. "Who else?"

"Second is Waldo Yang."

"Waldo Yang?" asked Lozano, with a frown. "I know that name."

"You should," said Daniels. "Your testimony sent him to prison for aggravated assault and domestic violence twelve years ago."

Lozano sat back in his seat. "I remember. That was one of my last cases as a detective. Guy was a hardcore bastard. Did a number on his girlfriend and pistol whipped a neighbor who tried to help."

"He got out two months ago."

"Terrific," said Lozano, writing the name.

"Third is Ester York. Convicted of drunk driving and vehicular manslaughter. Killed two people driving down the wrong side of the highway. Insisted she wasn't drunk even though her blood alcohol was over a one at the scene."

"She's considered violent?" asked Rem.

"No, but she sent angry emails to the judge and Alba during her time in jail, telling them God knew the truth and would exact his revenge."

"Nice lady," said Rem, sipping his coffee.

"Fourth is Jarrod Massey," continued Daniels.

Rem sat up. "Jarrod Massey?"

Daniels scratched his head. "Yeah. Remember him?"

"Sure as hell do. You testified in his trial," said Rem. "He knocked you over the head and would have shot you if his gun had been loaded." His face furrowed. "When was that?"

"It was one of our first cases as detectives. He was convicted of assaulting a police officer, possession of a deadly weapon, and burglary. Did eight years. Got out six months ago."

"Shit. That guy was an asshole," said Rem. "He threatened everybody, even the witnesses."

"I'm pretty sure the drugs ruined his mind," said Daniels. "He told the jury he thought I was a large bird of prey swooping down to eat him and he was only defending himself."

"He was aiming for insanity," said Rem.

"He failed," said Daniels. "But he's out now, so God help Big Bird."

Lozano scribbled. "Who's the fifth?"

Daniels studied the paper. "Les Rhodes. Attempted Homicide. Almost killed his best friend with rat poison. Did fifteen years. Threatened Hendrix in court during the trial and after."

"Another nice guy," said Rem.

"And the sixth?" asked Lozano.

"This one hits your other criteria, Cap." He looked at the paper. "Maia Chambers. Died in prison. Two years ago. Committed suicide with her bedsheets. Convicted of prostitution and drug possession with intent to sell. Did a year before she offed herself." He looked at Rem. "You recognize that name?"

"Maia Chambers?" Rem frowned, but then he snapped his fingers. "Yes." He rubbed his chin. "Shit. I remember her now. Crazy lady."

"How'd you get involved?" asked Lozano. "Isn't that Vice's area?"

"Yeah, it is." Rem shook a finger at Daniels. "But you were out of town with Marjorie not long after you met. I helped out in Vice while you were gone because they were short-handed." He shook his head. "It's coming back now. We arrested her on the street, picking up johns, and selling cocaine. Went nuts when we arrested her. Almost scratched my eyes out. Alba offered her a plea deal, but she refused. I testified at her trial, along with a few others who turned on her. She wasn't happy. They dragged her kicking and screaming from the courtroom."

"She sounds charming," said Daniels.

"She killed herself?" asked Rem.

"Yeah."

"Any connection to the number left at the scene?" asked Lozano. "Is there a date that matches?"

"Not that we know of, but again, we still need the full files for all of them." Daniels put the paper in his lap.

"It may not be a date," said Rem. "We need to keep an eye out for other possible matches." He sipped his coffee.

"Well, it's not a case file. The numbers don't match up," said Daniels.

"Wouldn't it be nice if it were that easy?" said Rem.

Lozano huffed. "Well, keep looking."

"At least we've got six solid names to look at, and not a hundred and six," said Rem.

Daniels folded the sheet. "We'll check them out, but there's something to consider here."

"What?" asked Lozano.

"If we truly do have a psycho going after the people who put him or her away," said Daniels, "or is pissed about a death, then all three of us are connected to a potential suspect."

Lozano put down his pen.

Daniels put the paper in his shirt pocket and leaned back. "Not to freak you out, but one of us could be the next on his list."

Rem stopped in mid-sip and put his coffee down. "See, this is why I don't invite you to parties."

Chapter Fifteen

DANIELS RETURNED TO HIS desk and Remalla helped himself to some more coffee. "You really think we could be targets?" Rem asked.

Daniels took the paper from his pocket and put it on the desk. "Only if we're barking up the right tree. It may be none of these people."

"But if it is..." Rem put his coffee on the desk.

"Then it's something to consider." He thought of Marjorie and J.P.

Rem nodded. "You thinking of the family?"

Daniels nodded, not surprised Rem had picked up on his worry. "Yeah, I am."

"You could ask them to get out of town for a few days until we're sure."

"It's not that easy. Marjorie can't just take off whenever she wants."

Rem sat. "I know." He rubbed his jaw. "If this guy just wants you, though, I doubt he'd hurt them."

Daniels leaned in, his elbows on his desk. "That's comforting. Thank you."

"How's the wedding planning going, by the way? You set a date yet?"

"I'm staying out of it as much as possible, although I told Marjorie I'd be perfectly happy going in front of a justice of the peace." He shook his head. "With everything happening now, that might be the way to go. Less to worry about." He fiddled with the piece of paper, envisioning his wedding being interrupted by a crazy psychopath with a gun.

Rem sighed. "We're getting way ahead of ourselves here. Let's check the files first. Could be Jarrod Massey moved to Alaska and is deep sea fishing in the Bering Sea."

"Let's hope." Daniels read the list. "You want to take the last three names and I'll take the first three?" He showed the paper to Rem.

Rem read it. "You should take Jarrod, since you arrested him. I'll take Ester."

"How do you want to handle Maia?"

"I'll check relatives and any mention of a significant other who might have been pissed about her death. See if that number pops up anywhere."

"Okay."

Rem frowned. "First though, I'm starving. You hungry?"

"A little, yeah."

"Then you're in luck. I'm buying. Whatever you want from the cafeteria, it's yours."

"The cafeteria?" asked Daniels. "Lucky me. I should have bought a lottery ticket."

Rem smirked. "How about a fancy bran muffin or one of those ugly green shakes you like?"

"You know they don't make green shakes downstairs. I think you're referring to their milkshakes."

"Even better. I'll get you one of those."

Daniels snorted. "Don't tell me. Is this going to be one of those times you buy me something and you end up eating it yourself?"

"I can't let good food go to waste."

Daniels smiled. "Get me a tuna sandwich and an apple. Oh, and one of those nice shakes I won't touch, but you will."

"Perfect." Rem stood. "Anything else? Something to drink?"

"I'll stick to my water. Thanks."

"Be right back."

Rem disappeared, and Daniels focused on pulling up the old files on Jackson, Yang, and Massey. Fifteen minutes later, Rem returned, a bag in hand and talking on the phone. He put the bag on his desk.

"You keep me posted. Okay?" he said. "Don't do anything stupid, please."

Daniels looked up.

"Okay. Talk soon." Rem hung up and sat in his seat. "You're not going to believe this."

Daniels sat up. "What?"

Rem told him how Jill and Madison had gone to Jace's, found the place trashed and had called the police. Jace was nowhere to be found.

"You're kidding," said Daniels.

Rem put his cell on his desk. "Jill did her mental connecting thing, like she did with the Artist, and she's pretty convinced it's Rutger."

"What did they tell the cops?"

Rem picked up his coffee. "Just that they're friends. Stopped by to say hello and found the place like it was."

Daniels tensed. "You think Danni was with Jace?"

Rem shook his head. "Don't know. Let's hope to God Rutger didn't kill Jace."

Daniels considered that. "Well, if he did, he likely would have left the body behind. Rutger wouldn't lug Jace downstairs and into a car. The man's the size of a wrestler. And somebody would have seen it."

"If Rutger used his mojo, maybe he could have moved the body pretty easily."

Daniels pointed. "Maybe. Maybe not. The last time Jace and Rutger got into it, Rutger didn't use his mojo on Jace, remember?"

"I know. We thought it was weird."

"Maybe he can't use it on Jace, and that's why Jace's place is trashed."

Rem expelled a gust of air. "Who the hell knows? Jace could have killed Rutger for all we know. Hid the body and disappeared with Danni."

"You think he'd do that?"

"Rutger murdered his best friend. I sure as hell would have been tempted."

"Yeah. I know." Daniels sat back, thinking. "If Jill's senses are accurate, then that means Rutger's back on the radar." He studied Rem, who stared at his coffee, his face furrowed. "Would you feel better if we went over there?"

Rem put his cup down. "Nah. There's nothing we can do. Besides, Jill and Madison are on their way to Jace's bar to see if he went there."

"Well, you know Jill. If Jace is in a hundred-mile radius, she'll find him."

"That's what worries me. If she finds Jace or Rutger, there's no telling what could happen. Said if she doesn't have luck at the bar, she's going to try and find Sonia."

"Good luck with that. Sonia will only be found only when she wants to be."

"I know." Rem paused. "I gave Jill some background info on Jace. Figured she could use it to check out a few other places."

"You sure about that?"

"I tried keeping stuff from her before and it blew up in my face. She's hell bent on figuring this out, and I can't stop her." He ran a hand through his hair. "It scares the crap out of me, but hell, Marjorie manages with you chasing after bad guys every day. I figure I can do the same."

"Marjorie doesn't know about bad guys that move objects with their mind, nor will she. You know this guy. Jill doesn't. You have every right to be worried."

Rem let go of a ragged breath. "At least we talked before she left."

Daniels nodded. "I know you're scared, but thankfully, your mental state is a lot better than yesterday."

Rem dropped the pencil, his face somber. "I told her I loved her."

Daniels raised a brow. "That's a big step. How'd she handle it?"

"Pretty well, considering how pissed she was with me. Luckily, she told me the same."

Daniels relaxed. "It's about time."

Rem smiled softly. "You're just going to have to put up with me, though, because I can't help but think of Jennie in this giant mess. So, if I go quiet on you..."

"I'll snap you out of it. Throw some coffee in your face or something. Or maybe that fancy milkshake I assume you bought. If it's in the bag, by the way, it's melting."

Rem picked up the food. "I guess we should eat, huh?" He reached inside.

Daniels pushed the paper with the names aside. "She'll be okay, partner. But don't be surprised if she finds Jace."

"And if she does?" Rem pulled out a wrapped sandwich.

"Then we'll figure out, like we always do." He took his sandwich from Rem. "Where are Jill and Madison staying, by the way?"

Rem opened his wrapper. "With me, of course, assuming they want to. Jill has a key. Madison can take one of the rooms upstairs. And it will make me feel better knowing they have a place to go."

Daniels held his food, an odd feeling of discomfort blooming. "Okay. Just keep me updated."

Rem hesitated, ready to bite into his sandwich. "You worried too?"

"When it comes to Rutger, I worry about all of us."

"I know." Sighing, Rem bit into his lunch.

Chapter Sixteen

DANIELS FOLLOWED REM INTO his house. Rem flicked the lights on and went inside. "You could have gone home to Marjorie. It's been a long day."

"Nah. It's fine. Marjorie's sister is coming over. They're ordering in and watching some sort of rom-com. I prefer this by comparison."

Rem tossed his keys on the front table, unholstered his weapon, and put it in a safe in the front closet. "You want to be here when Jill and Madison show. You're just as curious as I am."

Daniels took off his jacket and threw it on a kitchen chair. "I admit. I'm curious. Are they on their way?"

Rem grabbed a beer from the fridge, handed it to Daniels and took one for himself. "They're picking up some food. Should be here soon."

Daniels unscrewed the top of his beer. "They tell you anything?"

"Haven't found Jace, Sonia or Rutger. That's all I know. Said they'd fill us in with details when they got here." He opened his beer and took a swig. Putting the beer down, he eyed the upstairs, his jaw set. He glanced at Daniels. "You mind if I ask you for a favor?"

Daniels put his beer on the kitchen table. "Since when do you ask if I mind?"

Rem raised the side of his lip. "It's a little weird..."

"Nothing you say surprises me anymore, partner. What's up?"

Rem tilted his head toward the stairs. "The room with Jennie's closet. I opened a box. It's where I found the bracelet." He paused. "I left the box open on the bed and, well, if Madison sleeps up there..."

"You want me to go put the box away?"

Rem gripped his beer. "I know it's silly, but I don't need to go up there and get set off again by finding something else that will throw me. The timing isn't good."

"No problem." Daniels took another sip of his drink and put the bottle down. "I'll be right back."

"Thanks."

Daniels headed up the stairs and entered the bedroom where Rem had put Jennie's things. Flicking on the light, he saw the open box on the bed. He went over to it and grabbed the lid. Before he closed it, he glanced inside, seeing her personal items, and the memories swirled. He remembered Rem putting her things in the box, trying to be so damn stoic, but unable to keep the tears at bay. Once they'd put everything away, they'd both gotten roaring drunk, and Daniels had stayed the whole weekend, unable to go home because of the lingering effects of the hangover.

Spying an object in the box, his heart fell. Sitting next to a bottle of shampoo and a hairbrush was a small snow globe, no bigger than the hairbrush. Daniels pulled it out and shook it, and yellow mustard-colored flakes flew up, dusting a hot dog within the globe. He remembered vividly giving it to Jennie for a birthday as a joke, telling her when Rem was working late hours, she could shake the hot dog and think of him.

She'd laughed and Rem had made the comment that it should have been a taco. Jennie had kept it on her desk at Rem's.

He shook it again, and as the flakes drifted, a well of emotion bubbled up and his eyes watered, remembering their shared time together as couples. Those were good times, and he missed them, too.

He cleared his throat and sniffed. "God, Daniels," he said to himself, "You can't even do this yourself." Holding on to the snow globe, he hesitated. He kept the globe and put the lid back on the box and returned it to the closet. Closing the door, he studied the globe again, wondering if Rem would mind.

He left the room and went back down the stairs, seeing Rem in the living area on the couch, with the TV on, looking lost in thought. He glanced up when Daniels returned. "Thanks again," he said.

Daniels debated, but then held up the globe. "I found this."

Rem narrowed his eyes to see it, but then smiled. "It's hard not to reminisce, isn't it?"

Daniels shook it again. "Would you mind if I keep it?"

Rem watched the globe, his eyes faraway, and Daniels wondered if he was asking too much.

"Of course not. She'd want you to have it."

"I'll put it on my desk at work. Would that bother you?"

Rem smiled softly. "Not at all. It's the perfect place for it. Although I still think it should have been a taco."

Daniels shook his head. "When I find one with a taco, I'll be the first in line to buy it, but the hot dog will have to do for now." He turned and put it on the front table to remember to bring it home with him. "Thanks."

"You're welcome."

Daniels found his beer and sat in a chair beside the couch. He tried to lighten the melancholy mood brought on by the globe. He didn't need Rem spiraling down. "I hope they're here soon. I'm starving."

Rem checked his watch. "Should be. They weren't that far away."

On cue, a key sounded in the lock and the door opened. Jill walked in with Madison behind her, holding two boxes of pizza.

"Speak of the devil," said Rem, standing.

Daniels stood too. "How'd it go?" he asked, walking over. He took the boxes from Madison.

Rem walked over to Jill, and she took a second before moving close and giving him a quick kiss. "It's really good to see you after a frustrating day."

Rem smiled, and Daniels could sense his partner's mood improving. "You guys want a beer?" he asked.

"God, yes," said Madison. She looked around the house. "This is nice."

"Thanks," said Rem. "It's actually my Aunt Audrey's, but she's moved into assisted living, so I'm staying here for her."

"Plenty of space," said Madison. "You could use some artwork, though."

Rem took Jill's jacket. "Yeah, well, when I get time to hit the local art shows, maybe I'll pick something up."

"I don't think she means velvet paintings with dogs playing cards," said Daniels.

Rem smirked.

"This is cute." Madison picked up the snow globe with the hot dog and shook it. "Very pop art."

Daniels met Rem's gaze. "Yeah, well," said Daniels, "I have a more eclectic style."

"You bought it?" she asked

"Yup. Made me think of Rem," said Daniels.

"I can see why," said Jill. "I'm starving. Let's eat."

They sat down with the pizza and their beers and dove in while Hitchcock's *Vertigo* played on TV. Jill told them about going to Jace's and calling the police, and then going to the places Rem had suggested to find Jace or Sonia. They'd had no luck with any of it.

"We talked to several people," said Madison. "And nothing. No one's seen or heard anything about either of them."

"Not really a surprise," said Rem. "If they're trying to lie low, they won't go to the expected places."

"You still calling him?" asked Daniels.

"Yes," said Jill. "No answer, and no voicemail." She wiped her hands with a napkin. "I don't understand what is going on. Where is he?"

"Anybody tried Danni?" asked Rem.

Jill and Madison shared glances. "No. You have her number?"

Rem grabbed his cell. "I think I added it when Jace was hiding Danni. Yeah. Here it is." He dialed and listened, then frowned. "Going to voicemail."

Madison's shoulders fell. "Well, at least you can leave a message."

Rem left a short voicemail, asking them to get in touch and even leaving his address in case they needed a place to go and hung up.

"They show up, you're going to have a full house," said Daniels.

"There's plenty of space. We'll make it work," said Rem.

"It's also risky. You'll all be in one place. Makes it easier for Rutger," said Daniels.

Jill took a swig of her beer. "Or it makes it harder." She massaged her temples.

"Still have a headache?" asked Madison.

"I'm not sure it's a headache," said Jill.

Rem put his slice of pizza down. "Are you picking up on something?"

"It's just a sense of...I don't know...I hate to say foreboding." She closed her eyes, and then opened them. "Sonia came to see me for a reason. She wanted me to get all of us together. Maybe because Rutger wants the opposite."

"Then why didn't she do it sooner?" asked Daniels. "She's had ample opportunity."

"Maybe not," said Jill. "Rutger's actions have brought us out into the open. Sonia knows who we all are now, and where we are. I'm not sure she knew that before Rutger struck."

"Sonia strikes me as a lady who knows everything," said Rem, biting into his pizza.

"I wish she did. Then maybe she could tell us where the hell Jace is," said Madison.

Jill took a breath and leaned against a pillow, holding her beer. "How's your case going? I hope you're having better luck than we are."

Rem shrugged. "We've narrowed down our pool of suspects. Going to head out for some face-to-face time tomorrow. That should be interesting."

Daniels drank his beer. "Unfortunately, Jarrod Massey is not deep-sea fishing."

"Nor is Waldo Yang," said Rem. "Figures."

"Well, at least we know Les Rhodes is in upstate New York, running a retreat for planetary peace. That's one suspect down." Daniels reached for another slice.

Jill's brow creased. "Who are these people?"

Rem recounted to her about their case and potential suspects.

"You honestly think one of these people could come after one of you?" asked Madison.

"It's a long shot, but you have to be prepared for the worst," said Daniels.

"It's the number connection we need to find," said Rem. "That's the key."

"You think it's a date?" asked Jill.

"Could be, but so far, nothing," said Rem, licking his fingers.

"And this woman, Maia Chambers, you think somebody's mad because she killed herself?" asked Madison.

"Stranger things have happened," said Daniels.

Madison shook her head. "Police work sucks. I'm glad I'm an artist. I can paint in my studio and shut out the world."

Jill tossed her napkin on the table. "I wish the bad guys would do more of that. It might do them some good."

"We'd at least get a wider selection of velvet paintings," added Rem.

"And hot dog snow globes," said Madison.

Daniels chuckled and stood, grabbing an empty pizza box. "Anybody want another beer?"

All three said yes at once.

"Be right back," he said.

"I'll help," said Rem standing. They headed into the kitchen. Daniels put the empty box on the table, and Rem opened the fridge when the doorbell rang.

Rem stopped and Daniels turned. Jill stood in the living room.

"Expecting anybody?" asked Daniels.

"Nope," said Rem. He jumped when the knock became several slams, and Jace's voice boomed from the other side of the door. "Anybody in there?"

"Shit," said Rem, closing the fridge.

Daniels kept his hand by his weapon just in case, and Jill and Madison ran toward the door.

Rem walked over, gesturing for Jill and Madison to stay back, and put his hand on the knob and eyed Daniels, who nodded, standing to the side. Rem opened the door, his eyes widening. "Jace?"

Daniels peered around the side and saw Jace, his clothes disheveled and blood-stained, holding his side with a bloody bandage on his arm. His long, wild hair hanging in his face, Jace stared with a grimace of pain, sweat, and exhaustion. "Can I come the fuck in?"

Chapter Seventeen

JACE GRITTED HIS TEETH, waiting for Remalla to open the door further. "I'm not getting any younger out here."

Remalla snapped out of his shock, and Daniels swiveled around the door frame, checking the area and Jace. "Hell. You're a mess. Come on in."

He reached out to take Jace's arm, but Jace winced and pulled back. "I'm okay."

Rem widened the door and stepped back. "Yeah. You look great."

Jace took painful steps inside, and Daniels pulled out a kitchen chair. "Have a seat."

Rem closed the door, and Jace sat with a gasp. His ribs were on fire. He held his side and cursed.

"What the hell happened?" asked Rem. He went to the sink and wet a dishcloth under the faucet.

"I fell down the stairs." He tried to shift in the chair to get more comfortable and bumped his injured arm. He groaned again.

Daniels sat across from him. "Must have been a helluva flight of stairs." He flicked a glance toward the entry. "I'm sure you have a story to tell, but you have some ladies here who've been looking all over the city for you."

Jace turned with effort. Even his neck hurt. He saw two women, one small and blonde and the other tall and brunette. Despite his aches and pains, a strange sense of relief came over him, and he tried to stand, but it hurt too much.

The blonde one came over. "Take it easy. Relax. You're hurt." She put a hand on his shoulder. Warmth shot through his arm, and he eyed the brunette. "Don't tell me. Jill and Madison?"

The brunette nodded. "Jace Marlon?"

"That would be me, only I've had better days."

Remalla came over with a wet towel. "Let's see your arm."

Jace tried to cope with the two women who were likely the sisters from his dreams. "Leave it. It's fine."

"The hell it is." Remalla squatted beside him and tried to remove the bloody bandage. His face blanched when he removed part of it, and Jace cursed. "This is a mess. You need a doctor."

Madison leaned in. "Oh, my God. What happened to you?"

Jace winced again as Remalla used the towel to clean the slash in his arm. "Damn it. What are you doing? Digging for treasure?"

"Give it to me," said Madison.

Rem hesitated, but then gave it to her. "Be careful. He may bite."

Madison pulled a chair over. "Not with me, he won't."

Jace groaned, knowing she was right. He was not going to growl at his sister, no matter how little he knew about her. Feeling her touch against his skin, he gritted his teeth once more, but stayed quiet.

"You need stitches," said Madison.

"Not right now, I don't," he said, feeling a sliver of sweat trickle down his face.

Jill sat at the table. "You hungry?"

"I'll get you some water," said Daniels, standing.

"I'll get what's left of the pizza," said Rem.

Jill took Daniels' seat. "How do you know who we are?" she asked.

Jace studied her, trying to forget what Madison was doing to his arm. "I've dreamed about you for a while now."

Jill nodded. "Me, too."

"Me, too," said Madison, dabbing at his arm.

Daniels put a glass of water in front of him. "Drink it."

Rem gave him a plate of pizza, and Jace's stomach growled. He hadn't eaten since breakfast. But then he thought of Danni, and his stomach curdled, curbing his appetite. "Thanks." He picked up the water with his free hand and his fingers shook.

"Take it easy," said Jill.

He drank slowly, and the cool liquid quenched his brutal thirst. He drained the glass.

"I'll get some more," said Daniels.

"You know we're siblings?" asked Jill.

Despite his worry for Danni and waning appetite, Jace knew he needed to eat. He picked up a slice of pizza. "You're my sisters in my dreams, but don't know much else." He took a bite.

Jill and Madison shared a glance. "We share the same birthdate," said Jill. "All three of us. Same year, too."

Jace stopped in mid-chew. "We do?"

"It seems we're triplets," said Madison.

Jace finished chewing and swallowed. "You're sure?"

Jill confirmed his date of birth.

"I wasn't even sure if that date was accurate," said Jace. "It was just on a slip of paper in my pocket when I was found in a fire station at the age of two. And I have no idea where I was born."

"The date must be accurate, and I suspect you were born in New Britain, Connecticut. The same place we were born." Jill gestured at Madison.

Jace still felt like this was from a dream. "Then how'd I end up here?"

Jill shook her head. "I don't know. That's another mystery to solve, along with Rutger, who it seems is also a sibling, which might make us quads."

At the mention of Rutger's name, Jace tensed. He sucked in a breath when Madison scraped harder against his injury with the cloth.

"Sorry," she said. "You moved." She spoke to Rem. "He's going to need some clean cloths. You have any?"

Rem nodded. "Yeah. Hold on."

"You honestly think we're quadruplets?" Jace asked with another grimace. "Seriously?"

Jill sat back. "It makes sense. Madison and I somehow were adopted as babies. You got out when you were two, and Rutger..."

"He didn't get out. And now he's pissed at us," said Jace. "But why? It's not like it's our fault for whatever happened to him."

"There's so much we don't know. Why are we quads? Who are our parents? Why did Rutger stay, and we got sent away? How does Sonia play into all of this?" Jill pointed. "Why did he come after our loved ones and not us? And now you get attacked."

Daniels put a fresh glass of water in front of him. "What happened, Jace? Did Rutger do this? Where's Danni?"

Jace rubbed his eyes. Fatigue washed over him, and he could still see Danni crying in his arms.

"I sent her away," he said. "I had to get her out of here." After the fight at his home, he'd gotten her out of the bathroom. She'd been hysterical, likely reliving what had happened to her, but he'd calmed her down, told her to grab some things, and then taken her to a seedy hotel, where they'd rented a room, and Jace had talked to her about getting out of town. It had taken some convincing, but she'd finally agreed.

"Where'd she go?" asked Daniels.

Rem returned with some linens. "These are old pillowcases. Use these." He handed them to Madison.

Jace took a gulp of water. "I don't know, and I don't want to know. Told her to get on a plane and disappear. It's the only way to keep her safe." He could still hear her pleas to stay with him, and he shut his eyes. It had been pure torture to send her away, but at least he knew she was safe from Rutger. "Told her to text me when she ended up somewhere. I ended up getting a text from her telling me you'd called. That's how I knew you were here."

"We've been trying to reach you all day," said Madison. "We went to your place, and knew you'd been in some sort of fight. We called several times but couldn't reach you."

"Yeah. I know. I switched phones. Never set up the voicemail."

"You might want to fix that," said Jill. "Especially right now."

He twisted in his seat to get comfortable and gasped when pain shot through his side.

"What is it?" asked Jill. "Is it your ribs?"

"Yeah. I think a few are broken," said Jace.

"You need to go to a doctor," said Rem. "Make sure you're okay."

"There's no time for doctors. This guy is out there, and I can't afford to sit on my ass if Rutger ends up coming after someone else."

"So, this was Rutger?" asked Daniels.

Jace bit his lip through the pain as Madison hit a sensitive area of his arm. He forced himself to breathe through it. "Yeah, it was him. Showed up on my doorstep this morning. Said he wanted to talk. Said Jill and Madison were coming to meet me, and there was something I needed to know. I refused. I think he just wanted me out of the apartment. It didn't sit right, especially after what happened with Danni. It felt more like he was luring me out for some purpose."

"You think he planned to kill you?" asked Rem from the kitchen sink. He turned the running water off and wrung out another dish towel. He came over and handed it to Jace. "Here. For your face."

Jace took it with his free hand and held it over his eyes and nose, feeling the cool relief. His head was throbbing. He wiped the sweat from his skin and then rubbed the back of his neck. "I don't know, but thinking back on it now, yes, I think he may have been there to kill me. Fortunately, I don't go down easy. He got away, but he took it worse than me."

"He's injured?" asked Jill.

"I'm sure he's got a broken nose, maybe even a broken jaw, and I slashed him across the belly. If I got lucky, maybe I got a couple of his ribs, too." He grimaced again when his own ribs pulled.

"Our theory may be holding up then," said Daniels.

"Looks like it," said Rem.

"What theory?" asked Jill.

"Rutger can't use his mojo on Jace," said Rem.

"Mojo?" asked Jill. "Oh, you mean the whole throwing shit around stuff? Maybe he's just not as capable as you think."

"Oh, he's capable," said Jace. "I've seen it. I expected him to use it, but it never happened. Maybe it has something to do with why I can't use my own personal mojo on myself, which would be nice right about now."

"I was wondering about that," said Daniels.

"Wondering about what?" asked Madison. She looked up. "You have mojo?"

"You all do," said Rem. "Haven't you all figured that out by now?"

They went quiet. "I'm not sure what to believe anymore." Jill tipped her head. "What can you do?" she asked Jace.

Jace held his breath when Madison hit a nasty part of his arm and couldn't talk.

"He can heal people," said Daniels.

Jill's face fell, and Madison stilled.

"It's true. He can," said Rem. "Daniels has experience."

Daniels raised a hand. "I cut my palm open. Probably needed stitches, but Jace here waved his fingers over it, and within minutes, it was fine."

Jill dropped her shoulders. "Come on. That's all you've got? You probably had a paper cut, which hurts, I know, but it doesn't require stitches."

"He helped Sonia. Saved her life when Rutger tried to kill her," said Rem.

"Is that true?" asked Madison.

Jace dropped his face cloth and held his head. "Pretty much. Had the ability since I was a kid, although I didn't really understand it."

"Eat some more pizza. You need your strength," said Daniels.

"I'm almost done with your arm," said Madison. "I like your tattoos by the way, but this is going to leave a scar, so the tattoos aren't going to be as pretty." She dabbed again with the wet cloth and picked up a pillowcase. She laid it over the injury and wrapped it. "This really needs more than what I can do. You have any antiseptic?"

"Ah, hell," said Jace, imagining more pain. "Just leave it."

"You don't want it to get infected," said Madison.

Jill straightened and picked a leaf off Jace's shirt. "You guys can enjoy your special powers, but for right now, I'm sticking to the skeptic camp."

"You have your own gifts," said Rem. "How can you deny theirs?"

"My gifts aren't that special. I think most people could do what I do. I just tune in more."

"If you say so," said Daniels. "But I think you've got more mojo than you think."

Jace set his jaw as Madison put pressure on his arm. "Damn it."

"Sorry. It's bleeding," said Madison.

Jill spoke to Rem. "Is there someone who can come over and patch him up?"

Rem raised a brow and Daniels pointed. "What about—," started Daniels.

"Doc Martin?" finished Rem. "You have his number?"

"Yeah. I do." Daniels stood. "Give me a sec." Pulling out his phone, he stood and left the room.

"Who's Doc Martin?" asked Jill.

Rem took a seat beside Jill. "When Daniels was injured in the shoulder, he followed up with a doctor at the hospital. They hit it off. Martin thought it was cool Daniels was a cop. He even came into the station not long after Daniels returned to duty. We gave him a tour, and he took us to lunch."

"You think he'd come over and help Jace without reporting any of this?" asked Jill.

"You kidding? We tell him this is top secret stuff, he'll love it. He told us he'd always wanted to work for the CIA. Chose medicine instead. More money in it, plus he wanted to help people instead of kill them."

"That's a good quality to have," said Madison. She secured a second pillowcase around Jace's arm. "That's the best I can do for now. Did you have any disinfectant?"

"Oh, yeah. Let me check in the bathroom." Rem left the kitchen. "I'll look for something to help with the pain, too."

Jace expelled a breath, glad Madison was finished, although his arm throbbed. "You two should leave."

Jill crossed her arms. "Where exactly are we going to go?"

"Anywhere. Just away from Rutger. Let me deal with him."

Jill snorted. "That's very brotherly of you, but we're not going anywhere."

Madison sat beside him. "It wouldn't fix anything. You know he's planning something."

"Yes. He's planning something with us, which is why you both should leave. I almost took him once. Next time I face him, I'll be more prepared." Jace picked up his slice of pizza, hoping he could finish it.

"Yes. You will be," said Jill. "Because we'll be with you. Like you said, there's something about us being together that scares him. Maybe it's time to figure out what that is. We run and we give him exactly what he wants. Fear."

"You think we won't be scared if we all end up facing him together?" asked Madison.

"Together, we can handle him," said Jill. "It might be terrifying, but it will be better than running."

"How the hell do you know that?" asked Jace.

Jill crossed her arms. "Despite my doubt, if we all really have some sort of ability, then that must work in our favor. Rutger's nervous, which makes him vulnerable. Sonia knows that, which is why she orchestrated this."

"Sonia's had her chances. She could have told me everything when I asked her about it," said Jace.

"You sure about that? Because I'm not." Jill leaned in, her voice low. "We need to consider something else. Sonia could have told Rem and Daniels what she told me, but she didn't. I think she's trying to protect them. Which means we may need to as well."

"You mean keep them in the dark?" asked Madison.

"If it means saving their lives, then yes," said Jill. "They have a case of their own to keep them busy. Let them do their jobs, and we'll do ours. And when the time comes to face Rutger, we'll do it alone."

Jace studied Jill, knowing that tone and attitude. She reminded him of him. Something in his gut told him she was right. If Rutger was going to be stopped, it would be up to them to stop him, and Daniels and Rem would likely only get in the way. He sighed and clutched his ribs with a grunt. "Fine with me. We go it alone."

He and Jill waited for Madison. Jace half expected her to disagree, but she straightened, her eyes glimmering, and held out a pinky. "Alone."

He almost chuckled that she wanted a pinky promise, but he raised his pinky and so did Jill, and they linked them together.

"Alone," they said in unison, and pulled their pinkies apart.

They sat back just as Rem returned. "Good news. Doc Martin's on his way. And look what I found." He waved a bottle of rubbing alcohol. "In case the good doctor needs it."

Jace slumped in his seat, his ribs protesting, and cursed.

Chapter Eighteen

JILL DRIED OFF WITH a towel, feeling better after a grueling day. Doc Martin had left an hour earlier after stitching up Jace's arm, confirming his broken ribs, and telling him to get some rest. He'd written out a prescription for a painkiller and a sedative and Rem had run to the drugstore and picked it up.

They'd put Jace in one of the bedrooms upstairs and, despite his injuries, he'd managed to get a hot shower. Once Rem had returned, he'd found one of his uncle's old t-shirts and a pair of sweats for Jace to change into. Jace had argued about taking the medication, but Jill and Madison argued back. He'd wilted under the pressure and fallen asleep in his room within fifteen minutes of taking the pills.

Rem had set Madison up in the other bedroom upstairs, and she'd gone to bed soon after, exhausted after a long day.

Daniels had thanked Doc Martin, who'd looked as eager to help as a school kid just before the start of his summer break. Daniels had offered to pay him, but he'd declined, happy to have done his part in whatever secret espionage was playing out. He'd left, saying mum's the word and promising to follow up with Jace in a couple of days.

Fatigue had caught up to Jill, and she'd disappeared into Rem's room to take a much-needed shower. After drying off, she donned a nightgown, brushed her teeth and stepped into the bedroom. Rem sat at the edge of the bed, kicking off his shoes.

"Feel better?" he asked.

"Much." She ran a hand through her wet hair and shook it out. "Daniels go home?"

"Yeah. And Jace and Madison are asleep."

"Good. They need it."

"So do you." He stood and pulled off his shirt.

Admiring his muscular physique, she leaned against the door frame. "I've missed you."

Tossing his shirt into the laundry pile, he watched her. "I've missed you, too." He walked over to her. "You feeling okay after this afternoon?"

His nearness made her body warm, and she wanted to reach out and pull him in. "You mean after meeting my long-lost brother, who'd been attacked by my other long-lost brother, while hanging out with my long-lost sister, along with you and me saying I love you?" She cocked her head. "I'd say it's been a full day."

He offered that crooked grin that made her heart swell. "Oh, I don't know. Could have been worse. We could be at my old apartment, in which case, we'd probably be sleeping on the floor."

"Well, thank goodness for Aunt Audrey."

"Thank goodness."

They stared for a second and she could feel her cheeks flush. She smiled softly. "I know what you're thinking."

He reached out and took her hand. "You thinking the same thing?" he asked. "Or are you still mad at me?"

She stepped close and put her arm around his back. "Oh, I'm pretty furious."

His eyes darkening, he brought his hands up and pushed her hair away from her shoulders. "You're pretty gorgeous when you're mad."

Moving closer, she brought her face to his and she could hear his breathing pick up. "I bet you could help me get over it, though."

He ran his fingers down her neck to her shoulders, where he pulled the strap of her nightgown down. "What did you have in mind?" He lowered his head and trailed soft kisses down the nape of her neck to her collarbone.

She tilted her head back, and the warmth in her body turned to raw heat, and her heart rate picked up. "That's a good start," she said, her breathing escalating.

"You sure you're not too tired?" he whispered against her skin. His fingers trailed down her arm, and he moved his lips to her ear, where he nibbled her lobe.

Moaning softly and enjoying his touch, she gripped his back and savored the sensations of his mouth on her skin. Leaning against him, she raised her hand and slipped off the other strap of her gown and let it fall to the floor. "I think I have a little energy left."

A deep sigh escaped him, and he groaned softly. He moved his hands down her body and caressed her back and stomach. "Thank God," he said against her, and bringing his lips to hers, he slanted his mouth over hers in a hungry kiss.

•••••••••

The next morning, Jill stood in Rem's kitchen, holding her coffee. Having a long day ahead of him, Rem had left an hour earlier. Letting Jace and Madison sleep, Jill had sat at the dining table, thinking. Now that she, Jace, and Madison were together, what was their next step? How would they find Rutger? How would they get the answers to all the questions about their past?

Coming to no conclusions, she'd made another pot of coffee, expecting Jace and Madison to wake soon, and then stared out the window in the kitchen, hoping an idea would pop into her head. When that failed, she decided to make some breakfast. She needed to do something to keep her busy.

Surprised to find a pancake mix in Rem's pantry because the main things on Rem's grocery list were usually coffee, beer, popcorn, taco meat, and hot dogs, she took advantage of the benevolent favor of the food gods, and make some pancakes.

She found a pan and put it on the stove, and turned to see Madison standing in the kitchen. Jill jumped and held her chest. "Shit. You scared me."

Wearing a bathrobe, her hair disheveled and her face still creased with sleep, Madison searched for a coffee cup. "Some psychic you are."

Jill rolled her eyes. "They're in the cabinet, above the toaster."

Madison looked and found one.

"You sleep okay?" asked Jill.

"Really well, considering. I kind of wanted to not get up and be lazy, but I smelled the coffee." She poured some into her cup. "How'd you sleep?"

Jill thought of Rem and smiled. "Just fine."

Madison eyed her sideways while sipping her drink. Lowering the cup, she grinned. "You two obviously made up. How much sleep did you actually get?"

Jill's cheeks warmed. "Enough. You want some pancakes?"

Madison chuckled. "Nice diversion. You're better at this sister thing than you realize."

Jill found some chocolate chips on a shelf. "I can add chips." She held the bag.

Madison shook her head. "Sure. What the hell. Let's live it up."

Jill pulled the ingredients together, and Madison sat at the table. "I take it Jace is still in bed?" asked Madison.

"Yes."

"You sure? Something tells me he'd sneak out in the middle of the night and try to solve all our problems by hunting Rutger down and strangling him with his bare hands."

Jill whisked together the pancake mix. "I thought of that. I had Rem peek in on him before he left. Jace was snoring like a truck driver."

"Good. Poor guy needs it." She sipped her coffee and scratched her head. "I hate to get serious when we just woke up, but have you been thinking the same thing I have?"

Jill checked the heat on the pan. "You mean what next?"

Madison nodded. "We can't exactly stay here and play house, although it sounds kind of nice."

Jill sighed. It did sound enjoyable just to hang out and get to know her new family. "I know. I figure when Jace wakes, we'll talk. There has to be something logical for us to do. I mean, we made it this far, but where do we go from here?" She added batter to the pan, and it sizzled.

"We need to find Sonia. She's got secrets. I think she knows all about us."

"You got any ideas on how to do that?"

Madison went quiet, and Jill wondered what she was thinking. The lull continued as Jill eyed the pancake. Finally, Madison spoke. "Maybe we shouldn't take the logical approach. Maybe it's time to consider something else."

"Like what?"

Madison put her cup on the table. "Our gifts."

"Our gifts?" Jill checked the pancake and flipped it. "You mean Jace's supposed ability to heal and your supposed ability to do what Rutger does?"

"Why do you keep saying supposed?"

Jill hesitated. "Look. I get it. There are things out there that can't be explained. Strange phenomena, ghosts, UFOs, Sasquatch, you name it, but most of it is bogus and the result of people's overactive imaginations."

Madison stood, picked up her coffee, and walked closer. "Excuse me? We just found out that we are probably quadruplets, our parents are not our biological ones, and that our lives are in danger from an insane sibling and the only woman who has answers is a grandmotherly chick with chubby cheeks who gives us jewelry. Are you saying that's a product of our imagination?"

Jill jabbed at the pancake and sighed. "Well, when you put it that way..."

"Then cut us some slack when it comes to believing we have some unique traits and stop downgrading yours. In fact..." Madison tapped on her lips.

Jill removed the pancake and put it on a plate. "In fact, what?"

Madison pointed. "I think that's where we start."

"What do you mean?" She started to add more batter when Madison stopped her.

"Hold off on that pancake for a second." She grabbed Jill's elbow. "Let's try something."

Jill scowled. "I'm hungry."

Madison put her mug down and turned off the heat. "Come here."

"Madison—" Jill wanted to argue, but Madison pulled her by the arm and Jill went with her into the living room. "What are you doing?"

"Sit. Get comfortable. Cross your legs or something. Whatever you do when you meditate."

Jill dropped her jaw. "You want me to meditate? I'm making pancakes."

"They're not going anywhere. And no, not necessarily meditate. Maybe focus is a better word."

"Are you serious? Now?"

"Yes. Now. Let's just try. If this works, you may be the key to finding Sonia, or even Rutger."

An itch of apprehension made Jill squirm. Some part of this had occurred to Jill, but she'd disregarded it, preferring to rely on solid investigative techniques. Plus, she didn't like opening herself up. She'd already gotten a glimpse of Rutger and it hadn't been pleasant. She'd kept him at bay since then, but didn't know how long it would last. Focusing on him would only make it harder to keep him out. "This won't work."

Madison turned serious. "Don't give me that crap. I know you can do it. You just don't want to." She paused when Jill looked away. "What's the matter? Are you worried about Rutger? Could he hurt you if you do this?"

Jill sat on the couch. "I don't know if he could hurt me physically, but who knows? We're moving into uncharted territory here. But mentally, it's no picnic." She paused. "But I see your point. It's worth a try."

"Good. I'll be here to help if you need it." She sat next to Jill. "You want to come up with a safe word?"

Jill frowned. "A safe word?"

"Yeah. In case you get in too deep, and you need me to pull you out."

"You're serious?"

"Yes. It's a good idea." She pursed her lips. "Let's see. How about pancakes?"

Jill dropped her jaw. "Pancakes? That's your safe word?"

"You have a better one?"

Jill closed her eyes, not believing she was doing this. "Fine. Pancakes." She opened her eyes and straightened. "But if I agree to do this, it goes both ways. I practice, then you practice."

Madison's face fell. "What, me?"

"Yeah, you. You want me to believe, then show me the goods. Make me a believer. I want to see what you can do."

Madison paled. "Crap."

"It's not so fun when your ass is on the line, is it?"

Madison sighed, but nodded. "Deal."

Jill almost deflated. She half hoped Madison would refuse, and then so could she. But Madison looked just as determined as before. "Fine," said Jill.

"Good. Now get comfortable. Go to your happy place, or whatever it is you do."

Jill stared at Madison like a teenager whose mother told her to put on a coat when it was freezing outside, as if it wasn't obvious. "My God," said Jill. "You are freakishly irritating."

"And you are freakishly slow. Come on. The pancake is getting cold."

Jill made a face at Madison. "Okay. Okay." She leaned back on the couch, getting comfortable. Crossing her legs, she shifted, trying to relax. It was weird doing this with Madison watching, but also comforting at the same time. *Pancakes*, she thought to herself. *Pancakes*. Taking a deep lungful of air and blowing it out, she closed her eyes.

••••••••••

A thick fog surrounded her. A soupy mix of heavy clouds shifted and churned, preventing her from seeing anything. Jill walked through it, and the fog twisted and twirled. An eerie silence enveloped her, and Jill debated whether to speak. Would anyone hear her? Would her voice only be muffled by the heavy, low-lying mist?

She kept walking for what felt like hours. Brief glimpses of faces occasionally swirled in front of her. She saw her father, and then her mother, or what she remembered of her. Then Rem's face appeared, and she smiled, feeling his love. His face dissipated and she saw Jace and Madison standing in the distance, their arms outstretched, calling to her. It was the first sound she'd heard, and she turned to follow it. She picked up her pace, eager to reach them, but the distance never seemed to shrink. It almost felt like they were getting further and further away. She started to jog, trying harder. But the faster she moved, the farther away they got. Realizing it was pointless, she stopped, breathless. She couldn't reach them. The fog overtook them, and Jace and Madison disappeared into the mist.

Frustrated, Jill turned, ready to return. This exercise was pointless. The fog was not releasing any secrets, and she was tired and hungry. Her mind wanted to stop. Moving back through the clouds, her anxiety inched up a notch when she realized she didn't know where she was. How did she get back? Would anyone find her? Was she lost?

Rem's face appeared again in the shifting of the fog, and she relaxed. Rem would show her the way home. Following him, her fear eased, and calm returned. But the longer she walked, the more uncomfortable she became. She should have been back by now. Wanting to reach Rem, she raised her arm, and almost touched him, when his face morphed, his eyes, nose and smile shifting and changing, until they became a sneer. His dark hair turned blonde, and his brown eyes went blue, and Jill stared into the face of Rutger.

Her body went numb, and she couldn't move. She feared if she did, he would see her and chase her, and she had nowhere to go. Her body tingling with terror, she willed herself to stay calm and wait. Rutger remained almost as still as Jill, but then he shifted and walked away. Still anxious, Jill forced herself to follow. Did he know she was there? Was he leading her? She had no idea. Moving through the clouds, he seemed relaxed, almost serene. As he moved, the fog lifted, and Jill's vision improved, and suddenly, Rutger walked into a room. It looked like a hotel room, with a small kitchenette and dining table. There was a worn couch and a beat-up TV and there were dirty plates stacked in the sink.

Jill stayed silent, not wanting him to see her. A sudden intense pain shot through the bridge of her nose, and she held it, feeling it throb. The movement caused a slice of heat to shoot through her abdomen and she ran her hand over it, wondering where the pain was coming from. Rutger sat at the small table, shirtless, his body lean and sinewy. He moved slowly, holding his belly, and Jill saw his bruised face and the bandage across his midsection, dirty and bloody, and she knew then that she was feeling his injuries. His nose was broken and swollen and his eyes puffy. Jill gritted her teeth against the discomfort and stayed quiet.

Rutger took a drink of something, and Jill tasted orange juice. She saw a piece of paper and pen on the table, a picture, and a green stone. She moved slowly, trying to see the picture. Rutger, moving gingerly, picked up the stone, and held it. Jill inched forward. If she could get just a little closer...

A sudden movement from Rutger made her gasp as light flashed in her head and hot white pain sliced through her gut. The noise alerted him, and he swiveled in his seat, and stared right at her.

He didn't speak, but she heard him clearly. "Well. Looky, looky."

The pain shifted to fear, and she tried to get out. Where was the fog? How did she return?

He stood, still holding the stone, and encroached. "Not bad, Jill. You're getting the hang of it, aren't you?"

Her terror ratcheted up. *How do I get out? How do I get out? He can see me.* She searched for an escape, but there was none.

He moved closer. "Funny thing about newcomers," he said. "They're all excited about the journey until they find what they're looking for, and then they realize where they truly are."

Jill stepped back, frantic. Her heart rate tripled and sweat prickled on her skin. Her voice locked up.

He walked up to her and she wanted to scream. "Be careful, Jill. Just because you're my sister doesn't mean I won't remind you of your place and put you back in it."

Her entire body shook, and she wanted to cry. Her stomach clenched, and she fought the urge to throw up. A pressure against her shoulder fought for her attention, but she focused on Rutger. Then she heard the distant sound of her name being called, and she thought her mind was playing tricks on her.

Rutger tipped his head. "They're looking for you Jill. Too bad they won't find you." He lifted a finger and brought it to her face. "You're in my world now."

He lightly touched her cheek, and his fingertip burned. She heard her skin sizzle, and the terror was so intense she drew back, her voice unlocked, and she screamed as loud as she could. "Pancakes."

And she opened her eyes.

· · · · ●· ● · · · ·

Jill sat, aware of the couch beneath her. Madison was shaking her shoulder, and Jace was sitting on the coffee table in front of her, his hand gripping her wrist. Their eyes were wide, and Madison looked as terrified as she felt.

Jill blinked, breathing hard, and shivering.

"Jill," yelled Jace. "Jill, are you back?"

Madison shook her shoulder again. "Jill, are you okay?"

Jill shook her head, trying to acclimate; Rutger's sneer was still visible in her mind. "Where am I?" Her voice shook.

"You're at Remalla's," said Madison.

"What happened?" asked Jace. He wore a T-shirt that said *Man of the House* and a pair of gray sweatpants with holes in them. His arm was bandaged, and he held his ribs with his free hand. "Where the hell did you go?"

Jill still felt partly detached, like she was still in the clouds. "Where's my necklace?" She reached for her neck. "I need my necklace."

"What necklace?" Madison's eyes widened. "Sonia's necklace?"

Jill nodded, wiping away an unshed tear, her fingers shaking.

"Where is it?" asked Madison.

"On the nightstand. In Rem's room." She tried to relax, but her heart wouldn't slow.

"I'll get it." Madison ran out.

Jace moved to sit next to her, sucking in a breath when he moved. "What the hell were you doing?" He looked closely at her. "And what happened to your cheek?"

Madison ran back in with the necklace. "Here. Hold it."

Jill took the stone and put it in her hand, feeling instantly more connected to the room and the people in it. Rutger's face faded from her mind. She took slow, deep breaths.

"You better now?" asked Madison.

Jill nodded and swallowed. "That was awful."

Jace grimaced, and Jill didn't know if it was from his ribs or Jill's attempts to contact Rutger. "You're an idiot. What were you thinking?"

Madison smacked him on the arm. "Don't call her an idiot."

"Was this your idea?" he yelled.

"And don't yell at me," said Madison. "It was an experiment."

Jill's cheek burned, and she touched it. Wincing, she pulled her hand back.

Madison shifted to see. "Did he do that to you?" She stood. "I'm going to get some of that rubbing alcohol."

Jill didn't bother to argue. She still felt rattled. Taking another breath, she shook out her hands.

Jace eyed her, his face unpleasant. "You shouldn't have done that."

She squeezed her temples as a headache bloomed. "It was a good idea. I had to try."

"He could have killed you."

Madison returned with the alcohol and a tissue. "Let me see."

"I'm okay." Jill waved her off.

"Did you see him?" asked Jace.

The fear had subsided, but it flared again at the question. Rutger had been in her face, and he'd touched her. The memory made her skin break out in chills. "Yes. He was there. I followed him."

Madison held the alcohol. "Where did he go?"

Jill closed her eyes, remembering. "He was in a hotel room. Small and run-down. Dirty. I felt his injuries." She held her stomach, remembering. "He has a broken nose, swollen eyes and his stomach is bad. He needs a doctor, I think."

"Good. I got the bastard," said Jace.

"I made a noise, though, and he saw me." Jill cursed. "And I didn't know how to get out." She bit her lip. "And then he touched me." She could hear the sizzle of her skin again and bit back a well of emotion, but a tear still escaped, and she wiped it away.

"He left that mark on you? Shit," said Madison.

"I'm okay." Jill sniffed and straightened. "I'm better."

"This is by far the dumbest thing ever," said Jace.

"No. It wasn't," said Jill. Madison handed her the tissue, and she dabbed her face, careful to avoid her burning cheek. "Madison was right. We have to use what we have to catch him. It's the only way to find him." Feeling more centered, she thought back to her vision. "I saw something else. He sat at a table. There was a piece of paper and a picture, and he was holding a green stone. I tried to look at the picture..." She squinted, trying to recall.

"What did you see?" asked Madison.

"It was a photo. I didn't get a clear look at it. It was a woman. Acting silly, but I didn't get a good look at her face."

"What about the paper? Was he writing something?" asked Madison. "Maybe it was from the hotel. Did you see a name or address?"

"I don't know, but he wasn't in a type of hotel that has stationary."

Jace scoffed. "Yeah. This is super helpful. You saw a picture of an unidentified woman, a piece of paper, a green rock, and a dirty hotel room. Let's call the cavalry. We've got him in our sights."

Madison swatted at Jace again. "Would you stop? At least now we know she can reach him. It took a while, but she got there."

Jill held the bridge of her nose. "How long was I out?"

"Close to an hour," said Madison.

Jill looked up. "What? Are you kidding?"

"No," said Madison. "It took you a while to get deep. I almost roused you, but then Jace came down. He wanted to stop you, but then you showed signs that you were connecting, so we let it continue. Then you started shaking and sweating. We tried to pull you out, but you wouldn't break loose. Jace even yelled at you. I grabbed you and shook you, but you wouldn't open your eyes. You were making this awful keening sound, like you were terrified, and then you said pancakes, and you were back."

"I said pancakes?" Jill remembered shrieking the word in her head.

"What the hell does pancakes mean?" asked Jace.

"It's our safe word," said Madison. "We were going to make some."

Jace dropped his jaw. "Son-of-a-bitch. Are you two crazy?"

"It worked," said Madison. "She came back."

Jace scowled. "Well, thank God for pancakes."

"You are in a foul mood this morning," said Madison.

Jace yelled. "That happens when I wake up to find my two new siblings playing with the devil, and one of them almost gets taken by him. Not to mention I'm starving, and my ribs hurt."

Jill rubbed her eyes. "He's right. We need to eat. I feel a little weak."

"I'll get you some water," said Madison.

"No. I'll get up. I need to stand. Move around." Jill put her feet on the floor and Jace took her arm and helped her up. She wobbled for a second but found her balance.

"You need to clean your cheek," said Madison.

"I'm sure it's fine," said Jill.

Jace guided Jill with his arm. "I think you need to see it for yourself. Then you might understand why I'm upset."

He led Jill to the bathroom, with Madison following. Looking in the mirror, a jolt of shock ran through her. Her cheek had a long, raised area of skin, blistered, raw and red. It looked like a third-degree burn. "Oh, hell," said Jill. She touched it and winced. "What did he do to me?"

"Now you see what I'm talking about?" asked Jace. "This guy is no joke. If you hadn't gotten out when you did, there's no telling what he could have done."

"Here," said Madison. "Use this to clean it." She held out the alcohol.

"Never mind that," said Jace.

"She needs to disinfect it," said Madison. "We'll need a bandage, too."

"I said never mind." Jace raised a hand. "Let me work on it."

"What are you doing?" asked Jill, pulling back.

He frowned. "You want us to work on our gifts? Well, let me work on mine. Stay still." He raised his hand and held his fingers over her cheek. Her skin began to warm and tingle, and the pain faded.

Madison's eyes went wide. "No way."

Jill stared too and saw the redness diminish and the blistering subside. She didn't know what to say.

Jace dropped his hand. "Give it a minute or two, then it will be gone. Hopefully, you won't have more than a small scar."

Jill touched her cheek, and what had been a raw and seeping wound was now only a pink inflammation. "I don't believe it."

Jace watched her through the mirror. He spoke in a serious tone. "And that is why you fail."

She glared back at him, as did Madison.

"Sorry," he shrugged. "I'm a *Star Wars* fan."

Jill sighed. "Great. Now I'm going to have to put up with both you and Rem." She looked back in the mirror, still in shock. The wound continued improving, and the redness was fading.

"That is amazing. Do you believe in mojo now?" asked Madison.

Jill touched the healed area. "I...I...guess I don't have a choice. I'm stunned."

"Can we get those pancakes now?" asked Jace, leaving the bathroom. "And I definitely need some coffee."

"Just a second," said Jill, turning from the mirror.

Jace turned with a grimace, holding his side. "What now?"

"You and I have had our shot, but she hasn't." Jill poked Madison in the arm. "Now it's your turn."

Madison narrowed her eyes. "Seriously? Now?"

Jill nodded. "A deal's and deal. You saw mine. Now I want to see yours."

"Son-of-a...," said Jace. "Can we eat first?"

Chapter Nineteen

REM GOT OUT OF the car and closed the door. "Is this it?"

Daniels got out on the driver's side. "This is the address."

Rem surveyed the structure. "This is a church."

"I can see that." Daniels walked up beside him.

"This is where Massey lives?"

"According to his parole officer."

"Huh. Well, I guess it's better than the street." Rem took the stairs up to the front. The sign at the entrance read *Our Lady of Sorrows Church,* and a list of service times were noted below it. He opened the door and walked in, seeing a large sanctuary with a carpeted walkway and pews on either side of it. At the back was an altar and a cross with flowers at the foot of each.

"It's quiet in here," said Rem.

"It's a church. They're not usually loud," whispered Daniels. He pointed. "There's a side door. Let's head over there."

Rem followed Daniels as he walked out and headed down a carpeted hall-way, which veered left, and Daniels approached a row of doors and a sign leading to an office. "Here we go," said Daniels. He opened the door.

A receptionist with purplish red hair sat at a desk reading a book. Rem caught a glance at the title. *His Mighty Sheath of Love.* She stared up at them over her readers. "Can I help you?"

Rem tried to ignore the book and put an elbow on a counter adjoining the desk. "We're looking for Mr. Massey? Is he here?"

She squinted. "Reverend Massey? Yes. Of course. He stepped out of the office, but I think he went to the garden. You're welcome to check."

"Reverend Massey?" Daniels raised a brow.

"That's what they call him," said the receptionist. "The garden is straight across. Just go out and turn right and the door outside will be just down the hall on your left."

Rem nodded. "Okay. Thanks. Enjoy your book."

She stared and went back to her reading. "You're welcome and I will."

Daniels and Rem left the office and turned right down the hall. "Reverend Massey? What's up with that?" asked Rem.

"Don't know. The file said nothing about him being ordained."

"Nowadays, you can get ordained in minutes on the internet. That might explain why he has a receptionist reading soft porn at her desk."

The hallway brightened as the wall became a window, and they could see a green garden adorned with various types of flowers. Daniels opened the door. "He gets ordained on the web, hires an erotica fan, and suddenly has a congregation months after getting paroled from prison? Hard to believe."

Rem walked through the door. "Ever heard of Jim Jones?"

"Jarrod Massey is no Jim Jones. He'd be lucky to get a kid to buy him a lollipop."

"People change." Rem spotted a man kneeling in the dirt, pulling weeds. "That must be him."

"People change, but some stripes don't come off." Daniels approached the kneeling man. "Excuse me. Are you Reverend Massey?"

The man turned and looked up, squinting in the sun. Rem realized this couldn't be Jarrod Massey. His face looked older, and the lines around his eyes crinkled when he smiled. The reverend stood and took off his gardening gloves. "Why, yes. How can I help you?" He took out a rag and patted his sweaty forehead.

Daniels showed his badge, as did Remalla. "We're looking for Jarrod Massey."

"Police? Is something wrong?" asked the Reverend.

"That's what we're here to find out," said Daniels. "Are you a relative?"

The reverend nodded. "Yes. I'm Jarrod's brother, Paul." His face fell. "Is Jarrod in trouble?"

Rem stepped into some shade and admired a pretty rose. "We just need to talk to him."

"Does he live here?" asked Daniels.

"Yes. I told him he could take the room upstairs, above the office. It's quiet and he can keep to himself if he chooses. And it's not far from where he's been working."

"He's working nearby?" asked Daniels.

"He works at the grocer down the street. He's trying hard to stay on the straight and narrow since getting out of prison. I vouched for him so he could stay here, as long as he checks in and I know where he is, and he holds down a job. It's been working so far. He even came to a service last week. I'm hoping this environment will help lead him back to the church. I pray for it every day."

Daniels regarded Rem, who shrugged. "That's very nice, but we need to talk to him. Is he here?"

"I think so. He worked early this morning, and he came back to get something to eat, but he's returning to work this afternoon."

"You think so? Aren't you keeping track of him?" asked Rem.

The reverend picked up a pulled weed and tossed it in a bag. "I'm quite sure he's upstairs. I trust him to follow the rules."

"Yeah, well, if he'd had a loaded gun instead of an empty one eight years ago, he might be dead." Rem shot a thumb at Daniels. "So, forgive me if I question his rule-following."

The reverend's face softened. "Forgiveness is required in God's teaching and paramount in reaching the gates of heaven, so you are forgiven."

Rem saw a weed and pulled it. "I appreciate that." He tossed the weed into the bag.

"Where can we find your brother?" asked Daniels.

"Paul. I'm headed out." A male voice called from a distance. Rem and Daniels turned to see a man standing by the door to the garden.

The reverend raised a hand and waved. "Jarrod, come on over."

A younger version of the reverend walked over and stopped in front of them. "I got to go or I'm going to be late."

"Jarrod Massey?" asked Daniels, flashing his badge.

Jarrod paled and flicked a glance at Rem, who also held a badge. "What's this all about? Am I in trouble?"

"You remember him, Jarrod?" asked Rem, pointing at Daniels.

Jarrod narrowed his eyes. "Ah, hell. You're the cop who arrested me." He raised a hand. "Hey, man. I'm clean. No drugs. Haven't seen any of the old crew. My brother's keeping tabs on me. And I've got a job."

"Where were you Saturday morning between ten and twelve and Monday morning between five and eight?" asked Daniels.

"Working. I went in at six on Monday. Ask Paul. He'll vouch for me," said Jarrod. "I didn't do anything. Right, Paul?"

The reverend wiped the back of his neck with the cloth. "He's correct, detectives. He went to work on both days. He came back for lunch on Monday around noon. I saw him."

"That's great, but you believe he's actually at work. We'll need to verify your whereabouts with your employer," said Daniels.

"Do what you gotta do, but I didn't do anything," said Jarrod.

"What's this all about?" asked the Reverend.

Rem saw another weed and pulled it. "You had any contact with Judge Hendrix or your prosecutor, Lyla Alba? From your court case? Any phone calls, notes, visits?"

Jarrod's jaw dropped. "That? You think I killed them?"

"You threatened them. Me, too," said Daniels. "Plus, a witness or two. That makes you a suspect."

Jarrod shook his head. "Hey, man. Different time. Different place. I ain't that guy no more. Right, Paul?"

"Still think I'm a bird of prey?" asked Daniels.

Jarrod held out his hands. "It was the drugs, man. They messed with me. I'm different now."

"I sure hope so," said Rem. "Because if we find out you're lying..."

"I'm not lying. I swear." Jarrod smoothed his shirt nervously, and Rem noticed his fingers were shaking.

"Go to work, Jarrod. I don't want you to be late," said the reverend. "I think these detectives have asked their questions."

"Right. Okay." Jarrod ran a hand through his hair. "I'll see you tonight."

"See you tonight," said the reverend.

Jarrod looked between Rem and Daniels, turned and left.

Rem watched him go. "I'm hurt. He didn't say goodbye."

"That was rather rude, wasn't it?" asked Daniels. "I don't think he likes us."

Rem tipped his head. "Comes with the territory."

The reverend dropped his rag to the ground. "You two should come to a service. We'd love to have you join us."

"Thanks, Reverend. Once we stop chasing bad guys, maybe we'll check it out," said Daniels. "You ready?" he asked Rem. "Let's go talk to the grocer."

"I'm ready. You sure there's nothing about Jarrod that we need to know?" Rem asked the Reverend. "If you do, now's the time to tell us."

The reverend smiled. "I trust my brother. He's had his issues, but he's getting his life back together."

Daniels pulled out a card. "If that changes, give us a call."

The reverend took the card and put it in his shirt pocket. "God bless you two. Enjoy your day."

Daniels nodded. "You, too."

Rem followed Daniels out of the garden and back into the hallway. "Well, what do you think?" he asked.

"I'll know what I think after we talk to the grocer. Good brother Paul may have no idea what his brother's doing while he thinks he's at work."

Rem waved at the receptionist, still reading as they walked by. She eyed them over her readers and went back to her book. "You see his hands? They were shaking."

"Yeah, but he could have been nervous because of us. We catch him violating parole, he's back in jail."

"Makes me wonder if he's got something to hide."

"Let's go find out."

They walked back through the sanctuary and returned to the car.

• • • • • • • • • •

"What do you want me to do?" asked Madison.

They'd finished their pancakes, and she and Jill were sitting in the living room again. Jace remained in the kitchen, finishing his second helping and waiting for the painkillers to kick in.

"I don't know. This isn't my forte. What do you usually do?" asked Jill.

Madison clenched her hands together. "I'm not really sure. It just sort of happens."

"But when? There's got to be a catalyst or something that triggers it. Think. What's going on when something moves?"

Madison thought back, recalling memories she'd rather forget. "High emotion. Like anger or fear."

Jill considered that. "We don't want to create that, but it's good to know. How can you pull in that kind of energy without being scared or angry?"

"Look at you, talking about energy. I'm impressed."

"I know, but it's the word that makes the most sense, doesn't it?"

"Yes, I guess it is."

Jill scanned the room and grabbed a magazine from a side table. It was a popular tech magazine with the well-known guru and CEO of Steele and Stone Industries, Grayson Steele, on the cover. Rem never seemed to have the time to read it. She put it on the coffee table in front of Madison. "Here. Let's start small. See if you can move this."

Madison shook out her hands. "Do we really have to do this? I mean, maybe I got the short end of the stick here and this is really not all it's cracked up to be."

"Like you said, it's time to find out. If we want to find and confront Rutger, we have to know our strengths. So, let's learn more about yours."

Madison sighed. "Okay."

"Focus," said Jill. "Concentrate on the magazine."

Madison stared at the coffee table, gripping her knees, her brow creased.

"Relax," said Jill. "You're not trying to rip it in half."

Madison bobbed her shoulders and arms and moved her head side to side. "Okay." She stared again, her face less tense.

"Let the energy build. See it move across the table." Jill held her breath.

"I'm trying."

"Do or do not. There is no try."

Madison eyed her. "Really?"

Jill shrugged. "Sorry. Rem's *Star Wars* quotes are rubbing off on me."

"You and Jace are a lot alike, which makes me worry." Madison went back to focusing on the magazine.

"About what?"

Madison paused. "Am I more like him?"

"You might look like him, but that doesn't mean you act like him."

Madison stared at the floor.

"You know that, don't you?" asked Jill. "You're not suddenly going to the dark side simply because he did."

"I don't know. Sometimes I wonder."

"Madison, don't be silly."

She studied her hands. "I had a dream last night."

Jill put a hand on her wrist. "We've all been having dreams."

"This one was different."

"How so?"

Madison's face darkened. "He was there, as usual. As were you and Jace. He threatened you both. Said if I didn't do as he wanted, he'd kill you. I was terrified."

"What did he want you to do?"

Madison closed her eyes. "Use my strengths to protect him. You and Jace were in danger. Rem and Daniels showed, and he...he...wanted me to stop them. To hurt them. Or he would hurt you." She looked up at Jill, her eyes haunted. "And I considered it. For a brief moment, I...I...was desperate."

Jill's heart sank. "Madison, it was a dream."

"I know, but some part of me wonders—"

Jill squeezed her hand. "I've known you for what? Less than a week? And I can tell you I'd trust you with my life."

"I feel the same. But if our lives are threatened by this man, how far are we willing to go to protect each other?"

Jill considered the question. "I don't think we'll really know that until we face it in reality, and not in some dream."

"You think he's manipulating us? In our dreams?"

"Maybe. Maybe not. Maybe we're just forcing ourselves to work through our issues so that when the real thing happens, we'll be more prepared."

Madison rubbed her thighs. "I hope that's all it is."

"How's it going in here?" asked Jace, sipping from a cup of coffee. "Any progress?"

"None so far," said Madison. "I think you and Jill got all the talent."

"Nonsense," said Jace. His demeanor had improved. "Keep trying."

"Let's go again. Focus on the magazine," said Jill. "Clear your mind and relax."

Madison exhaled a deep breath and stared.

"There you go," said Jace. "You can do it."

"Breathe," said Jill. "Don't contract, expand."

The magazine shifted slightly on the table, and Jill jumped. "It moved."

"You got this," said Jace. "Don't stop." He stepped closer.

Madison focused her gaze, taking deliberate breaths. The magazine slid about an inch.

Jill hooted. "That's fantastic. Keep going."

Madison tried, but deflated. "This is too hard. It's a lot of work to move something so flimsy only an inch."

"You're making it difficult," said Jace. He came over and stood beside her. "You're thinking too much. See it as easy. Like you're picking it up with your hands. Try it again."

Madison rubbed her temple. "Okay." She raised her hand out. Several seconds passed. "Move, you stupid thing."

The magazine vibrated on the table. "There you go," said Jace. "Nice job. Don't stop." He put a hand on her shoulder, and the pages flew open. The magazine slid across the table, zipped through the room, and landed on the floor in the entry.

Jill jumped back. "Holy shit."

Madison, her eyes wide, said the same.

"Rock on, sis. That was perfect. Now all you need is practice." Jace drained his mug. "I'm going to get some more coffee." He walked out, picked up the magazine with a groan, and put it back on the table. "Try it again. Make it hover and go all the way to the kitchen."

Madison's face scrunched, and even Jill was doubtful. "There's no way...," started Madison.

Jace held up a finger. "Ah, ah. Don't say it. You should see the shit Rutger can do. This is just the tip of the iceberg. Try it again." He turned and went into the kitchen. "See if you can hit me with it."

Madison bit her lip, but then took a deep breath and focused once more, holding out her hand. "I can do this," she whispered. "I can do this."

After trying for a few seconds, the magazine shifted only slightly, and Madison dropped her arm. "Why is it so hard one time, and so easy another?"

Jill eyed Grayson Steele's face, then Madison, and a thought popped in her head. "Jace. Come back in here."

"What?" Jace poked his head out of the kitchen.

"Come back. I want to try something," said Jill.

Jace returned with a fresh cup of coffee and munching on a dry pancake. "What are you thinking?"

"Try again, Madison," said Jill.

Madison moaned, but raised her hand again. After a few seconds, the magazine slid a short distance.

"There you go," said Jace.

"Good. Don't stop," said Jill. "Jace. Put your hand on her shoulder. Like you did before."

Jace, curious, carefully put his coffee cup down and rested a hand on Madison's shoulder. The magazine shot across the table and back onto the floor.

"Perfect. Keep focusing," said Jill, and she inched closer and placed her hand on Madison's other shoulder.

The magazine shook, pages fluttering, and rose. It hovered in the air.

"Oh, my God," whispered Madison.

"Make it move," said Jill quietly, as if speaking louder would break the spell.

Madison turned her hand, and the magazine turned in the air.

"You got it now," said Jace. "Now throw it somewhere. With force."

Madison smiled, flicked her hand, and the magazine flew higher, reversed direction, and flew back into the room, hitting Jace in the chest and falling to the floor.

Jace grabbed his ribs and bellowed a curse.

"You told me to hit you with it," said Madison.

"You did it," said Jill. "You really did it. That was amazing."

Madison rubbed her hands together in satisfaction. "Let's hit something else."

"Did you see what happened, though?" asked Jill. "When we touched you, it helped."

Jace held his ribs. "Lucky me."

Madison went quiet, thinking. "That's true. When you touched me, I felt a warmth, like I was heating up." She swiveled and pointed. "You know, that happened to you, too."

"To me?" asked Jill. "When?"

"You remember, Jace? When you came in the room this morning, and Jill was meditating?"

Jace ate the rest of his pancake. "It's hard to forget."

"Everything was fine, and then you sat and took her wrist. That's when you reacted, Jill."

Jill recalled her vision. It had been mundane at first, and she'd been looking to return, when it had suddenly changed. "The three of us together makes a difference."

"Maybe that's why that asshole doesn't want us together," said Jace, rubbing his side.

"Maybe it was just Jace," said Madison. "He was the one who changed things when he came into the room."

Jill tipped her head. "I guess there's one way to find out."

They eyed her with interest.

She smiled. "Let's keep practicing."

· · · · · · · · · ·

Rem entered the squad room carrying a paper bag and headed for his desk. "Well, that was a giant bust." He sat and opened the bag. "God. I'm starving."

"It wasn't a total waste of time," said Daniels, sitting at his desk. "We know Massey was at work."

Rem unwrapped the food and picked up a hamburger. "But he's also a delivery driver. He had deliveries both mornings. Could he have swung by Hendrix and Alba's?"

"Nobody saw a delivery truck."

"He could have switched cars." Rem bit into his food.

Daniels slid his jacket off. "Maybe." He opened his desk drawer and pulled out a granola bar. "Waldo Yang was a bust, though."

"Can you believe he's back with that chick he beat up? What the hell is wrong with the world?"

"She vouches for him, though. Says he was with her during the times of Hendrix's and Alba's deaths."

Rem spoke through a mouthful of burger. "You believe her? I think she'd defend Charles Manson if he were her boyfriend."

Daniels shook his head. "I know. She's not too reliable." He took a bite of his bar and took a swig of water from a bottle on his desk. "We can at least clear Foster Jackson. Guy's been in traction for a month."

Rem licked mustard off his finger. "That'll teach him to race a horse without a lesson."

"You'd think that would be a given."

"You'd think, but nobody asked us."

"And you think Ester is off the list?" asked Daniels.

Rem nodded. "For sure. She got a degree in jail. Now she helps other addicts with therapy. She's got solid alibis for both mornings."

"That's something, at least." Daniels sat forward. "What about Maia Chambers? You find anything?"

Rem chewed a french fry. "Just that her mother lives in Florida and her father in New York. I talked to the dad, but he couldn't offer much. Said he'd never had much of a relationship with Maia. Haven't got a hold of the mother yet. There was one interesting thing about Maia, though. She had a baby in jail."

"What?"

"Apparently, she was pregnant when she was arrested. Gave birth during her stay."

"Really. What happened to the baby?" asked Daniels.

"Mother took her. It was a girl."

Daniels' brow raised. "Any chance that number at the scene matches the baby's birthdate?"

Rem grabbed another fry. "I looked, but no cigar. It was close, though."

"How close?"

"Two weeks prior."

"You think that might mean something?"

Rem shrugged. "Maybe. Need to talk to the mom to find out. I'll try her again this afternoon. But do you really think either the mom or dad would come down and kill Hendrix or Alba?"

"Who's the baby's dad? Any idea?"

Rem sucked from his cup of soda. "None. Not in the file."

Daniels fell back in his seat. "Wonderful." He rubbed his face. "Lozano's not going to like this update."

"Probably not." Rem took another bite of his burger.

Lozano's office door opened, and he poked his head out. "Glad you two are back. I want to know how it went." He held the door open.

Rem chewed. "This day just keeps getting better."

"Doesn't it though?" Daniels picked up his granola bar. "Let's get this over with."

Rem grabbed his burger and carried it into the office. He took his usual seat and Lozano sat at his desk.

"How'd it go today?" asked Lozano. "Any possibles?"

Rem eyed Daniels. "I'm eating. You tell him."

Daniels rolled his eyes. "Fine." He went through their day, telling Lozano that no one so far seemed to be good for the murders, but Massey and Yang couldn't completely be ruled out, nor could a mad relative of Maia Chambers.

Lozano grunted. "You're telling me that of the six, the three we're all connected to have not yet been ruled out?"

"No. They haven't. But we haven't found any smoking guns," said Daniels. "It may not be any of them."

"We could put a tail on Massey and Yang," said Rem. "See if that leads anywhere." He ate the last bite of his burger.

Lozano grabbed a pen from his drawer but knocked it on the side of his desk. The pen fell and Lozano reached to pick it up. "We could do—"

A loud pop sounded and the window behind Lozano shattered, as well as the glass wall behind Rem and Daniels.

Lozano fell forward, and Rem flew out of his seat along with Daniels and hit the floor.

Chapter Twenty

SONIA SAT IN CONTEMPLATIVE silence, her eyes closed, and head bowed. Her mind would not settle, though. Holding the black obsidian stone, she tried to relax. After a jarring meditation the previous night, she'd hoped the obsidian would protect her against psychic attack and negativity, plus help relieve her of the constant stress she seemed to be under.

Sighing deeply, she opened her eyes and stared at the closed door to her room. Since asking for Peter's help, she'd kept to herself, allowing him to work. She'd questioned her decision repeatedly, but ultimately knew it was for the best. If something happened to her, then someone else needed to know the truth. She hoped she had not burdened him with too much. He'd spoken little since she'd given him the project, talking to her only when he needed clarification or couldn't read her writing. She'd waited, knowing at some point he would find her, and have several questions. Would he be angry? Would he want to leave? Could she get him to understand?

Knowing these questions were only making it more difficult for her, she tried again to relax, but the visions from last night returned. The realness of it had frightened her, but she suspected she knew why. The energy she'd felt from the siblings had increased, and she sensed they'd found each other. Rutger knew it too, and it was creating a turmoil of emotion, elation, worry and fear. It was the only explanation.

Sonia again wondered if she'd done the right thing in speaking with Jill. She'd hoped but failed to stop Rutger on her own. She hadn't been strong enough. Now, she needed the very people she'd been trying to protect to stop him. It had been the thing she'd been wanting to avoid, but she'd had no choice.

The only option now was to let Jill, Madison and Jace connect and hope they found their way, and hope Rutger didn't interfere too soon. She could sense his awareness of them, and he'd tried to stop their reunion, but had failed. His energy felt scattered and weak, but she knew that wouldn't last. Whatever had happened, he would recoup from and come back that much stronger.

Perhaps that had been the reason for her strange vision. Sonia remembered the pain and the attack, seeing blood, feeling the heat, and hearing the screams. It had been vicious and unrelenting, and the energy had bloomed, ready to unleash itself. But she couldn't see why. Where did it come from? Did Rutger start it, or one of the other three? And those detectives. They'd been there, too. She hadn't liked that. She'd hoped Jill would keep them out of it, but Sonia had her doubts. For some reason, they remained a part of the unfolding story.

Squeezing her temples, she dropped her head, thinking of Peter, the siblings, Rutger, and the detectives. Something was building. Something big. And she was powerless to stop it.

· · · ● ● · ● · · ·

Daniels stayed flat as shattered glass rained down. Everything went quiet, and he lifted his head. "Rem?" He saw his partner lying on the ground beside Lozano's desk.

Rem raised his head and shook the glass out of it. "I'm okay. You?"

"Fine. How's Lozano?"

Rem stayed low and moved forward through the glass. Daniels did the same, trying not to get cut. Raised voices traveled from the other room.

Rem scooted up and Daniels came up beside him. Lozano lay on his belly.

"Captain?" asked Rem.

Lozano grunted.

Footsteps sounded, and Daniels heard crunching glass. Daniels recognized the two detectives who ran in with their weapons pulled. One was Mellenbuehl and the other Georgios. Others ran up behind them. "What the hell happened? You guys okay?" asked Mellenbuehl.

Daniels stayed down. "Shots fired. Outside the window. Don't know from where. Lozano's down. Get an ambulance."

Lozano mumbled. "I'm okay." He reached for his head.

"Shit." Mellenbuehl pulled back, looking out the window.

"I'll contact Shorty. Clear and check the area." Georgios ran off, keeping his head down.

Rem patted the Captain's arm. "Captain. It's Remalla. Can you hear me?"

Lozano raised his head, and Daniels could see a trickle of blood running down Lozano's cheek.

"I'm not deaf, Remalla," said Lozano. "Yeah, I can hear you."

Rem coughed. "He can't be too injured. He's still grumpy."

Daniels inched forward. "Are you hit, Captain? There's blood."

Lozano, his face sweaty, tried to sit up. "I think it's just a crease. Bastard barely missed."

"Take it easy," said Rem. "Stay down."

They sat up along with Lozano, staying under the bottom of the window.

Mellenbuehl peered in. "Ambulance is coming. We're checking outside. Can you guys make it out?"

"Give us a sec, Mel," said Daniels, his voice shaky.

"I don't need an ambulance," said Lozano, holding his head.

"You're bleeding, Cap. You need to get it checked," said Rem. He held his hand, pulled on something, and grimaced.

"You hurt?" asked Daniels.

"Piece of glass in my hand. Nothing serious." He leaned his head against the wall. "You think he's gone?"

Daniels dusted the glass off of his pants, careful not to get cut. "He ought to be, unless he wants to be found. The entire building is going to be out looking for him."

"Shit. That was close," said Rem. "If the Cap hadn't bent down for that pen..."

"Yeah. I know," said Daniels.

"I'm in the damn room," said Lozano. "And how do you know I was the target?"

"You're the one who's hurt," said Daniels.

Lozano pulled his bloody hand back.

"You probably need stitches, Cap," said Rem.

"And you need a haircut, but I don't see you getting one," griped Lozano. "And I wasn't the only person in this room. He could have been targeting any of us."

Rem sighed, and Daniels closed his eyes.

"Looks like Massey and Yang's odds just improved," said Rem. "Although I think Yang's the front runner.

"Don't forget Maia Chambers. She's not off the list yet either," said Daniels.

Lozano pulled out a handkerchief and held it over his injury. "Looks like you two have more work to do."

· · · · ● · ● · · ·

Rutger eyed the house. The sun was setting beyond the trees, and the neighborhood was quiet; the only activity was an occasional jogger or dog walker. He held his stomach, sore from his encounter with Jace. After a busy, but productive, day, he'd finally walked into an E.R., giving them a crazy story about being in a bar fight and offering false identification from a man whose wallet he'd stolen. The picture on the I.D. looked enough like him to pass the nurses' inspection, and they'd treated him and sent him on his way. His eyes were bruised, his jaw swollen, and his stomach bandaged, but he'd be good as new in no time, which gave him plenty of opportunity to plan.

Staring at the house, he knew who was in it and who his target was, and all that mattered now was the timing. The pieces were falling into place and although there'd been a few hiccups, he'd successfully navigated the pitfalls. Sonia thought that by bringing the siblings together, she'd mounted a significant army, but Sonia didn't have all the puzzle pieces. There were a few missing, and those few would make all the difference.

Smiling, he put his hands in his pockets and pulled out the green piece of Jasper. He stared at it for a second, rubbing his fingers over it before returning it. Then he turned and walked down the sidewalk.

Chapter Twenty-One

REM OPENED THE DOOR and entered his home, with Daniels behind him. "Marjorie make it to her sister's okay?" Rem asked. He stopped short when he almost walked into one of his dining chairs. "What the...?" He moved the chair out of his way, then almost tripped on a framed picture of him and his mom lying on the floor. It normally hung on the wall in his bedroom.

"Someone doing some redecorating?" asked Daniels. "And yeah. She's good. Although this business of her having to leave when I get nervous is wearing thin."

Rem picked up the frame and put it on the entry table, wondering why it was there. "Someone took a shot at us today. I think your nervousness is justifiable." He looked around. "Where the hell is everyone?" He spied the dining table and the chairs all splayed out away from it. "And what the hell is going on around here?" He returned all the chairs to their proper places.

The back door opened, and Jill came in. "Hey, guys." Her cheeks were flushed, and she smiled. "How was your day?" She came up and gave Rem a kiss.

Rem cocked his head, since he was not used to her displaying public affection. Even Daniels raised a brow. She opened the fridge and pulled out a beer. "You guys want one?"

"Yeah, we do," said Rem. "What's up with—"

Madison ran in, flustered, and breathing hard. "I did it. I moved the rock. And you weren't even there."

Jill handed Rem and Daniels a beer. "That's great. You're definitely getting better. Here..." She handed a beer to Madison. "That's for Jace. You want one?"

Madison jumped with excitement. "Are you kidding? Yes. We need to celebrate." She looked over. "Hey, Rem. Daniels. You guys just get in?"

Jill grabbed two more beers for her and Madison.

Daniels uncapped his beer. "Yeah. Thought we'd stop by and say hi."

"What have you guys been up to?" asked Rem. "And why is this house a mess?"

Jill grabbed his arm. "Come on. We'll show you."

Rem let himself be dragged out into the backyard. Aunt Audrey had had a small garden and an old swing set, and Rem had done little with either. The garden was overgrown, and the swing set rusty. There were a couple of lawn chairs and a small table on a back porch, and he opened his beer, took a swig, and put it on the table. Jace leaned against a porch rail, holding his side.

"Jace," said Daniels, coming up next to Rem. "How are the ribs?"

Jill handed Jace his beer. "They're still there. I've been wanting one of these all day." He raised the bottle. "But they made me wait."

Madison swatted him on the arm just above his bandage. "You can't get drunk while we work on this."

"Says who?" asked Jace. He opened his beer and took a big swallow.

"What exactly are we out here for?" asked Rem.

"Show 'em, Madison," said Jill.

Madison drank some of her own beer and added the bottle to the table. "Now that I have an audience, I'm nervous."

"Don't be silly," said Jill. "Just be careful with the neighbors. We don't need to deal with that."

Madison flexed her fingers. "Okay. Here goes." She held out her hand.

Rem waited, and Daniels drank his beer.

One of the swings on the old swing set began to rock back and forth. Rem watched with interest, and Daniels lowered his beer. The rocking picked up until it was swinging high in the air, going back and forth.

Rem eyed the trees, looking to see if they were swaying, but there was no wind. He glanced at Daniels, who continued to stare at the swing. Madison stood focused, her arm outstretched, and then the swing abruptly stopped, coming to a motionless position as if someone had grabbed it and halted its movement.

"Not bad," said Jill.

Rem pointed. "Did you do that?" he asked Madison.

Madison did a fist pump in the air. "Damn right. Pretty good, huh?"

"Practice the rock again," said Jill.

Jace grunted and pushed off the rail. "I'm using the john. Try it without me around." He walked by Rem, whose mouth hung open. "I'd be careful," said Jace in a mumble. "She's still working on her aim."

Rem tried to fathom what he was seeing. "Do you believe this?" he asked Daniels.

Daniels gripped his beer. "I'd thought I'd seen everything, but now I come to your place and Madison Vickers is practicing psychokinesis in your backyard." He shook his head. "I'm half expecting fairies and unicorns to stroll through here, too."

Madison shifted her focus to a medium-sized rock on Rem's porch steps. The rock shook and then slowly raised.

"Hell," said Rem. "I could almost deal with Rutger because everything always happened so fast and then it was over, but this..."

"Pretty cool, isn't it?" asked Jill. "Let it hover, and then see if you can bring it to the table over here." The rock raised to the height of the rail and then hovered in mid-air. "Perfect," said Jill. "You're needing us less and less. Now move it over. Slowly."

Rem watched in disbelief as the rock moved, slowly at first, and then picked up speed.

"Careful," said Jill.

Rem dodged sideways when the rock whizzed by him and hit the side of the house.

"Damn it," said Madison, clenching and unclenching her hands. "It's still hard to control it, especially when the three of us aren't together."

"It's your first day. Take it easy on yourself. We'll practice more later. Right now, we need to eat." Jill turned and headed inside. "I'll heat the oven."

Madison sighed and followed her into the house.

Daniels and Rem stood, openmouthed, on the porch. Rem didn't know what to say. Daniels drank from his beer and leaned against the rail. "Well, this has been one hell of a day. You come home thinking your big news is you got shot at, only to learn that no, it's actually not such a big deal after all."

Rem tucked his hair back and stood on his back step. "What the hell have we gotten ourselves into?"

Daniels made an anxious chuckle. "I wish I knew, partner. I wish I knew." He eyed the rock. "But I think the bigger question is, how do we get ourselves out of it?"

Rem could only shake his head. "At least you're not dating one of them."

Daniels pushed off the rail. "There is that. But I'm stuck with you, so I don't see myself getting a reprieve." He nudged Rem. "Come on. It's been a long day. And Jill was right. We need to eat." He turned and walked into the house but stopped and looked back before entering. "You think we might be lucky enough that one of them could cross their arms and blink their eyes and we get a steak dinner?"

Rem huffed. "Shit we've seen, maybe we should ask." Drinking his beer, he followed Daniels back inside.

· · · · · · · · · ·

The five of them sat at the dining table, eating lasagna and salad with bread. "This is delicious," said Rem.

"Jace ran out to the Italian place down the street," said Jill. "I figured we needed more than pizza tonight."

Jace slid some lasagna onto his fork. "That's the last time I go out in this shirt, though. I need to either get my own stuff or stop at a store. I look ridiculous."

They'd warmed the lasagna in the oven while Jill and Madison filled them in on their day and how they'd used objects around the house to help Madison practice. Now that they were finally eating and Rem had had some time to digest their news and what he'd seen in his backyard, he had some questions.

"You guys are stronger together?" he asked.

"Seems that way," said Jace, slathering butter on his bread.

"Then how come Rutger can't use his mojo on you?" asked Rem. "And does that mean that you can't use your mojo on him? And if that's the case, what does it matter what you three can do if you can't do it around him?" He took a bite of lasagna.

Jill stopped in mid-chew. Jace and Madison looked just as uncertain.

"That's a good question," said Daniels, wiping his mouth with a napkin.

"We don't know that we can't use our stuff against him, do we?" asked Jill.

"We don't know anything," said Jace. "All we can do is hope. But Remalla's right. If we meet up with this guy, and we can't do shit, we're screwed."

"But he can't do anything either," said Madison. "That helps."

"That's not true," said Jace. "He hurt Sonia when I was there, and he slammed a door on Danni, so maybe he can't use it on me, but he's still dangerous."

"But maybe if it's the three of us together, that might be the tipping point," said Jill. "Remember what happened with the meditation, when Jace showed and took my wrist."

"What meditation?" asked Rem.

"You can't compare it to your meditation," said Jace. "It's not the same as being physically in the room with him. You can't be face to face with Rutger, say 'pancakes' and bounce right out of it."

"Pancakes?" asked Daniels. He eyed Rem. "What did we miss?"

Rem stabbed some lettuce with his fork. "I don't know. But that reminds me. I have a pancake mix in the pantry. We should make some for breakfast." He poked at a tomato. "And what meditation?"

Jill waved. "It was nothing."

"Nothing?" said Madison, her eyes wide. "You connected with Rutger."

Jill scowled at Madison.

Rem put his fork down. "You did what?"

Jill's shoulders fell. "It was just an experiment. I wanted to see if I could locate him." She rubbed her cheek.

Rem bit back a curse and tried to play it cool. "You sure you want to do that?"

Jill pushed the food around on her plate. "I think we have to. We can't stay here forever. At some point, we have to deal with him. I tried to see where he was, but didn't have much luck. But maybe this will get him to react, or at least show him we're on to him."

"React how? You want him to come here?" Rem gripped his beer bottle. "What exactly are you going to do if he does? Is Madison going to throw a rock at him while you go into a trance, and Jace tries to heal his violent ways?"

Jill tapped her fork on her plate. "I don't know, Rem. This is as new to us as it is to you."

Rem set his jaw. "It's not exactly new to me and Daniels. The guy's kicked our asses more than once. So, if you're planning on confronting him, you better be damn sure you play to win, or else you're all going to wind up dead."

The table went quiet.

"I'll play to win. I guarantee that," said Jace. "Which is why you two should disappear. If our abilities are no help when we confront him, then it's better I face him alone."

"We're not disappearing. And we don't know what will happen when we face him. For all we know, we may get stronger," said Madison. "He didn't want us to get together for a reason. I doubt it's because he dreads us telling boring stories from our childhoods."

"We're not leaving, Jace. We're in this together," said Jill.

"Any of you have a gun?" asked Daniels.

"I have mine in my backpack," said Jill.

"A lot of good it will do you there," said Rem.

"I don't like guns," said Madison.

Jill put her fork down. "I don't believe that a gun's going to stop him. At least not when it comes to us."

"Well, it would sure as hell make me feel better," said Rem. "If he does show and your gifts go kaput, it's going to work a lot better than one of Jace's punches." He met Jill's gaze, and he could tell she was frustrated. Looking more closely, he noticed something. "What happened to your face?"

Jill raised her hand and touched her cheek.

"It looks like you have a scar."

"It's nothing," said Jill. "Madison winged me with a rock and Jace healed it."

Rem noticed Madison look down at her plate and Jace frown. "Really? You guys did have an interesting day." Something told him there was more to the story, but he didn't pursue it.

Jill picked up her water. "What happened to your palm?"

Rem eyed the cut on his hand where he'd removed the glass. "It's nothing."

Daniels straightened. "We got shot at today." He picked up some bread and his knife. "Can you pass the butter?"

········

Jill wasn't sure she heard right. "You got what?"

Rem jabbed some lasagna with his fork. "Shot at, by a gun. In Lozano's office. Lozano was grazed, but he'll be okay."

"Are you joking?" asked Madison.

Daniels stopped before taking a bite of his bread. "No. I like a good joke, but not when it comes to almost getting killed."

"Did you catch the guy?" asked Jace.

Rem swallowed and sat back. "Nope. He shot out Lozano's window and disappeared. The three of us were in the office at the time, so we have to assume the target could have been any of us."

"Is this related to your current case?" asked Jill.

"Pretty sure it is," said Daniels. They continued to eat as he went through the suspects they'd talked to that day and why they might want them dead.

"Did anyone follow up with them after the shooting?" asked Jill.

Daniels tossed his napkin on the table. "Yeah. We had a couple of officers talk to Massey and Yang afterwards. Massey was at work, and Yang was at home."

"According to his girlfriend," said Rem.

"Exactly," said Daniels, "and we don't have a lot of confidence that she's telling the truth. And if Massey was out on a delivery, it wouldn't be hard to swing by, take a shot at us, and drive off. We don't have enough to hold them, but we've got patrols watching them, and we're going to bring both of them in tomorrow for questioning. See what happens."

"And what about this Maia Chambers? Why is she still on your list?" asked Jill.

"Because we haven't definitively ruled out the pissed relative theory," said Rem. "Shit. I was supposed to call the mom this afternoon."

Daniels sipped his beer. "You were a little distracted. You can call tomorrow."

"That's how you hurt your hand?" asked Jill.

Rem eyed his injury. "Just a piece of glass. No big deal."

"You want me to look at it?" asked Jace.

Rem pushed his plate back. "You know, between flying rocks, meditations to contact Rutger and getting shot at, I think I've handled all I can today. I'll stick with my body's natural healing process, but thanks, though."

Jace finished his beer. "No problem."

Daniels stood. "I'll clean up if you guys want to resume," he waved a hand, "you know, whatever it is you want to call it." He picked up his plate.

"You going home tonight? If someone's really aiming for you, do you think that's wise?" asked Jill.

"Daniels is taking the couch tonight. Marjorie and J.P. are at her sister's. We figure there's safety in numbers. Hopefully, tomorrow, we'll figure out if it's Yang or Massey and put this case to rest." Rem stood. "I'll help you clean up."

"Thank God, you're okay. Why didn't you call me?" asked Jill, standing and picking up her plate.

"You've got enough on your mind. Plus, it's all over the news. Figured you'd hear about it soon enough." Rem carried his plate over to the sink.

Jill followed and stood next to him. "You sure you're okay?"

He looked over at her, reached up and touched her scarred cheek. "You sure you're okay?"

Guilt crept up Jill's spine, remembering her lie. Should she tell him the truth? "I'm fine."

Rem started up the sink. "Then go finish..." He glanced back at Daniels, who brought over his and Madison's plates. "What did you call it?"

Daniels set the plates down. "Whatever it is they were doing out there."

"Yeah. That." Rem picked up a plate and rinsed it under the water.

Jill nodded, knowing there was more to be said, but it would have to be said later. She spoke to Madison. "You ready?"

Madison rose from the table. "Maybe we should take a break. We've been going at this all day."

Jace took the last bite of his second helping and swallowed it down with the last slug of his beer. "I agree." He stood with his plate. "Plus, Danni is supposed to call, and I want to talk to her."

Jill considered her options, thinking about the next day. "Let's practice until Danni calls, then we'll call it a day." She squeezed Rem's wrist. "Thanks for cleaning."

"You're welcome. And don't break any windows." Rem handed a plate to Daniels, who loaded the dishwasher.

Madison's shoulders slumped, but she followed Jill out to the backyard, along with Jace. The door closed behind them. "I'm kinda tired. Can't we pick this up tomorrow?"

Jill walked down the porch steps. "That's not why I asked you out here. We need to talk."

Jace joined her at the bottom of the stairs. "About what?"

Jill touched her cheek, remembering Rutger's touch. "About what's next."

"What do you mean?" asked Madison. She came down the steps and joined them.

Jill paced, thinking. "We can't drag this out. Once Rem and Daniels solve this case, it makes it harder for us to keep them out of it. We have to up the ante."

Jace crossed his arms. "What are you thinking?"

"Rutger's weak right now. We should take advantage of that. For the moment, he's calling the shots, but maybe we should start calling them instead." Jill stopped pacing and faced them.

Madison's eyes rounded. "What are you proposing?"

Despite the sliver of fear that made her shiver, she made a decision. "After Rem and Daniels leave for work tomorrow morning. I'm going back under to find Rutger. And I'm going to confront him." She bit her lip.

"The hell you are," said Jace. "You can't face him alone."

"I can face him long enough to find out where he is." Jill remembered the dirty hotel. "It can't be that hard. All I need is a name."

"Jill, you saw what he did to your cheek. If he gets a hold of you, and you can't get out..." Madison put a hand on her chest.

"It was new to me this morning," said Jill. "I didn't know where I was. But I'll do better the next time."

"What makes you think that?" asked Jace.

Jill recalled Rutger's stony eyes. "He's cocky. He's used to control. He thinks I'm weak and scared. I'll use that. I'll let him feel strong and dominant." She paused. "I think there's some part of him that likes that I'm there." She cocked her head, feeling a strange certainty. "In fact, I think there's some part of him that wants us to join him. He wants us to be angry and want revenge, the same way he does. I think that's why he killed Rick, Donald, and Justin." She paused. "He wants us to be as miserable as he is, which in some weird way makes him feel more connected to us."

"You mean he wants us to be like him? To go to the dark side?" asked Madison.

Jill nodded. "Yes. Remember your dream? Where you feared that very thing?"

"What dream?" asked Jace.

"I think that's what he wants," said Jill. "So maybe that's what we give him."

"Jill, are you crazy?" asked Madison.

Jill's mind whirled. Could doing this help them find Rutger? Could they convince him they were on his side?

"Actually, I think it's the sanest idea I've had since we started this." Jill rubbed her jaw. "And once we get him thinking we're on his side, then we...we..."

"We, what?" asked Madison. "Find him and kill him?"

"Damn straight," said Jace. "And what dream?"

"I don't know if I like this," said Madison.

Jill pointed. "Tomorrow. We're going to try. And not a word to Rem or Daniels, otherwise, they'll want to get involved. Okay?"

Madison and Jace stood silently. "If you go too deep, we're pulling you out," said Jace. "No exceptions. I don't care if I have to burn your other cheek myself."

Jill nodded. "Understood." She held out a pinky. "Tomorrow, we're going to find Rutger."

Jace held out his own pinky. Madison hesitated. "Are you sure we shouldn't mention it? Maybe they should know."

"It's to keep them safe. We can't handle Rutger if we have to protect them," said Jill. "Okay?"

Madison, her face somber, held out her pinky and sighed. "Okay."

Chapter Twenty-Two

SONIA ADDED A TEA bag to her hot water, along with a squeeze of fresh lemon. Eyeing the clock, she saw it was almost midnight. Unable to sleep, she'd come into the kitchen to get some chamomile tea. Passing Peter's door, she'd seen his light still on and debated knocking, but then changed her mind. Something told her to wait and let him come to her.

Sipping her tea, she flicked off the kitchen light and planned to return to her room when she heard a noise and saw Peter standing by the couch, lighted only by the soft lamp on a side table.

"Peter," she said.

He stood there quietly and then sat on the sofa. "We need to talk, Sonia."

Feeling her guilt well up, she braced herself for the upcoming conversation. She sat across from him, holding her tea. "Okay."

"I've read through your notes and made a few of my own. What I have learned is...surprising."

Sonia bobbed her tea bag in the water. "I suspect it is."

He looked up, his eyes dark hollows in the light, and she knew she'd not been the only one who'd had trouble sleeping. "I need to hear it from you. In your own words. All of it," he said.

Sonia held her breath. "You have what I wrote."

"That's not enough. Writing it down is not the same as speaking it aloud. There are things you might say that you might exclude on paper. I need to hear both versions."

She held her mug, debating her response, wanting to refuse because she'd given him ample information. "Peter..."

His eyes did not waver, and she felt his sadness.

"I understand." Taking a deep breath, she did as he wished, and thought of where to start. She took a sip of her tea and thought back. "Many years ago, I was asked to work as a nanny in a secluded household. The request was unusual, but many things in our community are, so I didn't ask too many questions. Two esteemed members of our Council contacted me directly, and I met with them. I was told that the position would require the utmost secrecy for reasons known only to them, but that it was for a good reason, and that the safety of our community depended on it. I, of course, believed them. I had no reason not to." She paused and took another sip of her tea.

"I was brought to a large home with gardens and statues and manicured lawns. It was beautiful, and I was excited to be trusted with such an important assignment." She sighed. "Anyway, when I arrived, I was given my own room and then taken down to a full floor below the house. There was even a secret stairway. I was given a key and told that only approved staff could come and go. When they took me down, I was shocked to see two toddlers, both boys, around twelve months old. They were adorable. They had all the amenities they needed. A kitchen, bathroom, two bedrooms, and even a little patio where they could play outside. It was hidden from above, and surrounded by thick shrubs and vines, to hide any sounds of laughter or tears. They told me the boys were to stay in that part of the house and no one was to know of their existence. I thought it was odd, but they assured me it was necessary to keep the children safe. I believed them." Sonia eyed her tea. "Little did I know what that assignment would do to me and to them."

Peter nodded and picked up a file and pen from the coffee table. He opened it. "You didn't mention the name of the Council members who hired you. Who were they?"

Sonia hesitated. "I'm not sure I should say."

Peter clicked the pen. "Are they even still alive?"

Sonia shook her head. "No."

Peter tipped his head, waiting. Sonia smiled softly, appreciating Peter's tenaciousness. He wasn't as laid back as she'd assumed. "The man who'd hired me was Emerson, but there was another man who came around often. His name was Arnuff."

Peter scribbled in the file.

"Have you heard those names before?" she asked.

"No."

Sonia bobbed her tea bag and removed it, placing it on the saucer. She wondered how the Council would take it if Peter came snooping around, asking questions.

"Did you have any knowledge of the children's parentage, or where they'd come from?"

"At the time, no, but as I stayed, I became privy to more information. Plus, I overheard a few things. Over time, they trusted me more, maybe because they simply became too self-confident, believing they couldn't be caught, or even if they were, could easily cover up the truth."

"When was it you discovered who the boys were?"

Sonia recalled the incident. "I'd been taking care of them for almost a year. They were good children. Sweet-natured and well-tempered. One of the odd things about the situation was that they didn't have names. Emerson always referred to them as C and D. I never knew why. I asked, but was rebuffed, and basically told it wasn't my concern. So, I gave them my own names. I called them Cason and Dean. But only behind closed doors." She shook her head. "I remember asking when their birthdays were, so we could at least acknowledge that, and I was told they shared the same birthdate. They were fraternal twins." A heaviness in her heart she'd carried for years flared as her mind returned to the fateful day when she'd learned the truth.

"I threw a birthday party for them when they turned two. Emerson frowned upon it, saying it was unnecessary and frivolous, but he allowed it, and I invited the staff who had privileges to the bottom floor. I had party hats and cake and gave the boys some toys. It was fun." She drank her tea, her stomach unsettled. "I remember I'd left one of the presents upstairs, and I'd gone to look for it. The little party was winding down, but the boys were still knee deep in cake. Nina, one of our housekeeping staff, stayed with them while I went upstairs. I went into the office, looking, when I heard arguing. I recognized the voices as Arnuff and Emerson, and I had the urgent intuitive hit that told me to hide. I'd learned enough by then to listen to that urge, and I slipped into a closet, just before they came into the room."

Sonia closed her eyes, still hearing their angry words. "They were talking about the boys. One was saying the experiment was a bust and they should end it, the other saying the opposite. One wanted to get rid of the boys and all evidence of what they had done. The other wanted to continue to see where it might lead. He said something about how they had another group of offspring showing excellent promise, and that C and D could be the back-up in case that group failed." She put the saucer down and gripped her cup.

"One mentioned two other babies, females. They'd called them A and B, and how they'd successfully sold them, and how they might do that with C and D, but the other disagreed. Said they'd gone too far with D at this point, and the experiment should continue." She held her head. "I couldn't believe what I was hearing."

Peter made notes on his paper. "Is that when you decided to remove Jace?"

Sonia stared off, her mind weary. "I agonized over what to do. After hearing that conversation, I worried ceaselessly. I didn't know what they meant by an experiment, but it was obvious why the boys were kept out of sight. I couldn't understand why. They seemed like completely normal children to me. But then, one day, Emerson came down and took the boys away. I asked why, but he said nothing. It scared me to death. I half expected to never see them again. I paced the halls, waiting for their return. After a full twenty-four hours went by, I got desperate, and I went into the office, and searched the files. I had to know what was going on."

Peter's face fell. "And that's when you learned the truth?"

The emotion of that day returned, and her chest tightened. "A lot of it. I read about how they'd been doing DNA testing with unwitting mothers. They were trying to create some sort of hybrid child with a variety of abilities. For what purpose, I'm still not sure, even now, though I've heard theories." She put her teacup on the table. "They were using their own DNA, likely because they were powerful men, and I'd heard about their own unique abilities, although I was rarely a witness to them. One of them was the father of Case and Dean, plus the two other girls, all born to the same mother who'd died in childbirth. The girls were given away, since they'd wanted the boys only."

Peter watched her, his face unreadable. "What did you do then?"

"It's in the file, Peter," said Sonia, wringing her hands.

"I need you to tell me."

Sonia cursed, and Peter raised a brow, but never dropped his gaze.

"Fine." She paused. "The next day, the boys were returned. They were sullen and reserved, though, and extremely tired, as if they'd not been allowed to sleep. Case cried through the night, and Dean...he...I don't know...acted out. His normal kind demeanor had vanished, and he threw his toys and pinched me. I couldn't understand it. That's when I made my decision. Whatever was happening had to stop. I would have to get them away from there."

Sonia rocked back and forth, hating the memories. "I planned to sneak them out. I arranged to take some time off to visit my sister on the west coast. My plan was to get us all to the airport, and then I'd get them on the plane, and we'd disappear. The day came, and I was a wreck. There was a window of time where I had the boys to myself, and I could feasibly get them out of the house. That day came, though, and it all fell apart. Dean had thrown a toy at Case and split his lip. It was bad and there was a lot of blood. I wasn't sure what to do. I had plane tickets and suitcases for the boys in the trunk of my car. Nina, the housekeeper, showed up when she was supposed to be gone. I told her I was taking the boys to the doctor."

"I thought they couldn't leave the premises," said Peter.

"Only if given permission and if so, with an escort, or for a medical emergency, and then only to a certain doctor."

"What did Nina do?" asked Peter.

"She wanted to contact Emerson, and I told her not to worry him and I would let him know. I took the boys to the car, Case wailing and Dean fighting me and crying. He didn't want to leave. Nina came and took him, saying she'd watch him, and looking at me as if she knew my plans. Something in her eyes told me to go with Case." Sonia picked up her tea, her hands shaky.

"Take your time," said Peter.

Sonia took a sip and collected herself. "I was so torn. I didn't know what to do. I didn't want to leave Dean behind, but some part of me told me I could come back for him, and to get Case out, so I did." She paused and stretched her neck. "I should have listened better to my intuition."

"Did you take Case to the doctor?"

"I took him to a friend who was a doctor. He patched up the lip, saying it wasn't too serious, and I headed to the airport, questioning everything. I wanted to go back for Dean, but I knew if I did, I would never get Case out, so I got on the plane."

A tear escaped her eye and ran down her cheek, and she wiped it away. "I got to San Diego, found a hotel, and stayed there a couple of days, telling my sister I was delayed and wondering what the hell I was doing. Case was fine. I bought him a few toys, and he kept busy. His lip healed, and he kept asking why I was crying. I knew I had to act quickly. Case loved fire trucks, so I went to a fire station, and with tears streaming down my cheeks, I wrote his birthdate on a piece of paper and put it in his pocket so they would at least know how old he was, and I let him go." Sonia held her hand against her mouth, as more tears fell. "It was the worst day of my life, at least up until then. But at least I knew he was safe."

Peter stood and went into the bathroom and returned with a box of tissues. Sonia took one and dabbed her face. "Thank you."

"You think that's why they named him Jase or Jason, because that's what they thought he was saying?" asked Peter.

Sonia stifled a sob. "Yes."

Reading through the report, Peter waited while she pulled herself together. "This is where I got confused. You were allowed to return. Why?"

Sonia cleared her throat and sniffed. "I went to my sister's afterward, waiting the whole time to see if the police would show at my door, but they never did, which I guess makes sense since no one really knew of the children's existence. About a week later, I got a phone call. It was Emerson."

"What did he say?"

"He wanted me to return."

"Why?"

Sonia shook her head. "He told me I'd done him a favor. He was the one who'd been pushing to end things and Case leaving was of benefit, although Arnuff disagreed. I asked about Dean and he told me that Dean would have to stay. Arnuff insisted. Dean had shown the most promise, and his development was crucial to whatever experiment they were conducting."

"They told you all of this?"

"They understood then that I was aware of much more than they realized. Emerson wanted me back because of what I knew and because Dean missed me and was asking for me. By returning, I could monitor him and ensure he was treated well, but Dean could not leave. I would not be permitted off the grounds with him. I wanted to tell him no. I wanted to tell him I would tell the Council. Instead, I agreed." Sonia twisted her tissue.

"Why didn't you tell anyone?"

Sonia moaned. "I planned to. I thought that once I returned and ensured Dean was okay, I would contact a member of the Council and let them know what was happening. I had it planned out. But once I got back, I realized it would not be that simple."

Peter studied the notes. "You say they threatened you? How?"

Sonia recalled that day and shivered. "After I arrived, I found Dean and was happy to see he was fine, although he kept asking about Case. It broke my heart. I already began to think of ways to get him out too, and then I was summoned upstairs." She took a breath to steady herself. "Arnuff was in the office. He was not as pleased with my return as Emerson was, but he told me that Emerson had convinced him to keep me on. He told me that if I ever attempted to take Dean, he would not hesitate to hurt me or my family. He threatened my sister, and he threatened to find Case and take care of him, too. He said it wouldn't be hard. And if I dared to tell anyone what was going on, they would have no choice but to remove Dean from the picture."

"Remove him?"

"Yes." Sonia rubbed her temples. "I felt a horrible pain in my head when he said it, and I knew then what he meant. Dean would suffer a terrible accident and would not recover." She pulled another tissue from the box. "I realized then I should have never returned, but it was too late. He told me if I left, I would suffer a similar fate."

"He would kill you?"

"He never used those words, but yes. That was the message. I told myself that by staying, I could keep an eye on Dean and at least try to offer some sense of normalcy to the boy. And that's what I did. I stayed, watching him grow up, and doing my best to soothe and comfort him each time after they'd return him after a night or two away. But I saw what it was doing it to him. He internalized all of it. Became angry and sullen. As he got older, he didn't understand why he couldn't leave. He wanted friends and freedom. Emerson and Arnuff rarely saw him and the only ones in his life were me and Nina, and a security man they'd hired to watch the door, but he barely spoke to Dean. But then Nina left, and they hired..." She looked at Peter warily.

Peter set his jaw, his eyes haunted. "...my sister."

Sonia stilled and spoke quietly. "Yes. Your sister."

Peter studied the paper and then closed the file and sat back. "How come you never told me this?"

Sonia studied her hands, which she clenched together. "When I hired you, I didn't think it was pertinent."

"Don't give me that bullshit, Sonia. You knew exactly what you were doing. You were using me to find Dean, or Rutger, or whatever you want to call him. My question is why? How does my sister play into all of this?"

Sonia exhaled a deep breath and straightened, knowing he deserved the truth. "Because Dean fell in love with her."

Chapter Twenty-Three

DANIELS RESTED HIS HANDS on the back of a chair, and Remalla stood beside Waldo Yang, whose dark greasy hair hung in his face.

"I told you. I had nothin' to do with any shooting," said Yang. "I was home all day yesterday. Ask Delana. She already told you."

"Delana's got an ugly black eye this morning, which she didn't have yesterday," said Daniels. "That tells me that maybe Delana is not saying everything she knows because she's scared of you." Daniels pointed. "And if she is lying and we find out, that makes her an accessory. I wonder if she knows that and if it's worth protecting you."

"She's not lying." His face furrowed. "And she fell off of her bike yesterday. I didn't touch her."

"Sure, she did," said Remalla. "And you could also tell me you showered today, but we know that's not the truth." Remalla got in Yang's face. "Just tell us what happened, Yang. You got pissed at Hendrix, Alba and Lozano, and took matters into your own hands. Tell us now, and maybe we can help with the prosecutor. But if you make us keep looking, and we find you've been holding back, and you murdered two people and took a shot at a police officer, then your new home will be behind bars, and you'll be the one getting the black eyes."

Yang threw out his hands. "I'm telling you. I didn't shoot nobody. I was at home all day yesterday. Don't you have cameras or something to show I didn't do anything?"

Rem regarded Daniels, who let go of the chair and crossed his arms. "If we had that, would we be talking to you right now, Yang?" asked Daniels.

The door opened, and Mellenbuehl stuck his head in the room. "You two got a second?"

Rem glared at Yang. "Sure."

They walked out and closed the door. "Any luck?" asked Mel.

"None," said Daniels. "He's sticking to his story. What about Massey?"

"Same," said Mel. "Insists he was at work. Was out on deliveries, but says he was nowhere near the station. His boss vouches for him, too. We're trying to put the pressure on, but he's not cracking."

"Yeah, neither is Yang," said Rem.

"We want to keep trying, but he's insisting on leaving. Says he's got to get to work. You want us to keep pushing?" asked Mel. "Says if he can't go, he wants a lawyer."

Daniels cursed. "We don't have a choice. Let him go, but tell him to stay in town."

"Will do. What about Yang?" asked Mel.

Rem eyed the door. "Let him sit and think for a bit, then we'll go back in. See if he's loosened up. He's definitely nervous, so it makes me think he's not telling us something."

Daniels smirked. "It might have something to do with Delana's black eye. She talks and tells us, then he's violating parole."

"Think we should bring Delana in? See what she has to say?" asked Rem.

"Probably not a bad idea."

Rem groaned and rubbed his neck. "God. What time is it? Is this day over yet?"

"It's not even noon," said Daniels.

"Shit," said Rem.

An officer poked his head out of the squad room. "Hey. Rem, Daniels. There's a phone call for one of you."

"I got it," said Rem. "Hopefully, my house it still intact." He jogged off.

Mel's brow furrowed. "He doing some renovations?"

Daniels chuckled. "Something like that."

"Alright. I'll go talk to Massey. Tell him he can go," said Mel.

Daniels frowned. "What's your read on him, Mel? You think he's good for it?"

"Honestly, based on his demeanor and answers, he's not striking me as our guy, but hey, I prefer cheese whiz over the real stuff, so what do I know?"

"You and Rem have a lot in common."

Mel smiled. "I'll go talk to Massey."

"Thanks," said Daniels, and Mel walked back down the hall as Rem returned, jogging faster and holding Daniels' jacket. "What is it?" asked Daniels, seeing Rem's face.

"We got another one," said Rem, handing Daniels his jacket.

Daniels dropped his jaw. "You're kidding? Another body?"

"Gunshot to the chest. Let's go."

· · · · ● · ● · · · ·

"Are you sure about this, Jill?" asked Madison. She sat next to Jill on the couch.

Jace sat on the other side of her. "You don't stay long," he said. "Get in and get out."

Jill took Madison's hand. "Yes. I'm sure. I've had this eerie feeling all night that something's ramping up, and if we don't take the initiative, we're going to be too far behind to catch up." She squeezed Madison's fingers. "It will be okay. Don't worry." She smiled, conferring confidence, unsure if she was feeling it herself, but she couldn't let Madison know that.

"Pancakes, remember? That's the safe word," said Madison.

"Can we go with something other than pancakes?" asked Jace.

"Why?" asked Madison.

Jace frowned. "Because it's stupid. How about good old-fashioned 'help?' That usually works in my experience."

Madison sighed. "Fine. 'Help,' or 'Pancakes.' Whatever. Just make sure you use it."

"I will," said Jill. She settled back on the couch and relaxed. "Ready?"

Madison and Jace nodded. "Ready," they said in unison.

Jill took a deep breath, rested back against the pillows, and closed her eyes.

· · • • • • • • · ·

The fog returned—a deep haze overshadowed the landscape, and Jill walked silently, seeing little of any detail around her. It was silent, and she wondered where to go. She stopped walking and just focused. Rutger was here. She just needed to find him.

The clouds swirled, and she waited, an itch of anxiety flickering in her stomach. The fog continued to churn, gaining intensity. Her hair whipped as the wind picked up, and then the mist took shape, and a cool brisk breeze made her shiver.

Blinking, she watched the mist coalesce, take form, and then she was back in the dirty hotel room. She didn't move and slowed her breathing, fearful of being seen. Turning, she took in her surroundings, seeing the worn couch, chipped coffee table, beat up TV and thin carpet. Facing the dining table where she'd seen Rutger sitting before, her heart raced. But he wasn't there. The room was empty.

Frightened that he was nearby and ready to jump out when she was vulnerable, she told herself to calm down and reached out with her senses. Rutger had a definitive feel about him that was hard to miss, and she didn't detect it. Forcing herself to get moving, she took a step forward and stopped, waiting, but nothing moved. She took another step.

Approaching the dining table, she saw a dirty plate and a half-filled coffee cup. The piece of paper and pen were still there, but the stone was not. Next to the paper was a small worn black book, dirty from use, as if it had been opened and closed hundreds of times. She searched for the picture but didn't see it. Stepping closer, she reached out and shifted the paper aside, looking for anything that might indicate where this hotel was located.

Glancing around and behind her, she kept her senses on high alert but saw and sensed no one. Another paper poked out beneath the one she'd moved. A scribble of handwriting across the center caught her attention, and she pulled it out, reading it, her heart beating fast. It was an address. She re-read it, committing it to memory.

A creak sounded, and a sense of foreboding crept up into her throat. Was Rutger returning? She eyed the black book. She wanted to open it, but the feeling of dread intensified, and it was time to get out. Her fingers shaking, she made a hasty decision, and quickly opened the book. She saw names. There were several listed in the book. Her stomach curdled, and feeling ill, she flipped through the pages. She saw her name, Madison's and Jace's. She read Sonia's name, Rem and Daniels, and Justin, Donald, and Rick's. And then she flipped a page and saw several others. She raised a hand and covered her mouth. "No," she said to herself.

"Interesting reading, Jill?"

Jill swiveled, and the book skittered across the table and fell with a slam to the ground. Rutger stood near the couch, his eyes wide with fury.

Sneering, he advanced on her. "I was going to save this for later, but now you've pissed me off." He raised his hands, and before Jill could move, he grabbed her by the throat and slammed her up against the wall.

Jill tried to cry out, but he squeezed hard and held her tightly enough that she couldn't speak. Kicking out, she pulled at his wrists, her nails ripping at his skin, but he only stared, unaffected by her desperate attempts to get away.

With her airway pressed shut, black spots appeared before her eyes, and she knew if she didn't do something, she'd die here, and Jace and Madison would only have a limp body lying on a sofa in Rem's house. Remembering the black book, her rage bubbled up. Seeing his angry eyes, and the bruises beneath them, she let go of his wrists and punched his swollen nose. He cried out, closing his eyes and loosening his grip, allowing Jill to suck in some air. He squeezed again, but the momentary respite provided her enough forethought to kick, landing a blow to his midsection, where she knew he'd been injured.

He let go and doubled over, raging and bellowing, and she opened her mouth, sucking in air and coughing, but screamed *help* as loud as she could, although it emerged as a whisper. *Help* she cried again. *Pancakes.* Temporarily free, she pushed past him, but he grabbed her and threw her back again. She deflected a blow as his arm came up, and she ducked beneath, trying to escape, but he tackled her and brought her to the floor, knocking the small dining table over along with everything on it. Flailing, her hand connected with his face, and enraged, he drew back and slapped her. Her head swam, and she heard and sensed Jace and Madison calling for her. The pressure on her arms indicated they were trying to pull her out, and she made one last grasp for freedom by clawing at the carpet. She pulled away, but he yanked her back. Holding her down and getting in her face, he spoke in a low and furious tone, his face a mask of acrimony. "You're not going anywhere."

Something inside her snapped, as if all the fear and pain this man had caused suddenly solidified into one solid mass of disgust, weariness, and utter doneness. Without thinking, she gathered her saliva and spit in his face, making a direct hit on his cheek. Feeling her resolve gather and build, she glowered back, narrowing her eyes. "I'll go wherever the *fuck* I want." Her flailing hand found an object on the carpet, and she gripped it, feeling the pen from the table that must have fallen, and she swung it up and rammed it into his shoulder, burying it deep. He shrieked, his arm buckled, and blood spurted. Jill thought of Jace and Madison calling to her and closed her eyes.

· · · · **·** · **·** · · ·

Jace shook Jill hard, shouting her name and seeing her neck bruise and swell. "Jill," he yelled.

"Jill," Madison gripped her shoulder. "Come on. Come back. You can leave. You can do it. Please."

Jill eked out a whispered *help* and what sounded like pancakes. She shuddered and groaned, her arms flailing and moaning softly.

"He's got her," said Madison. "Damn it." She smacked Jill's cheeks.

Jace leaned over and yelled, his heart racing. "Jill, listen to me. Get the hell out. Now." He held her head. "Why the hell isn't she coming out of it?"

"I don't know," said Madison.

Jill suddenly gasped, her eyelids creased, and then her eyes opened, and she raised a hand to her throat, sputtering and trying to breathe.

Jace moved back, letting her sit up as she doubled over, coughing hard.

"Jill," said Madison, her eyes frantic, "Are you okay?"

Jill's cheek reddened, and Jace could see the outline of a handprint on her skin. Breathless, he sat on the coffee table, facing her. "What happened?" Her neck began to turn a deep purple.

Jill struggled to speak, and when she did, it came out as a whisper. She coughed some more.

"We tried to get you out, but we couldn't reach you," said Madison. She touched Jill's cheek. "My God. What did he do to you?"

Jill's coughing slowed and she breathed easier. "I'm okay," she whispered.

"No, you're not," said Jace. "Did he choke you?"

"Looks like he slapped her," said Madison.

"Never mind," said Jill. "I got out." She blinked several times and held the stone around her neck. "I'm better now."

Jace swore. "I swear to God, when I get a hold of this guy, I'm going to break his fucking neck." He touched her bruised skin. "He damn near killed you."

Jill felt her neck and grimaced. "But he didn't. I got away. And not without doing some damage of my own."

"I'm going to get you some ice," said Madison.

"Leave it," said Jace, raising a hand. "Let me work on it."

Jill held her breath as Jace hovered his hand over her, but he moved slowly and let the heat build. Resting his palm against her gently, he focused on her neck and the swelling, and then moved up to her cheek, which was now a garish red, and he could imagine how it stung. Jill began to relax, and her shoulders dropped. After a few minutes, Jace lowered his hand. "That should help. Feel better?"

Jill gently rubbed the tender areas, her face more relaxed. "Yes. Thank you."

The bruise remained, but the swelling had improved and her cheek's redness had faded. "It'll get better with more time," he said.

Jill sighed, holding her head in weariness.

"Now, please tell me this hell you just put us through was worth it, and you got something," said Jace. He set his jaw. "Or I'm going to have to hold back from killing you myself."

Madison took Jill's elbow. "You sure you're okay?"

Jill held her stomach, swallowed, and looked up. "It didn't exactly go according to plan. I failed at playing meek. But I'm okay, and I got something."

Jace waited. "What did you get?"

Jill stood, lost her balance, but Jace grabbed her arm.

"Come on," said Jill, straightening. "We're going."

"Going where?" asked Madison.

Jill swiveled her head and grimaced. "I've got an address."

Chapter Twenty-Four

DANIELS ENTERED THE HOUSE, following Rem. It was small but in a quiet neighborhood, with sprawling lawns and long driveways. The victim lay in the living room, face down, blood pooled beneath his chest. A member of the forensic team walked through, taking pictures. The living area was clean and tidy, and the body lay between the sofa and the coffee table. It was a man of average height and build, with short and wavy blonde hair, wearing pajamas and a robe. An open, empty file folder sat on the table.

Rem studied the area. "We have any idea who this guy is?"

Villanueva stepped in from the bedroom. "Not yet. Haven't found any identification."

"M.O. fits the others?" asked Daniels.

"The gunshot wound fits. Looks like he took a shot to the chest. Close range. Casing was found beside the table."

"Who found the body?" asked Daniels.

"Anonymous call. Somebody heard a gunshot."

Rem smirked. "You find the number anywhere?"

Villanueva shrugged. "No. Not yet at least, but it's always been left in an obvious place before."

Daniels looked around the house, seeing a teacup on the counter by the sink in the kitchen. "Anybody else live here with him?"

"We think so, but we're checking," said Villanueva. "Both bedrooms appear to be in use, and there are some women's clothes and toiletries in one of them, but we don't know who it belongs to, unless this guy likes to dress in drag. It wouldn't be the first time I've seen it."

"Yeah," said Remalla. Someone called Villanueva's name, and he walked into the opposite bedroom. Rem pushed his hair back. "Think it could be a copycat?"

"Maybe," said Daniels. "The number was never released to the press, so unless we find it, that makes the most sense."

"Maybe somebody got pissed and offed him, trying to make it look like it's our courtroom killer." Rem shook his head.

A woman, her hair, hands and feet covered, and wearing a jacket identifying herself as Dr. Venners from the coroner's office and holding a bag, entered to examine the body and Rem and Daniels stepped back. "Hey, Doc," said Rem. "How's it going?"

"Just another day on the job, Remalla." She kneeled next to the body.

Daniels nudged Rem. "Well, any thoughts on the vic?"

Rem watched the doctor work. "What I think is that I'd like to know who he is, and then we can figure out if he has any connection to the Judge and Alba."

"And if he doesn't?" asked Daniels.

"Then I guess Yang and Massey are still in the hot seat and we've got a copycat on our hands. But if he does, and that number turns up..."

"Then Massey and Yang are cleared, since they've been with us since this morning," said Daniels.

"I guess so," said Rem.

"Which leaves Maia Chambers."

Rem's face fell. "You really know how to ruin a guy's day."

"Stay positive, though. Maybe it's a copycat."

"How's that staying positive? That just gives us a second killer to find."

"Hey, you wanted me to cheer you up? That's all I got for you."

Rem huffed. "Some partner you are." He hooked a thumb in his belt loop. "You know, it's probably not Maia, either, which means we've been chasing our tails on this, and we're going to have to start from scratch."

"Either way, it looks like it's going to be a slow day for good news." Daniels tipped his head. "There's an empty file folder on the coffee table. What do you think that means?"

"I don't know. Maybe he liked file folders."

Daniels squinted. "Really? That's all you got? Did you consider that maybe there was something in it? Who carries around an empty file folder?"

"Weirdos," said Rem. "God knows we've seen enough of them."

"Or somebody took it, whatever it was."

Rem gestured toward the body. "It could have been anything from his favorite porno pics to his grandmother's dessert recipes. There's no telling."

"It's something to consider, though. Why would the killer take it?"

Rem scratched his jaw. "I think the bigger question is why is this guy dead, and who the hell is he?"

"I've got something," said the doctor.

Rem and Daniels walked closer as the doctor leaned over the victim, inserted a tweezer, and pulled something from the victim's mouth. It looked like paper.

"What the hell?" asked Rem.

"Is there anything on it?" asked Daniels.

The doctor opened the crumpled paper, and Daniels saw something scrawled on it. "It's a number," said the doctor, reading it. "0212."

"Shit," said Rem. "It's our guy. There goes our copycat theory."

"Looks like Yang and Massey are off the hook," said Daniels.

"Lucky me," said Rem.

"There's something written on the back," said the doctor.

"What is it?" asked Daniels.

The doctor turned the paper as Villanueva returned, holding a small badge with a picture on it. "We got a name for the vic. Found some I.D.."

Daniels read the name on the paper from the victim's mouth and his jaw fell. "Oh, hell."

"His name's Peter Chambers," said Villanueva.

Rem's eyes widened. "What?"

"Peter Chambers," repeated Villanueva.

Daniels straightened.

Rem checked the badge Villanueva held to confirm the name. "Did you hear that?" he asked Daniels. "Peter Chambers?" He pointed. "As in Maia

Chambers?" He rubbed his forehead and groaned. "What the hell is going on here?"

"I've got one better for you, partner," said Daniels.

"What the hell can beat Peter Chambers?" asked Rem, his arm outstretched.

Daniels stared, still not believing it. "The name on the back of the paper..."

"What about it?" Rem's eyes widened. "Please tell me it's the name of our killer."

"I hope not."

"What do you mean?"

Daniels hesitated. "It's Sonia Vandermere."

· · • • • • • • · ·

Jace drove up the street, but seeing police cars, forensic and coroner's vans, he pulled over, not far from the house.

"What the hell?" asked Jill from the backseat.

"What's going on?" asked Madison.

"It seems that whatever Rutger was going to do, it's done," said Jace. "Damn it."

Jill surveyed the scene. "That's Rem's car. Crap. He and Daniels are on the scene."

"Those vans suggest somebody's dead," said Jace. "Am I wrong?"

"No. You're not wrong," said Jill.

"I don't suppose you saw anything else on that paper, did you?" asked Jace. "Do we know who's dead?" He held the steering wheel. "Could we be so lucky that it's Rutger?"

Jill touched her neck. It was still bruised, but it had improved and the redness on her cheek was gone. She went still. "It's not him. I have no idea who it is." She moved her hand to her head and closed her eyes.

"Is there something else?" asked Madison.

Jill stayed quiet, but then opened her eyes, looking distant. "No. Nothing."

Jace looked back at her but stayed quiet.

"What do we do now?" asked Jace. "Call Rem and Daniels? Find out who's dead?"

"No," said Jill, tersely. "They can't know we're here. Too many questions."

They sat in the car, watching the activity in the house. "Well, this is fun," said Jace. "Anybody want to get some lunch? Catch a movie?"

Madison rested her elbow on the door. "There's got to be something we can do." She exhaled. "This is so frustrating."

A rap on the door made them jump. Jace turned along with Jill and Madison and stared at a familiar face in the window next to Jill. His jaw fell open.

"Oh, my God." Jill reached over and opened the door.

Sonia Vandermere slid into the backseat, her eyes red and puffy and her cheeks tear stained. She sniffed and held a handkerchief to her face. "Hello, dears," she said with weariness, and she burst into tears.

Chapter Twenty-Five

DANIELS HUNG UP THE phone. "That was Villanueva. Fingerprints at the scene belong to Peter Chambers, plus another set of prints not yet identified."

Rem sat up with his phone to his ear. "You thinking they're Sonia's?"

"Odds say they are."

"You honestly think she's a murderer?"

"No. But we have to go where the evidence leads."

Rem left a voicemail and hung up. "I still haven't got a hold of Maia's mom."

Daniels tapped on a paper. "I also looked into the house. It's a rental. Under a corporate name." Daniels read from it. "It's called EOE International. I'm looking for a contact number."

Rem put his phone down. "Right now, the only thing we have that leads us to Sonia is her name on that paper. We can't even put her at the house."

"We actually can. The neighborhood canvas revealed a few people who've seen a woman come and go from the residence. She matches the description of Sonia."

Rem leaned back in his seat. "So put on a flowery dress, chunky jewelry and a pair of sunglasses and how hard would it be to look like her?"

Daniels paused. "You really think someone's trying to frame her?"

"You really think she's our courtroom killer?" He pointed toward Lozano's office. "You think she'd try to shoot us through the window?"

Daniels bounced a pen on his desktop. "No. I don't, but whether or not she pulled the trigger, she's involved. And we have to figure out how."

Rem put his hands behind his head. "Well, if Peter Chambers is related to Maia Chambers, and let's assume he is—"

"Probably wise," said Daniels.

"Then, assuming it's not Sonia, somebody killed Peter, the Judge and Alba. But why Peter?"

"Don't know. Family issues are the most likely reason. Maybe a falling out. Maia had issues. Maybe Peter practiced some tough love. Once we get a hold of Peter's next of kin, we can ask."

"And if that's the case, why frame Sonia? How is she involved in all of this? And who made the anonymous call? Sonia?"

"I don't know. Those are the million-dollar questions," said Daniels. "You thinking about Rutger? Could he be involved?"

Rem shrugged. "We have to consider that, but we haven't seen any evidence, unless he's trying to put it to Sonia, by making her look like a killer."

A chill ran through Daniels. "What if this is his way of hurting her, like he hurt the others? What if she's close to Peter? Rutger gets to her by killing Peter and deliberately makes it look like one of the courtroom killings."

"But he doesn't know—"

"How do you know he doesn't?" Daniels knew Rem was referring to the paper with the number on it. "Considering who he is."

Rem's forehead creased, and Daniels raised a brow at him. "Exactly," said Daniels.

Rem groaned. "If that's true, then we still have to find the person who killed Hendrix and Alba, and now Rutger. He's already wanted for the murder of Jace's friend Justin. Do we now include him as a suspect in this? And if so, how do we explain that to Lozano?"

Daniels picked up the hot dog snow globe he'd put on his desk the other day and shook it. "Maybe we keep the Rutger theory to ourselves? At least for now." He watched the mustard flakes drift. "Have you called Jill?"

Rem watched the flakes, too. "No."

"She'll want to know about all of this."

"I know. I figure I can tell her tonight. We'll tell all three of them. That ought to be fun. Letting them know Sonia's a suspect in a murder investigation, oh and, by the way, maybe Rutger's framing her."

Daniels opened his mouth to speak, but hesitated.

"What?" asked Rem. "You think it's a bad idea to tell them?"

"No, no. They should know." He shook the globe again and put it down.

"What are you not saying?"

Daniels pursed his lips. "It just strikes me as weird, don't you think, the three of them in your house, while all of this is going down?"

Rem scoffed. "Weird? The whole thing is certifiably insane. I've got Madison floating rocks through my backyard, Jill doing strange meditations and Jace healing all their injuries. Weird doesn't even cover it. I feel like we're in the Twilight Zone."

"You think they're telling us everything?"

"I'll admit. It's crossed my mind. I know Jill too well and I know she's not just sitting in the house in the lotus position. And did you buy that story about her cheek being injured by a rock?"

Daniels chuckled. "That smelled funny to you, too?"

"Like bad chicken."

Daniels thought about it. "What do you think they're hiding from us?"

"They're trying to find Rutger, and I suspect they don't want us involved if they do."

"Probably smart. It's going to be really awkward if we have to arrest them."

Rem stared off. "Or worse."

Daniels picked up his water. "If they go after Rutger, are we going to stop them if they break the law? Or are we going to look the other way?"

"Considering the things he's done, and may still be doing, I'd be open to averting my eyes."

"Even if it meant your career? We're cops. You willing to forget that?"

Rem held his gaze. "We're not talking about your run-of-the-mill bad guy. He's not someone you can toss in jail and throw away the key."

"So, we shoot him in cold blood?"

Rem rested his elbows on his desk. "I guess it depends on the situation."

"That's the whole problem with this. Considering his talents, he could be considered a threat without ever having a weapon, but how do you prove that in a court of law?"

"Let's just hope if, or when, the time comes, we'll make the right decision. Whether it's us or anybody else."

"Would you lie to protect Jill?"

Rem rubbed his jaw. "I'd lie to protect you. I suspect I'd do the same for her."

"Let's hope it doesn't come to that."

"Yeah. Let's hope."

The squad door opened, and Lozano walked in, a white bandage on the back of his head.

"Captain, what are you doing here?" asked Daniels. "You're supposed to have the day off."

Rem's phone rang, and he answered it.

"Another dead body was found this morning. Where else would I be, Daniels?" He walked by their desks. "Head into my office and let me know where we are on this."

Rem held up his hand over his phone. "I've got Maia Chambers' mom on the line. Be there in a sec."

Daniels nodded, stood and followed Lozano. Pieces of plywood covered the broken window behind Lozano's desk and the wall across from it. Daniels sat, trying not to think about being shot at the last time he'd been in there. He gave Lozano the update on Peter Chambers and finding Sonia Vandermere's name at the scene.

"Why do you think the paper was in his mouth?" asked Lozano.

"We don't know, Cap. Did the killer put it there, or did Chambers do it before he died? We're not sure."

"But we know now that Peter is connected to Maia? These deaths are connected to her?"

"Seems that way," said Daniels.

"What about the number? Any ideas?"

"Not yet."

Lozano moved some papers on his desk. "And what about your partner? If this is related to Maia, you think he's at risk? He arrested and testified against her." He tipped his head at the plywood. "That shot may have been meant for him."

Daniels massaged his tense neck muscles. "I know. It's on my mind, but Jill's staying with him and he's either with me or her. It makes me wonder, though."

"What?"

"Why did this guy take a shot at us through the window? His M.O. is close range in the chest. Why suddenly decide to fire at us from a distance?"

"Maybe because, like you said, he can't get up close, so he tried it another way."

"It's possible," said Daniels, shifting in his seat. "It just doesn't sit right."

Lozano pulled out an apple from his desk drawer. "Well, keep an eye on Remalla. If you think we need a patrol at his house, let me know. We don't need any more casualties on this one. We've had enough."

"I hear you, Cap."

The door opened, and Rem entered, breathless and his eyes wide. "Guess what?"

Daniels straightened. "What?"

Rem came in and closed the door. "I talked to Maia's mom. Remember I told you Maia had a child in jail?"

"Yeah. Her mom took the baby, right?" asked Daniels.

"She did. But the baby had complications, probably due to mom's drug use. Baby died two weeks after birth."

Daniels held his breath. "Don't tell me...what was the date?"

Rem held up a piece of paper with the numbers from the crime scenes on it. "Feb. 12th."

Chapter Twenty-Six

JILL PACED IN THE living room. Madison watched her from her seat on the sofa. "You're going to wear a hole in the rug."

"Have you seen this rug? I doubt Rem would notice."

Madison sat up and clasped her hands together. "What do you think we should do? Sonia's resting in my room. She can't stay here without telling Rem and Daniels."

They heard a door close above and footsteps come down the stairs. Jace came around the corner. "She's finally asleep."

"She's exhausted and grief-stricken. I'm worried about her," said Madison, feeling weary after an emotional day. "She didn't look good."

"Did you believe her story?" asked Jace. "About finding the body?"

"Why wouldn't we?" asked Madison. "Why would she lie?"

Jace put his hand against the wall. "I know we all want to believe she's this sweet benevolent lady who gives out random pieces of jewelry and woo-woo advice, but the truth is, none of us really know her or her connection to Rutger. It's possible they could be in on it together."

Jill stopped pacing. "I don't believe that."

"Neither do I," said Madison.

Jace scowled. "Well, excuse me if I have to consider it. She knew Rutger was dangerous. She knew he was coming after us. If she'd bothered to warn us, maybe Justin would still be alive."

Jill slid her jacket off and threw it on the couch. "I don't think she necessarily knew where to find us until the crimes were committed, and even if she had known, would any of us have thought she was serious? You would have laughed her out of your bar."

"I would have still appreciated the warning," said Jace. "And we still don't know how she's connected to us. And who is this Peter that died? How does she know him and did she kill him?"

"She said she found him and called the police," said Madison.

"Then why leave the scene if she's innocent?" asked Jace. He pushed off the wall and went to look out the window. The sun had gone down, and Madison could only see the reflection of the living room lamp in the glass. Jace sighed. "None of it makes sense."

Jill resumed her pacing. "I think there's the obvious answer. Rutger did this."

"You think he did this, but you can't be sure," said Jace.

Jill turned toward him. "I saw the address, remember? It was on a piece of paper in his room."

Jace raised his voice. "Maybe because he knew Sonia was staying there. For all we know, she gave the address to him. Hell, maybe she arranged for Rutger to kill this Peter guy, and maybe even Rick, Donald, and Justin. We don't know anything, unless you saw more in that vision than you're saying." He held a stony glare at Jill.

Madison waited for Jill's answer, wondering the same thing.

Jill studied the floor. "I saw a book."

Jace stepped closer. "A book? What book?"

Jill shut her eyes, as if remembering hurt. "It was a small black book. I looked through it."

"What did you see?" asked Madison.

The front door opened, and Madison jumped in her seat. Rem and Daniels entered. "Hey," Rem said to them, tossing his keys on the front table.

Daniels closed the door.

"Glad to see my house is in one piece," said Rem, standing in the entry, facing them. He looked around. "No broken dishes or cutlery stuck in the walls."

The three of them didn't move.

Rem put his hands in the pockets of his worn jeans. "You guys have a good day?"

· · · · •· • · · ·

Daniels looked between each of the siblings, but no one said a word. "Well, we had an exciting day. Anybody care to hear about it?"

Jace grumbled. "I'm going to start dinner." And he walked past Rem and Daniels.

Rem raised a brow. "Start dinner? Do we have something to start?"

Madison stood from the couch. "We went to the grocery store." She glanced at Jill. "I'm going to help Jace." She headed into the kitchen.

Rem watched her leave. "I'm getting the distinct impression no one wants to hear about our day."

"You ought to be a detective," said Daniels.

"Good thing I already am," said Rem.

Jill stood by a chair and picked up a pillow and picked at the fringe.

"Everything all right?" asked Rem.

Jill hugged the pillow. "We've just been talking. Wondering what to do next."

"You come to any decisions?" asked Daniels.

"No. Not really."

Rem walked up to her. "Anything we can help with?"

Jill held the pillow tighter. "I wish."

Daniels rolled his shoulders, tired after a busy day. "You know you can tell us, right, if there's something going on?"

She looked over, her expression guarded. "Why would you say that?"

"Because it's true," said Rem. "Daniels and I know that you guys are gearing up for something. We know you want to find Rutger, and we know you're not just sitting on the sidelines, and—" He frowned, reached up and tipped her jaw. "What in the hell? What happened to your neck?"

Jill shrank back, but Daniels could see the distinct yellowish mark of a fading bruise. Looking closely, he saw more than one.

"Nothing," said Jill. "It's fine."

Rem tried to look, but Jill put her hand to her throat. Rem spoke to Daniels. "Do you see that?"

"Yeah. I do." Daniels moved closer. He'd been in law enforcement long enough to know what those bruises looked like. "It looks like someone put their hands on you."

Jill cursed and tossed the pillow on the couch. "It's nothing, and I am really fine. There's nothing to worry about. Jace..." She cringed and shut her mouth.

Rem glared. "Jace what?" His eyes glimmered. "He worked his magic, didn't he? Which means that this..." he waved a hand at her, "...was actually much worse, wasn't it?"

"Rem—" Jill started, but Rem stomped out of the room. "Wait."

Daniels followed Rem, who flew into the kitchen. Jace held a package of hamburger buns, and Madison held a patty of meat.

Rem jabbed out a hand, pointing back at Jill. "Do you want to tell me what the hell is going on here? Why does Jill have bruises around her neck?"

Madison's face froze, and Jace tossed the buns on the counter.

Jill ran into the room. "Rem, please. You're overreacting."

"I don't think he is," said Daniels.

"Why don't you ask her?" asked Jace, his face stony.

"I'm asking all of you," said Rem, his voice raised. "You have a scar on your cheek from yesterday and now it looks like somebody strangled you? Please don't give me the 'I got injured by a rock' crap, because that shit won't sell."

Jill touched her neck. "Why didn't you guys tell me I still had visible bruises?"

Madison put down the patty. "Really? You're blaming us? Based on what we saw earlier and how bad it was, your current state is a remarkable improvement."

"What are you saying?" asked Rem. "If you'd known, you'd have covered them up? To hide it from us?"

Jill dropped her hand. "Yes. Because you'd freak out, which is exactly what you're doing."

Rem dropped his jaw. "Yes. I typically freak out when I find out someone tried to strangle my girlfriend, and then find out she's trying to cover it up. Call me crazy."

"It's not just that, though, is it?" asked Daniels. "You don't want us to know who did it."

Rem took a deep breath and gripped the counter. "Ok. I'm trying to be calm."

Jill, Madison, and Jace eyed each other, but none of them spoke.

"Who did this?" asked Rem. "And who hurt your cheek yesterday?"

Jill exhaled. "Rem...you don't understand..."

"Well, then help me." Rem shook his head. "What are the three of you keeping from us?"

Madison looked away, wiping her hands on a towel. Jace continued to scowl, and Jill bit her lip.

"You know it's going to come out, eventually. It always does. You should know that, Jill," said Rem.

Jill closed her eyes, her lips pursed in a thin line.

"Jill, please," said Rem, his face softening. "What the hell is going on?"

"We need to tell them," said Madison.

Jill, her body tense, shifted her stance. "Madison, just—"

"She's right," said Jace. "They need to know." He paused. "And not just about your neck."

Jill's face colored.

Frustrated, Rem slammed his fist on the counter. "Just tell me."

Footsteps sounded from the entry, and Daniels pivoted, reaching for his weapon, but stopped.

"She's just trying to protect you, Detective."

Rem startled and turned. Seeing who it was, his heart stopped.

Sonia Vandermere walked into his kitchen.

Chapter Twenty-Seven

"WHAT IN THE...?" ASKED Daniels.

"Holy shit," said Rem. He looked at Jill.

"Sonia, I thought you were resting," said Madison.

Sonia walked to the dining table and sat. "It's hard to rest, dear, when the energy is so unsettled."

Daniels noticed her red eyes and blotchy cheeks.

"Can I get you some water?" asked Jill.

Sonia nodded. "Actually, if you have some tea, that would be nice."

"I'll get it," said Madison.

"We have tea?" asked Rem, watching Sonia.

"We got some at the grocery," said Jill.

Daniels tried to stay cool. "How long has she been here?"

Everyone went quiet again until Jace spoke. "Since we picked her up at the crime scene."

Jill moaned.

"Excuse me?" asked Daniels.

"What?" yelled Rem. "The crime scene from today? You were there?"

Madison put a pot on the stove to boil some water. "Yes. We were there."

Daniels couldn't help but chuckle.

Rem stared with his mouth open. "What am I missing here?"

"Apparently, a lot," said Daniels. "We are way behind the curve, and I thought we'd rounded it."

Rem walked to the side of the table and sat across from Sonia. "You know you're a suspect in a murder investigation? You want to tell me why you're hiding in my house?"

Jill came over and put a hand on Sonia's shoulder. "Rem, stop. We brought her here."

"And apparently she didn't object. Nor did any of you. You realize all three of you could be charged with aiding and abetting?" Rem gestured at them.

"Oh, come on," said Jill. "Sonia didn't kill anybody."

Daniels leaned against the counter. Watching Sonia, he saw her eyes well with tears.

"You sure about that?" asked Rem.

"Of course, she didn't," said Madison from the stove.

"It's a fair question," said Jace. "You guys seem to think she's some sort of fairy godmother, but fairies can be evil, too."

Jill yelled. "That's absurd. What is the matter with you?"

"She wouldn't kill anybody," added Madison.

Jace pushed off from the counter. "Justin is dead, and so are Donald and Rick. How can you stand there and act like she's so innocent?"

Sonia sat quietly as Jill and Madison started yelling and Jace yelled back.

Daniels grabbed a napkin from the counter and handed it to Sonia, who silently cried while the siblings yelled.

Rem put his fingers to his mouth and blasted out a loud whistle. Everyone went still. Rem paused and eyed Daniels, who didn't know what to do.

"Sonia," said Rem, his voice softer. "We need to talk."

Sonia dabbed her eyes. "I know," she whispered.

"We need to know what happened today. With Peter," said Daniels.

Jill sat beside her. "You don't have to talk to them. You can have an attorney present."

Rem shot a hard stare at Jill.

Jill shot one back. "She should know her rights. Don't give me that look."

Sonia sniffed. "It's okay, dear. I don't mind. There are things you all need to know."

Madison took the pot off the burner and poured hot water into a cup with a tea bag. "You want any sugar or cream?" she asked.

"No, dear. Thank you."

Madison brought the tea over and put it on the table as Sonia reached out and took her hand. Madison went still.

Sonia paused and smiled softly. "You're much clearer now than before. You've been practicing, haven't you?"

Madison squeezed Sonia's fingers. "Yes. I have. I took your advice. I am stronger than I thought."

"You always were, dear." Sonia regarded the three of them. "All of you are."

Madison pulled out a chair and sat, still holding Sonia's hand.

Jace, his face somber, stayed behind the counter. "I'm going to start the hamburgers." He grabbed the patty of meat Madison had left on the plate.

Sonia studied him, her eyes shimmering. "I remember dropping you off at the fire station like it was yesterday." A tear trickled down her cheek.

Jace stopped, holding the patty. "What?"

Sonia sat up. "You were only two, and you liked fire trucks, so I took you over and you walked right in." She wiped her eyes. "I cried for a week."

Jace didn't move. "You're the one who left me there?"

More tears fell. "Yes. I was."

Jace squeezed the patty. "You abandoned me?"

Sonia cried softly. "I was trying to save you."

Daniels watched the interplay between Jill, Madison, and Jace, seeing their expressions of doubt and fear. "You need to tell them what happened, Sonia."

Rem leaned back, sighing. "I think it's time. For them, and for us."

Sonia fidgeted with the napkin. "I know it is." She cleared her throat, wiped her eyes, and took a deep breath. "This is harder than I thought." She stared into her tea. "It all started years ago..."

They sat and listened as Sonia went through her history as Rutger and Jace's nanny. How she'd called them Dean and Case and how she'd learned of their strange beginnings along with Jill's and Madison's.

Daniels listened as she talked about the DNA experimentation the siblings supposedly resulted from—how she took Case and left Dean behind, and then returned to help raise Dean—finding it all hard to believe.

"How long did you stay? After you returned?" asked Rem.

"I stayed until...well...until I couldn't stay anymore." She'd shredded the napkin, and Daniels grabbed another and handed it to her.

"What does that mean?" asked Jill.

Sonia sipped the remains of her tea. "As Dean got older, he became harder and harder to handle. He would erupt out of nowhere, angry and frustrated. And then he got sick. He was in bed for a long time, and Emerson refused to let me get him medical attention. Thankfully, he recovered, but I noticed soon afterward that something had changed."

"I'll get you some more," said Madison, picking up Sonia's mug.

"Thank you," said Sonia.

"What changed?" asked Daniels.

"I would come downstairs to find things scattered all over the place. Books on the floor, tables overturned, broken plates."

"Sounds familiar," said Rem.

"I didn't understand it," said Sonia. "Until Nina was injured."

"The housekeeper?" asked Daniels.

"Yes. She'd cleaned something, and Dean had gotten angry that she'd touched his things. He'd become very possessive and protective, but Nina didn't wilt easy, and she told him she was doing her job. He didn't back down though, and I came in to intervene and I saw a silver tray fly off a table and hit her in the head. It cut her, and she started bleeding. She ran from the room, and Dean did nothing. Only smiled. I knew then what had happened. The scattered items suddenly made sense. The experiments Emerson and Arnuff had conducted were becoming evident. Dean had done it with his mind." Sonia squeezed her temples. "Nina left afterward. And that's when we hired Maia."

Daniels sat up, and Rem's brow creased. "Did you say Maia?" He glanced at Daniels. "As in Maia Chambers?"

Daniels' jaw dropped. "Son-of-a..."

Rem fell back against his seat. "I don't believe this."

"Believe what?" asked Jill. Her eyes widened. "Is this the woman from your current case?"

"There's our connection," said Daniels, shaking his head in disbelief. "So, Maia knew Rutger, or should I say Dean?"

Sonia frowned. "Oh, yes. He fell in love with her."

Rem snorted. "Of course he did."

"What happened?" asked Jill.

Madison heated more water. "This Maia was the new housekeeper?"

"Yes, dear. I have no idea why she was hired. She was young and beautiful and impulsive, and terrible at cleaning. Dean took one look at her and was instantly smitten. He was a young man by then, and perhaps that's why she was hired."

"What? To keep him occupied with female pursuits?" asked Jace, who still stood beside the counter and who'd said little during the conversation. "Probably smart."

"I'm sure they thought it was," said Sonia, "but it quickly turned on them. I don't think they expected him to fall in love with her."

"How long did it last?" asked Rem.

"I don't know that it ever ended, at least not for Dean," said Sonia. "Whenever I was there, I could see what was happening. If I told her to work, Dean would get angry with me. He was protective of her, and she would look at me with this cold satisfaction in her eyes. She knew I had no power over her. I think Emerson realized that perhaps they'd allowed Maia too much leeway, and he told me to fire her. I tried to talk to him about how that could be a bad idea, but he told me it was nonsense. Dean was well under their control. By then, though, I think he and Arnuff were far too overconfident, but there was little I could do."

"Did you do it?" asked Madison from the stove.

"Yes. I fired her." Sonia leaned on the table, lost in thought. "Dean was furious and there was no consoling him. He threw me out of the room, almost tossing me physically." She sighed. "A week later, he was gone. I came into the house, and I instantly knew. I didn't feel him anymore. Emerson's office was in shambles and the downstairs was wrecked, except for the clothes and personal items he'd taken. The security man had been injured but luckily recovered."

"He'd gone through the office?" asked Rem. "Is that how he learned about Jill, Madison, and Jace?"

"I'm sure it was. I don't know how he located Jill and Madison, but I'd been asked to detail my account with Jace, so if he found that information, he might have found Jace that way. But keep in mind, he didn't start hurting people at first. I suspect he took off with Maia when he left."

"Thought he'd play house. Start a family? All that fairy tale stuff?" asked Jace.

"He'd never had any of that before," said Sonia. "Deep inside, he craved it. But then the realities of life set in."

Madison poured more hot water into Sonia's cup with a fresh tea bag. "Maia wasn't ready to put down roots."

Sonia fiddled with her napkin. "I found him once, a few years after he'd escaped. I simply looked for Maia. She'd been hard to locate. They moved around a lot, and from what I learned, were experimenting with drugs and alcohol. He was doing all the things he couldn't do before."

"Makes sense," said Daniels.

"He didn't want to see me, though. He was furious and belligerent. Told me I'd taken his brother away from him. The only other soul he'd had in this world. He tossed me out. Told me to leave him alone." Sonia paused. "I decided to talk to Maia. I found her one day alone, and I asked her about Dean. Wanted to know if they were happy. She laughed in my face and told me Dean was fun for now because he could do cool things. But beyond that, it was none of my business."

"Sounds like a healthy couple," said Jill.

Madison brought the fresh cup of tea over. "How long did it last?"

"I tried to keep tabs on them, but it was difficult. A few more years passed, but eventually, I learned from sources, namely Peter, Maia's brother, about their break-up. Peter didn't know Dean's story, but I'd befriended Peter hoping to hear about Maia. He told me his sister had found another boyfriend, but then had been arrested soon after for drug possession and assaulting a police officer."

Daniels shot a glance at Rem, who shook his head.

"She fought it and ended up in jail. I tried to reach out to Dean but couldn't find him. I'd hoped he was okay, but had no idea the extent of his fall." Sonia sipped her tea.

"What do you mean?" asked Jace.

"Someone reached out to me. Who it was is not important, but that was when I knew I was not the only one keeping tabs on him. Apparently, he was still of interest to...well...certain people." She gazed at Jill with sad eyes. "I was told he'd located you, and he'd been responsible for Rick's death. That's when I tracked him, hoping to find him and stop him, but my overconfidence was my downfall. I should have learned from Emerson."

Jill fell back in her seat and crossed her arms.

"What about me and Madison? You couldn't warn us?" asked Jace.

"I was very much at the mercy of those who knew more than I did. I had to wait to hear from them. I tried to find you both, but I had limited information on Madison until I was told about Donald's death. I wanted to find you, Jace, but I didn't know your name. I hated it, but I had to wait for Dean to strike before I could act."

Jace hung his head.

"I'm sorry. I wish I could have done more for all of you." Another tear welled up, escaped, and fell down her cheek. "And now I've failed Peter, too."

Jill sat up and patted her hand. "Why don't we take a second and let you catch your breath?"

Sonia waved her hand. "I'm okay, dear. I've been through a lot in my life. I'll manage." She held the napkin to her nose.

"Sonia," said Rem, "was Peter helping you to find Rutger?"

Sonia exhaled and nodded. "Yes. He'd been assigned to assist me. I'd hoped his connection to Maia would help me connect to Dean, but it didn't. Peter didn't know anything about Maia's involvement in all of this. He'd been estranged from his sister when she took her life, and he feels...felt...the guilt of that."

Rem held up a finger. "Hold up a sec. You said assigned. Who's doing the assigning? Who are these people you report to?"

Sonia fiddled with her tea bag. "There are certain things you need to know. That is not one of them."

"These people can help corroborate your story," said Daniels. "You may need them."

"And if they choose to step forward, that will be up to them. I have no say in the matter." Sonia sipped more tea.

"If you told us who they are—," said Rem.

"I'm telling you only what you need. No more, no less." Sonia said, her face flat, and Daniels could see that would be the end of that conversation.

Rem narrowed his eyes. "Suit yourself."

Daniels considered something else she'd mentioned. "You said you'd hoped Peter would help you 'connect' with Dean. What exactly does that mean?"

Sonia gripped her cup. "It's complicated."

"Try us," said Rem.

Sonia hesitated and spoke to Jill. "You and I have similar abilities."

"We do?" asked Jill.

Rem rested his elbows on the table, frowning. "Does this have something to do with the bruises around her neck?"

Sonia sighed. "I can't get as close as Jill can, but I have a mental connection. We can talk telepathically. That is, if he chooses to. Dean has a remarkable ability to block people out." She looked over at Jace. "As do you."

Jace dropped the patty he was molding. "What do you mean?"

"I saw what happened when you attacked Dean," said Sonia. "He couldn't fight back, at least not the way he wanted to. He couldn't use his skills against you. I suspect you were blocking him without even realizing it."

Jace wiped his hands and held his ribs. "Guy can still throw a punch."

"It's better than throwing you against a tree," said Daniels, absentmindedly rubbing his own ribs.

"Or throwing a rock at your head," said Rem.

"Is that true for all of us?" asked Madison, who'd returned to her seat beside Sonia.

"Sadly, no," said Sonia. "But what I'm not sure about is the three of you together."

"Madison moved things with Jace present. And I connected with Rutger with Jace there," said Jill.

"He wasn't blocking you," said Sonia. "In fact, he may even amplify it. Make you stronger. That's just a theory, though."

Jace snorted. "Lucky me. I don't even know I'm doing it." He picked up the patty again.

"Subconsciously, you do," said Sonia.

"So, you connected with Rutger?" Rem asked Jill. "Is that what you've been calling your meditations?"

Jill slumped in her seat. "I didn't quite realize how deep I would go."

Sonia patted her hand. "It's shocking, isn't it, when it first happens? I should have warned you." Sonia moaned softly. "There are a lot of things I should have done."

Jace grunted, but finished the patty and started a new one.

"I guess we understand the whole 'I did it for you' now," said Madison. "In some sick way, he thinks he's helping us."

"He wants us to feel the same pain he's felt. And in his warped way of thinking, our pain makes him feel better. Maybe he's convinced himself that he's helping us, too," said Jill.

Sonia rested her hand over Jill's. "I wish I could have helped more. But I have to tell you that the strength I feel from all of you now is admirable. You may have bent, but you haven't broken."

Jill squeezed Sonia's fingers and nodded. Jace didn't respond.

Daniels stood. "I need a beer."

"Times two," said Rem.

"Times three," said Jill.

"I'll get one for everyone," said Daniels, opening the fridge.

Rem clasped his hands together. "I don't understand how Rutger was able to physically hurt Jill when he's not even present in the room."

"I don't get it either, but it's scary as hell," said Madison. "We almost didn't get her back."

"Madison...," said Jill.

"Wonderful," said Rem.

"It's like another sense, only more developed," said Sonia. "Since they are siblings, they have an even stronger ability to connect. I can't see or touch him physically, but Jill can. But if you don't know how to use it properly, it can be very dangerous."

"As I've learned," said Jill, holding her neck.

"Why couldn't I block him?" asked Jace.

Sonia held a chunky yellow stone on her necklace. "You may have been with Jill, but you weren't with her in Rutger's space. You can't go there, so you can't block him from there. You have to be physically with him." Sonia spoke to Jill. "And you can't go back there again. It's too dangerous."

Daniels handed Jill a beer, and she took it. "It's how I found you, though. I saw the address on his table."

"I'm not saying there aren't benefits to it," said Sonia, "but Dean is very strong and angry. He holds a grudge against all of you...and me, too." Sonia tipped her head at Daniels, who was about to close the fridge. He saw the look, got the message, and grabbed another beer. He twisted the cap and handed it to Sonia.

"Thank you, dear. I think you have a touch of ESP yourself." She took a long gulp.

Jill smiled, and Madison raised a brow.

Daniels returned to his seat. "I ought to. It keeps us alive in this job, plus it helps me when he needs his Taco del Fuegos." He nodded at Rem. "Otherwise he gets really pissy."

"That keeps you alive more than the job stuff," said Rem.

"Probably," said Daniels.

"Why is he taking his anger out on us?" asked Jace. He sat his beer on the counter while he made another patty. "Why make us miserable?"

Sonia put her beer down. "Because you got out. You had families. Parents. Normalcy."

Jace mumbled. "If you can call it that."

Sonia pushed her empty teacup back. "The manner in which you were raised does not matter to him. You had what he did not. That's not your fault, but he doesn't care. He's enraged and when Maia left him, he needed a place to direct his ire, so he directed it at you, and consequently, pushed away the very thing he's wanted all this time. People. Connections. Relationships." She crumpled her napkin. "I've tried many times to reach out to him, to get him to see that, and I thought and hoped I could get him to understand, but I failed." Her emotion returned. "And I'm so sorry."

"Don't do this to yourself, Sonia," said Jill. "You raised him. How can you expect yourself to not want to save him? He's like a son to you, and you're the only mother he's ever known."

"Is that why you're still alive?" asked Jace. "Is that why we're all still alive? Because in some messed up way, he still hopes we can be a family?" He mashed a patty and Daniels wondered if those patties would ever become hamburgers.

Sonia held the napkin to the corner of her eye. "It's possible. If you were to reach out and tell him you wanted a relationship with him, he might respond, but it could also blow up in your face. He might be too far gone to help."

"He's killed four people," said Jace, squeezing a patty hard enough for it to poke out through his fingers. "I'd say he's past the point of redemption."

"Maybe six people," said Rem. "If our theory holds up."

Jill paled and gripped her beer.

Sonia's face tightened. "Six? What do you mean?"

"Judge Hendrix and D.A. Alba," said Daniels. "Our boy hasn't been sitting on the sidelines."

"Why them?" asked Sonia.

"Because of Maia," said Rem. "Did Peter tell you about the baby?"

"What baby?" asked Sonia.

"Maia had a baby girl in prison," said Daniels. "Her mother took the child, but the baby died two weeks later. A number was left at the crime scenes. 0212. Rem learned today from Maia's mom that that was the date of the baby's death."

Jill put down her beer. "You're kidding."

"You think it was Rutger's child?" asked Madison.

"It's looking pretty obvious," said Rem. "Did Peter know about the baby?"

Sonia shook her head. "No. He never mentioned it."

"God. He's angry about his upbringing, then gets close to having a family of his own, and it's all taken from him again. No wonder he's furious," said Madison.

"Life happens. Get over it," said Jace, his voice raising. He shoved a plate of mangled patties aside and wiped his hands. "Don't take your shit out on me because I got left at a fire station when I was two."

The room went quiet, and Daniels picked at the label on his beer. "Rem arrested and testified against Maia. Is that the reason we keep getting pulled into all of this?"

"You testified against her?" asked Sonia.

"Lucky me," said Rem.

Sonia stared off, thinking. "I just assumed, with Jill's involvement with the Artist and you two becoming close, that it was just a natural occurrence. And then you were assigned to Madison's case, which I found unusual. Did he somehow plan that? I don't know."

"He sure as hell planned it when Justin was murdered," said Daniels. "He made sure we got assigned to that one."

"Is Rem in danger?" asked Madison.

"He's had ample time to get to me, but I'm still walking around," said Rem.

Sonia spoke to Jill. "Did you see anything else in your encounter with Dean?"

"You said you saw a book," said Jace.

Jill sank in her seat. "Yeah. I did. A black book." She winced and touched her head.

"You need some peppermint oil, dear? It will help," said Sonia. "Detective, do you have the bottle I sent you?" She looked at Rem.

Daniels raised a brow. "Seriously?"

"Hold on. I'll get it." Rem stood. "You can use some, too," he said to Daniels. "You look like you need it."

"Just get me another beer. That'll work a lot better than a smelly oil." Daniels waved his bottle.

Rem smirked. "Hold that thought about the black book." He left the room.

"You said you also saw a green stone and a picture?" asked Madison. "On his desk?"

Jill nodded. "Yes. I didn't get a good look at the picture, though, but it was of a woman. From a distance, her arms out, like she was acting silly."

Sonia sucked in a breath. "How big was the stone?"

"Not big," said Jill. "It would fit in the palm of your hand. It was smooth and a lighter green color."

Sonia put her hand over her mouth. "It's the piece of Jasper I gave to Maia. She gave it to Dean because he liked it. I didn't know he kept it."

"How sweet," said Jace. "Let's all sigh together." He took a long pull on his beer.

Rem returned with the oil and handed it to Jill. He stopped and grabbed another beer and handed it to Daniels and, seeing Jace's almost empty bottle, gave another to him.

Jill dabbed some oil on the back of her neck and forehead, and Rem returned to his seat.

"What was in the book?" asked Daniels, opening his beer.

Jill closed the oil and put it down. "Names."

"What names?" asked Daniels.

Jill rubbed her neck gently with the oil on her fingers. "I didn't see them all. I was in a hurry. But I saw Rick's, Donald's and Justin's. Plus, all of us and Sonia. It's possible I saw Peter's, but I can't be sure." She sighed. "I saw Rem and Daniels, too."

"How nice," said Rem.

"What about Alba and Hendrix?" asked Daniels.

"I don't know," said Jill. "There were more, so it's possible."

"What exactly does that mean, though? Some of them are dead, but others aren't," said Madison. "Does that mean he's planning to kill us?"

"I don't know, dear. I'm not even sure he knows." Sonia took the oil and opened it. "Do you mind?"

"Help yourself," said Rem. "We'll pass it around."

Daniels took a sip of his second beer. "What happened with Peter this morning, Sonia? Did you find him? Did you make the anonymous call to report it?"

Sonia added some oil to her own forehead and neck and took a deep breath. "Peter and I talked last night. I told him much the same as what I've told you. He wasn't happy to hear about Maia's involvement. He thought I was using him. I explained to him my motives, but I'd accepted his doubt. I'd given him a file folder with a lot of this information. I'd asked him to research the names, go through the story, and see if anything came up for him. I'd hoped he might see something that I didn't." She rubbed her hands together. "He'd gone through it and had several questions, most of which I answered."

"Most?" asked Jill.

"There are some things, like you, that he didn't need to know." Sonia's emotions surfaced again. "We went to bed, agreeing to pick up our discussion in the morning. I was up early, unable to sleep, and I went for a walk. I was gone for maybe an hour. When I came home…" She hesitated and sniffed. "…I found him." Another tear escaped. "It was terrible. I was distraught. Peter didn't deserve that."

"You left the scene?" asked Rem.

"I had to." Sonia wiped her tears. "I couldn't answer all the questions the police would have. Plus, I knew I would be a suspect. I think Dean hoped I would be put in jail. It would keep me from helping all of you."

"So, he is planning something, and he wants you out of the way," said Jill.

"I can only suspect," said Sonia.

"The file folder was empty, Sonia," said Daniels. "Did Rutger take it?"

A fresh sob escaped Sonia. "He must have. It was there last night."

"Was there anything in it he might read that he shouldn't?" asked Rem. "Anything that might make this thing worse instead of better?"

Sonia held her napkin to her mouth. "Oh, dear."

Daniels leaned in, anxious. "What is it?"

She closed her eyes. "I mentioned one thing in the file. Perhaps I should have left out."

"What was it?" asked Rem.

Sonia expelled a puff of air. "A potential way to kill him."

Jill and Madison's eyes widened, and Jace straightened. Daniels dropped his jaw.

Rem leaned back, took a gulp of his beer, and put the bottle on the table. "That ought to make him happy."

Chapter Twenty-Eight

HIS NECK TIGHT FROM strain, Rem grabbed some of the oil. "I think I need some of that, too." He dabbed some on his fingers and massaged his neck.

"What was mentioned?" asked Daniels. "About how to kill him?"

Sonia bit back a sob. "It was only a suggestion made by someone to be used as a last resort. I didn't have any real plan to act on it. My hope has always been to get him to see reason. Dean just has a misdirected perspective on life. He's been through so much."

"Oh, give me a break, Sonia." Jace stabbed out a hand. "This guy is a lost cause. He had a hard life. His girlfriend broke up with him and his child died. It's terrible. I get it. But none of it justifies what he's done to us or to you. So stop taking pity on him because it's making me sick." He shoved the plate of patties and it slid it off the counter and shattered on the floor. Jace pointed. "If there's a way to kill him, then please fill me in, because I'll be the first one to use it." Breathless, he crossed his arms and turned away.

Rem eyed the mess. "Guess we won't be having hamburgers tonight."

"Jace," said Madison. "If there's a way to reach him, don't you think we should try?"

Jace swiveled, his face angry. "No, actually. I don't. Did you see what he did to Jill's throat? That is not a man who wants to play nice, Madison. This man wants us dead. The longer this goes on, the madder he becomes. And if we don't act soon, we'll all regret it. Maybe even lose somebody else we love. Maybe somebody in this room. Forgive me if I have to be the one to offer tough love, but this guy is not my brother, and if he tries to hurt me or anyone else, I will gladly kill him." His gaze darted around the room. "Can anybody here say any different?"

Rem watched everyone's reactions, already knowing his answer. "What was it, Sonia? How can we kill him?"

Sonia's face furrowed, and her fingers tightened over her beer. "This is not exactly legal, detectives. You sure you want to know?"

"Nothing's happened yet. We're just talking," said Rem.

Daniels traced a seam on the table. "You and I both know that won't fly in a court of law, Rem. We're talking about it, so we have prior knowledge."

"I don't know anything," said Rem. "Do you?"

Daniels raised a brow. "You sure about this?"

"Keep in mind," said Jace. "Rem could be next on his list. I'd say it's worth a listen."

Daniels paused, and Rem waited. "It's cool if you want to leave the room."

Daniels peeled off a piece of the label on his beer. "Like you said. Nothing's happened yet."

"And maybe nothing will," said Jill. "None of us knows how this will end."

"What is it, Sonia?" asked Jace.

Sonia swallowed. "I have access to a poison. It's potent and quick and leaves no trace. It would be quite effective if he were to ingest it." She dropped her head.

"You sure it's real?" asked Rem.

"Oh, it's quite real, detective," said Sonia. "And don't ask me where I would get it, where it comes from, or who would give it to me, because I won't tell you."

"Probably for the best," said Jill.

"Poison?" asked Jace. He thought about it. "We'd have to get close enough to give it to him."

"There was no discussion as to how to administer it. I was only notified that it was an option. Nothing more." Sonia took a long drink of her beer.

"You have this poison now?" asked Jill.

Sonia swallowed. "No, but I know where I could get it."

"And you mentioned this in the file that Peter had?" asked Daniels.

"I did," said Sonia. "But nothing about my source. It was only mentioned as a suggestion."

"I don't think that distinction will matter much. He'll take it as a betrayal and it will likely seal your fate," said Rem. "If he didn't want to kill you before, he probably will now."

Sonia closed her eyes. "It's not me I'm worried about. I've lived my life. I'm worried about all of you."

"You get a hold of that poison, I'll figure out how to get it in him," said Jace. "I won't waste time wondering if, when, or what he might do." He put his hands on the counter. "And you can do whatever you like with that information, detectives."

"Let's just take this one step at a time," said Rem. "We don't even know where he is."

"Well, we know he killed Peter, Hendrix, and Alba. What do we do with that?" asked Daniels.

"We can connect him to Maia, so we'll just tell Lozano," said Rem. "Rutger's already wanted for Justin's murder. Might as well add the rest to the list."

Daniels rubbed his face. "You think it's possible to bring him in?"

"You'll never bring him in," said Jace.

Madison stood and picked up the broken dish and the mangled patties. "I guess we need a plan." She found a trash bag under the sink and opened it. Jace squatted and helped her clean.

"Can you get a hold of that poison?" asked Jill.

Sonia stilled. "You really want to go down this path?"

"We don't have a choice," said Jace. He picked up a handful of meat and dumped it in the bag Madison held.

"He'll be expecting it, though," said Rem. "If he's read the file."

"Maybe we tell him one thing, but do another," said Madison. She tossed the last shards of the plate into the bag and closed it. Jace got a wet rag and wiped the floor.

Daniels glanced at Rem. "This is the part we should probably not be listening to."

"Hell, we're already harboring a fugitive," said Rem. "How much worse can it get?"

"If you can think of a better way, detective, let us know." Jace finished cleaning the floor and washed the rag under the faucet.

"How would that work?" asked Jill.

"You give him the right bait, it might draw him out," said Madison. She tied the bag closed and headed to the back door. "I'll take this out to the garbage bin."

"I don't like this," said Sonia.

"He killed Peter, Sonia. Shot him point blank in the chest. He stabbed Rick, Donald and Justin," said Jill. "You know he won't come willingly, and you know we can't stop him on our own. And even if we could, what do we do? Put him in prison? And what prison would that be?"

"She's right," said Rem. "Much as I hate to admit it, we don't have many options. If we don't take him down, he'll take us down."

"If we do it in self-defense, though. Cold-blooded murder is another story," said Daniels.

Jace dropped the rinsed rag and turned off the faucet. "You want to wait for him to try to kill us first?"

Rem finished his beer. "I don't really think it's an issue. I don't see a scenario where we meet up with this guy and he doesn't try to kill us."

"I'm not sure about that," said Daniels. "We've met with him three times and he hasn't killed us."

"He broke your ribs and gave me stitches. I'd say that's probable cause. Plus, he killed a judge and a D.A. Let's be honest, we take a shot at this guy, who's going to blame us?" asked Rem.

"Taking a shot is one thing. Poison is another," said Daniels.

"I don't care what method we use," said Jace. "Just so long as the bastard goes down."

"This is awful," said Sonia, holding her stomach.

"Why don't you go lie down," said Jill. "You've been through a lot today. Get some rest."

Rem stood and stretched. "Technically, we should bring her in."

"Yeah. We should," said Daniels. "But I'm starving, and our hamburgers are in the trash."

"I agree. All this light-hearted talk is making me hungry," said Rem.

"We got a couple of frozen pizzas. We could heat those," said Jill. "And I certainly hope you're not suggesting that you'd take Sonia into the station."

"She's a suspect," said Daniels. "We can't keep her here."

"That's ridiculous," said Jill. "No one will know she's at Rem's. And if you bring her in, that makes her an easy fall guy."

"We know Rutger did it. She'll be released," said Rem. "But she'll still need to be questioned."

"It's okay," said Sonia. "I'll go."

Rem hesitated, hearing his stomach rumble. "You promise not to pull a disappearing act, we'll wait until tomorrow." He looked at Daniels. "You okay with that?"

Daniels shrugged. "Hell. Why not? She's not staying at my house."

"I'll warm the oven," said Jill, standing. "Where's Madison?"

"I'll check." Jace stepped outside.

Daniels stood, too. "I have another question, Sonia."

Sonia sat up. "What is it?"

"These abilities Jace, Madison, and Jill have. How did they get them? How do you have yours? Exactly whose DNA are they experimenting with, and why?"

Sonia didn't answer.

"Who exactly are you people?" Daniels asked.

"A logical question. Let's see if we get an answer," said Rem, waiting for Sonia's response.

Jace ran in from the backyard. "We've got a problem. Madison is gone."

Chapter Twenty-Nine

REM SHOT OUT FROM behind the table and followed Daniels out into the backyard. The lights were on, but visibility was low and long shadows harbored numerous hiding places.

Jace opened the bin and pulled out the garbage bag. "She made it out, but she didn't make it back."

Rem searched the area with Jill and ran out into the front, but there was no sign of Madison. "Where could she be?" asked Jill.

Daniels joined them after checking the alley and the house. "She's not inside or out back."

"Check with the neighbors," said Rem. "I'll go here." He pointed. Jace came out, and Daniels told him to stay inside with Sonia in case Madison returned. Daniels ran to the neighbor on the opposite side from Rem, and Jill went across the street.

They spent the next several minutes searching, but found no sign of Madison.

Rem met Daniels on the front porch. "Nothing. You?"

"Nothing," said Daniels.

Jill returned from her canvas and shook her head. "Nobody saw anything. I tried to call her, but she's not answering."

Jace opened the door and stepped out. "Any luck?"

Rem shook his head.

"Shit," said Jace. "He took her, didn't he? That bastard walked right up and grabbed her while we were sitting inside talking about him." He kicked at a porch chair and it toppled over. "Son-of-a-bitch."

"Now what do we do?" asked Jill.

"What do you think?" Rem asked Daniels. "Call Lozano?"

Daniels ran a hand through his tousled hair. "We probably should. Put out a missing-persons on her."

"Missing-persons? What good is that going to do?" asked Jace. "If Rutger's got her, then nobody's going to find her. And if someone sees her, Rutger could easily eradicate the threat. You're more likely to end up with an injured or dead cop on your hands."

Sonia joined them on the porch, her hands clenched. "She's gone, isn't she?"

"Yeah, she's gone." Jace cursed. "I should have taken out the damn trash."

"Nobody saw this coming," said Jill. Pacing, she stared at the ground. "Think. What can we do? Why did he take her?"

"And how come nobody knew he was here?" asked Jace, looking at Sonia.

Sonia paled and held on to the door frame.

Jill ran over and grabbed her arm. "Sonia, sit down. You look like you're going to faint." She righted the chair and guided Sonia to sit.

Sonia took a deep breath. "I should have felt him, but it's not always that easy. He's good at blocking his presence, and my emotional state isn't helping."

"That's terrific," said Jace.

"We'll find her," said Jill.

"We need to get more people looking," said Rem.

"I agree," said Daniels. "But Jace is right. It could get someone hurt."

Rem pulled out his phone. "I don't think we have a choice."

"Don't forget about Sonia," said Daniels. "We'll have to explain what she's doing in your house."

"We'll figure it out," said Rem. He started to dial when a phone rang.

"That's me," said Jill, grabbing her cell from her pocket and checking the display. "It's an unknown number." She answered. "Hello?" Her face paled.

Sonia flattened a hand on her chest. "It's him."

"Where is Madison?" asked Jill, pausing. "Don't hurt her."

"We should try to trace it," said Daniels.

Rem put his phone away. "I doubt he'll give us enough time."

"Wait," said Jill. "Let me talk to her. I want to know she's okay." She listened. "Hello? Hello?" She waited. "Shit. He hung up. Damn it."

"What did he say?" asked Jace.

Jill set her jaw. "He wants to meet. Me and Jace. At midnight. He'll call later with the address. No cops, or Madison will end up like Hendrix, Alba, and Peter."

"There's no way in hell you two are going in alone," said Rem.

"We can't risk Madison's life," said Jace.

"She's already at risk," said Daniels. "You go, then you'll all be at risk. You know that."

"We can't have an army of cops at the door," said Jill. "She'll be dead before we even get there."

"Who said anything about an army?" said Rem. "Daniels and I will back you up."

"He'll know you're coming," said Jill.

"Maybe not," said Sonia. "There may be a way." She spoke to Jace. "Your ability to block him might conceal the detectives' presence long enough for them to get close."

Jace hesitated. "I don't even know how I'm doing that."

"I can give you some pointers. I suspect you'll be a fast learner." Sonia looked between the two of them. "You realize what you'll have to do?"

Jill made eye contact with Jace. "We'll have to kill him."

"Either you or us," said Rem. He spoke to Daniels. "Looks like self-defense may not be an issue."

"Can you get a hold of that poison?" asked Jace.

"How are you going to get him to take poison?" asked Jill. "You planning on toasting him with a drink?"

Jace glared. "If it works, then maybe yes. Remember what you said before? Letting him think we were on his side. Like Madison said. Draw him out. He said something to Sonia about losing his brother and how it upset him. Maybe we can use that." He raised a brow at Sonia. "We need that poison. Can you get it?"

Sonia wrung her hands, but her gaze didn't waver. "Let me make a phone call." She stood and went inside the house.

"You sure about this?" Daniels asked Rem. "Our ass and our career are on the line if this goes bad. Even if it goes well, we'll likely be directing traffic for a while."

"I don't like it," said Rem. "But we don't have a choice. This guy has got to go down, but with as few casualties as possible." He leaned on the rail. "If Jace can get us in undetected, maybe we can take him down before Jill and Jace have to worry about using any poison. But if it comes to that, I'd prefer they have it." He spoke to Jill. "I assume you'll bring your gun?"

"Not leaving without it," said Jill.

"We need the address, so we can prepare," said Daniels. "When's he calling?"

"He didn't say," said Jill.

"Let's hope it's sooner rather than later," said Rem.

Jill went quiet. "Maybe I can find out."

Jace shook his head. "Oh, hell, no. You're not going back there. I'll end up losing both of you."

Jill sat in Sonia's seat. "It's a good idea," said Jill.

"Are you talking about confronting Rutger again? In your mind?" asked Rem. "No way. Jace is right. It's too dangerous."

"If I can find Madison's location, that gives us the upper hand," said Jill.

"It doesn't help us if you're dead," said Jace.

"It's not worth the risk," said Daniels.

Jill's face fell. "It would be different this time."

"How do you know that?" asked Jace. "It could also be worse."

Jill bounced her knee. "Because I wouldn't connect with him. I'd connect with Madison."

Jace glowered at her.

"It's worth a shot," said Jill.

"Rutger is with Madison. How do you expect to avoid him?" asked Jace.

Jill stood. "All I need is a location. I may be able to get in and get out before he even knows I'm there."

"You *may*," said Jace. "*May* being the crucial issue. You don't know."

"I have to try," said Jill. "We're talking about Madison's life."

"We're talking about yours, too. You heard what Sonia said," said Rem.

Sonia stepped back onto the porch. "It's done. You two can pick it up." She held out a piece of paper to Jace.

"Pick it up? I thought we couldn't know who, what, where, or when?" Jace took the paper.

"You won't know any of those things. It will be in a mailbox at this location, in thirty minutes and in a manilla envelope. Simply drive by and check the mail."

"Whose house is it?" asked Jill.

"It doesn't matter," said Sonia. "I just need you two to pick it up."

"Jace can pick it up," said Jill. "I can stay here."

Sonia stared at Jill. "No, you will not. I need you to go. Remalla and Daniels will stay with me." Her gaze softened. "I know what you want to do, Jill, and I commend you for your bravery, but Madison needs you right now. She needs both of you." She adjusted her necklace. "And I am just as capable. I'll do it myself. I'll look for Madison."

"Sonia. No. You can't," said Jill.

Sonia took Jill's wrist. "I can and I will. I'm not fragile. I may look it right now, but I'm tougher than I appear. Plus, I can get out more easily. I don't have the physical connection you do. It's harder for him to get to me."

"Doesn't that also make it harder for you to get the location?" asked Rem.

"If it were just Dean, that may be true, but Madison will be the key," said Sonia. "You two need to go."

"I don't like this," said Jill. "We should be here."

"There would be nothing for you to do," said Sonia. "Besides, I work better alone." She paused. "Now go."

Jill and Jace hesitated until Jace turned. "I'll get the keys." He went inside.

"Please be careful, Sonia," said Jill.

"I'm always careful. I'll have these two. They'll help."

Rem shrugged. "Don't know what the hell I'm going to do. Do you?" he asked Daniels.

"Not a clue," said Daniels.

Jace returned with the keys. "Let's go."

Jill nodded. "Okay." She stopped in front of Sonia. "You're sure about this?"

Sonia patted her arm. "I'm very sure."

Jill took her hand and squeezed her fingers. "Please don't die," she whispered.

Sonia moved close and put her hand on Jill's cheek. "I don't plan to." She pulled back. "These detectives have enough on their plate. I don't intend to give them more."

"That's kind of you," said Rem.

Daniels grunted. "Less paperwork for us because God knows we're going to be buried in it after tonight."

"Let's hope that's all we're buried in," said Rem.

Jace walked up to Sonia, his back straight, but his eyes somber. "I know it's a long shot, but thank you for trying."

Sonia's eyes softened, and she reached out and touched his wrist. "I know you're struggling with what I did, and who I am." She paused. "But I want you to know, for what it's worth, that I always thought of you as a son." Her voice caught, and she put her hand to her mouth. "Sorry."

Jace groaned, his eyes shimmering. "Damn it. Come here." He wrapped her in a bear hug and Rem heard him whisper, "I don't blame you. I know you wanted the best for me."

Sonia closed her eyes and hugged him back. "Thank you." She held him for a moment, then stepped back, wiped her eyes and squared her shoulders. "Now go. And don't be afraid. Trust your instincts. And don't worry about me. Just make sure you all come back alive." She looked around Jace's shoulder. "That includes you, too, detectives."

"That makes me feel better," said Daniels.

"We'll stay with Sonia," said Rem. "Once we figure out where Madison is, we'll get in touch and take it from there." He pulled his gun and checked the chamber, ensuring it was loaded, and re-holstered it. He spoke to Daniels. "Something tells me this is going to be a bumpy night."

Chapter Thirty

REM PACED OUTSIDE MADISON's bedroom door and checked his watch. "How long has she been in there?"

Daniels blinked his red eyes. "I don't know. At least forty-five minutes."

Rem stopped, unsure what to think. "Should we go in? How do we know she's not lying dead on the floor?"

Daniels shrugged. "I don't know. She told us not to disturb her. I figure if she was under duress, we would hear something."

"Hell. At this rate, Jill and Jace will be back soon."

"We have less than three hours until midnight. That's not a lot of time," said Daniels. "Let's hope this works."

Rem leaned back against the wall. "If we don't get an address, we'll have to sneak in with Jill and Jace when they go to meet Rutger."

"There's the possibility Madison won't be where Rutger is. What if he's holding her somewhere else?"

Rem groaned. "I have no idea. We'll just have to deal with that when the time comes. I just want this to end. Rutger's been a pointy thorn in our side for too long."

Daniels crossed his arms. "You really prepared to shoot him in cold blood?"

Rem rested his head on the back of the wall. "This guy can take our guns right out of our hands. If we don't shoot first, it may be too late." He glanced at Daniels. "You worried?"

"Terrified. Aren't you?"

"I've felt better." Rem paused. "Just between you and me, I'd rather be in Kansas."

"I hear you."

Rem faced Daniels. "Listen, you've got a kid and a fiancée to worry about. There are no hard feelings if you want to go home to them."

Daniels frowned. "I'm a cop, Rem. I don't get to go home when I get scared. This is part of the deal. Marjorie knows that."

"This was never part of the deal, and you know it," said Rem. "We're not dealing with your average perp."

"I think you just want to go in alone so you can get all the credit."

Rem smiled. "You caught me." He turned serious. "Just know that I'll back you up no matter what."

"Which is exactly why we're both going in, crazy perp or not." Daniels put his hand on the bedroom door. "And we're both coming out alive, and hopefully with a justifiable ending to all this. Okay?"

Rem nodded. "Okay."

The front door opened below, and Rem stepped away and peered over the bannister. He saw Jill and Jace enter, and Jill place a manilla envelope on the entry table. "They're back."

Jill raced up the stairs with Jace behind her. "What's happening?"

"Sonia's in Madison's room," said Daniels. "Said she thought it might help connect with her better." He paused. "Did you get what you needed?"

"Yeah. We did. It's downstairs," said Jace.

"Should we knock?" asked Jill, listening at the door.

"She said not to disturb her, so we haven't," said Rem. He checked his watch again. "But I'm beginning to wonder if we should."

"What's taking so long?" asked Jill.

Jace stepped closer. "I say we go in. We don't have all night, and I think we need to check on her."

"Go for it, but if she gets pissed, we're blaming you," said Rem.

Jace had put his hand on the knob when they heard Sonia cry out. Jace threw the door open and ran in. Jill went in behind him.

Sonia lay on her side, her skin pale and her eyes closed.

"Sonia," said Jill.

Jace squatted next to her and put a hand on her shoulder. "Are you okay?"

Her eyelids fluttered, and she seemed to be struggling to stay conscious, but she reached out and Jill took her hand. Rem stayed back with Daniels.

"She's trying to come back." Jill reached for her necklace with the black stone, took it off, and put it in Sonia's hand. "Hold this, Sonia." Sonia gripped the stone and made a whimper. "That's it. Focus. Can you hear me?"

Sonia blinked a few times, and her eyes fully opened.

"Can you sit up?" asked Jace.

Jill looked back. "Can you get her some water?"

"I'll get it," said Rem. He turned and headed down the stairs, ran to the fridge and grabbed a bottled water. Heading back to the stairs, he saw the manilla envelope. He stopped briefly, wondering what was in it, tempted to look.

Beside it was a retail catalogue and a couple of letters. A white envelope with his name and address on it caught his eye. It had no stamp or return address. Where had it come from? Had it been there earlier? He slid it out. The message was handwritten, and something about it made him squirm.

He put the water down and opened the letter.

·· • • •· • •·· •

Daniels squatted beside Sonia, whose face was slowly regaining some color. "You all right?" he asked.

She leaned back against the foot of the bed. "I'm better now."

"What happened? What did you see?" asked Jill.

"Did you see Madison?" asked Jace.

Sonia took a deep breath. "Thank you for the stone, dear. It's helping."

"Take your time," said Jill. "We're getting you some water."

Sonia nodded.

Daniels wanted to wait for her to recuperate, but he was acutely aware of the time. "Did you get a location?"

Sonia held her head. "I saw her. I saw Madison." She closed her eyes. "Oh, my. Poor dear. She's so scared."

"Is she with Rutger?" asked Jill.

"Yes. She is." Sonia opened her eyes. "They're in a house."

"Where?" asked Jace.

Sonia straightened. "It's older. Needs work. Away from here. There are hills and I saw trees." She squeezed her temples. "Madison's inside." She grimaced. "I smelled gasoline."

"Did you get an address?" asked Daniels.

Sonia scrunched her face. "I see a tree. Something to do with a tree."

Daniels had to forcibly prevent himself from groaning. "Anything else?"

"Where's Rem with the water?" asked Jill.

"There's something about that property," said Sonia. "It's important to him." Her eyes opened wide. "He's not planning to survive the night."

Jill squeezed her hand. "Think, Sonia. Where is this house?"

Sonia paused, her eyes closed. "Outside the city. Not too far. North. There's a gate. Old and rusty. Wait a minute." She touched her forehead. "There are words on the gate."

"What words?" asked Jace.

"It's a farm," said Sonia. "Something to do with fruit."

Daniels waited, listening, but something nudged at him. Rem had not returned with the water.

Sonia sighed. "I don't have a physical address," said Sonia. "But I would recognize it if I saw it."

Jace cursed. "We'll have to wait then until he contacts us."

"It's okay, Sonia," said Jill.

Daniels stood.

Sonia put a hand on her chest. "I can take you there, though. I think I can find it."

Daniels walked out of the room and over to the bannister. "Rem?" Not getting an answer, he ran down the stairs. Something was wrong.

He stopped when he saw the water bottle sitting on the entry table beside the manilla enveloped. "Rem?" he yelled louder.

Jill peered over the banister. "Where is he?"

Daniels saw an opened envelope and picked it up. Rem's name and address were handwritten on the front, but there was nothing inside.

Jill came down the stairs, her face anxious. "Something's happened. I can feel it. Where did he go?"

Daniels looked around, and that's when he saw the photo lying on the ground. He picked it up.

"What is it?" Jill looked at the picture. "Oh, my God."

It was a picture of Jennie, taken from a distance, standing at the side of the Grand Canyon, pretending to fall. He remembered it because the four of them had gone for a long weekend. A cold tendril of fear twisted in his stomach.

"That's the photo," said Jill.

"What?" asked Daniels, his skin prickling. He turned. "What photo?"

Jill turned white. "In my vision. With Rutger. I saw the photo of a woman on the table." She put her hand over her mouth, her eyes rounding. "Why is it here?"

"This is Jennie," said Daniels. Fear turned to fury. "Why the hell does Rutger have a picture of Jennie?"

"Oh, no." Jill covered her eyes. "Daniels, I saw something else. I didn't want to tell Rem."

Daniels resisted the urge to grab her. "What did else did you see?"

Jill dropped her hands to her throat, her face distraught. "I wanted to tell—"

Daniels yelled. "Damn it, Jill. What is it?"

"Her name," she shrieked. "Jennie's name. It was in the book."

Daniels couldn't breathe. Everything went cold, and his hair stood on end. He stared at the picture. "No," he whispered. "It's not possible." He forced air into his lungs and almost put a hand on the wall to support himself. "Jesus. No." He said again. *Had Rutger killed Jennie?* If he had and Rem knew... He closed his eyes and tried to think. Where had Rem gone?

Daniels opened his eyes and turned the picture over. Two words were written on the back. *Come alone.*

"Oh, shit," said Daniels, his fingers shaky. He raced to the front door and opened it.

His suspicions were confirmed. Rem's car was gone.

Chapter Thirty-One

MADISON TRIED THE DOOR, but it was locked. She banged on it, yelling for help, but heard nothing. Turning, she faced the room she was in. It looked like an old bedroom, with deteriorating curtains on the walls and a dilapidated mattress on the floor. A beaten-up wooden chair sat beside a nicked wooden table, where a lighted candle provided the only illumination in the room. The windows were shuttered, and she'd tried to pry the wooden slats free, but they hadn't budged. An occasional skitter on the warped floor confirmed that there were likely mice living in the mattress. That was bad enough, but the smell frightened her the most. The scent of gasoline permeated the room.

She stepped back and leaned against the door, wondering where she was. The last thing she'd recalled before waking up in this room was taking out the trash. She'd dumped the bag in the dumpster, and some strange heaviness had come over her and she'd found it hard to breathe. She'd stumbled and fallen to her knees, trying to call out for help, but the oppression had overwhelmed her. Everything had gone dark. She had a vague memory of being carried away, but couldn't remember anything else.

The next thing she knew, she was here, but she'd felt a familiar presence. It was the same sensation she'd felt when she'd encountered the man in the woods after Donald had died. That same man was nearby, and she knew it was Rutger.

Trying the knob again, she called out and banged again, knowing it was pointless. Rutger had a plan, and she suspected he was using her to lure Jill and Jace.

Staring at the doorknob, she remembered the rock in Rem's backyard. Raising her hand, she did her best to clear her mind, trying to ignore her fear, but it was a challenge. She did her best to focus on opening the door, seeing the knob turning in her mind. Breathing deeply, she pushed outward, recalling the rock and how it felt to move it. Nothing happened at first, but she kept at it, hoping she could prevent whatever Rutger had planned.

She pushed harder, feeling the energy move through her, and almost yelled in relief when the knob turned. Focusing harder, she turned the knob more. There was a click, and the door opened.

Relief soared through her, and she took a step toward it, but stopped short when the door swung open, and she saw Rutger leaning against the frame.

He smiled at her. "You've been practicing."

Madison stepped back, her heart thumping fast.

"I'm afraid it's too little, too late, though. Your time is running out." He checked his watch. "Quickly."

"What am I doing here?" she asked, trying to keep her voice from shaking.

He stared, his face impassive. "It's the beginning of the end, sis. It's what you and the others have been waiting for."

"What do you mean?" she asked.

"You'll see," he said. "It won't be long now." He straightened. "I have some unfinished business to deal with, but then we'll get to the main event." He paused. "When the time comes, I'm going to need you to make a phone call."

Intuitively, Maddie knew what he wanted. "I'm not going to let you use me as bait to hurt anyone."

He grinned. "Then you'll have a decision to make. It's the phone call or watch another suffer. What will you do, Maddie?" He checked his watch. "My first guest is due here soon. It's the phone call or his life. The decision will be yours."

Madison's dream flickered in her head. "Don't ask me to do that. No one needs to get hurt."

"Oh, yes, they do. Enjoy your time to consider your decision. I'll be back." He started to shut the door.

"Wait," said Madison. "Can't we talk?" She took a step closer, despite her terror.

His face remained flat. "Why? So you can try to convince me you care? Did you really think that would work? Talk is cheap, Maddie. I prefer action. And this action is long overdue." He flicked a thumb at the table. "And be careful with the candle. Knock it over and this place will go up like the Hindenburg. You're lucky the fumes haven't ignited."

"Don't do this," said Madison. "Please. Think about what you're doing."

He stepped back and started to close the door. "Thinking is all I ever do. I'm looking forward to when the thinking stops." He swung the door closed, but poked his head in. "And by the way, I turned the knob. Not you." He shut the door, and Madison heard the lock click into place.

· · · · •• · • • · ·

Daniels yanked his phone out and dialed Rem's number. It rang with no answer. The voicemail picked up. "Shit. Shit. Shit," said Daniels, closing the door. He stabbed a finger at Jill, who bit her lip in worry. "Talk to Sonia. Get that address."

She nodded and ran up the stairs.

Daniels heard the beep and left a message. "Rem. Listen to me. Don't do this. He's waiting for you. You go in there alone, you're a sitting duck. Please, tell me where you're going. Let me help. I need you to call me back. Please." He paused and took a breath. "We'll do this together. I saw the picture and you're doing exactly what he wants." He hung his head. "I don't want you dead, partner. Please, call me."

He hung up, praying Rem would get in touch, but also knowing what his partner would be feeling right now. Rem would want revenge, and Rutger knew it.

Daniels took the stairs two at a time. Sonia was standing, and Jace was holding her elbow. "Sonia," he flew into the room. "We have to find that house. Now."

"She says she can take us there," said Jill. "Go get the car."

"Where the hell is Rem?" asked Jace.

"We'll tell you on the way. Come on. We have to hurry," said Jill, guiding Sonia.

"I'm okay, dear. I can walk," said Sonia. "Hurry, detective. We don't have much time."

"Grab my keys," said Jill. "We'll take my car."

Daniels flew down the steps, grabbed Jill's keys from the table, ran out to the driveway, and jumped into the car. He started the ignition, and the engine roared to life. He could see Jace and Sonia step out onto the front porch with Jill behind them.

He checked his phone again, prepared to dial Rem's number once more, when it rang. It was Rem. His fingers shaking, Daniels answered. "Rem? Where are you?"

He heard heavy breathing, and a sputtered voice. "He killed her," Rem stammered. "That bastard killed her." He could barely get the words out.

Daniels' heart sank, and he bit back his own anguish. "Let me help you, buddy. Don't do this alone. Please tell me where you're going."

"He had a fucking *picture* of her," Rem yelled. "Oh, God." His voice fell again. "All this time. All this time..." His pained voice trailed off.

"Rem." Daniels tried to keep his voice calm. "You're playing right into his hands. You can't face him alone. He'll kill you. It's what he wants. Just tell me where you're going." He heard a strangled sob. "Rem...please." He closed his eyes, knowing if he didn't get through to Rem, he'd likely never see his partner again. "Let me help you."

Rem's breath caught, and he moaned. "I'm going to kill him, Daniels. I am going to find him and kill him. He'll pay for what he did to her. If I get close enough, I am going to rip his throat out. I want him to know the pain. I want him to die."

"I know, Rem. I know," said Daniels. "I get it. Just, please, wait for help."

Jace and Sonia reached the car, and Jill opened the door.

"There's no more waiting," said Rem, his voice stronger. "I'm doing this. Alone."

Daniels pleaded. "Rem, you can't. I don't want to lose a partner tonight. Losing Jennie will be mild in comparison."

There was a brief pause, and Daniels heard Rem's labored breaths before he heard a quiet whisper. "I'm sorry," and the line went dead.

Chapter Thirty-Two

REM TURNED DOWN A dirt driveway, passing under a wrought-iron gate. His headlights illuminated the words on the gate, but he didn't bother to read them. His mind was a whirlwind of pain, fury, and grief. He could still see the picture of Jennie, standing at the edge of the canyon, playfully holding out her arms and smiling. He didn't understand it at first. Why would her picture be in the envelope? But then he'd pulled out the other piece of paper. The number 0212 had been on it, written in pencil, plus a list of names. Rick, Donald, Justin, Hendrix, Alba, Peter...and Jennie.

It had taken him a second, but then it had hit him, and the realization had almost brought him to his knees. Everything had gone silent, and all he could hear was the rushing of the blood in his ears. It felt like he'd been stabbed in the heart, and he'd fought to breathe as his vision swirled. He'd almost bellowed in anguish. It couldn't be true. It couldn't. Rutger had taken Jennie's life? He'd stared again at the picture, disbelieving the truth, and he'd flipped it over, hoping and praying there was some mistake, and it wasn't really her. But he'd seen the words *Come alone*, and he'd known. It was not a mistake.

Looking back at the sheet of names, he'd seen the address. The pain and grief had turned to rage, and he'd dropped the picture, unable to look at it, and grabbed his keys and ran for the car. He knew then that Rutger would die.

He drove as the memories swam in his mind. Jennie had been hit by a drunk driver while on her way home from a girl's night out. What had Rutger done to cause it? What had Rem missed? How had he not known that the woman he loved had been murdered? He'd slammed his palm on the steering wheel, multiple times, and picked up his speed, driving recklessly through the city streets, running red lights and stop signs. Tears stung his eyes, but he bit them back, too enraged to cry.

Daniels had called, but he hadn't had the strength to answer, but then, knowing what he was about to do, he understood it might be his last talk with his partner. He'd called back, emotional and in despair, but unable to give his partner what he wanted. Rem would face Rutger on his own.

After the call, he'd turned off his phone, and as the city lights faded, Rem found himself on quieter roads. The asphalt turned to farmland with wide stretches of open fields and patches of trees, and he'd found the turnoff. He drove down the long dirt driveway and came to a stop in front of an old farmhouse. The windows were dirty and shuttered, the steps to the entry sagged and the railing around the porch had fallen down. No lights were on that he could see, but he saw what looked like the flicker of candlelight through a cracked piece of wood.

He stopped the car, killed the ignition, and opened the door. All he heard were the peaceful sounds of an evening in the country. The crickets chirped, and the frogs croaked, but he heard nothing else.

Leaving his phone in the car, he pulled his weapon and held it at his side. Looking around, he saw nothing and walked toward the front door.

· · • • • · • • • · ·

Daniels drove like a madman, allowing Sonia to direct him, praying that she knew where Rem was headed and that it was in the same place as Madison. If Sonia had seen Madison and Rem was headed somewhere else, then the game was lost. Maybe not for Madison, certainly for his partner. But he couldn't let himself think the worst. It made sense that Rem was heading toward Rutger, and Rutger would be with Madison.

Jill tried to call again, but Rem's phone went to voicemail. Jace sat with Sonia in the back seat. After telling him about Jennie, he'd remained quiet.

"Get off the highway. Here," said Sonia, pointing.

Daniels jerked the wheel, tires squealing, seeing the patches of open land appear in his headlights and under the occasional streetlamp, and prayed they'd get there in time.

· · • • · • • • ·

Rem approached the front door and didn't bother to knock. He opened it and the creaking door swung wide. Stepping inside, he immediately smelled gasoline, and he saw an open kitchen on his right, with lighted candles perched on a countertop. What would have been used as a large family room stood empty in front of him, illuminated only by the candles. A cement floor with bits of debris and a broken brick fireplace were all that greeted him. Off the main room was a hallway and Rem could see a closed door, but beyond that, it was darkness.

Footsteps sounded and Rem went still, eyeing the hall, waiting, his weapon in his hand.

The footsteps neared, and Rutger turned the corner, wearing a T-shirt, jeans and his customary hoodie, but his head was uncovered. He stopped when he saw Rem, crossed his arms and leaned casually against the door frame.

"Glad you got my message," he said.

Rem itched to raise his weapon and shoot, but he knew what this man could do, and he forced himself to wait for a vulnerable moment to take the shot. He did his best to keep his cool, but he rubbed his thumb against the metal of his gun. "I got it."

"Sorry to be the bearer of bad news, but it was time you knew." He straightened. "I'd been dreaming of telling you. It's been almost two years now."

Everything in Rem screamed to kill this man, but he needed some answers. "Why?" he asked, his throat almost closing. "Why Jennie?"

Rutger's face hardened. "Grief needs to be shared, don't you think? And since you put Maia behind bars, which led to her and my child's death, I thought it was an appropriate response."

Rem tried to think through his outrage. "I did my job. What happened to her wasn't my fault, and it sure as hell wasn't Jennie's."

"Bad things happen to good people all the time, detective. I've learned to live with it. I figured you, Jill, Jace and Madison could use a dose of it, too." Rutger stepped out from the hallway.

Rem braced himself, but Rutger stayed near the perimeter. "You're in-sane," said Rem. "You had your chance to live a normal life."

Rutger swiveled, his face a mask of anger. "You're right. I did." He raised a hand. "This house? I bought it for me and Maia. I even named it for her. I used to call her my pretty peach." He chuckled with disdain. "I thought we'd live here and raise a family, but then she left. Told me she'd found someone else. Moved on. I didn't expect that to last, though. Maia frequently tired of men and always came back to me. But this time was different. It was around that time, while I waited, that I decided to find my siblings. I found Jill first. She was knee deep in trying to find a serial killer in Seattle, but was happily involved with someone." Rutger stared off. "It pissed me off. I was tired of being miserable. She shouldn't escape it any more than me, so I killed Rick." He smiled, but his eyes never changed. "I'd felt like I'd found my calling. No one was looking for me. They all blamed the Artist."

Rem held his breath, trying to understand this madness. "She's your sister. Why hurt her?"

He shot Rem an evil look. "Because it made me feel better. What part of that is so hard to understand?" He snickered. "And just because she's my sister doesn't make her worth saving. She has her faults, just like me." He cocked his head and the side of his lip raised. "Did she tell you about Neil Wilder?"

Rem's heart thudded. "Who the hell is that?"

"Doesn't really matter anymore, because you'll be dead and so will she, but just so I can have the satisfaction of telling you, Neil Wilder is a man who's taken an interest in Jill and Jill didn't turn him down." He made a tsk-tsk sound. "Women can be cruel creatures."

"You're a liar," said Rem.

"Believe what you want, but you should know by now that I don't lie." He shook his head. "It happens to the best of us, but it doesn't matter. Not anymore."

Rem's body trembled with anger and disbelief. He steered the conver-sation away from Jill. "Why did you try to shoot me through the window? Why not just kill me like you did everyone else, and leave Jennie out of it?"

Rutger's eyes narrowed and flashed. "Something about you pisses me off. Maybe because I see myself in you. The man I could have been." He sneered. "I wasn't aiming at you through that window. I was aiming at Lozano. I wanted to make you suffer a little more before I killed you. Maybe it was an overreach on my part, but I tend to be impulsive. I got greedy, though, and tried to take out Lozano and your partner with one shot. If I hadn't hesitated one second too long, they'd both be dead now, and you'd be begging me to kill you."

"You're insane."

"I am," he said. "Tends to happen when you're an experiment gone bad." He stepped from the wall, his posture rigid. "Now," he said. "Let's get to the good stuff." He smiled smugly. "After finding Jill, I wanted to go after Madison next, but not long after Rick's death, I discovered Maia was in jail. I hoped again that maybe I could still have what I wanted. I just needed her to get released, and then I learned she was carrying my child. Imagine my elation. I thought maybe things would be different." He clenched his hands into fists. "But then my baby was born. I knew Maia's mother was taking her, and I planned to wait until Maia was free, and we'd pick the child up together, come back here, and raise her. But then..." He stopped and swallowed. "It all went away." He eyed Rem with a hard gaze. "The baby died, and Maia took her life soon after."

Rem shook his head. "None of that is my fault."

Rutger's face twisted. "Yes, it is. If it hadn't been for you, and Hendrix and Alba, she'd never have been in jail. Her stupid brother Peter, Sonia's little helper, left her there and did nothing. After I shot him, he kept moaning about Maia, so I stuffed the paper in his mouth to shut him up. Maia was no more than a piece of dirt on his shoe. After I lost her, I sought the people responsible, and I targeted you first. But then I saw you one day, with Jennie, laughing and smiling, and I knew what I was going to do."

Rem clenched his gun, eager to use it.

"I wanted you to know my grief. I wanted you to hurt. So, I waited for my chance, and the time came when she was alone, driving down a street. I was following her, and all it took was a slight course correction. My gifts made it easy. I saw the driver coming toward her, and I even saw the slight weave he made while he drove in his lane, and I simply jerked his wheel and hers, at just the right time, and then…" He offered a contented chuckle. "…it was over."

The bile rose in Rem's throat and before he could stop it, he bellowed in outrage, raised the gun, and fired.

· · · · ● · ● · · · ·

Madison stood at the door, listening. She'd tried with no luck to turn the handle, and that's when she'd heard the voices. Two men were talking. She almost banged on the door, but Rutger's words haunted her. Was this the person Rutger would harm if she didn't make the phone call? Indecision tore at her heart. What should she do? Listening against the wood, she tried to make out what was said, or who it was. The words were hard to discern, but she recognized Rutger's voice and the other sounded like Remalla. Her heart thudded harder. Had Remalla found her? Were Jace and Jill nearby? Or was it Rutger's plan to threaten Remalla's life in exchange for her compliance?

Desperate, she reached for the doorknob again. She had to get out of here before it was too late. Focusing, she tried again to turn the lock when she heard a shout. Two loud shots rang out, and she jumped back from the door.

· · · · ● · ● · · · ·

Daniels stopped in front of a rusty iron gate. They were on Pine Street, which matched with Sonia's description of a road named after a tree. Jill looked out the window and read the name on the gate. "Pretty Peach Farm." She looked back. "That sounds like your fruit reference."

"It's definitely a farm," said Jace.

"This is it," said Sonia. "I'm sure of it." She wrung her hands. "Hurry, detective. There isn't much time."

Daniels wrenched the wheel, and the car bounced along the dirt driveway. In the distance, as the headlights beamed, he saw Rem's car. "That's him." He pulled over and stopped.

"What are you doing?" asked Jace.

"I can feel Madison nearby," said Jill. "She's in the house."

Daniels turned off the ignition and headlights. "We'll go in from here. I don't want to announce our presence if we don't have to." He spoke to Sonia. "You stay here. Wait for us. I'll leave the keys. Get out if you need to."

Jill popped the glove compartment and pulled out a gun and a flashlight. "Take them, Sonia. If you need the gun, don't hesitate to use it."

"I could never use a gun," said Sonia.

Jace exited the car and leaned into the window. "You do what you need to do to protect yourself. If he comes here, shoot him."

"But what about you, Jill?" asked Sonia. "Don't you need it?"

Jill raised her pant leg and unholstered another weapon. "I came prepared."

"Oh, dear," said Sonia. "What about the flashlight?"

"Can't use it. It could give away our position," said Jill.

Daniels pulled his own gun, his eyes adjusting to the moonlight. He spoke to Jace and Jill. "You find Madison. I'll find Rem."

Jill and Jace stood beside him. Jace held the manilla envelope and ripped it open. He reached in and pulled out a plastic-capped syringe filled with a dark liquid and tossed the envelope aside. "Just get me close to him," he said to Jill, tucking the syringe into his back pocket.

"Be careful with that thing," said Jill.

Jace growled. "You worry about you and Madison. Let me deal with Rutger."

Sonia stuck her head out. "Please, be careful. Remember, Jace. You can block him, but you might block Jill and Madison, too. Do your best to just focus your attention on him. That will help."

"I don't think that's going to be a problem," said Jace.

Daniels watched the house, eager to move. "You both watch your backs. This guy won't go down easy. If you can get Madison out, then do it. We can deal with Rutger later."

"The hell we will. After what he's done, that bastard dies tonight," said Jace. "If Rem hasn't killed him already."

Daniels checked his weapon. "You ready?"

Jill inspected her gun. "I'm ready."

A shout and two shots blasted through the silence. Daniels startled and cursed, then took off in a sprint.

Chapter Thirty-Three

RUTGER TWISTED AWAY, THE bullets narrowly missing him and hitting the wall. The gun flew out from Rem's hand and skittered across the floor toward Rutger. A heavy force gripped Rem's chest, and he was lifted and shoved backward, slamming against the fireplace and hitting his head. Blood gushed down the side of his face and neck, and he was momentarily stunned.

Dizzy, but pushing himself to his knees, Rem searched for his weapon, and stopped cold when he saw Rutger pick it up. Rutger studied it and then aimed it at Rem. "I think our little chat is over." He cocked his head for a moment, like he was hearing something. His eyes narrowed, and Rem thought he heard him curse and mutter 'Sonia,' and then he stomped to the closed door in the hallway. He waved a hand, and it opened.

Rem heard a female voice and Rutger yanked Madison out by the arm.

"Looks like our party is starting early," said Rutger. "But there's always plan B."

He shoved Madison down the hall. She shrieked and fell.

"Leave her alone," said Rem, wiping the blood from his face. "If you need to take somebody, take me."

Rutger sneered. "Don't worry. I'm taking all of you." He held the gun on Rem. "Get in the room, Detective."

Rem hesitated. "We weren't finished talking."

"Maybe not, but our time is up." Rutger raised a hand, and Rem was violently pulled forward, dragged across the ground, and tossed into the room.

Madison screamed, and Rutger yelled at her to shut up.

Bumped and bruised, Rem lay on his side, his head bleeding and his ribs aching.

Rutger raised the weapon. "No hard feelings, detective, but I need you out of the way." Rem heard the cock of the gun, saw Rutger take aim, and he rolled as Rutger fired at him. He felt a pinch of pain in his leg, and he banged against the far wall. He waited for the final shot, but none came.

"That ought to do for now," said Rutger. He grabbed the doorknob. "Give my regards to Jennie." He cocked his head, and the candle slid off the table and landed on the floor. A flicker of flame caught, ran across the room, and ignited the curtains.

Madison screamed again.

"It's been fun," said Rutger, and he closed the door behind him.

· · · ·•·•· · ·

Madison hit the ground hard in the hallway at the same time as Rem was thrown into the room. She screamed, Rutger fired and then the hallway brightened with instantaneous light and heat, and she knew what had happened. Rutger had ignited the gasoline.

She tried to run when an invisible hand held her ankle, and she couldn't get free. Rutger closed the door and reached for her, yanking her up beside him and dragging her to the room next to the one she'd been in.

"Don't. Please."

He shoved her into a dark area with no light.

"I'd leave you with him, but this will give me more time." He paused. "No hard feelings. For the record, I did you a favor with Donald. And personally, I think we could have been friends."

Madison pleaded. "You don't have to do this."

"Yes, I do." And he slammed the door shut on her.

Madison ran up to it, trying to open it, but it wouldn't budge. She banged on the door, yelling for help, feeling the heat build and smelling the smoke coming from the other room. Rem would burn to death in minutes, and she would be next if they didn't get out.

Desperate, she pounded again on the door.

· · · ·•·•· · ·

Daniels jumped up the front steps of the house. The door was open, and he ran in, swinging his gun wide, looking for Rem. The room was empty though and lighted only by two candles on a kitchen counter.

Jace and Jill ran up behind him just as they heard pounding and a scream for help.

"It's Madison," said Jill, running toward a dark hallway.

Daniels smelled smoke. Seeing another closed door, he saw a bright light beneath it.

Jill and Jace ran to an adjacent door, where Madison screamed again.

"Hold on," yelled Jace, and he slammed his shoulder into the wood. The frame cracked, and he hit it again. The wood buckled and gave way.

"Rem," yelled Daniels. Where was he? Something about the other closed door scared him and he tried it, but it was locked. He banged on it. "Rem."

Jace pulled Madison out. "He's in there," she screamed. "Rutger threw him in and set the room on fire."

Daniels holstered his weapon and slammed on it with his fist. "Rem, can you hear me?" The smoke curled out from beneath the door and fear slammed into Daniels' chest. Sweat trickled down his back. He tried the door again, hoping his partner was still alive.

Jill put her gun in her waistband, ran over, and yelled against the frame. "Rem?"

"Let me try," said Jace, pushing Daniels aside. He banged his shoulder against it, but the door didn't budge.

· · · · ● · ● · · · ·

Rem bit his lip against the pain. The pinch in his leg had intensified into wicked burning agony, but besides his injuries, the heat was rapidly escalating. The curtains were fully engulfed, and he raised his hand against the flames, which licked up the walls and onto the ceiling.

He had to get out of there, but his leg throbbed, and he was losing blood fast. He thought he heard voices, but the sound of the fire muffled everything. Sliding against the floor, he pulled himself to the wall farthest from the flame and closest to the door. The fire grew, and his skin burned with the heat.

Coughing through the haze of smoke, he took off his jacket and covered his mouth. Sweat poured off of him, and he realized that this was it. The hot air was making it harder to breathe and his eyes began to burn and water.

Desperate, he made a last-ditch effort to reach for the door. His vision swam, and he could barely move his arm, much less his body, when he heard a loud bellow and a crack. The frame gave way. The door flew inward and Jace fell into the room.

····•··•···

Daniels held his arm up against the heat and flame, and saw Rem lying on the floor beside the door, holding his jacket over his mouth as blood ran down his sweaty face and a circle of it pooled beneath him.

Daniels squatted beside him and grabbed an arm. "Help me get him up."

Jace stood and came over. He took Rem's other arm, and they yanked him to a standing position. Daniels got under him and threw Rem's upper body over his shoulder and carried him out. The flames licked higher as the ceiling caught and ignited.

Daniels ran out into the main room as Jace closed the broken door as best he could. Daniels headed for the front door. "We have to get out of here."

"Go with him," Jace yelled at Jill and Madison.

The door that had been open up front was now closed and Daniels tried to open it, but it wouldn't move. "Shit," he yelled. "It's locked."

Jill ran up and tried it. "He's stopping us from leaving."

Madison banged on a thick slat of wood beside the door. "Try here."

Jill saw it was a shuttered window. Avoiding the shards of broken glass, she pushed and shoved on it, but it didn't move. Kicking out, she busted out the glass and continued to kick against the wood.

Smoke curled into and enveloped the room, and Daniels coughed. So did the rest of them.

"Let me try," said Jace. He tried to break the door open, but it opened inward, and he didn't have enough strength. He tried to ram the covered window with his shoulder, but the wood didn't budge.

"Shoot it out," said Daniels, coughing.

Jill reached for the gun at her waist, but it flew out of her hands and fell at her feet at the same time as Daniels' weapon leaped from his holster, fell on the floor and dragged across the cement.

Jill swiveled, ready to pick up her weapon, but stopped. Daniels turned and saw Rutger standing opposite the room from them, holding a gun.

The intensity of the smoke increased, and Daniels was finding it harder and harder to breathe. He stepped back, still holding Rem, who moaned and coughed. Slowly, Daniels lowered Rem and put him on the ground near the exit. He grabbed Rem's jacket and wiped his partner's face with it, trying not to show the alarm he felt at seeing the amount of blood running down his partner's leg. "Hang in there, buddy." He put the jacket back up to Rem's face and tied it around Rem's neck to help it stay in place. Then he turned and faced Rutger.

Rutger grinned. "Welcome to the party,"

· · · · ●· ●· · · ·

Jace took a step forward, his mind racing. "What are you doing? This place is going up in flames." He had to almost yell as the sound of the encroaching fire made it hard to hear.

"Keep your distance," said Rutger. He held a gun and aimed it. "The farther the better. I don't need you hampering me, but even if you did, you can't hamper this." He waved the gun.

"You're crazy," yelled Jill. "Are you going to let us all burn to death?"

Madison held her arm over her mouth. "Let us out of here."

"Yes, Jill. That's exactly what we're going to do," said Rutger. "Consider this our ultimate send off. We'll all go out in a blaze of glory." He paused. "Too bad Sonia isn't here. After reading her notes and her plan to poison me, it would have been fitting. But maybe it's for the best. She'll have to live with the loss, which will finally do what I couldn't. Destroy her."

The ceiling above them began to burn, and heat bloomed in the room. Jace took another step closer. "Let them go. I'll stay." He coughed and wiped the sweat from his brow. "We'll go down together."

"No," said Madison. "We're all getting out. You, too," she said to Rutger. "There's still a chance to make this work. We are not your enemies."

Jace slid his hand into his back pocket and pulled out the syringe. He didn't know how close he could get to Rutger while Rutger held the gun, but he wanted to be prepared. He popped the plastic lid off the needle.

Jill came up beside him, standing close enough that he could feasibly hand the syringe to her without Rutger seeing it.

"Rutger. Dean. Please," said Jill. "Don't do this. It doesn't have to end this way."

"Give us a chance to be a family," said Madison. She held her mouth and coughed. "It doesn't have to be like this."

Flames escaped from the room where Rem had been held and the old wallpaper was peeling and curling up the wall. Jace knew they didn't have much time. The smoke alone would take them first.

Rutger stood there, as the pop and crackle of the fire grew, and the ceiling began to creak and moan.

"My family is dead," said Rutger, and he looked over at the kitchen. The candles on the counter began to move and slide toward the edge.

· · · · · · · · · · ·

Jill saw them and realized what would happen. "No," she yelled. The inhalation required almost made her double over with coughing.

Jace shot forward, intent on stopping Rutger. The gun discharged, and Madison screamed. Jace slammed Rutger into the far wall, fighting for the weapon.

Daniels dashed over, grabbing for the candles. They'd slowed in their momentum, and he stopped one, but the one on the further end perched on the edge, and almost stopped, but it tilted and went over. Jill pulled Madison back as the kitchen lighted up in flames.

Daniels pitched backward, holding his arms up as the flames flickered to life. The curtain over the kitchen window ignited, and the fire ran up the wall to the ceiling.

In Jace's attempt to take the gun, the syringe flew from his grasp and Jill saw it bounce across the floor. She lunged for it, and almost had it when Rutger, flailing against Jace, kicked out and knocked it away.

Daniels jumped into the fray, trying to help Jace. The gun discharged again, and Jill felt a sting in her arm. The bullet had barely missed her.

Seeing the syringe on the floor near the kitchen, Jill reached for it again, but the heat and fire reared up and Jill fell back. Looking behind her, she saw Madison leaning against the fireplace, her eyes shimmering in the light, and Rem, his face ashen, still lying against the wall. His jacket had fallen from his face, but he'd made no attempt to fix it.

There was a loud crack and Jill looked up, seeing the fire engulf the ceiling. "Get back," she yelled.

Jace struggled with Rutger, who still held the gun. Daniels had gotten behind Rutger, attempting to pull him away, but hearing Jill's shriek, he saw the ceiling, let go and dodged back, as a piece of fiery beam fell into the room.

Without Daniels' hold on him, Rutger fell forward, knocking Jace back; the beam narrowly missed them. The shift in Jace's balance gave Rutger the advantage, and he punched out and connected with Jace's injured ribs. Jace grunted in pain, but kept his grip on the gun.

Jill frantically searched for her own weapon, knowing it was nearby on the ground, but the smoke was making it hard to see and almost impossible to breathe. Holding her elbow against her mouth, she got down on all fours. Daniels did the same. She looked for Madison but didn't see her, and hearing a guttural yell, she saw Rutger kick and knock Jace back against the wall, causing Jace to lose his hold on the gun. Rutger stepped back, cocking and aiming the weapon.

"No," screamed Jill.

A multitude of shots rang out.

Daniels yelled and jumped around the flaming beam but stopped.

Rutger jolted and bucked, his back arching. His body stilled, and he fired randomly, but away from Jace, who stood frozen against the wall. Rutger's arm fell and, losing his hold on the gun, his knees buckled, and he crumpled to the floor.

Jill, kneeling and dizzy from the smoke, sat in shock, the fire raging through the kitchen and encroaching fast into the main room, and turned to see Madison sitting beside Rem, who held Jill's gun in his hand, aiming it toward Rutger. Rem stared for a moment, blinking and coughing, then dropped his arm.

Jace shot forward, jumping over Rutger, and ran toward the door. Daniels, momentarily stunned, dodged more fiery debris, grabbed Jill's arm and pulled her back toward Rem.

Jace, his shoulder bloody, rammed against the door again, but it didn't budge.

Jill, barely able to see through the smoke, and her breathing becoming more labored, couldn't get enough oxygen to speak. She held her shirt over her mouth as Madison coughed and sputtered. She kicked out at the window, but the slat across it was heavy and the fresh wood wouldn't move.

Daniels took the gun Rem held and aimed it when shots rang out. They all dropped low, and Jill tried to see where they were coming from. Additional shots were fired and Jill saw the wood at the door lock begin to splinter and crack.

"She's shooting at the door," said Daniels, his voice raspy. He aimed his gun as well, and fired several rounds, low and toward the ground. The wood splintered more.

Jace raised his foot and slammed it against the frame. The lock began to give and the wood around it splintered more and broke. Daniels joined him, standing and kicking at the door. It cracked, snapped, and Jace grabbed and pulled. The lock gave way, and the door swung open just as the roof groaned and more debris fell.

"Go, go, go," yelled Jace. Jill grabbed Madison, and they ran as Jace and Daniels picked up Rem and followed them out, just as the ceiling collapsed.

Chapter Thirty-Four

DANIELS RACED PAST SONIA, who stood on the porch, holding Jill's gun and the flashlight. Carrying Rem with Jace's help, they got to the grass, lowered Rem, and collapsed to the ground, coughing and gagging.

Jill and Madison sank to their knees, soot-covered and gasping.

Sonia ran over, bobbing the flashlight, her face frantic. "Are you okay? I saw the fire. I tried to open the door."

There was a loud pop and crash, and Daniels saw a wall crumble as smoke billowed from the doorway and roof. A window shattered, and the inferno grew, completely engulfing the house.

Jill crawled over and took the gun from Sonia and put it in the back of her waistband. "We're okay," she said, her voice rough from the effects of the smoke.

Daniels, after getting some deep breaths of clean air, made it to Rem's side. He blinked and wiped his burning eyes. His partner's eyes were closed, and his sweaty face was pale, bloody, and dark with soot. "Rem," he tried to speak, but he coughed instead.

Rem didn't respond.

"Sonia," Daniels sputtered, "bring the flashlight." Sonia aimed the light and Daniels got a closer look at Rem's leg. "Shit," he said. "He's been shot."

Jace stumbled over, blood running down his arm. "How is he?"

"Not good," said Daniels. He pulled his belt off and wrapped it around Rem's leg, making a tourniquet. He looped it through and pulled, trying to slow the bleeding.

Jill checked his pulse. "Daniels, it's weak." She put her cheek against his mouth. "God. I don't think he's breathing."

Daniels held pressure against his partner's leg, but a freezing gust of terror ran through his veins. He tried not to think about how much blood Rem had lost. "Come on, Rem. Don't do this."

Jill hovered over Rem, tilting his jaw back and opening his airway. A jagged spasm made her cough, and it took her a few seconds, but then she began mouth-to-mouth, giving him two full deep breaths. Rem's chest rose and fell.

Daniels checked Rem's pulse, trying to stifle his own urgent need to cough but failing. Jill was right. He could feel a heartbeat, but it was faint and rapid. "Rem, listen to me. Now is not the time. You need to breathe." He stared upward. "Jennie. Help me out here. Don't take him yet. Please."

Madison crawled over, and Sonia kneeled beside Daniels, her hand over her mouth.

Jace, after another round of coughing and spitting into the grass, scrambled over and put his hands, palms down, on Rem's midsection. "Keep working on him," he said, his voice gruff from the smoke.

"Madison, put your hand on Jace," said Sonia. "He needs all the help he can get."

Madison moved to Jace's side and held his shoulder, while Sonia held the other.

Jace closed his eyes and focused on Rem as Jill continued mouth-to-mouth, stopping only if she needed to catch her breath or cough.

The house burned behind them, but Daniels barely noticed as he held pressure on Rem's leg, continuing to check Rem's pulse, praying it wouldn't stop beating.

"It's okay to come back, Rem," said Madison, quietly. "Please don't leave us."

Jill gave him two more breaths, and Daniels eased slightly on the pressure before tightening it again. He checked Rem's pulse and was encouraged when it felt stronger. "I think it's working."

Jill was about to give another breath when Rem tensed and gasped, attempting to breathe. Jill pulled back and held him, waiting to see if Rem would take over. "That's it. Keep going," said Jill, stroking his cheek. Rem sucked in a labored breath and coughed harshly.

"There you go," said Daniels, a rush of relief coursing through him. "Come on, partner. Breathe."

Jace didn't move, but continued to focus on Rem, until another round of coughing erupted from him, and he had to stop.

Rem made another sputtered breath and made a garbled moan.

"We need to call nine-one-one," said Madison.

Daniels did a quick evaluation in his mind. "Let's get him in the car. By the time an ambulance gets out here and gets him back, it could easily be an hour. We can take him and get him there in half the time." He eyed Madison. "Go pull the car up."

Madison nodded and jumped up. Sonia ran with her with the flashlight, although the fiery house provided plenty of illumination.

Daniels watched Rem, ensuring he continued to breathe. "I'll stay with him in the back seat and keep putting pressure on his leg. Jace, stay with me, and keep working on Rem if you can." Daniels spoke to Jill, who held Rem's head in her lap. "Jill. Call Lozano and the fire department when we get in the car."

Rem's breaths came slowly, interrupted by his hacking and gasping. His eyes opened, but he couldn't seem to focus.

"Rem, can you hear me?" asked Daniels.

Rem mumbled, his eyes blinking and then closing.

"We're going to get you to a hospital. Hang in there," said Daniels, feeling his own lungs burning, and he fought the urge to cough again but lost.

"I think we all need a hospital," said Jace, returning to Rem's side.

"I know," said Daniels. The burning house cracked and popped, and Daniels could feel the intense heat on his back. He eased the pressure briefly on the belt and tightened it again. Rem groaned and gripped at the grass. He coughed again and mumbled something. Daniels thought it sounded like Jennie.

The car pulled up next to them and the headlight beams brightened the ground.

Jill jumped up and opened the back door.

"Ready?" asked Daniels.

"Let's do it," said Jace, and they lifted Rem and eased him into the back seat. Jill slid into the front with Sonia and Madison, and Madison put the car in reverse and shot out of the driveway.

Chapter Thirty-Five

JILL RESTED AGAINST THE pillow in a bed in the emergency room, a bandage on her arm and an oxygen mask over her face, breathing evenly, but still coughing. Madison lay in a bed beside her, her face soot-covered but also wearing an oxygen mask.

She wondered where Jace was, but suspected he was nearby. Daniels had been taken for a chest X-ray, and Jill assumed that she or Madison would be next. After the amount of smoke they'd inhaled, the doctor wanted them to stay the night for observation. Jill worried about Rem. She'd heard nothing after they'd wheeled him in and taken him away.

Coughing again, she lifted the mask. "You okay?" Her voice was hoarse, and her eyes still burned.

Madison nodded, lifting her own mask. "I'm okay." Her voice didn't sound any better than Madison's. "Where Jace?"

"I don't know."

A male voice boomed through the E.R. "I am fine. Where are my sisters?"

Jill sat up, her body aching. "I think we found him."

Madison sat up, too. Curtains had been pulled around them and Madison tried to say 'Jace,' but it came out as a croak.

The curtain swung open and Jace stood there, his face dirty and his clothes filthy. His hair hung in his face, and he had a bloody bandage on his shoulder. Seeing them, his face dropped in relief. "You two okay?"

"We're fine," said Jill. "Where's your oxygen?"

Jace held his chest and coughed. A nurse came over. "You need to lie down, sir. Go back to your bed. We're finding you a room and we need to finish with your shoulder. It shouldn't be much longer."

"They want us to stay overnight. Can you believe that?" asked Jace, his voice strained and his eyes bloodshot. "Where the hell are Daniels and Remalla?"

"Daniels is getting a chest x-ray. I guess we all are," said Jill. "I don't know where Rem is. I haven't heard anything." Her chest hurt from talking and she put the mask back on her face.

"Sir, you need to go back to your bed," said the nurse.

"I'll go back in a second," said Jace, his face pale despite the dirt and soot. "Can you check on a Detective Remalla? He was brought in with a gunshot wound to the leg."

"You need to rest," said the nurse.

Jace sat in a seat beside Madison's bed. "Here. See. I'm resting. I promise. I'll go back to my bed in a second. We just need to know the detective's status. Please."

The nurse looked between the three of them and sighed. "Give me a second."

"Thank you," said Jace.

The nurse swung the curtain shut and left.

Exhausted, Jace's shoulders relaxed, and he laid his head back against the chair.

"You sure you're okay?" asked Madison.

Jace blinked at the ceiling. "I dozed off. Had a horrible nightmare. Flames everywhere. Heat and smoke, and you two were in the house, and I couldn't get you out." He closed his eyes and cleared his throat. "It wasn't pleasant."

Jill tried not to rub her burning eyes. "I guess some habits die hard."

Jace opened his eyes. "I needed to know you were okay."

Jill tried to take a deep breath but ended up coughing some more. "I'm worried about Rem."

"He'll be fine," said Jace. "He felt stronger to me when we brought him in."

"You're sure?" asked Jill.

"Well, I'm not a doctor, but I know what I felt."

"Rem's tough. He'll survive," said Madison.

Jill met Jace's gaze, thinking about what Rutger had done to Jennie. "I hope you're right," she said.

"It might take some time, but he'll manage," said Jace. Jill debated telling Madison about Jennie, but decided there would be another time and place. Besides, she had a different question on her mind. She recalled the burning house, and Madison sitting beside Rem. "Madison," she paused. "Can I ask you something?"

Madison looked over. "What is it?"

Jill almost gave in and rubbed her weary eyes. "When Jace and Rutger were fighting, how did Rem get the gun? There's no way he could have reached it."

Madison pulled her mask down. "I was standing by the fireplace, terrified, watching the flames and feeling the heat, expecting to die, and I looked at Remalla, lying back against the wall. His eyes were glassy and lost, and I thought I should be with him. He shouldn't die alone. I ran over and sat beside him, and that's when I saw it. Your gun was lying on the ground, and he was staring at it, and I knew that's what he wanted. And I focused like I did with the rock, and the gun slid over, right into his hand, just as Rutger took the gun from Jace."

Jace sat up. "You gave him the gun?"

Madison stifled a cough. "Yes. I don't know how I did it, because I could just have easily thrown it back into the fire."

"You saved our lives," said Jill.

Madison pushed up on the bed. "I think we all saved our lives. Sonia was right. We couldn't have done it alone."

Jace held his bandaged arm. "Where is Sonia, by the way?"

"How's your injury?" asked Jill, remembering Jace rushing Rutger and the gun firing.

"It's nothing," said Jace. "Just a graze. Probably need a few stitches."

"You're damn lucky he didn't shoot your head off," said Jill.

"It was that or burn to death. I chose the former and took my chances," said Jace.

The curtain moved, and Jill expected to see the nurse, but a different head popped in.

"Sonia," said Madison.

"Hello, dears." Sonia looked behind her and darted in, closing the drape. "How are you? These silly hospitals. They don't want you to talk to anybody."

"How did you get back here?" asked Jace.

Sonia walked up to Jill's bed. "I find a frail old lady like me looking for her lost sister who's been injured works wonders. Some nice orderly is trying to find my sister right now."

Jace grunted. "You mean your mom, who's having hip replacement surgery?"

"That works too, dear," said Sonia.

"Sonia, if you're old and frail, then I'm a lost cause," said Jill.

Sonia sat on the edge of Jill's bed. "It's all about perception, dear." She sighed. "You sure you're all okay? Nobody would tell us anything."

"Us?" asked Madison.

"Captain Lozano is waiting to hear about his detectives. There's a sea of blue out there. I told him I'd do a little investigating for him."

"He should hire you," said Jill. "You'd be masterful at undercover work."

"Oh, dear. I'd never be good at taking orders," said Sonia.

"I'm guessing Remalla's in surgery, but I think he'll be fine," said Jace. "Jill says they took Daniels for a chest x-ray and apparently we're all next. And they want us to stay overnight, which is silly."

Sonia shook her head. "You've all been through a terrible trauma. I don't think it's silly at all. You inhaled a lot of smoke, and you need to be checked. Let the doctors do their jobs." She patted her chest. "Besides, it will make me feel better."

Jill thought of Rutger. "Sonia, how are you? You've been through a trauma, too."

Sonia went quiet and studied the sheet on the bed. "It's been a long couple of days, actually months, or, if I'm honest, years."

"I'm sorry about Rutger. Despite what he did, I know you were close to him." Madison paused. "Is there something you want done with Rutger's body once they find it?"

Sonia swallowed. "Oh, that's...that's a tough question." She slid her hand over the sheets and Jill could feel Sonia's emotions rising.

"Would you like us to take care of it?" asked Jill.

Sonia hesitated. "Would you mind?"

Jace scowled. "You'll understand if I decline."

Sonia eyed him with sadness. "I understand your anger, and that's your decision to make, but in the end, he was your brother, and as deranged and mad as he'd become, I will always believe there was a part of him that was good." She cleared her throat. "It would be helpful for each of you to find some closure with all of this. Scatter him somewhere pretty. With wide open spaces. He would have wanted that."

"I couldn't give a shit about what he wanted," said Jace.

"I know he did horrible things, Jace, but he also brought us together," said Madison. "None of us would have had any idea about each other without him. That's one good thing he did." Madison nodded at Sonia. "I'll do it. I'll scatter his ashes if they don't want to."

"I'll help you," said Jill. She reached over and took Sonia's hand. "For Sonia."

Sonia smiled and dabbed an unshed tear from her eye. "Thank you."

Jace looked away, his shoulders slumping. "I'll think about it."

Picking up on Sonia's pain, Jill fought back her own tears. "There's something else. We lost your pois..." She lowered her voice. "...I mean, the syringe, in the fire. I suspect it melted and was destroyed."

"Let's hope so," said Jace. He rubbed dirt off his face with the sleeve of his shirt, which was almost as dirty. "That's all we need is for the police to find it."

"No matter," said Sonia. "Even if they found it fully intact, I doubt they'd know what it was, and even if they did, they wouldn't know if it came from you or Dean, unless you choose to tell them."

"Mum's the word," said Jace. "Right?"

"I didn't know it was there in the first place," said Madison.

"I don't even know what you're talking about," said Jill.

Sonia smiled softly, nodded, and looked between them. "It's good seeing you all together. I know I can't take any credit, but I feel a small measure of pride." She sighed. "Like you said, Madison. Dean did something good."

"He wanted us defeated and disempowered," said Jill. "Instead, he got exactly the opposite."

Jace coughed and held his chest.

"You need your oxygen," said Madison.

The coughing spasm passed. "Later," said Jace. "I need to ask something." He spoke to Sonia. "When are we going to hear the truth? This whole..." he waved his hand, "...shitstorm. Dean and us. You and...whoever you worked for. What we can do? What Dean could do." He studied her. "Who are we, and where do we come from?"

Sonia paled and opened her mouth to speak, when the curtain slid open and the nurse stood there, holding a chart. "Jill Jacobs?"

"Yes," said Jill.

"You're up. Chest x-ray." An orderly pushed up a wheelchair.

"Where's Daniels?" asked Jace. "And how's Detective Remalla?"

The nurse offered him a flat stare, as if she'd dealt with numerous patients like Jace. "Detective Daniels is being settled into a room, just like you all will be. But I pray you won't bitch as much as he does." She eyed Jace pointedly. "The other detective is stable. Considering the amount of blood loss, he was doing well when they brought him in. He's in surgery, though, so that's all I can tell you." She put a hand on her hip. "I believe that's your cue to get back in bed and start breathing some oxygen." She raised a brow. "Am I right? Or do I need to raise my voice?"

Jace's face fell. "Fine."

Jill almost smiled. She slid her legs over to stand and get in the wheelchair. "Sonia, will you be here later?"

There was no response. Jill looked, as did Jace and Madison, but Sonia was gone.

Chapter Thirty-Six

REM SAT IN HIS wheelchair, looking over a small pond on the hospital grounds. Three ducks swam together, creating ripples of water, cresting silently over the surface. He sighed.

"Here you go," said Daniels, walking up and holding a Styrofoam cup of coffee. "It's officially Doctor and Daniels approved. I even added sugar."

Rem took the coffee. It was his first cup since waking up in the hospital three days earlier. "Bless you," he said, taking the drink.

"You're welcome." Daniels sat on a bench beside him. "Pretty day."

"Yeah." Rem sipped his coffee.

"Doctor still planning on letting you out of here tomorrow?"

Rem nodded. "So far as I know."

"You start physical therapy on your leg?"

"Did a little this morning. Hurt like hell. But we'll pick it up full force after I go home."

"That ought to be fun. But I bet you're ready to get back on your feet."

Rem set his coffee on the arm of his wheelchair. "I suppose." He rested his elbow beside the coffee. "You talk to Lozano?"

"I did. Once I got out of the hospital and slept for two days." Daniels stared up at the clouds. "He seemed satisfied with all of it. Rutger killed Hendrix, Alba, and Peter, and also Justin Tenley. I told him about Rick Henderson and Donald Vickers, too. Sonia's cleared and the current case is closed. Now there's just the paperwork to start this afternoon. It'll keep me busy until you get back."

"You forgot someone," Rem said quietly.

Daniels paused and frowned. "Sorry. I mentioned Jennie too. Lozano knows."

Rem watched the ducks, still wondering why his life had been spared, and not Jennie's, but he kept his thoughts to himself.

"You haven't said much since you've been here." Daniels shifted toward Rem. "You want to talk about it?"

Rem's heart thumped. "Not really. No."

Daniels nodded. "Okay." He studied his hands. "Jill's supposed to come by. Should be here soon."

Rem watched a duck waddle out of the pond. "How are Jace and Madison?"

"Fine. They spent a night in the hospital like me, and will have to check-in with their doctors. Jace is flying out soon to see Danni. Madison is going home."

"What about Sonia?"

Daniels shook his head. "Nobody's knows. Jill said she showed up in the hospital E.R., but she disappeared afterward." He straightened the cuff on his shirt. "Which sucks because I needed a statement from her."

"Figures. Probably never see her again."

"I guess we'll never know who she really is, or where Jill, Jace, and Madison come from."

"Or who she works for," said Rem. "One of life's great mysteries."

"Truth is stranger than fiction, isn't it?"

"Shit we've seen, that's an understatement."

Daniels chuckled.

They sat for a few quiet minutes, enjoying the sunshine. Rem appreciated Daniels letting him sit with his thoughts, although he knew there would be more to say, but he just didn't have the strength to say it.

Footsteps encroached, and Rem saw Jill walk up. "Hey," she said. "The nurse said I'd find you out here."

"Thought Rem could use some sun. He's looking a little pale," said Daniels. "How are you feeling?"

"Good," said Jill. "Still have the occasional coughing spasm, and sometimes my voice goes a little hoarse, but I'm better."

"Yeah, me too," said Daniels. He slid over. "Have a seat."

"Jace and Madison say hello," said Jill. "Madison's still a little tired, so I told her to stay home. Jace is at the bar, even though I told him to rest, but he's excited to see Danni, so he's getting things in order."

"I'm glad they're doing well," said Rem.

Jill clenched her hands and eyed the pond.

Daniels looked between the two of them. "You know, that coffee looks good. I think I'm going to get some for myself." He stood. "You want any?" he asked Jill.

"No. I'm fine. Thanks."

"Okay," said Daniels. "I'll be back." He patted Rem on the shoulder and walked away.

Rem waited, wondering what to say.

"How are you?" asked Jill.

He adjusted his sitting position, trying to get comfortable. "Hanging in there. Ready to get out of this wheelchair."

"I bet. Have you been doing any walking?"

"They got me up and moving this morning. I took a few steps and almost fell over."

"Yeah, well, give it time. You'll be back up and running around before you know it."

He nodded. Another duck hopped out of the water, following his friend. A few silent moments passed. "We gonna keep doing the small talk thing?"

She crossed her legs. "It's terrible, isn't it? I'm not good at it."

"Me neither." Pausing, he looked over. "What's on your mind?"

She smiled. "I was going to ask you the same thing."

"You really want to know?"

She hesitated. "Gosh. Now I'm nervous." She pulled on a button from her shirt. "Yes. I want to know."

He held her gaze, a thousand questions running through him, but only one kept tugging at him. "Who's Neil Wilder?"

Her jaw dropped. "Neil...? How do you know about Neil Wilder?"

Rem recalled Rutger's satisfaction in telling him. "Take a wild guess."

Looking puzzled, her eyes rounded. "You're kidding. Rutger?"

"Told me right before he shot me."

"Hell."

"And as much as I hate to jump into the rabbit hole that asshole dug for me, I can't help but ask."

She expelled a breath. "It's no big deal. I met him about a month ago at a bar. I was out with friends. We've since shared a cup of coffee and a dinner, but that's it. He tried to kiss me, but...I...I...it took me by surprise, and I spilled coffee on him. Then all this happened, and I haven't seen him since."

Rem absorbed the news, unsure how he felt. But that seemed normal now. He didn't know what to think about anything anymore. "You like him?"

"As a friend, yes."

He hesitated. "Did you tell him about me?"

She paused, and he caught her flinch. "No." She moaned. "And before you ask why, I don't know why. I should have told him. It should have been the first thing out of my mouth." She swept a hand through her hair. "I think maybe I was lonely, and the attention was nice, and I justified it by saying we were just friends."

Rem scratched on the side of his Styrofoam cup, etching marks in its side. "It's hard being long distance, and we hadn't seen each other in a while."

"It's not that hard. And it isn't fair to him, or to you. I'm sorry."

He considered his next words. "Do you want to stay long distance?"

"What do you mean?"

He swiveled his chair to face her. "Is this working for you?"

Jill picked at something on her jeans, and he waited. She spoke quietly. "With everything that's happened, I don't know what's working for me any-more."

Swallowing, he nodded. "I hear you." They sat for several seconds in si-lence, and Rem wondered what to say before he finally spoke. "Listen. You and I have been through a lot."

Jill chucked wearily. "You could say that."

"You've found out that your family is not biological. You don't know who your parents are or understand your origins. You suddenly have two siblings you've just met. You all have these unique...skills...that you're not quite sure how to handle, and you almost died in a fire by your estranged brother's hand." He shook his head. "It's a mess."

She nodded.

"And let's not even start with me. I'm a loaded gun with a broken trigger. And I don't even know if..." He stopped and shut his mouth.

She leaned forward. "What? You don't know if what?"

He watched the ducks.

"You don't know if you want to be a cop anymore?"

Shrugging, he pursed his lips.

She reached over and took his hand. "It's understandable. It's how I felt after Rick died. Nothing made sense. And after learning what Rutger did to Jennie, it's like grieving all over again."

"He took Rick, too," he said, softly. "I know how you feel now."

"Rick had still been murdered, not killed in a supposed car accident."

His chest tightened, and he didn't trust his voice.

Her thumb moved over his hand. "Be easy on yourself. Just take it one day at a time."

She sat with him for a bit and until he began to feel calmer. "Can I be honest?" he asked.

"You know you can."

He fiddled with his medical bracelet. "I think we need some space. Or, at least, I do. Everything is upside down and I can't think straight, much less maintain a healthy relationship, especially from a distance."

Her face furrowed, and she gripped his fingers. "Hell. This whole thing sucks." She took a second. "But you're right. I think we both need it."

Rem put his other hand over hers. "It's true. It sucks. But it will do us both some good. We can figure a few things out and try and find some stable ground again." He saw her eyes shimmer. "Doesn't mean I don't love you, though."

Her hand tightened over his. "I feel the same." She sniffed. "But don't count us out yet, Remalla. Who knows what the future holds?"

He smiled. "Probably vampires and werewolves."

A tear trickled down her cheek, and she wiped it away. "Doesn't seem so crazy anymore, does it?"

Sadness bubbled up, and he took a shuttered breath. "No. It doesn't. Not anymore." He cleared his throat, hearing the ducks quack. "So, when are you headed home?"

She moaned softly. "Tonight, actually. It's why I needed to talk to you."

He didn't want to think about potentially not seeing her again. "Your dad okay?"

"He's struggling. Now that I know what I know, he's got some questions to answer, and he's dreading it. But he can't avoid it anymore."

"God help him. He has no idea what he's in for."

"I think he does, which is why he's dreading it."

Rem removed his hand from hers, and she sat back.

He sighed softly, his chest tightening. "Don't be a stranger, okay?"

Her eyes welled with tears. "You either. Keep me updated. I want to know how you're doing." She pulled a tissue from a pocket and dabbed her nose. "And don't be afraid to ask for help if you need it."

His own tears surfaced. "I'll figure it out. Daniels won't let me fall off the cliff, or at least he won't let me bounce off the bottom and hit twice."

"You know you can always call me if you need to."

"I know, and I will." He cleared his throat and wiped his eye.

They remained quiet for a moment, collecting themselves, until Jill stood. "I guess I should go." She squatted beside his wheelchair. "Shit. I'm going to miss you."

Rem studied her face. "You're a one-of-a-kind Jacobs. Don't let anybody ever tell you different. Especially not Neil Wilder."

She grinned, her eyes sparkling. "Don't worry. Neil's got nothing on you, and he never will." She reached up and stroked his cheek, then leaned in and kissed him.

He kissed her back, smelling her flowery scent, and reached up and stroked her jaw. "Take care of yourself, Jacobs," he said, his voice gruff.

She tweaked his chin with her thumb. "You too, Remalla. Don't eat too many hot dogs." Another tear escaped over her lashes.

"The hot dogs I can handle. It's the tacos you need to worry about."

More tears spilled down her cheeks, and she smiled. Leaning back in, she gave him one more quick kiss and squeezed his hand. "Be safe," she whispered.

"You, too." The words caught in his throat, but he clenched her fingers and then let her go.

She straightened, wiped her eyes with her tissue, and walked away.

· · · ● ● · ● ● · · ·

Daniels pushed the wheelchair down the hall. Jill had left a little earlier, telling Daniels goodbye before she'd gone and letting him know what had happened with Rem.

Daniels had waited, drinking his coffee in the cafeteria, and giving Rem some time, but then had headed back out. Rem had given him grief about getting a sunburn, but Daniels could see Rem's red eyes and the fatigue and sadness behind them.

Now, on the way back to his room, Rem remained quiet, and Daniels made little effort to talk. Waiting at the elevator, Rem shifted in his seat and winced.

"You all right?" asked Daniels. The doors opened, and he pushed Rem in.

"A little sore. Just need to get out of this chair."

Daniels hit the button. "We'll get you back in bed, and you can rest." He swiveled the chair back to face the elevator door. "You want anything from home when I pick you up tomorrow?"

Rem pulled at his gown under the robe he wore. "Clothes would be nice."

Daniels nodded. "I'll pick out your finest pair of holey jeans and your best stained shirt. How's that sound?"

"Don't forget the filthy tennis shoes."

"The ones where your big toe sticks out? Perish the thought."

Rem carefully massaged his injured leg. "I'm still pissed you threw out my clothes and my other pair of sneakers."

The elevator slowed and came to a stop. "Sorry, buddy, but I draw the line at blood-soaked garments. Into the trash they go."

"There is such a thing as a washing machine."

Daniels waited for the doors to open. "How about you don't get shot again? Then you don't have to worry about your clothes getting tossed."

"I'll see what I can do," Rem mumbled as Daniels pushed the chair.

Daniels turned the corner and headed toward Rem's room. The hall was quiet and the only noise was the beeping from a nearby machine and the phone ringing at the nurse's station.

"You heard Jill's leaving?" asked Rem, his voice quiet.

Daniels took his time meandering down the hall. "Yeah. She told me." He paused. "How are you handling it?"

Rem put his elbows on the armrests. "I could easily say I'm fine, but you'd know I'd be lying."

"You two have a lot to work through. It's good to take some time. Figure out what you both want. Doesn't mean it's forever, though."

"Yeah. I suppose."

They reached Rem's room, and Daniels steered Rem inside and toward the bed. Daniels stopped and put on the brake. "You need some help?"

"I think I can manage." Rem pushed up and slowly stood.

Daniels pulled back the bedsheets as Rem turned and sat on the bed. His face tensed, and he held his leg.

"Go slow," said Daniels, moving the wheelchair to the side.

Rem took a second and then lifted his wounded leg and brought it up on the mattress, then fell back against the pillows, his face pale.

"You want to leave the robe on?" asked Daniels.

Breathing harder, Rem looked down at himself. "It's fine. Leave it for now."

Daniels nodded and pulled the sheets up, covering Rem. He found the call button and put it next to Rem's hand. "Here. In case you need the nurse."

"Thanks," said Rem.

Daniels studied him. "Sit up. You look like you're uncomfortable."

Rem groaned and attempted to sit up, and Daniels fluffed his pillows and re-situated them. "That's better."

Rem rested back on the bed with a huff. "You're nicer than my mother, although she'd get me some orange juice."

Daniels rolled his eyes. "Pulp or no pulp, your highness?"

"No pulp."

"Pulp, it is. Give me a sec. I think they have some in the family room." He turned to leave.

"Hey," said Rem.

Daniels paused and looked back, seeing Rem peering up from his sheets and pillows. "What? You want a croissant too?"

Rem pushed the blankets down. He opened his mouth, hesitated, but finally spoke. "I told Jill I didn't know if I could be a cop anymore."

Daniels stood still, but his heart rate picked up, and his blood raced. Standing by the door, he didn't answer, but found a chair and pulled it up next to Rem's bedside. He sat and interlaced his fingers, considering his answer. "That's not surprising." He hung his head. "To be honest, I don't know if I do either."

Rem pushed up higher in the bed. "Are you serious?"

"Why wouldn't I be?" He waved a hand. "Look what it's cost us. You've almost been killed twice. I've been shot, my family's been threatened, and Marjorie has had to take J.P. and get out of town more than once. We lost Jennie to a psychopath who was pissed at you for doing your job." He shook his head. "I think we'd be crazy not to consider it."

Rem leaned back and stared at the ceiling. "I was worried about telling you."

"You shouldn't have been."

Rem hesitated and scratched his head. "Funny thing, though..."

"What's that?"

Rem looked over. "It's hard to imagine not being one. You know?"

Daniels nodded. "I know. Me, too." He lifted a brow. "I hear the circus is hiring. Ever thought of being a clown?"

Rem's eyes widened. "Clowns are terrifying. All that makeup and crazy hair and clothes."

"Who said anything about makeup? You'd fit right in."

Rem made a face. "What are you going to be? The lion tamer?"

"I deal with you every day, so hell, why not?"

"I'd feel bad for the lions."

"They'd be fine. I'd give 'em a clown every morning for breakfast."

Rem snorted.

Daniels went quiet, and so did Rem. After a moment, Daniels straightened, sat back, and crossed his arms. "I have an idea."

"What's that?"

"How about, once you're up and around, we take a few days? Go up to Lozano's cabin. Fish and drink some beer, relax and recharge. No business allowed. No Rutger, no flying objects, no women. Marjorie's been wanting to have her mom come stay for a few days and help with wedding planning, and that will be a perfect time for me to get out of the house. Then, if we want to talk about our options, we can. And if we don't, we don't." He cocked his head. "What do you say?"

Rem adjusted a pillow. "Lozano's cabin, huh?"

"I think it's a great idea."

"Can I do the grocery shopping?"

Daniels narrowed his eyes. "Only if I can join you. I can't eat hot dogs and tacos every night. But I'll buy the beer. How's that sound?"

Rem's eyes lighted up. "Now you're talking."

"I thought you'd like that."

Rem settled back on his pillows. "I'd be a fool to pass that up."

"Then it's settled. I'll talk to Lozano about it." He checked his watch and debated his next words. "I want you to know something though, before I head back to the station and plow into paperwork."

"What's that?"

"Whatever you decide, whether I do the same, is fine with me. You know that, don't you?"

Rem's jaw tightened.

"You do what you want to do, but take some time with it. Don't...don't..." He tried to think of how to say it, but decided to be straight. "...don't let Rutger take something else you love. Okay?"

Rem's fingers curled in the sheets, and he took a heavy breath. "Okay," he whispered. "I'll try."

Daniels patted Rem's arm. "Good."

"You really know how to tell it like it is."

Daniels smiled. "I learned it from my partner."

"There's another thing you should know." Rem wiped a tear-filled eye. "It's going to be another year before I can go near that closet."

Daniels squeezed Rem's wrist. "I think that's a good idea. I doubt I could handle it, either."

Rem sniffed and wiped his face. "You're a good partner, Daniels. Something tells me I'm stuck with you."

"Cop or no cop, that's for damn sure." He swallowed, collecting himself. "You need anything else before I leave this pleasure palace? Still want that orange juice?"

"Nah. I'm gonna try and sleep. You go home. Just don't forget me tomorrow."

"Perish the thought."

Rem chuckled. "Thanks for the pep talk."

Daniels nodded. "You got it." He stood and put the chair back. "I'll be back in the morning. Don't throw any wild parties and get kicked out before I get here, okay?"

Rem grinned, and his face had more color than when they'd entered the room. "No promises. I think Nurse Williams on the night shift is itching to find a reason to dance with me."

"She must be burly if she's planning to hold you up the whole time."

"If I were a betting man, I'd take her against you in an arm-wrestling match."

Daniels smirked. "Remind me not to piss off Nurse Williams."

"You've been warned."

Daniels headed to the door. "I'll see you later. Get some rest. And don't worry about the future, okay? Everything will work out."

Rem settled back and got comfortable. "All I want to do right now is crash. I feel like I haven't slept in weeks." He closed his eyes.

Daniels watched him, hoping he'd said what Rem needed to hear. "See ya," he said. Rem mumbled something, half asleep, and Daniels sighed, flipped the lights off, and left.

Chapter Thirty-Seven

Jɪʟʟ ᴢɪᴘᴘᴇᴅ ᴜᴘ ʜᴇʀ bag and tossed it on the floor in the entry of Rem's home. Hearing footsteps on the stairs, she looked to see Madison coming down them. "You get some rest?"

Madison made a half-yawn. "Yes. I did."

"How's your breathing? Any problems?"

"I'm good. Stop worrying. I'm just tired."

"You have any issues? You get back to the doctor, okay?"

"God. You're like the mother I never had." Madison stepped to the bottom. "You got everything?"

Jill checked the two bags. "Pretty much, but I didn't bring a lot though."

"When's your flight?"

"This evening. We've got some time."

Madison nodded and headed toward the kitchen. "You want some water?"

"Sure. Thanks."

Madison opened the fridge and pulled out two bottles of waters. "You talk to Rem?"

Jill took the water and sat in a kitchen chair, trying to sound cheery. "I did."

Madison sat across from her. "And?"

Jill debated her answer. "And it was fine."

Madison narrowed her eyes. "Oh, hell. You two broke up, didn't you?" Her shoulders fell.

Jill cracked her water open and took a drink. "Not really." She sighed and the heaviness in her chest increased. "But kinda, sorta, yeah." She bit her lip and held her head. "It made sense. He's reeling right now. And, I sort of am too." She paused. "It's hard trying to be there for someone else when you need to take care of yourself first. Especially when I'm not here."

Madison frowned. "I'm sorry, Jill." She leaned forward. "But you know, if you wanted, you could be here."

"I've thought about it. But with my family, and my dad, it just never seemed like the right time." Jill played with the cap from her bottle. "And now, after all of this, and us, and what we know and don't know. To be honest, I'm not sure where I belong anymore."

Madison groaned and rubbed her shoulders. "It's confusing, isn't it? Not knowing where we come from? It messes with your head."

"And I'm guessing Sonia won't be telling us."

"I wonder where she is. And why she left."

"I don't know. We may never know."

The two sat silently pondering, when the doorbell rang, and Jill heard the door open and a male voice speak. "Anybody here?"

Jill stood and peered around the corner. "Jace. I thought you were at the bar and then headed to see Danni?"

Jace walked in and shut the door behind him. He threw a backpack on the floor. "About that." He saw Madison. "Hey, Maddie."

"Hey, Jace. Feeling better?" asked Madison.

Jace took his studded leather jacket off and tossed it over a chair. "Feel better than I have in a while, knowing Rutger's gone."

Madison sighed. "Don't forget. We need to scatter his ashes when we get them."

Jace went to the fridge and grabbed a can of soda. "You agreed to that. Not me."

"I know," said Madison. She looked at Jill. "Any ideas?"

Jace sat beside Jill. "How about a dog park? That's a wide-open space." He opened his soda and took a gulp.

"You're not helping," said Jill.

"I'm completely serious," said Jace. "You think he deserves better than dogs shitting on him every day?"

"You didn't want to help scatter so you don't get a say," said Madison. "Jill and I will figure it out."

"Suit yourself," said Jace.

"Can we think about it later?" asked Jill. "I've reached capacity on decision-making right now." She eyed Jace. "What were you saying when you came in? Are you going to see Danni?"

Jace grinned. "I am. I was about to tell you. You and I are on the same flight."

Jill raised a brow. "We are?"

"Guess which city Danni disappeared to?" asked Jace.

"You're kidding," said Jill. "She went to Seattle?"

Jace dug through a pocket in his jacket. "She did." He pulled out two airline tickets. "I told her to sit tight, and I'd come to her. Nice, huh? You'll get to meet her."

Madison looked at the tickets. "Why do you have two? Is one Jill's?"

"I have mine," said Jill.

Jace chuckled, looking pleased with himself. "Nope. One's yours."

Madison's eyes rounded. "What? Why do I have a ticket?"

Jill took the ticket. "That's a great idea." She spoke to Madison. "You can come with us."

"Come with you?" Madison sputtered. "But...but...I have to go home."

"Why?" asked Jill. "You can paint anytime. Take a few days and go on a trip. When's the last time you had a vacation?"

"You can meet Danni, and we'll all have some fun," said Jace. "It's an open-ended return, so you can come back when you want."

"You can stay with me," said Jill. "I have an extra bedroom. It'll be perfect."

"I haven't packed for a trip," said Madison. "All I have are the few things I brought with me here."

"We have plenty of time," said Jill. "We'll leave early, stop by your place, and you can get what you need, then we'll head to the airport. It won't take that long."

Madison fidgeted. "Are you sure?"

"I wouldn't have bought the ticket if I wasn't sure," said Jace. "I mean, if I'm going to Seattle with Jill, you sure as hell should come with us. We have some catching up to do."

"Will Danni mind?" asked Madison.

"I already told her. She's excited to meet you guys," said Jace. "But I'm planning on some one-on-one time too, so don't be surprised if you two are on your own for a while."

"I can show you around Seattle. It'll be great," said Jill.

"I can pay for the ticket," said Madison.

Jace shrugged. "Forget it. Buy me and Danni a nice fish dinner and we'll call it even."

Madison hesitated, but then smiled. "Okay, then. I'm in."

Jill clapped. "That's great. This is exciting." Madison nodded and held her hand over her mouth. Jill saw her eyes fill. "Maddie, what is it?"

"What'd I do wrong?" asked Jace.

Madison sniffed. "No. It's not that. It's just...I...I've never had this before. You know?" She wiped her eyes. "Like a...family."

Jill reached over and took her hand. "Well, you do now."

Jace groaned, and Jill saw him set his jaw.

"What? Are you getting emotional, too?" She asked him.

His eyes shimmered. "She's right. It's nice...you know...to have this."

Jill took his hand too.

Jace squeezed her fingers. "No matter what happens after today, you two are my people."

Madison's eyes welled up more, and a tear ran down her cheek.

Jill tried not to get emotional, but failed. "God. Look at us. We're a mess." She stood and grabbed some napkins and handed them out. "No matter what we've been through, I'm thankful that it at least ended up in finding you two." She wiped her eyes and blew her nose.

Jace blinked teary eyes. "I sure as hell would like some answers, though."

Madison dabbed her nose. "I think those disappeared with Sonia."

"God. I wonder where she went," said Jace. "And why not tell us the truth?"

Jill, more composed, returned to her seat. "Maybe she couldn't."

"That woman did whatever the hell she wanted," said Jace. "Disappearing saved her ass. She knew we wanted answers."

"Maybe one day," said Madison. "You never know. Sonia could show up on our doorstep, out of the blue."

"That would be like her, wouldn't it?" Jill checked the time. "If we're going to stop by Madison's, we should probably leave in about an hour, so we don't have to rush."

Jace tossed his crumpled napkin on the table. "I'm ready when you guys are. If you want, we can leave now and get some lunch on the way."

The doorbell rang.

Jill stilled, and Jace and Madison looked toward the door.

"You expecting someone?" asked Jace.

"No. Probably a delivery," said Jill, standing.

"You don't think...?" Madison stood, too, her eyes wide. "What if...?"

"You're hoping it's Sonia?" asked Jace. "Yeah. Right."

Jill went to the door just as it rang again and looked out the peephole. "It's not Sonia."

"Who is it?" asked Jace.

"I don't know," said Jill, opening the door.

A tall, lithe older woman with silver hair swept up into a smooth chignon stood at the entry. She wore a sleek red pantsuit with a navy scarf, and she tossed the end of the scarf over her shoulder. Two women and a man stood behind her. Jill didn't recognize any of them. "Can I help you?"

"Jill Jacobs?" asked the woman, holding a small clutch purse under her arm.

A small pulse of pain, like the beginning of a headache, blossomed in Jill's temples. "Yes?"

One of the women from the back looked around and studied Jill.

"Do I know you?" asked Jill.

Jace and Madison came over and stood behind her.

The woman walked in. "You must be Jace and Madison." She put her clutch on the entry and removed her scarf. "We have much to discuss."

"Who are you?" asked Jace.

Jill stepped back as the two women and the man walked in behind the older woman. The man answered. He was tall with a lean build and dark, wavy hair. "Don't mind her. She likes to barge in and disrupt people's lives. It's her calling card."

"I am Morgana," said the woman. "And these are my associates. Ramsey, Gillian, and Sarah. We can get to the pleasantries later, but we're here to talk." She looked around. "Do you mind if we sit?" She stepped into the living room.

Jill held her mouth open, unsure what to say. This strange woman had just taken over, like it was her own home.

The man, who Jill guessed was Ramsey, leaned in. "Just do as she says, and we'll get this over with, and then Sarah and I can continue what was supposed to be a vacation."

"Oh, get over your complaining, Ramsey," said Morgana. "Although I should be used to it by now. It is one of your strengths."

"It's fine, hon," said the taller of the two women, patting his arm. "It's good we're here. I still remember when you told me. It's a little jarring."

"Those were the days," said Ramsey. He winked at her, and she smiled back.

Jill shut the door and stared.

"Who are you people?" asked Jace.

"Sonia sent us," said the taller woman who'd spoken to Ramsey. She had shoulder-length brown hair and soft bangs that fell to her eyebrows. "I'm Sarah and this is Gillian." She gestured toward the shorter woman with long, dark hair and pretty eyes.

"Sonia? You know Sonia?" asked Madison.

"Yes. I do," said Morgana. "For longer than I'd like to admit." She went to the window and looked out. "Your detective friends aren't here, correct?"

"No," said Jill. "Not until tomorrow."

Morgana turned back. "Then let me preface this by saying that what you are about to hear stays in this room and is not to be repeated. If it does, then we disappear and even if you found us, we would deny everything, and you would look...well..."

"Like idiots," said Ramsey.

"I was going to say foolish, but that will work." Morgana walked to the sofa. "Have a seat."

Jill's mind whirled, and she followed Madison into the living area. Sarah stood beside her, and Jill could feel that strange pain bloom in her head. Sarah whispered to her. "Don't worry. The pain dissipates after a while. Gillian can help with that."

Jill almost stopped cold, baffled at Sarah's words, but Sarah had stepped away and walked over to Jace.

"When Morgana's finished, you and I will need to talk," she said to Jace. "We have a few things in common."

Gillian regarded Madison. "I'm Gillian," she said, shaking Madison's hand. "I'll talk to you about meeting my brother, Royce."

"Royce?" asked Madison.

"He couldn't join us today," said Morgana. "He's currently...out of the country."

"You could say that," said Ramsey. He eyed the coffee table and chuckled. "Look at that, Gillian. Your husband's on the cover."

Jill saw the magazine that Madison had practiced with a few days earlier. "Grayson Steele is your husband?" she asked Gillian.

Gillian studied the magazine. "I told him he should have worn the other shirt. He looks better in blue." Gillian spoke to Sarah. "Remind me to call him when we're done. He's dying to know what happens."

Jace entered the living room, his expression as confused as Jill felt. "Who the hell are you people?" He scoffed. "What is this? Some sort of secret, experimental military thing?" He waved at the magazine. "Backed by some private tech millionaire guru?"

Ramsey snorted. "You're gonna wish it was. It would be a lot simpler. I'll give you this much. It's got nothing to do with the military and if you'd mentioned genetics or DNA, you'd be a lot warmer, although that doesn't even cover it." He raised a brow. "Let me ask you this. You enjoy science fiction? Because you're about to get a taste of it."

"Enough, Ramsey." Morgana approached Jace, her posture stick straight. Jill couldn't help but admire her composure and confidence. Morgana stopped in front of him and offered a steely glare. "The people here have origins very similar to your own." She tilted her head. "You want to know who you are? Then sit down, Mr. Marlon."

Jace set his jaw, but didn't argue, and sat on the sofa.

Jill didn't speak either, and she and Madison took a seat beside Jace.

Morgana watched them, her eyes like a hawk, and glanced at the other three in the room.

Ramsey leaned against the wall with his hands in his pockets and Gillian and Sarah sat in the chairs across from the couch.

Morgana faced Jill, Jace and Madison. "You understand what I told you about keeping this a secret, and the repercussions if you don't?"

Jill hesitated, and shared a look with Jace and Madison, both of whom seemed unnerved. "Yes," said Jill. "I think you made it clear."

"Sure. Why not," said Jace. "It's about time we heard the truth."

Madison nodded.

Morgana raised a brow. "Excellent." She smoothed her shirt. "Then let's begin."

Want more Daniels & Remalla?

If you're a fan of these two bantering detectives, then get ready, Their story continues in the *Detectives Daniels & Remalla* series - 10+ books of paranormal mystery, an engaging found family you'll root for, and the dangerous cases that haunt them.

Start with *Shadows and Secrets* - the books 1-3 omnibus collection. Includes *Haunted River*, *Of Breath and Blood* and *Of Body and Bone*.

Or if you prefer, start with book one, *Haunted River*. Enjoy an excerpt of *Haunted River* below.

Who are Morgana and her friends?

Jill, Madison and Jace share a unique history with Morgana's group. Uncover the truth about their startling origins with Ramsey and Sarah's story in the complete *The Red-Line Trilogy Boxed Set*, or start with book one, *Red-Line: The Shift*.

Dive into Gillian and Grayson's origin story in *Curse Breaker*, book one in Bishop's sister series to *The Red-Line Trilogy* called *The Fletcher Family Saga*. Or grab all four books in this series in *Red-Line: The Fletcher Family Saga Boxed Set*.

Want more from J. T. Bishop?

Subscribe to her newsletter at jtbishopauthor.com and get two Daniels and Remalla prequel novellas, *The Girl and the Gunshot*, plus *The Magic of Murder*, and future books for **free**, in addition to extra content.

Follow J.T. on her Amazon Author Page to be notified of new releases.

Did you know there's also a Daniels and Remalla Prequel Novel?

Murder Unveiled, a Daniels and Remalla standalone, is a prequel novel to *Haunted River*. It follows the events of *The Family or Foe Saga*.

If you're a fan of Daniels and Rem, and love to read in order, then start with *Murder Unveiled*. But if not, this book is designed to be read at any time.

Curious? Enjoy an excerpt of *Murder Unveiled* below.

A Note from J. T.

I love to hear from my readers about their experiences with my books, and I'd love to know what you thought about *Fourth Strike*. Wrapping up this series with Jill, Madison, Jace and Rutger is bittersweet. I am especially fond of Sonia, too. Fans keep asking if Rutger is really dead, and as of now, he is. But you never know with me. Stranger things have happened, and when is anyone ever truly dead when it comes to the mind of a writer?

I hope you enjoy Detectives Daniels and Remalla as much as I do. Originally, this was their series, but I switched it to the *Family or Foe* saga, because these books were more centered around the stories of Jill, Madison, Jace and Rutger, and they deserved their own title. But now, it's the detectives' turn, and future stories will focus on them, which is exciting for me because I love writing their characters. I think you're going to like what's in store for them.

And I think you can tell I enjoy tossing in a little paranormal into my books. It adds a bit of secret sauce if you ask me. This will continue into the Daniels and Remalla series and they'll encounter a few villains who may surprise you. This allows me to explore some creative opportunities when it comes to bad guys, and boy, it's fun. I've always had a curiosity about the paranormal and thought it would be interesting to include it in what would normally be a mainstream storyline. Basically, if you read my books, expect the unexpected.

Reviews are a huge plus and big help for an author, plus for potential readers. I would love it if you could please take a couple of minutes to leave a quick review for *Fourth Strike*. And if you'd like, please leave a few comments, too.

As always, thank you for your time and readership. It is deeply valued and appreciated.

Now, on to the next book!

Books in Chronological Order

A<small>LTHOUGH</small> <small>RECOMMENDED</small> <small>BUT</small> <small>NOT</small> required, in case you prefer to read in order...

Prelude to The Shift, a short story (subscribers only)

Red-Line: The Shift

Red-Line: Mirrors

Red-Line: Trust Destiny

Curse Breaker

High Child

Spark

Forged Lines

· · · ● · ● · ● · · ·

The Girl and the Gunshot, a novella (subscribers only)

A Hamburger Christmas, a novella

The Magic of Murder, a novella (subscribers only)

First Cut

Second Slice

Third Blow

Fourth Strike

Murder Unveiled

Haunted River

Of Breath and Blood

Lost Souls

Of Body and Bone

Lost Dreams

Of Mind and Madness

Lost Chances

Of Power and Pain

Lost Hope

Of Love and Loss

Lost Lives

Dominion

Lost Time

Illusions

Lost Love

Vendetta

Black Bird

Acknowledgements

THANK YOU TO EVERYONE for the amazing support I consistently receive from family and friends. These books are a labor of love for me and I receive such joy sharing them with family and fans alike.

I love writing about strong family and friendship and the bonds that hold them together. Plus, my fascination with the unknown thrown into the mix makes for a satisfying story and hopefully, adds a little more thrill for my readers.

Hearing your feedback, and how you've enjoyed my books, I want to thank you. When it comes down to it, knowing I've helped someone escape for an hour or two and get lost in another world makes all the difference.

Here's to more stories, more fun, and more time for yourself. If you can have a little of that each day, you're on the right track.

About the Author

AWARD-WINNING AUTHOR, J.T. BISHOP, is a writer of mystery thrillers with a paranormal edge. Growing up, she read Stephen King, Mary Higgins Clark, and Dean Koontz, devoured every episode of the X-files and watched plenty of TV shows with great partnerships that leave you wanting more. She loves tangled relationships, unexpected twists and turns, heart-stopping love stories and the complications that come with all the above. Throw in a little supernatural fun and she's hooked. Her evil plan is to hook you, too.

She's the author of The Red-Line Trilogy and its sister series, The Fletcher Family Saga, which features touches of urban fantasy, light sci-fi, and paranormal romance. She's also happily writing mystery thrillers featuring two charismatic detectives who may occasionally encounter a supernatural villain or two, and a crossover series which follows the exploits of a gifted, but troubled, paranormal P.I. and his spunky sister.

All the above keeps her busy, but in her spare time, she loves good movies, tasty food, an unfortunate sugar addiction, and traveling.

Enjoy an Excerpt from Haunted River, Book One in the Detectives Daniels and Remalla Series

DETECTIVE GORDON DANIELS PUT the phone down, shaking his head.

"Who was it?" His wife, Marjorie, entered the kitchen, putting on an earring. Her smooth blonde hair brushed her shoulders. "Rem?"

Daniels chuckled. "He's on the road and bitching up a storm. Thinks he's lost."

Her earring secured, she smoothed her t-shirt. "You can't be surprised. You didn't exactly give him the full story."

"I haven't been here since I was a kid. I told him what I remembered."

"We've been here a week. You've had ample time to give him an update."

Daniels shrugged. "And ruin a perfectly good opportunity to get him away from the city for a bit?"

She stood up on her tiptoes and gave him a quick kiss. "You mean have him help you get this place out in the middle of nowhere cleaned up and sellable? Does he know that part?"

"He knows I need to get it ready to put it on the market. I figure we can hammer out the rest of the details once he's here."

"Uh-huh. Is he actually lost?"

"Not really. He's at the fork in the road."

"Where we took the wrong turn on the way in?"

Daniels sighed. "We weren't lost. I just wanted to get the lay of the land."

She frowned. "Sure you did. And J.P. wasn't crying, he was just curious about how to make water come out of his eyes."

Daniels smiled and pulled her into his arms. "I think J.P. is curious about a lot of things."

She hugged him and rested her head in the hollow of his neck. "I'm sure. Like how to get fed, cleaned, and entertained. Not unlike his father."

"J.P. asleep?"

She nodded against him.

He rubbed his jaw against her hair. "Care to be entertained?"

She squeezed his waist and laughed. "Rem will be here any minute."

"You're a lot more confident than I am. I give him an hour, at best."

"If he's at the fork, he's just down the road."

"I know."

Smiling, she looked up. "I'm going to miss you." She squeezed his arm. "And your sexy muscles."

Daniels kissed her forehead. "You've been looking forward to this trip for a while. It will be fun. You need to hang with the girls." He flexed a bicep. "My muscles will still be here next week."

"They better be." She rested her hands on his chest. "You're sure about this? You think Rem will mind helping you with J.P. for the week?"

"Mind? Nah. He's looking forward to it. Plans to teach J.P. how to throw a curve ball and make a hot dog."

"He's eleven months old."

"No time like the present."

"Well, if you need anything..."

"We won't need anything. We'll be fine. Go on your girls' trip and relax. Rem and I will get this place into shape, and I'll get it on the market. I'll meet you back home next week, with J.P. and Rem right behind me."

"You sure you can handle it?"

Daniels rubbed her shoulders. "He's my son, babe. Of course, I can handle it."

"I was talking about Rem."

He grinned and stepped back. "I've survived this long."

She opened the fridge and grabbed a bottle of water. "How's he been? Any better?"

Daniels grabbed a banana from the counter. "Still has his moments, but he's hanging strong."

"Good. After everything that's happened, I was halfway wondering if he'd go off and become a mountain man somewhere."

"Rem?" asked Daniels. "He can barely handle a salad, hates sleeping bags, and jumps when he sees a bug larger than a fly. I don't think mountaineering is in his future, much less leaving the comforts of home."

"He still seeing the shrink?"

Daniels peeled the banana. "Up until the last month or two. Don't think he's seen him since."

She twisted the cap and drank some water. "As long as he's still talking to you. When that stops, then I'll worry."

"No need. I won't let it get that far, anyway. I can tell when he's getting stressed, which he hates."

She reached over and took his hand. "Be careful he doesn't bite."

"Oh, he bites, but so do I. I just need to be sure to talk to him when he's not hungry. Then it might get ugly."

Marjorie nodded. "I know. That's why I feed him so often. Have to make sure to keep you safe."

"And that's why I love you." He squeezed her fingers and took a bite of the banana.

She checked her watch. "I should get going. I don't want to leave too late. I don't like driving around here at night. Feels spooky."

"You're right. I don't want you to rush. What time is your flight tomorrow?"

"Bright and early. We leave at eight a.m."

"You'll meet at the airport?"

"I'll meet Melanie there. We'll have dinner tonight at the airport hotel and head out in the morning. We'll meet the rest of the ladies when we get to Fort Lauderdale."

"It'll be a blast."

The doorbell rang and Daniels heard a yell from the front. "Anybody there?" The bell rang again. "Daniels? Marjorie? Satan? Bigfoot?"

"Guess who?" asked Daniels.

"I think he found us." She poked him in the arm. "There's still time. You can leave him on the front porch."

Daniels put his banana down and headed toward the door. "I'd only find him babbling on the steps tomorrow morning. It's not worth the cost of the straight jacket I'd have to buy."

"Good point."

Daniels reached the door and opened it. Rem stood on the other side, his long black hair disheveled and his face white. "Where the hell did you invite me? I'm halfway expecting the name of this place to have something to do with a Black Lagoon."

Marjorie joined Daniels at the door. "You're close. We're actually on the Black River."

Rem's jaw dropped. "You're kidding?"

Daniels swung the door wide. "Nope. She's not. Come on in."

Rem stomped in, wearing hiking boots and carrying a backpack and a duffel bag. He dropped them on the floor. "Were you aware of this, Marjorie? I expected more from you. You're supposed to warn me when Daniels is keeping secrets."

"Sorry, Rem," said Marjorie. "But I needed your help with J.P. I figure it was worth a few spiders and a potential Bigfoot sighting." She raised a brow when he jumped and brushed something off his sleeve. "I hope I can still consider you a friend."

Rem glared. "You're lucky I like you, and you're cute. You, on the other hand," he pointed at Daniels, "are not so attractive."

Daniels raised his hands in mock seriousness. "Ah, come on, partner. Consider it an adventure. It's nice to get out in nature. Good for the soul. Besides, it's not like we're camping. We've got bathrooms and showers. How's it any different from Lozano's cabin?"

"Adventure? We deal with enough adventure in our jobs. And Lozano's cabin is half an hour from civilization. What's wrong with a sandy beach and five-star service?"

Daniels closed the door. "How about this? Once we get this place cleaned up and ready to sell, we'll look online at some five-star resorts, then we can pretend we're there."

"Online?" Rem shook his head. "How do you plan to look online when you have no Wi-Fi?"

"Details," said Daniels.

Rem's eyes widened. "Details? I was just kidding. Do you seriously not have Wi-Fi?"

Marjorie patted Daniels' chest. "I think that's my cue. I need to hit the road."

Daniels hugged her and gave her a quick kiss. "You got everything?"

"It's all in the car. Just need my purse."

"You know where you're going? Got your cell?" asked Daniels.

"I got it," said Marjorie, grabbing her purse from a chair beside the door.

"What good is a cell out here?" said Rem. "Might as well use it as a paperweight."

Daniels ignored him. "Call me when you get to the airport."

"I will," said Marjorie. "Call me if you need anything. Love you."

"We're not going to need a thing," said Daniels. "Rem and I are going to be fine, and so's J.P. Love you, too."

"Take it easy, Rem," Marjorie said as she opened the door to leave. "Try to have fun. Take care of J.P. and don't let him catch too many fly balls or eat too many hot dogs."

Rem swiped at his pant leg. "I'll try, but no promises. I see a creature or something with too many legs, it's every man or baby for himself."

Marjorie bit back a smile, and Daniels shook his head. "I'll walk you to the car."

"Keep an eye out for a woman in a white dress on the way out," said Rem.

Marjorie stopped, and Daniels looked back. "What?" he asked.

Rem took his jacket off and shook it out. "I saw her near the fork. Tried to help her, but she disappeared into the woods. Just goes to show how crazy this place is. God knows what she's running from. The lady looked in distress, plus she was all wet, like she'd fallen in your Blue River."

"Black," said Daniels.

"Whatever," said Rem.

Marjorie shot a glance at Daniels. "Did you say a woman in white?" asked Marjorie.

"On the road?" asked Daniels. "Near the fork?"

Rem paused. "Did I stutter? Yeah. Just now. On the way in." He narrowed his eyes. "What? Something wrong?"

Marjorie held her chest. "Oh, my God. You saw the Lady of Black River."

Enjoy an Excerpt from Murder Unveiled, the Prequel to Haunted River

DANIELS LOOKED FOR REM. After finishing his talk with Dominique, he asked Reynolds to arrange for someone to take her home. She didn't want to walk out the front door where the remaining guests could see her, so she left through the back with an officer.

He spotted Rem walking down the hall and Daniels joined him. "What's the update?" asked Daniels.

Rem's face fell. "You were right."

"Aren't I usually?"

"Almost as often as me." He massaged his neck. "I met Robert Clifford. Mr. Security Guy's got a chip on his shoulder bigger than Laroche's fortune, and he was sure we had the killer on video."

"Let me guess. We don't."

"Like you said. A case like this is never simple."

"Somebody tampered with it?"

"According to Robert, yes. There's no other explanation. He insists that no one else could access the equipment, but the room doesn't have a lock and its location isn't a secret."

"Could Robert have tampered with it?"

"He insists he didn't, but we can't rule him out. The guy thinks he's too smart to work for Rowan but can't protect the security system, much less his boss. With Rowan's kind of money, he could have done a lot better."

Daniels glanced at his notes. "Well, according to Dominique, Robert's definitely a suspect. He talks down to the staff and isn't well-liked. He and Laroche got into a shouting match last week, and she heard them argue tonight, but Dominique doesn't know what it was about."

"Maybe Laroche was thinking about making a change. I wouldn't blame him."

"It's something to check."

"Who else is on the list?"

Daniels read the names to Rem. "Robert's the only staff member listed. The rest are guests." He pointed at a name at the bottom that said *mystery guest*. "She knows all of them except this man. Said she'd never seen him before and didn't know his name. He's six feet, around sixty, has black hair with gray streaks and was wearing a tuxedo that was too small. Nobody else seemed to know him either, and he kept to himself during the party. We'll have to find his name on the guest list."

"Interesting."

"We should talk to whoever is still here."

Rem checked his watch. "It's four o'clock in the morning." He ran a hand over his face. "If our killer's hanging around, we won't find him tonight. We're not even sure how Laroche died or if anything was stolen."

"Let's introduce ourselves and ask a few questions. We'll tell them we'll be in touch, and not to go anywhere until this investigation ends."

Rem blew out a deep breath. "You mean put the fear of God in them?"

"Exactly."

"All right. Come on."

They headed up the hall toward the entry and stopped just before the main room. "Let's talk to the staff first," said Rem.

They entered the room with the long buffet table and a large crystal chandelier hanging over it. The food had been cleared and several of the remaining staff had paper plates containing cheese and bread and other items from the buffet. Daniels guessed they'd helped themselves to some leftovers. When Rem walked in with Daniels, a few staff members entered from the kitchen, including a large Black man wearing a white shirt and pants and a chef's hat. Daniels assumed it was Laroche's chef, Maurice. Emotional, he dabbed at his teary eyes with a napkin and wiped his nose. Rem introduced himself and Daniels and explained that someone would be in touch to speak with each of them within the next few days and not to go anywhere. While he spoke, a man with curly hair entered and sat beside a thin Asian American woman with long black hair that ran down her back.

Rem leaned closer to Daniels and whispered. "That's Robert, our security man."

Daniels nodded and made a note beside Robert's name on his list.

After Rem's speech, the staff said little. A few asked questions about Laroche and some wiped tears from their cheeks, especially Maurice, but most didn't say a word and quietly left.

"One room down," said Rem. "Let's go hit the guests."

Daniels crossed the hall and stopped outside a set of closed doors. He held out the list of names Dominique provided. "Let's see if we can put some names to faces." He opened a door and walked into a large, ornate room with big mirrors, elaborate wall sconces, and colorful wallpaper. About twenty people were in the room, some sitting on a long white leather couch or on tall-backed upholstered chairs, and others were sitting on the floor on an extravagant oriental rug. The rest milled about in small groups, talking to each other. Dressed in fancy clothes with lots of leather, lace, satin, and silk, and wearing expensive jewelry, they looked stunned and out of place, like captured wild animals pacing in a small enclosure at the zoo. Some were drinking from half-filled glasses, and champagne flutes were sitting on the mantel above an enormous fireplace, and on small tables set up around the room. Daniels had to assume the drinking and partying had come to an immediate stop at the discovery of Laroche's body. Some women had streaks of mascara running down their cheeks and most of the guests' pale faces implied they were still struggling with the news.

Everyone turned when he and Rem entered. Daniels introduced himself and Rem, and they showed their badges. Daniels looked for the mystery man in the snug tuxedo, but didn't see him. He made a note on his paper.

"It's about time someone came to talk to us," said a woman in the back of the room. She wore a lot of makeup, a long-sleeved black dress that sparkled in the light, and her dyed black hair was severely pulled back into a low bun on her neck. "We've been waiting for hours."

"We apologize for the wait," said Rem.

"Why did they close the doors?" asked a younger Black man with an afro wearing a lavender suit. He looked to be in his thirties. "Are we not allowed to leave?"

"Closing the doors prevents everyone from contaminating the crime scene," said Daniels.

"You can't force us to stay, you know," said a younger woman with long, dark brown hair, wearing a leather dress with plenty of exposed cleavage. "It's ridiculous you made us wait this long."

"Several already went home," said an older man with salt and pepper hair wearing an oversized navy suit. He eyed the other guests. "And if you all hadn't wandered around the crime scene, they wouldn't have shut the doors."

"Oh, be quiet, Henry," said the woman in the black dress. "What did they expect us to do? Rowan was murdered. Should we just stand around and do nothing? What if he'd still been alive? We could have performed CPR or something."

Another man in the back of the room, wearing a red suit with wide lapels and a white shirt unbuttoned almost down to his naval, chuckled. "The day you put your lips on Rowan's to save his life, Evelyn, is the day I'll sell you my Matisse."

Evelyn glared. "The rate you're going, Roger, you're going to need that Matisse to get out of bankruptcy."

Roger glared back and someone else in the room chuckled. Roger shot a look at Rem and Daniels. "If you two are looking for suspects, you've come to the right place. This room's full of them, and you can start with Evelyn."

Evelyn gasped, and a man standing beside her wearing black pants with a purple and white striped shirt, with several diamond rings on his fingers put his hand on her elbow. "Don't listen to him, Evelyn." He spat back at Roger. "You better include yourself on that list, Roger. I know how badly you wanted *The Crimson Tiger*."

"Maybe that's what killed Rowan," said a woman sitting on the couch. She wore a slim-cut white suit, spike heels, and her thick auburn hair was softly pulled back with clips. "The tiger was cursed, after all."

The room hummed with conversation, and Rem held up his hand. "Um, excuse me." He rapped loudly on a table beside him. "Everybody quiet down."

The conversation slowed and stopped.

"Listen," said Daniels. "We appreciate you all staying. We know it's been a long night. We do want to speak to each of you, one at a time. We know it's late, though, and you'd like to go home. But before you go, we'd like to learn your names and how you know Mr. Laroche. And if anyone saw anything suspicious tonight, we'd like to know that too."

"Victoria is wearing pearls with that atrocious dress," said Roger. "Is that suspicious enough for you?"

The woman in the leather dress scowled at Roger. "And Roger brought his lover to the party tonight while his wife stayed home. How's that for suspicious?"

Roger's eyes flared. "Becca and I are separated, you cow."

Victoria started yelling, and Roger yelled back. Evelyn chimed in with the man in the purple shirt, and then everyone was all talking at once.

Rem put his fingers between his lips and whistled loudly. Everyone stopped chattering. Rem raised a brow at Daniels, who shook his head. Looking at his notebook, he saw two of the names on Dominique's list were Evelyn Sinclair, who was in the black dress and Victoria Laroche, who was wearing the leather dress.

"Before you all come to blows over your devastation," said Rem, "why don't we take this one step at a time."

A man standing beside one of the tall-backed chairs made a snort. He had black hair slicked back with gel and wore a well-cut designer chocolate-brown suit with gold and diamond cuff links. He put his hand on the shoulder of a woman sitting in the chair. Her thick blonde hair brushed her shoulders, and she wore a shimmery pink satin dress with a diamond necklace, and mascara ran down her cheeks. When the man put his hand on her shoulder, she visibly pulled away and swiped a tear from her eye.

"My wife is very upset about Rowan, and I'd like to take her home," said the man.

"It's fine, Carlo," said the woman. "If I can stay and help the police, then I will."

Carlo frowned at her. "We need to get home to Mateo, Isabella." Daniels eyed his list and saw the names Carlo and Isabella Vespucci.

"What about the guests who've already left?" asked the man in the red suit. "Are you going to talk to them, too?"

"Of course," said Daniels. "We have a guest list. We'll be talking to each of them, plus the staff."

The man in the purple shirt crossed his arms. "I would hope so. That Maurice is crazy. You make one small comment about his crab dip, and he goes insane." He huffed.

"Be quiet, James," said Evelyn. "The less we interfere, the sooner we can get out of here."

James sighed. "You're right. Sorry. No more remarks about the crab dip. Or those truffles." He rolled his eyes. "Personally, I think Maurice dug those out of the alley. Atrocious."

"Sssh." Evelyn poked James in the arm. "Stop complaining."

"Asking the sun to stop shining would be easier," said Roger.

Daniels raised his hand before James could offer another ugly retort. "Yes. We're talking to everyone, but not about the food." Daniels eyed his list and saw the name James Montrose, who was Evelyn Sinclair's gallery manager.

"Pity," said James with a scowl at Roger.

Daniels didn't know who Roger was, and Dominique had not mentioned him, but he made a note to consider him a suspect.

The woman in the tailored white pant suit stood from the couch. "I apologize for my friends." She gestured at the group. "I know we sound awful, but it's been a hellish night. Rowan is dead." She paused and looked around the room. "And most of us knew him well. It's shocking that this has happened, and right under our noses."

Everyone slumped, and the energy left the room.

"We'd like to know who did this," she said. "And if it means answering your questions now or later, I'm sure we'll be happy to do it."

"Well said, Maria," said a man leaning against the mantel. He wore leather pants and a black narrow-cut silk shirt, which emphasized his muscular arms and narrow waist. A silver and diamond watch on his wrist sparkled in the light. "Rowan deserves better from us."

Roger snorted. "Says the man Rowan made rich."

"Be quiet, Roger," said Maria. "Hendrix is right. Rowan deserves better. He's dead, for heaven's sake. Can't we take five minutes to mourn him?"

Daniels studied the people in the room, who suddenly appeared sheepish. Isabella, who'd deflected her husband Carlo's touch, sniffed again, and wiped away another tear. "I can't believe he's gone."

Carlo set his jaw. "It doesn't surprise me at all."

"What's your name, Miss?" Daniels asked the woman in the white suit.

"I'm Maria Rossi. A long-time acquaintance of Rowan's." She stepped forward. "And I'd be happy to talk to you."

Daniels recognized the name. Maria Rossi was also one of Dominique's potential murderers. The name Hendrix wasn't on the suspect list, but he added it.

Victoria stood and smoothed her leather dress. "Are you sure, Maria? You don't have to say anything."

Maria patted Victoria's hand. "It's okay, Victoria. No need to worry." She looked around. "We all need to tell them the truth. Okay?"

No one would look her in the eye.

"Great," said Rem. He gestured toward the door. "Then let's get started."

www.ingramcontent.com/pod-product-compliance
Lightning Source LLC
Chambersburg PA
CBHW022022240626
47154CB00007B/2220